ARCTIC
TREACHERY

ARCTIC TREACHERY

Richard Woodman

Walker and Company
New York City

First published in the United States of America in 1987 by the Walker Publishing Company, Inc.

Published simultaneously in Canada by John Wiley & Sons Canada, Limited, Rexdale, Ontario.

Library of Congress Cataloging-in-Publication Data

Woodman, Richard, 1944–
    Arctic treachery.

    British ed. published in 1985 under title: The corvette.
    Sequel to: The bomb vessel.
    1. Napoleonic Wars, 1800–1814—Fiction. 2. Great Britain—History, Naval—19th century—Fiction.
    I. Title.
    PR6073.0618C6 1987   823'.914   86-28949
    ISBN 0-8027-0948-6

Printed in the United States of America

10 9 8 7 6 5 4 3 2 1

For my Mother

Contents

PART ONE

The Convoy

'. . . and there came a report that the French were away to murder a' our whalers . . .'

The Man O' War's Man   BILL TRUCK

London

'He has *what?*'

The First Lord of the Admiralty swung round from the window, suddenly attentive. He fixed a baleful eye on the clerk holding the bundle of papers from which he was making his routine report.

'Resigned, my Lord.'

'Resigned? *Resigned*, God damn and blast him! What does he think the Service is that he may resign it at a whim? Eh?'

The clerk prudently remained silent as Earl St Vincent crossed the fathom of Indian carpet that lay between the window and his desk. He leaned forward, both hands upon the desk, his face approximating the colour of the Bath ribbon that crossed his breast in anticipation of a court levée later in the morning. He looked up at Mr Templeton.

Considerably taller than the first lord, Templeton nevertheless felt his lack of stature before St Vincent. Although used to his lordship's anger, his lordship's power never failed to impress him. The earl continued, his deep frustration obvious to the clerk.

'As if I have not enough with the war renewed and the dockyards but imperfectly overhauled, that I have to teach a damned kill-buck his duty. Good God, sir, the Service is not to be trifled with like a regiment. It has become altogether too *fashionable*.'

St Vincent spat the word with evident distaste. Since the Peace of Amiens he had laboured to clean the dockyards of corruption, to stock them with naval stores and to end the peculation and jobbery which beset the commissariat of his rival, Sir Andrew Snape Hammond, Comptroller of the Navy and head of the powerful Navy Board. He had found suppression of mutiny in the Cadiz squadron an easier task. He could not hang every grasping malefactor who stole His Majesty's stores, nor break every profiteer in the business of supplying His Majesty's Navy. Yet his affection for his ships and their well-being demanded it, and his honest opposition to the worldliness of the London politicians had made him many enemies.

Lord St Vincent hunched his shoulders and wiped his nose on a fine

3

linen handkerchief. Templeton knew the gesture. The explosion of St Vincent's accumulated frustration would be through the touch-hole of his office, since his opponents stopped his muzzle.

'Be so kind, Templeton, as to add upon the skin of Sir James Palgrave's file that he is not to be employed again during the present war . . .'

'Yes my Lord.' St Vincent turned back to the window and his contemplation of the waving tree-tops in St James's Park. It was now his only eye upon the sky he had watched from a hundred quarter-decks. Templeton waited. St Vincent considered the folly of allowing a man a post-captaincy on account of his baronetcy. He recollected Palgrave; an indifferent lieutenant with an indolent fondness for fortified wines and a touchy sense of honour. It was perhaps a result of the inconsequence of his title. St Vincent, whose own honours had been earned by merit, disliked inherited rank when it eclipsed the abilities of better men. Properly the replacement of Palgrave should not concern the First Lord. But there was a matter of some import-ance attached to the appointment.

Templeton coughed. 'And the *Melusine*, my Lord?' St Vincent remained silent. 'Bearing in mind the urgency of her orders and the intelligence . . .'

'Why did he resign, Templeton?' asked St Vincent suddenly.

'I do not know, my Lord.' It was not the business of the Secretary's third clerk to trade in rumour, no matter how impeccable the source, nor how fascinating it sounded in the copy-room. But Sir James's hurried departure was said to stem from an inconvenient wound acquired in an illegal duel with the master of one of the ships he had been ordered to convoy. Templeton covered his dissimulation: 'And the *Melusine*, my Lord? It would seem she was in your gift.'

St Vincent looked up sharply. Only recent illness, a congestive outbreak of spring catarrh among the senior clerks, and including his Lordship's secretary Benjamin Tucker, had elevated Templeton to this daily tête-à-tete with the First Lord. Templeton flushed at his presumption.

'I beg pardon, my Lord, I meant only to allude to the intelli-gence . . .'

'Quite so, the intelligence had not escaped my recollection, Temple-ton,' St Vincent said sharply, and added ironically, 'whom had you in mind?'

'No one, my Lord,' blustered the clerk, now thoroughly alarmed that the omniscient old man might know of his connection with

Francis Germaney, first lieutenant of the *Melusine*.

'Then who is applying, sir? Surely we are not in want of commanders for the King's ships?'

The barb drove home. 'Indeed not, my Lord.' The clerks' office was inundated daily with letters of application for employment by half-pay captains, commanders and lieutenants. All were neatly returned from the secretary's inner sanctum where the process of advancement or rejection ground its pitiless and partial way.

'Bring me the names of the most persistent applicants within the last month, sir, and jump to it.'

Templeton escaped with the alacrity of a chastened midshipman while St Vincent, all unseeing, stared at the rolling cumulus, white above the chimneys of Downing Street.

Since the renewal of the war two weeks earlier, officers on the half-pay of unemployment had been clamouring for appointments. The lieutenant's waiting-room below him was filled with hopeful officers, a bear-pit of demands and disappointments from which the admiralty messengers would be making a fortune in small coin, God rot them. St Vincent sighed, aware that his very overhaul of the navy had caused a dangerous hiatus in the nation's defences. Now the speed with which the fleet was recommissioning was being accomplished only by a reversion to the old vices of bribery, corruption and the blind eye of official condonement. St Vincent felt overwhelmed with chagrin while his worldly enemies, no longer concerned by the First Lord's zealous honesty, smiled with cynical condescension. Templeton's return broke the old man's bitter reverie.

'Well?'

'Three, my Lord,' said Templeton, short of breath from his haste. 'There are three whose persistence has been most marked.'

'Go on, sir, go on.'

'White, my Lord, Captain Richard White . . .'

'Too senior for a sloop, but he must have the next forty-four, pray do you note that . . .'

'Very well, my Lord. Then there is Yelland. He did prodigious well at Copenhagen . . .'

St Vincent sniffed. Whatever Yelland had done at Copenhagen was not enough to overcome the First Lord's prejudice. Templeton, aware that his own desire to please was bordering on the effusive, contrived to temporise: 'Though of course he is only a commander . . .'

'Just so, Templeton. *Melusine* is a twenty, a post-ship. Who is the third?'

'Er . . . Drinkwater, my Lord. Oh, I beg your lordship's pardon he is also only a commander.'

'No matter,' St Vincent mused on the name, trying to recall a face. 'Drinkwater?'

'I shall have to return . . .' began Templeton unhappily, but the First Lord cut him off.

'Read me his file. We may appoint him temporarily without the necessity of making him post.'

Templeton's nerve was near breaking point. In attempting to shuffle the files several papers came loose and floated down onto the rich carpet. He was beginning to regret his rapid promotion and thank his stars it was only temporary. He had forgotten all about his promises to his kinsman on the *Melusine*.

'Er, Nathaniel Drinkwater, my Lord, commissioned lieutenant October 1797 after Camperdown. First of the brig *Hellebore* sent on special service to the Red Sea by order of Lord Nelson. Lieutenant-in-command of the bomb tender *Virago* during the Baltic Campaign, promoted Master and Commander for his services prior to and during the battle of Copenhagen on the recommendation of both Parker and Nelson. Lately wounded in Lord Nelson's bombardment of Boulogne the same year and invalided of his wound until his present persistent application, my Lord.'

St Vincent nodded. 'I have him now. I recollect him boarding *Victory* in '98 off Cadiz before Nelson incurred their lordships' displeasure for sending that brig round Africa. Did he not bring back the *Antigone*?'

Templeton flicked the pages. 'Yes, my Lord. The *Antigone*, French National Frigate was purchased into the Service.'

'H'm.' St Vincent considered the matter. He remembered Mr Drinkwater was no youngster as a lieutenant in 1798. Yet St Vincent had remarked him then and had a vague recollection of a firm mouth and a pair of steady grey eyes that spoke of a quiet ability. And he had impressed both Parker *and* Nelson, no mean feat given the differences between the two men, whilst his record and his persistent applications marked him as an energetic officer. Maturity and energy were just the combination wanted for the *Melusine* if the intelligence reports were accurate. St Vincent began to cheer up. Palgrave had not been his choice, for he had commanded *Melusine* throughout the Peace, a fact that said more about Palgrave's influence than his ability.

'There's one other thing, my Lord,' offered Templeton, eager to re-establish his own reputation in his lordship's eyes.

6

'What is it?'

'Drinkwater, sir,' said the clerk, plucking the fact from the file like a low trump from a bad hand, 'has been employed on secret service before: the cutter *Kestrel*, my Lord, employed by Lord Dungarth's department.'

A gleam of triumph showed in St Vincent's eye. 'That clinches it, Templeton. Have a letter of appointment drawn up for my signature before eight bells . . . noon, Templeton, noon, and instructions for Captain Drinkwater to attend here with all despatch.' He paused reflecting. 'Desire him to wait upon me on Friday.'

'Yes, my Lord.' Templeton bent to retrieve the papers scattered about the floor. St Vincent returned to his window.

'Does one *smoke* a viper from his nest, Templeton?' The clerk looked up.

'Beg pardon, my Lord, but I do not know.'

'No matter, but let us see what Captain Drinkwater can manage, eh?'

'Yes, my Lord.' Templeton looked up from the carpet, aware that his lordship was no longer angry with him. He wondered if the unknown Captain Drinkwater knew that the First Lord's receiving hours were somewhat eccentric and doubted it. He reflected that there were conditions to the patronage of so punctilious a First Lord as John Jervis, Earl St Vincent.

'Be so kind as to have my carriage sent round, Templeton.'

The clerk rose, his bundle of papers clasped against his chest. 'At once, my Lord.' He was already formulating the letter to his kinsman aboard the *Melusine*:

My Dear Germaney,

In my diurnal consultations with his excellency The First Lord, I have arranged for your new commander to be Captain Nathaniel Drinkwater. He is not to be made post, but appointed as Job Captain so there is hope yet for your own advancement . . .

Chapter One

The Job Captain

'*Non, m'sieur, non . . . Pardon,*' Monsieur Bescond smote his forehead with the palm of his right hand and switched to heavily accented English. 'The shoulder, Capitaine, it must be 'igher. More . . . 'ow you say? Elevated.'

Drinkwater gritted his teeth. The pain in his shoulder was still maddening but it was an ache now, a manageable sensation after the agony of splintered bone and torn muscle. And he could not blame Bescond. He had voluntarily submitted himself to this rigorous daily exercise to stretch the butchered fibres of his shoulder whose scars now ran down into the right upper arm and joined the remains of an old wound given him by the French agent Santhonax. That had been in a dark alley in Sheerness the year of the Great Mutiny and he had endured the dull pain in wet or cold weather these past six years.

Monsieur Bescond, the emigré attorney turned fencing master, recalled him to his purpose. Drinkwater came on guard again and felt his sword arm trembling with the effort. The point of his foil seemed to waver violently and as Bescond stepped back he lunged suddenly lest his opponent notice the appalling quivering.

Mr Quilhampton's attention was elsewhere. The foible of Drinkwater's foil bent satisfyingly against the padding of Quilhampton's plastron.

'*Bravo, M'sieur, tres bien* . . . that was classical in its simplicity. And for you, M'sieur,' he said addressing Quilhampton and avoiding the necessity of using his name, 'you must never let your attention wander.'

Pleased with his unlooked for success Drinkwater terminated the lesson by removing his mask before Quilhampton could avenge himself.

'Were you distracted, James?' Whipping off his own mask Quilhampton nodded in the direction of the door. Drinkwater turned.

'Yes, Tregembo, what is it?'

Drinkwater peeled off his plastron and gauntlet. His shirt stuck to his lean body, still emaciated after his wounding. A few loose locks of hair had escaped the queue and were plastered down the side of his head.

'I brought it as soon as I saw the seal, zur,' rumbled the old Cornishman as he handed the packet to Drinkwater. Quilhampton caught sight of the red wafer of the Admiralty with its fouled anchor device as Drinkwater tore it open.

Waiting with quickening pulse Quilhampton regarded his old commander with mounting impatience. He saw the colour drain from Drinkwater's face so that the thin scar on the left cheek and the blue powder burns above the eye seemed abruptly conspicuous.

'What is it, m'sieur? Not bad news?' Bescond too watched anxiously. He had come to admire the thin sea-officer with the drooping shoulder and his even skinnier companion with the wooden left hand. To Bescond they personified the dogged resistance of his adopted country to the monsters beyond the Channel who had massacred his parents and driven a pitchfork into the belly of his pregnant wife.

'Mr Q,' said Drinkwater with sudden formality, ignoring the Frenchman.

'Sir?' answered Quilhampton, aware that the contents of the packet had transformed the *salle d'armes* into a quarterdeck.

'It seems we have a ship at last! M. Bescond, my best attentions to you, I give you good day. Tregembo, my coat! God's bones, Mr Q, I have been made a "Job Captain", appointed to a sloop of war!'

An elated James Quilhampton accompanied Drinkwater to his house in Petersfield High Street. Since his widowed mother had obtained him a midshipman's berth on the brig *Hellebore*, thanks to the good offices of Lieutenant Drinkwater, Quilhampton had considered himself personally bound to his senior. Slight though Drinkwater's influence was, Quilhampton recognised the fact that he had no other patron. He therefore accorded Drinkwater an absolute loyalty that was the product of his generous nature. His own mother's close ties with Elizabeth Drinkwater, had made him an intimate of the house in the High Street and it had been Quilhampton who, with Mr Lettsom, late surgeon of the bomb vessel *Virago*, had brought Drinkwater home after his terrible wounding off Boulogne.

To Quilhampton the Drinkwater household represented 'home' more than the mean lodgings his mother maintained. Louise Quilhampton, a pretty, talkative widow assisted Elizabeth Drinkwater in a school run for the poor children of the town and surrounding villages. Her superficial qualities were a foil to Mistress Drinkwater's and she was more often to be found in the house of her friend where her frivolous chatter amused five-year-old Charlotte Amelia and the tiny and newest arrival in the Drinkwater ménage, Richard Madoc.

James Quilhampton was as much part of the family as his mother had become. He had restrained Charlotte Amelia from interfering while her father sat for his portrait to the French prisoner of war, Gaston Bruilhac. And he had rescued her from a beating by Susan Tregembo, the cook, who had caught the child climbing over a fire to touch the cleverly applied worms of yellow and brown paint with which Bruilhac had painted the epaulette to mark Drinkwater's promotion to Master and Commander. That had been in the fall of the year one, when Drinkwater had returned from the Baltic and before he rejoined Lord Nelson for the fateful attack on Boulogne.

Quilhampton smiled at the recollection now as he looked at Bruilhac's creditable portrait and waited for Drinkwater to return from informing Elizabeth of their imminent departure.

That single epaulette which had so fascinated little Charlotte Amelia ought properly to have been transferred to Drinkwater's right shoulder, Quilhampton thought. Apart from concealing the drooping shoulder it was scandalous that Drinkwater had not been made post-captain for his part in extricating the boats after Nelson's daring night attack had failed. Their Lordships did not like failure and Quilhampton considered his patron had suffered because there were those in high places who were not sorry to see another of Nelson's enterprises fail.

Quilhampton shook his head, angry that even now their Lordships had stopped short of giving Drinkwater the post-rank he deserved. Allowed the title 'captain' only by courtesy, Commander Drinkwater had been made a 'Job Captain', given an acting appointment while the real commander of His Britannic Majesty's Sloop *Melusine* was absent. It was damned unfair, particularly after the wounding Drinkwater had suffered off Boulogne.

The young master's mate had spent hours reading to the feverish Drinkwater as he lay an invalid. And then, ironically, peace had replaced war by an uneasy truce that few thought would last but which made those who had suffered loss acutely conscious of their sacrifices. The inactivity eroded the difference in rank between the two men and replaced it with friendship. Strangers who encountered Drinkwater convalescing with energetic ascents of Butser Hill in Quilhampton's company, were apt to think them brothers. From the summit of the hill they watched the distant Channel for hours, Drinkwater constantly requesting reports on any sails sighted by Quilhampton through the telescope. And boylike they dodged the moralising rector on his lugubrious visits.

Gaston Bruilhac had been repatriated after executing delightful portraits of Drinkwater's two children and, Quilhampton recalled, he himself had been instrumental in persuading Elizabeth to sit for hers. He turned to look at the painting. The soft brown eyes and wide mouth stared back at him. It was a good likeness, he thought. The parlour door opened and Elizabeth entered the room. She wore a high-waisted grey dress and it was clear from her breathing and her colour that the news of their departure had caught her unawares.

'So, James,' she said, 'you are party of this conspiracy that ditches us the moment war breaks out again.' She caught her bottom lip between her teeth and Quilhampton mumbled ineffectual protests. He looked from Elizabeth to Drinkwater who came in behind her. His face was immobile.

'Oh, I know very well how your minds work . . . You are like children . . .' Her voice softened. 'You are worse than children.' She turned to her husband. 'You had better find something with which to drink to your new command.' She smiled sadly as Drinkwater stepped suddenly forward and raised her hand to his lips. She seated herself and he went in search of a bottle, waving Quilhampton to a chair.

'Look after him for me James,' she said quietly. 'His wound will trouble him for many months yet, you know how tetchy he becomes when the wind is in the south-west and the weather thickens up.'

Quilhampton nodded, moved by Elizabeth's appeal.

'This is the last of Dick White's malmsey.' Drinkwater re-entered the room blowing the dust off a bottle. He was followed by the dark-haired figure of his daughter who swept into the room in a state of high excitement.

'Mama, mama! Dickon has fallen into the Tilbrook!'

'What did you say?' Elizabeth rose and Drinkwater paused in the act of drawing the cork.

'Oh, it's all right,' Charlotte said, 'Susan has him quite safe. He's all wet, though . . .'

'Thank God for that. How did it happen?'

'Oh, he was a damned lubber, Mama . . .'

'Charlotte!' Elizabeth suppressed a smile that rose unchecked on the features of the two men. 'That is no way for a young lady to speak!'

11

Charlotte pouted until she caught the eye of her father.

'Perhaps,' said Elizabeth, seeing the way the wind blew, 'perhaps it would be better if you two went to sea again.' And then she began to explain to Charlotte Amelia that old King George had written a letter to Papa from Windsor and that Papa was to go away again and fight the King's enemies. And James Quilhampton sipped his celebratory malmsey guiltily, aware of the reproach in Elizabeth's gentle constancy.

Captain Drinkwater eased his shoulders slightly and settled the heavy broadcloth coat more comfortably. The enlarged shoulder pad which he had had the tailor insert to support the strained and wasted muscles of his neck did not entirely disguise the misalignment of his shoulders nor the cock of his head. The heavy epaulette only emphasised his disfigurement but he nodded his satisfaction at the reflection in the mirror and pulled his watch from his waistcoat pocket. It wanted fifteen minutes before six in the morning. Earl St Vincent, First Lord of the Admiralty, had already been at his desk for forty-five minutes. Drinkwater swallowed the last of his coffee, hitched his sword and threw his cloak round his shoulders. Picking up his hat from its box, he blew out the candle and lifted the door latch.

Three minutes later he turned west into the Strand and walked quickly through the filth towards Whitehall. He dismissed any last minute additions he should have made to the shopping list he had left with Tregembo and composed his mind for his coming interview with the First Lord. He paused only to have his shoes blacked by a skinny youth who polished them with an old wig.

As the clock at the Horse Guards, the most accurate timepiece in London, struck the hour of six he turned in through the screen wall that separated the Admiralty from the periodical rioting seamen who besieged it for want of pay. He touched two fingers to his hat brim at the sentry's salute.

Beyond the glass doors he stopped and coughed. The Admiralty messenger woke abruptly from his doze and almost fell as he rose to his feet, extricating them with difficulty from the warming drawer set in the base of his chair. This he contrived to do without too much loss of dignity before leaving the hall to announce Commander Nathaniel Drinkwater.

Earl St Vincent rose as Drinkwater was ushered into the big office. He wore an old undress uniform with the stars of his orders embroidered upon his breast.

'Captain Drinkwater, pray take a seat.' He used the courtesy title and motioned Drinkwater to an upright chair and re-seated himself. Somewhat nervously Drinkwater sat, vaguely aware of two or three portraits that stared down at him and a magnificent sea-battle that he took for a representation of the action of St Valentine's Day off Cape St Vincent.

'May I congratulate you, Captain, upon your appointment.'

'Thank you, my Lord. It was unexpected.'

'But not undeserved.'

'Your Lordship is most kind.' Drinkwater bowed awkwardly from the waist and submitted himself to the First Lord's scrutiny. St Vincent congratulated his instinct. Commander Drinkwater would be about forty years of age, he judged. The grey eyes he remembered from their brief encounter in '98, together with the high forehead and the mop of hair that gave him a still youthful appearance despite the streaks of grey at his temples. The mouth was a little compressed, hiding the fullness of the lips and deep furrows ran down from his nose to bracket its corners. Drinkwater's complexion was a trifle pale beneath its weathering but it bore the mark of combat, a thin scar down the left cheek from a sword point, St Vincent thought, together with some tiny powder burns dotted over one eye like random ink-spots.

'You have quite recovered from your wound, Captain?'

'Quite, my Lord.'

'What were the circumstances of your acquiring it?'

'I commanded the bomb *Virago*, my Lord, in Lord Nelson's attack on the Invasion Flotilla in December of year one. I had gone forward in a boat to reconnoitre the position when a shell burst above the boat. Several men were regrettably lost. I was more fortunate.' Drinkwater thought of Mr Matchett dying in his arms while the pain from his own wound seeped with a curiously attenuated shock throughout his system.

St Vincent looked up from the papers on his desk. The report of Commander Drinkwater's boat expedition into Boulogne was rather different, but no matter, St Vincent liked his modesty. A hundred officers would have boasted of the night's exploit and measured the risk according to the number of corpses in their boats. Palgrave would have done that, St Vincent was certain, and the thought pleased the old man in the rightness of his choice.

'Lord Dungarth speaks well of you, Captain.'

'Thank you, my Lord.' Drinkwater was beginning to feel uneasy, undermined by the compliments and aware that an officer with St Vincent's reputation was tardy of praise.

'You are perhaps thinking it unusual for a newly appointed sloop-captain to be interviewed by the First Lord, eh?'

Drinkwater nodded. 'Indeed, my Lord.'

'The *Melusine* is a fine sloop, taken from the French off the Penmarcks in ninety-nine and remarkably fast. What the French call a "corvette", though I don't approve of our using the word. Not an ideal ship for her present task . . .'

'No, my Lord?'

'No, Captain, your old command might have been better suited. Bomb vessels have proved remarkably useful in Arctic waters . . .'

Drinkwater opened his mouth and thought better of it. Before he could reflect further upon this revelation St Vincent had passed on.

'But it is not intended that you should linger long in northern latitudes. Since the King's speech in March it has been clear that the Peace would not last and we have been requested by the northern whale-fishery to afford some protection to their ships. During the last war it was customary to keep a cruiser off the North Cape and another off the Faeroes during the summer months while we still traded with Russia. Now that Tsar Alexander has reopened trade this will have to be reinstated. The whale-fishery, however, is sensitive. A small cruiser, the *Melusine* to be exact, was long designated to the task, principally because she was in commission throughout the peace.

'Now that war has broken out again her protection is the more necessary and the Hull ships are assembled in the Humber awaiting your convoy. That is where the *Melusine* presently lies. Her captain has recently become, er, indisposed, and you have been appoined in his stead . . .'

Drinkwater nodded, listening to the First Lord and eagerly wishing that he had known his destination was the Arctic before he despatched Tregembo and Quilhampton on their shopping expeditions. But there was also a feeling that this was not the only reason that he was waiting on the First Lord.

'During the peace,' St Vincent resumed, 'the French have despatched a vast number of privateers from their ports. These letters-of-marque have been reported from all quarters, most significantly on the routes of the Indiamen and already cruisers are ordered after them. That is of no matter to us this morning . . .' St Vincent rose and turned to the window. Drinkwater regarded the small, hunched back of the earl and tried to catch what he was saying as he addressed his remarks to the window and the distant tree-tops of the park.

'We believe some of these private ships have left for the Greenland Sea.' St Vincent spun round, a movement that lent his words a peculiar significance. 'Destruction of the northern fishery would mean destitution to thousands, not to mention the removal of prime seamen for His Majesty's ships . . .' He looked significantly at Drinkwater. 'You understand, Captain?'

'Aye, my Lord, I think so.'

St Vincent continued in a more conversational tone. 'The French are masters of the war upon trade, whether it be Indiamen or whalers, Captain. This is no sinecure and I charge you to remember that, in addition to protecting the northern whale-fleet you should destroy any attempt the French make to establish their own fishery. Do you understand?'

'Yes, my Lord.'

'Good. Now your written instructions are ready for you in the copy-room. You must join *Melusine* in the Humber without delay but Lord Dungarth asked that you would break your fast with him in his office before you left. Good day to you, Captain Drinkwater.'

Already St Vincent was bent over the papers on his desk. Drinkwater rose, made a half-bow and went in search of Lord Dungarth.

'Nathaniel! My very warmest congratulations upon being given *Melusine*. Properly she is a post-ship but St Vincent won't let that stop him.'

Lord Dungarth held out his hand, his hazel eyes twinkling cordially. He motioned Drinkwater to a chair and turned to a side table, pouring coffee and lifting the lid off a serving dish. 'Collops or kidneys, my dear fellow?'

They broke their respective fasts in the companionable silence of gunroom tradition. Age was beginning to tell on the earl, but there was still a fire about the eyes that reminded Drinkwater of the naval officer he had once been; ebullient, energetic and possessed of that cool confidence of his class that so frequently degenerated into ignorant indolence. Lord Dungarth wiped his mouth with a napkin and eased his chair back, sipping his coffee and regarding his visitor over the rim of the porcelain cup.

When Drinkwater had finished his kidneys and a servant had been called to remove the remains of the meal, Dungarth offered Drinkwater a cheroot which he declined.

'Finest Deli leaf, Nathaniel, not to be found in London until this war is over.'

'I thank you, my Lord, but I have not taken tobacco above a dozen times in my life.' He paused. Dungarth did not seem eager to speak as he puffed earnestly on the long cigar. 'May I enquire whether you have any news of, er, a certain party in whom we have . . .'

'A mutual interest, eh?' mumbled Dungarth through the smoke. 'Yes. He is well and has undertaken a number of tasks for Vorontzoff who is much impressed by his horsemanship and writes that he is invaluable in the matter of selecting English Arabs.' Drinkwater nodded, relieved. His brother Edward, in whose escape from the noose Drinkwater had taken an active part, had a habit of falling upon his feet. 'I do not think you need concern yourself about him further.'

'No.' In the service of a powerful Russian nobleman Edward would doubtless do very well. He could never return to his native country, but he might repay some of his debt by acting as a courier, as was implied by Dungarth. Vorontzoff, a former ambassador to the Court of St James, was an anglophile and source of information to the British government.

'I am sorry you were not made post, Nathaniel. It should have happened years ago but,' Dungarth shrugged, 'things do not always take the turn we would wish.' He lapsed into silence and Drinkwater was reminded of the macabre events that had turned this once liberal man into the implacable foe of the French Republic. Returning through France from Italy where his lovely young wife had died of a puerperal fever, the mob, learning that he was an aristocrat, had desecrated her coffin and spilled the corpse upon the roadway where it had been defiled. Dungarth sighed.

'This will be a long war, Nathaniel, for France is filled with a restless energy and now that she has worked herself free of the fervour of Republican zeal we are faced with a nationalism unlikely to remain within the frontiers of France, "natural" or imposed.

'Now we have the genius of Bonaparte rising like a star out of the turmoil, different from other French leaders in that he alone seems to possess the power to unite. To inspire devotion in an army of starving men and secure the compliance of those swine in Paris *is* genius, Nathaniel. Who but a fated man with the devil's luck could have escaped our blockade of Egypt and returned from the humiliation of defeat to retake Italy and seize power in France, eh?'

Dungarth shook his head and stood up. He began pacing up and down, stabbing a finger at Drinkwater from time to time to make a point.

'It is to the navy that we must look, Nathaniel, to wrest the

16

advantage from France. We must blockade her ports again and nullify her fleets. God knows we can do little with the army, except perhaps a few conjoint operations, and they have been conspicuously unsuccessful in the past. But with the Navy we can prop up our wavering allies and persuade them to persist in their refusal to bow to Paris.'

'You think it likely that Austria will ever reach an accommodation with a republic?'

'There are reports, Nathaniel, that Bonaparte would make himself king and found a dynasty. God knows, but a man like that might stoop to divorce La Josephine and marry a Hohenzollern or a Romanov, even a Hapsburg if he can dictate a peace from a position of advantage. *You* know damned well he reached for India.' Dungarth looked unhappily at Drinkwater who nodded.

'Yes, my Lord, you are right.'

'On land France will exhaust herself and it is our duty to outlast her.'

'But she will need to be defeated on land in the end, my Lord, and if our own forces . . .'

Dungarth laughed. 'The British Army? God, did you see what a shambles came out of Holland? No, the Horse Guards will achieve nothing. We must look to Russia, Nathaniel, Russia with her endless manpower supported by our subsidies and the character of Tsar Alexander to spur her on.'

'You purport to re-establish liberty, my Lord, with the aid of Russia?' Drinkwater was astonished. Enough was known of Holy Russia to mark it as a strange mixture of refinement and barbarism. Russian ships had served with the Royal Navy in the North Sea, their officers a mixture of culture and incompetence. Russian troops had served in the Dutch campaign and relations between the two armies had been strained, while Suvorov's veterans had established a name in Northern Italy as synonymous with terror as anything conceived in Paris. Only two years earlier Alexander's father, the sadistic Tsar Paul, had turned on his British ally and leagued himself with France in a megalomaniac desire to carve up Europe with Bonaparte. Although Alexander professed himself the friend of England and a Christian Prince, he was suspected of conniving at his own father's assassination.

'I am informed,' Dungarth said with heavy emphasis and a nod that implied a personal connection, 'that Tsar Alexander wishes to atone for certain sins and considers himself a most liberal prince.' Dungarth's tone was cynical.

'So Vorontzoff's man is of some use . . .?'

Dungarth nodded. 'Together with a certain Countess Marie Narishkine . . . Still, this is not pertinent to your present purpose, Nathaniel. It is more in the line of, er, shall we say, family news, eh?'

Drinkwater grinned. Clearly Edward was more than a courier and Dungarth had made him an agent in his own right. He wondered how Edward liked his new life and, recalling the man aboard the *Virago*, decided he would manage.

'Doubtless St Vincent mentioned that the late and unlamented Peace afforded the French every oppportunity to get ships away to cruise against our trade. This is the most dangerous weapon the French can bring against our sea-power. Look at the success enjoyed by privateers in the American War. Yankees, French and Irish snapped up prizes on our own doorstep, reduced our ports to poverty, raised insurance rates to the sky and induced the merchant classes to whine until the government rocked to their belly-aching. There won't be a captain in command of an escort like yours that don't bear a burden as heavy as that of a seventy-four on blockade duty. Mark me, Nathaniel, mark me. Loss of trade is loss of confidence in the Royal Navy and, bearing in mind the effort we must sustain for the foreseeable future, that augurs very ill.

'Now, to be specific, there are some whispers lately come from sources in Brittany that a number of ships, well armed and equipped, sailed north a year ago. They have not returned, neither has any news of them. Their most obvious destination is Canada where they may make mischief for us. But no news has come from the Loyalists in New Brunswick who keep a sharp eye on our interests. Neither have they been seen in American waters . . .'

'Ireland?'

'Perhaps, but again, nothing. The Norwegian coast provides ample shelter for privateers and was used by the Danes before Copenhagen but I am inclined to think they lie in wait for our whalers. Two disappeared last summer and although the loss of these ships is not remarkable, indeed they may simply have wintered in the ice, there is a story of some sighting of vessels thought not to be whalers by the Hull fleet last season.'

'You mean to imply that two whalers might have been taken by French privateers during the peace?'

'I do not know, Nathaniel. I only tell you this because these ships have not been heard of since they left France bound to the northward. It is a possibility that they have wintered in a remote spot like

18

Spitzbergen and are waiting to strike against the whale-fishery on the resumption of hostilities. It is not improbable. French enterprise has sent letters-of-marque-and-reprisal to cruise in most of the areas frequented by British merchantmen. Opportunism may sometimes have the appearance of conspiracy and most of us knew the peace would not last.'

'Do you know the force of these vessels?'

'No, I regret I do not.'

Drinkwater digested the news as Dungarth sat down again. 'There is one other thing you should know.' Dungarth broke into his thoughts.

'My Lord?'

'Captain Palgrave did not leave his command willingly.'

'I heard he was indisposed.'

'He was shot in a duel. A very foolish affair which I heard of due to the loose tongue of one of the clerks here who is related to your first lieutenant. It seems that Palgrave had some sort of altercation with one of the captains of the whalers. Nothing will be done about it, of course; Palgrave cannot afford scandal so he has resigned his command and he has enough clout to ensure the facts do not reach the ears of the Court. But it is exceedingly unusual that a merchant master should incapacitate the captain of the man-of-war assigned to give him the convoy he has been bleating for.'

'Perhaps some affair locally, my Lord, an insult, a woman . . .'

'I grow damnably suspicious in my old age, Nathaniel,' Dungarth smiled, 'but since you speak of women, how is Elizabeth and that charming daughter of yours. And I hear you have an heir too . . .'

The Corvette

Drinkwater leaned from the window of the mail-coach as the fresh horses were whipped up to draw them out of Barnet. Dusk was already settling on the countryside and he could make out little of the landmarks of his youth beyond the square tower of Monken Hadley church whose Rector had long ago recommended him to Captain Hope of the *Cyclops*.

From above his head a voice called, 'Why she flies like a frigate going large, sir.' Looking up he saw Mr Quilhampton's face excited by their speed, some eight or nine miles to the hour.

Drinkwater smiled at the young man's pleasure and drew back into the coach. Since his breakfast with Lord Dungarth it had been a busy day of letter writing and last minute purchases. There had been a brace of pistols to buy and he had invested in a chronometer and a sextant, one of Hadley's newest, which now nestled beneath his feet. They had seen the bulk of their luggage to the Black Swan at Holborn and left it in the charge of Tregembo to bring on by the slower York Stage.

He and Quilhampton had arrived at Lombard Street just in time to catch the Edinburgh Mail, tickets for which Quilhampton had purchased earlier in the day. He smiled again as he remembered the enthusiasm of Mr Quilhampton at the sight of the shining maroon and black Mails clattering in and out of the Post Office Yard, some dusty from travel, others new greased and washed, direct from Vidler's Millbank yard and ready to embark on their nocturnal journeys. The slam of the mail boxes, shouts of their coachmen and the clatter of hooves on the cobbles as their scarlet wheels spun into motion was one of affecting excitement, Drinkwater thought indulgently as he settled back into the cushions, and vastly superior to the old stage-coaches.

The lady opposite returned his smile, removing her poke bonnet to do so and Drinkwater suffered sudden embarrassment as he realised that not only had he been grinning like a fool but his knees had been in intimate contact with those of the woman for some minutes.

'You are going to join your ship, Captain?' Her Edinburgh accent was unmistakable as was the coquettish expression on her face.

'Indeed, ma'am, I am.' He coughed and readjusted his position. The woman was about sixty and surely could not suppose . . .

'Catriona, my niece here,' the lady's glove patted the knee of a girl in grey and white sitting in the centre of the coach, 'has been visiting with me in London, Captain, at a charming villa in Lambeth. Do you live in London, Captain?'

Drinkwater looked at the girl, but the shadow of her bonnet fell across her face and the lights would not be lit until the next stop. As she boarded the coach he remembered her as tall and slim. He inclined his head civilly in her direction.

'No, ma'am, I live elsewhere.'

'May one ask where, sir?' Drinkwater sighed. It was clear the widow was determined to extract every detail and he disliked such personal revelations. He answered evasively. 'Hampshire, ma'am.'

'Ah, Hampshire, such a *fashionable* county.'

As Mistress MacEwan rattled on he smiled and nodded, taking stock of the other passengers. To his left an uncomfortably large man in a snuff-coloured coat was dozing, or perhaps feigning to doze and thus avoid the widow's quizzing; while to his right a soberly dressed divine struggled to read a slim volume of sermons in the fast fading light. Drinkwater suspected he, like the corpulent squire, affected his occupation to avoid the necessity of conversation.

There was, however, no doubt about the condition of the sixth occupant of the swaying coach. He was sunk in a drunken stupor, snoring gracelessly and sliding further down in his seat.

'. . . And at the reception given by Lady Rochford, Catriona was fortunate enough to be presented to . . .'

The widow MacEwan's prattle was beginning to irritate him. The overwhelming power of her nonsense was apt to give the impression that all women were as ridiculously superficial. His thoughts turned to Elizabeth and their children and the brief note he had written to her explaining the swift necessity of his departure. Elizabeth would understand, but that did not help the welling sadness that filled his heart and he cursed the weakness acquired from a long convalescence at home.

'. . . And then the doctor advised the poor woman to apply poultices of green hemlock leaves to her breast and to consume as many

21

millipedes as her stomach could take in a day and the tumour was much reduced and the lady restored to health. Is that not a remarkable story, Captain? You are a married man, sir?'

Drinkwater nodded wearily, aware that the clergyman next to him had let his book fall in his lap and his head droop forward.

'Of course, sir, I knew you were, you have the unmistakable stamp of a married man and a gallant officer. My husband always said . . .'

Drinkwater did not attend to the late Mr MacEwan's homespun wisdom. He had a sudden image of Richard standing naked after his fall in the Tilbrook while Susan Tregembo rubbed him dry.

'. . . But I assure you, Captain, it was not something to smile about. She died of smallpox within a month, leaving the child an orphan . . .' Catriona's knee was patted a second time.

'My apologies, ma'am, I was not smiling.'

Drinkwater felt the coach slow down and a few minutes later it stopped to change horses at Hatfield. 'Your indulgence ma'am, but forgive me.' He rose and flung open the coach door, going in search of the house of office and, having returned, shouted up to Quilhampton.

'Mr Q, we will exchange for a stage or two.'

'Aye, aye, sir.' Quilhampton descended. The new horses were already being put to and the Guard was consulting his stage-watch. 'Half-a-minute, gentlemen.'

'Your boat cloak, Mr Q.' Drinkwater took the heavy cloak and whirled it round his shoulders. He reached inside the coach for his hat.

'I beg your forgiveness ma'am, but I am a most unsociable companion. May I present Mr Quilhampton, an officer of proven courage now serving with me. Mr Q, Mrs MacEwan.' He ignored Quilhampton's open jaw and shoved him forward. 'Have a care for the instruments.'

'Oh!' he heard Mrs MacEwan say, 'Honoured I'm sure, but Captain, the night air will affect you to no good purpose, sir and may bring on a distemper.' The speech ended in a little squeal of horror and Drinkwater grinned as he hoisted himself up. Mrs MacEwan had discovered Mr Quilhampton's wooden hand.

'All aboard!' called the guard mounting the box and raising his horn. He jammed his tricorne down on his head as the coach leapt forward. The blast of the horn covered his laughter. They had been less than the permitted five minutes in changing their horses.

Above the racing coach the sky was bright with stars. A slim, crescent moon was rising. The mail was passing through the market-garden country north of Biggleswade and the horses were stretching out. He did not encourage his fellow outsiders to converse, indeed their deference to his rank made it clear that Mr Quilhampton had been telling tall stories. He was left alone with his thoughts and dismissed those of Elizabeth and the children to concentrate upon the future. He was pleased to be appointed to the *Melusine* even as a 'Job Captain', a stand-in. It was a stroke of good fortune, for she would be manned by volunteers having been in service throughout the peace. All her men would be thorough-going seamen. The officers, however, were likely to be different, probably place-seekers and time-servers. Influence and patronage had triumphed once again, even in the short period of the Peace of Amiens. Worthy officers of humble origins had been denied appointments. *Melusine* was unlikely to have avoided this blight. He knew nothing about Palgrave beyond the fact that he was a baronet and had been compelled to resign his command after being seriously wounded in a duel. In the sober judgement of Nathaniel Drinkwater those two facts spoke volumes.

He shivered and then cursed the widow MacEwan for her sagacity. The night air and the cold had found the knotted muscles in his shoulder. Holding fast with one hand he searched for the flask of brandy in his tail-pocket with the other. The coach swayed as the guard rose to pierce the night with his post-horn. As he swigged the fiery liquid Drinkwater was aware of a toll-keeper wrapped in a blanket as he threw wide his toll-gate to allow the mail through.

The glorious speed of the coach seemed to speak to him of all things British and he smiled at himself, amused that such considerations still had the power to move him. His grim experience off Boulogne and the brush with death that followed had shaken his faith in providence. The ache in his shoulder further reminded him that he was going to venture into Arctic waters where he would need all the fortitude he could muster. Command of the *Melusine* and her charges would be his first experience of truly independent responsibility and, in that midnight hour, he began to feel the isolation of it.

He took another swig of brandy and remembered the melancholia he had suffered after the fever of his recovery had subsided. The 'blue-devils' were an old malady, endemic among sea-officers and induced by loneliness, responsibility and, some men maintained, the enforced chastity of the life. Drinkwater was acutely conscious that he owed his full recovery from these 'megrims' to the love of his wife and friends. This thought combined with the stimulation of the brandy to raise his spirits.

23

Tonight he was racing to join a ship beneath a cloudless sky at what surely must be twelve miles to the hour! His thoughts ran on in a more philosophic vein, recalling Dungarth's long speech on the ambitions of France and the defence of liberty. He might talk of freedom being the goal of British policies, but at this very moment the press was out in every British sea-port, enslaving Britons for service in her Navy with as savage a hand as her landowners had appropriated and enclosed the countryside through which he was passing. The complexities of human society bewildered and exasperated Drinkwater and while his ordered mind was repelled by the nameless perfidies of politics, he was aware of the conflict it mirrored in himself.

There were many in Britain and Europe who welcomed the new order of things that had emerged from the bloody excesses of the French Revolution. Bonaparte was the foremost of these, an example of the exasperation of youth and talent at the blind intractability of vested interest. Surely Dungarth had overplayed the real danger posed by Bonaparte alone? Yet he would sail in command of his 'corvette' to drive the tricolour of France from the high seas with the same eagerness that the mail-guard consulted his watch and urged his charge through the night. He suppressed the feeling of radical zeal easily. The excitement of the night was making him foolish. He had a duty to do in protecting the Hull whale-fleet. The matter was simplicity itself.

Then a precarious sleep swallowed him, sleep that was interrupted by sudden jolts and the contraction of aching muscles, and accompanied by the memory of Elizabeth's sadness at his departure.

They broke a hurried fast at Grantham after the terrifying descent of Spitalgate Hill and by noon had crossed the Trent at Muskham. Drinkwater rode inside for a while but, assaulted again by Mrs MacEwan who seemed desirous of information regarding the 'gallant and charming Mr Quilhampton', he returned irritably to the box. He did not observe Mr Quilhampton's look of joy as he again exchanged seats and he was thoroughly worn out by the time the mail rolled into the yard of the Black Swan at York.

'And what, my dear, did you think of Mr Quilhampton?' asked Mrs MacEwan staring after the captain and the tall young officer beside him.

'I thought, Aunt,' said the young woman, removing her bonnet and shaking her red-gold hair about her shoulders, 'that he was a most personable gentleman.'

'Ahh.' Mrs MacEwan sighed with satisfaction. 'See, my dear, he has turned . . .' She waved her gloved hand with frivolous affection while Catriona simply smiled at James Quilhampton.

Drinkwater took to his bed before sunset, waiting only to instruct Quilhampton to mind the baggage and engage a conveyance to take them to Hull the following morning. Quilhampton was left to walk the streets of York alone, unable to throw off the image of Catriona MacEwan.

The good weather held. The following day being a Sunday they were obliged to hire a private chaise but the drive over the gentle hills was delightful. Drinkwater was much refreshed by his long sleep at York where, by a stroke of good fortune, he had enjoyed clean sheets. They ate at Beverly after hearing mattins in the beautiful Minster, reaching Kingston-upon-Hull at five in the afternoon.

First Lieutenant Francis Germaney stood in his cabin and passed water into the chamberpot. His eyes were screwed up tight against the pain and he cursed with quiet venom. He was certain now that 'the burns' had been contracted in a bawdy house in Kingston-upon-Hull and he wondered if Sir James Palgrave were similarly afflicted. It would serve the God-damned smell-smock right for he deserved it, that pistol ball in his guts notwithstanding.

'Oh Christ!' He saw the dark swirl of blood in the urine. And their blasted surgeon had not been sober since the morning of the duel. Not that he had been sober much before that, Germaney reflected bitterly, but there had been periods of near sobriety long enough to attend the occasional patient and maintain an appearance of duty. But now, God rot him, just when he was wanted . . .

Germaney resolved to swallow his pride and consult a physician without delay. Mr Surgeon Macpherson with his degree from Edinburgh could go to the devil. As he refastened his breeches his eyes fell on the letter from cousin Templeton. Commander Drinkwater's arrival was imminent and Templeton indicated that the First Lord himself was anxious to brook no further delay. Germaney reached for his coat and hat when a knock came at the door. 'What is it?'

The face of Midshipman the Lord Walmsley peered round the door.

'Mr Bourne's compliments, sir, but there's a shore-boat approaching answering the sentry's hail with "*Melusine*".'

'God damn!' Germaney knew well what that meant. The boat contained the new captain. 'Trying to catch us out,' he muttered.

'That's what Mr Bourne says.'

'Get out of my fucking way.'

Drinkwater folded his commission after reading it aloud and looked about him. Beneath a cloudless sky the corvette *Melusine* floated upon the broad, muddy Humber unruffled by any wind. Her paint and brass-work gleamed and her yards were perfectly squared. She lay among the tubby black and brown hulls of the whalers and the squat shapes of the other merchantmen and coasters at anchor off the port of Hull, a lady among drabs.

Not a rope was out of position beneath the lofty spars that rose to a ridiculous height. Named after a Breton sprite, *Melusine* showed all the lovely hallmarks of her French ancestry. Drinkwater's spirits soared and although he knew her for a showy thing, he could not deny her her beauty. He clamped the corners of his mouth tightly lest they betrayed his pleasure and frowned, nodding to the first lieutenant.

'Mr Germaney, I believe.'

'Your servant, sir. Welcome aboard.' Germaney removed his hat and bowed. 'May I present the officers, sir?'

Drinkwater nodded. 'Mr Bourne and Mr Rispin, sir; second and third lieutenants.' Two young officers in immaculate uniforms bowed somewhat apprehensively.

'Mr Hill, the Master . . .'

'Hill! Why, 'tis a pleasure to see you again. When was the last time?'

'Ninety-seven, sir, after Camperdown . . .' Hill was beaming, his face ruddy with broken veins and little of his fine black hair left beyond a fringe above his nape. Drinkwater remembered he had been wounded when a master's mate in the cutter *Kestrel*.

'How is the arm?'

'An infallible barometer signalling westerly gales, sir.' They both laughed. 'I heard you was wounded off Boulogne, sir . . .'

'I am a trifle sagged amidships, Mr Hill, but otherwise sound. I have an excellent second for you. May I present Mr James Quilhampton, Master's Mate, lately qualified at the Trinity House of London and a veteran of Copenhagen.' He stepped aside allowing the little knot of officers to receive Quilhampton's bow. Drinkwater turned to Germaney who resumed the introductions.

'Mr Gorton, sir, whose six years are nearly up.'

'How many have you served at sea, Mr Gorton?'

'All of them, sir,' replied the midshipman, looking Drinkwater in

26

the eye. 'I was two years a volunteer before that, sir.' Drinkwater nodded with satisfaction. Mr Gorton seemed to possess more potential than either of the two commissioned lieutenants. He turned to the next youth, perhaps a year or two younger than Gorton.

'Lord Walmsley, sir.'

Drinkwater caught his jaw in time and merely nodded and turned to the next. Another seventeen-year-old, the Honourable Alexander Glencross essayed a bow and was received with similar frigidity. Drinkwater had the impression that neither of these two young gentlemen took their profession very seriously and was relieved to see two fairly commonplace specimens at the end of the line.

'Messrs Wickham and Dutfield, sir and Mr Frey.'

Mr Frey emerged from behind Dutfield where, Drinkwater suspected, the latter young gentleman had been holding him. Palgrave, it appeared, let his midshipman fool about and skylark. That was all very well but it led too often to bullying and Mr Frey was a child of no more than twelve years of age.

Germaney produced a purser named Pater, a bosun and a carpenter before drawing Drinkwater's attention to a disreputable figure half hidden behind the mizenmast.

'Mr Macpherson, our surgeon.'

'Macpherson of Edinburgh, Captain,' slurred the surgeon, his face wet with perspiration, his eyes watery with rheum, 'A votre service.' Drinkwater could smell the rum at a yard distant and noted the dirty coat and stained linen.

'Lieutenant Mount, sir,' Germaney ploughed on, distracting Drinkwater from the state of the surgeon. Macpherson's shortcomings would be the subject of some conversation between captain and first lieutenant, but later, and on Germaney's terms. 'Lieutenant Mount, sir, of His Majesty's Marines.'

'Royal Marines, Mr Germaney, you should not neglect the new title.' Drinkwater indicated the blue facings of a royal regiment. 'An improvement upon the old white, Mr Mount,' he said conversationally and paced along the line of scarlet and pipe-clayed soldiers drawn up for his inspection. Mr Mount glowed with pleasure. He had spotted the glitter of gold lace a good fifteen minutes before the midshipman of the watch and had turned his men out in time to create a good impression.

'Your men do you credit, Mr Mount. I would have them all proficient marksmen to a high degree and I should like you to take charge of all the small-arms training on the ship. I have a prejudice against the junior lieutenant being responsible for the matter. He is better employed with his division and at the great guns.'

Drinkwater looked round, pleased with the obvious stir this small innovation had caused. He strode forward to stand by the larboard hance. A solitary brass carronade marked the limit of the hallowed quarterdeck of Captain Sir James Palgrave and the non-regulation addition to *Melusine*'s long guns shone with an ostentatious polish.

'I hope, Mr Germaney,' said Drinkwater in a clear voice, 'that all this tiddley work ain't at the expense of the ship's true fighting qualities, eh?'

He was facing the men assembled in the waist and caught half a dozen swiftly suppressed grins.

'N . . . no, of course not, sir.'

'Very well.' He looked over the ship's company. They seemed to be made up of the usual mixture. Tow headed Scandinavians, swarthy Portuguese, three negroes, an Indian and an Arab amongst a herd of old and young from the two kingdoms and the emerald isle. 'Do your duty men and you have nothing to fear.' It was an old formula, hack words but good enough for the moment. And if it lacked inspiration it at least encapsulated all that was required of them.

'Pray take a seat, Mr Germaney.' Drinkwater hung his hat and turned to his first lieutenant. Captain Palgrave's hurried departure had made Drinkwater temporary heir to some handsome cabin furniture and a full decanter of rich malmsey.

He poured a glass for himself and the first lieutenant, aware that they had just inspected parts of the ship that he doubted Mr Germaney even knew existed.

'That cockpit, Mr Germaney, is an ill-ventilated spot at best. I want it white-washed as soon as possible. There are marks there, and in the demeanour of the young gentlemen, of a slackness that I do not like. Now, your good health.' They drank and Drinkwater looked shrewdly at the lieutenant. He was on edge, yet displayed a certain lassitude to the task of showing the captain round the ship. An officer intent on creating a good impression would have shown off some of *Melusine*'s good points rather than ignoring them. Well, it was no matter. For the present there were more urgent considerations.

'The ship is well enough, Mr Germaney, although I withhold my full approbation until I see how her people make sail and work the guns. What I am not happy about is the surgeon.'

A surprising and noticeable interest stirred Germaney.

'Tell me,' Drinkwater continued, 'how was such a slovenly officer able to hold his position under an officer as, er, punctilious as Captain Palgrave,' asked Drinkwater drily.

'I am not certain, sir. It seemed Sir James owed him some service or other.'

'Is the man perpetually drunk?'

Germaney brightened. Things were turning a little in his favour. 'I regret to say that that is most usually the case, sir. There is no confidence in him among the people.'

'That does not surprise me. His instruments were filthy with rust and his loblolly boys looked perilous close to being gangrenous themselves. Come, another glass of this excellent malmsey . . .' Drinkwater watched the first lieutenant shrewdly. In the few hours he had been aboard much had already been made clear. He did not find the weakness of his three lieutenants comforting.

'What made your late captain leave such a taut ship, Mr Germaney?'

Germaney was beginning to relax. Captain Drinkwater seemed amiable enough; a trifle of a democrat, he suspected, and he had a few bees in his bonnet, to which his rank entitled him. But there was little to mark him as special, as Templeton had intimated. If anything he seemed inclined to tipple. Germaney drained his glass and Drinkwater refilled it.

'Oh, er, he resigned, sir. He was a man of some wealth as you see,' Germaney indicated the richness of the cabin furnishings and the french-polished panels of the forward bulkhead.

'An odd circumstance, wouldn't you say, to resign command of such a ship on the outbreak of war?'

Germaney shrugged, aware of the imputed slight. 'I was not a party to Sir James's affairs, sir.'

'Not even those most touching his honour, Mr Germaney?'

Germaney moved uneasily. 'I . . . I do not understand what you mean, sir.'

'I mean that I doubt if Captain Palgrave engaged in an affair of honour without the support of yourself as his second.'

'Oh, you know of that . . . some damned gossip hereabouts I . . .'

'I learned at the Admiralty, Mr Germaney, and I do not need to tell you that the news was not well received.' The implication went home. It was fairly logical to suppose that Germaney would have served as Palgrave's second in the duel. Often a first lieutenant was bound to his commander by greater ties than mere professional loyalty. It was

29

inconceivable that a peacetime captain like Palgrave would not have had such a first lieutenant.

Germaney regretted his gossiping letter to Templeton and swore to have his cousin answer for this indiscretion. 'Was my name . . . am I, er . . .?'

'I think,' said Drinkwater swiftly, avoiding a falsehood, 'I think that you had better tell me the precise origin of the quarrel. It seems scarcely to contribute to the service if the commander of the escort is to be called out by the masters he is sent to protect.'

'Well sir, I er, it was difficult for me . . .'

'I would rather the truth from you, Mr Germaney,' said Drinkwater quietly, 'than rumour from someone else. You should remember that Hill and I are old messmates and I would not want to go behind your back because you concealed information from me.'

Germaney was pallid. The Royal proscription against duelling or participating in such affairs could be invoked against him. Palgrave had abandoned him and his thoughts would not leave the discomfort in his loins. Palgrave had his share of the responsibility for that too.

'There was an altercation in public, sir. An exchange of insults ashore between Captain Palgrave and the captain of one of the whale-ships.'

'How did this happen? Were you present?'

Germaney nodded. 'Sir James met Captain Ellerby, the master of the *Nimrod*, in the street. Ellerby was out walking with his daughter and there had previously been some words between him and Sir James about the delays in sailing. It is customary for the whale-ships to sail in early April to hunt seals before working into the ice in May . . .'

'Yes, yes, go on.'

Germaney shrugged. 'Sir James paid some exagerrated and, er, injudicious compliments to the daughter, sir, to which Ellerby took exception. He asked for a retraction at which Sir James, er . . .'

'Sir James what?'

'He was a little the worse for liquor, sir . . .'

'I should hope he was, sir, I cannot think an officer would behave in that manner sober. But come, what next? What did Sir James say?'

'He made the observation that a pretty face was fair game for a gentleman's muzzle.'

'Hardly an observation, Mr Germaney. More of a highly offensive *double-entendre*, wouldn't you say?'

'Yes, sir.'

'Then what happened?'

'Ellerby struck him with his stick and Sir James was restrained by myself and Mr Mount. Sir James said he would call for satisfaction if Ellerby had been a gentleman and Ellerby shouted that he would meet him if only to teach a gentleman manners . . . And so the unhappy affair progressed. Sir James was not entirely well the following morning and though he fired first his ball miscarried. Ellerby's ball took him in the spleen.'

'So the affair was public hereabouts?'

'As public as a Quaker wedding, sir,' concluded Germaney dejectedly.

'And hushed up, I don't doubt, with public sympathy supporting Ellerby and the town council firmly behind the move, eh?'

'Yes, sir. They provided a doctor and a chaise to convey Sir James away to his seat as fast as possible. It was not difficult to persuade him to resign, though damnably difficult to stop Macpherson leaving with him. But the city fathers would not hear of it. Macpherson had become too well-known in the taverns for a loud-mouthed fool. Until you told me I had supposed the matter hushed outside the town. I stopped all shore-leave, though I expect that by now the water-folk have spread the news among the men.'

'I don't doubt it. You and Mount stood seconds, did you?'

'Mount refused, sir.'

'Ahhh.' Mount's conduct pleased Drinkwater. It must have taken considerable moral courage. 'Well, Mr Germaney, your own part in it might yet be concealed if we delay no further.'

'Thank you, sir . . . About the surgeon, sir. It is not right that we should make a voyage to the Arctic with such a man.'

'No.' Drinkwater refilled the glasses. Germaney's explanation made him realise the extent of his task. The whale-ship captains, already delayed by government proscription pending the outcome of developments with France, had been further held up by Palgrave's dilatoriness, to say nothing of his arrogance and offensiveness. He knew from his own orders that the Customs officers would issue the whale-ships their clearances at a nod from *Melusine*'s captain, and he had no more desire than the whalers to wait longer. Delay increased the risk of getting fast in the ice. If that happened *Melusine* would crack like an egg-shell.

'But there is now no alternative. We will sail without delay. Now I desire that you send a midshipman to visit each of the whale-ships, Greenlanders they call 'emselves, don't they? He is to invite them to repair on board tomorrow forenoon and we can settle the order of sailing and our private signals. And tell the young gentleman that I would have the invitation made civilly with my cordial compliments.'

'Yes, sir,' said Germaney unhappily, 'and the surgeon?'

'Tell the surgeon,' said Drinkwater with sudden ferocity, 'that if I find him drunk I shall have him at the gratings like any common seaman.'

Two hours later Drinkwater received a round-robin signed by a dozen names stating that the whale-ship commanders 'Would rather their meeting took place ashore at the Trinity House of Kingston-upon-Hull . . .'

Drinkwater cursed Sir James Palgrave, annoyed that he must first set out to woo a set of cantankerous merchant masters who set the King's commission so lightly aside. Then he calmed himself and reflected they had little cause to love the Royal Navy. It plundered their ships of prime seamen, usually when they were entering the Humber after the hardships of an Arctic voyage. There was already a Regulating Captain set up in the city with all the formal machinery of the Impress Service at his finger tips. Drinkwater remembered the story of a whaler abandoned by her entire crew off the Spurn Head as the cruising frigate hove in sight to press her crew.

No, they had no cause to love the Navy hereabouts and suddenly the vague, universal preoccupation of the justice of the present war came back to him. And as quickly was dismissed as irrelevant to the task in hand.

The Greenlanders

The tie-wigged usher conducted Drinkwater through the splendid corridors of the Trinity House of Kingston-upon-Hull. His previous connections with the corporation had been with the Baltic pilots it had supplied for the Copenhagen campaign two years earlier. Their performance had been disappointing and had clouded his opinions, so that he had forgotten the Arctic connection of the brotherhood.

The usher paused for a second before a heavy door from beyond which came the noise of heated argument. Drinkwater caught the phrase 'two months late' and the angrier, 'what guarantee have we of a bounty . . .?' Then the usher opened the door and announced him.

Drinkwater advanced into the room. He was in full dress with cocked hat and sword. The room was lit by tall windows and rushes were strewn across the plain boarded floor. Sitting and standing round a long mahogany table about two dozen men in all shades of civilian clothing turned towards him. Their complexions varied from the effects of their diet, the privations of their calling and the present heat of their passions. He was acutely aware of a wall of prejudice and remained observantly circumspect. He inclined his head.

'I give you good day, gentlemen.'

'Huh!' A huge black bearded man who sat cross armed and truculent upon the nearer edge of the table turned his face away. Drinkwater kept his temper.

'Thou woulds't do better to keep thyself civil, Friend Jemmett.' A man in the dark green and broad-brimmed hat of a Quaker rose from a seat behind the table. He came forward and indicated an upright chair.

'Pray seat thyself, sir. I am Abel Sawyers, master of the *Faithful*.' The Quaker's voice was low and vibrant.

Drinkwater sat. 'I am indebted to you, Captain Sawyers.' He looked round the circle of faces. They remained overwhelmingly hostile, clearly awaiting his first move.

'I am aware, gentlemen, that there has been some disruption of your intentions . . .'

'Some disruption!' The big, black bearded man spoke after spitting into the straw for emphasis. 'Some disruption! We are nearly two months late, too late to qualify for the bounty, God damn it! I do not expect you to give a toss for our dependents, *Captain*, but by God do not *you* try to prevent us sailing by trading our clearances against men out of our ships.'

A chorus of agreement greeted this remark. Drinkwater knew the *Melusine* was short of a dozen hands but the idea of pressing men out of his charges had not occurred to him. Indeed he considered the deficiency too small to worry over. It seemed that Sir James Palgrave's iniquities extended to the venal.

'Aye, Cap'n, *my* guns are loaded and if you sends a boat to take a single man out of my ship I swear I'll not answer for the consequences,' another cried.

A further chorus of assent was accompanied by the shaking of fists and more shouts.

'First they reduce the bounty, then they take half our press exemptions and then they order us not to sail until there is a man o' war to convoy us . . .'

'Bloody London jacks-in-office . . .'

'The festering lot of 'em should be strung up!'

'Do they think that we're fools, Captain?' roared the bearded captain, 'that we cannot see they wish to delay us only to take the men out of our ships to man the fleet now that war has broken out again.'

'Gentlemen!' Drinkwater stood and faced them. 'Gentlemen! Will you be silent God damn you!' He was angry now. It was quite likely that all they said was true. There might yet be a frigate cruising off the Spurn to relieve the Hull whale-fleet of 'surplus men', pleading the excuse that they could recruit replacements in Shetland or Orkney as they were entitled to. Drinkwater would not have been at all surprised if the authorities had it in mind, but at least his presence made it more difficult if he refused to co-operate . . . 'Gentlemen . . .'

'Friends!' The mellow roar of Sawyers beside him seemed to carry some authority over the angry Greenlanders and they eventually subsided. 'Let us hear what Captain Drinkwater has to say. He has come hither at our request. Please continue, Captain.'

'I have been to the Custom House this morning . . .'

'We do not want you or your damned government orders,' said the bearded Ellerby again.

34

'Except in the matter of bounty, friend,' put in the Quaker Sawyers quickly, which drew a hum of 'Ayes' and showed the first split in the assembly's unanimity.

'*You* would sail alone, Jemmett, but I could not risk an encounter with a cruiser off the Spurn. Men have been reluctant to sail this year for fear of the press. Let us see what Captain Drinkwater says about the matter of his own complement.'

Drinkwater looked at the new speaker. Dressed in brown drab he had a heavily pocked face with thin lips and snub nose which was, despite its inherent ugliness, possessed of a certain charm, enhanced by the kindness of the eyes. He caught Drinkwater's glance and bowed from his seat.

'Jaybez Harvey, Captain, master of the *Narwhal*.' He smiled. 'Your colleagues are too eager to press our men and pay scant regard to any exemptions . . .'

Drinkwater nodded and felt the need to exonerate his service. 'There is a war . . .'

'If there was no wars, Captain, thou knowest there woulds't be no navies to press innocent and God-fearing men from their unfortunate wives and children,' reproved the Quaker Sawyers.

'This endless debate shows no sign of ending, Captain Drinkwater. Will you tell us, when you propose to sail?' A tall man dressed in a sky-blue uniform elaborately trimmed with fur rose from his place. A similarly dressed colleague joined him and the two officers picked up lavishly trimmed hats and made for the door.

'Commander Malim and myself will await your instructions at the White Hart. Perhaps you will oblige us with your company at dinner, Captain.'

'And where are your ships, sir?' asked Drinkwater sharply, aware that the two officers, commanders of two vessels belonging to the Hudson's Bay Company, threatened to break the meeting up.

'Off Killingholme where they have been at a short scope this past sennight.'

Drinkwater restrained them from leaving as a babble of talk engulfed the whale-captains round the table.

'Be silent!' he bawled, 'may I suffer you to be silent for a moment!' Eventually the noise diminished.

'This morning I visited the Custom House and authorised the release of your clearances.' He paused as this revelation found its mark. At last the Greenlanders fell silent. He turned to the pock-marked Harvey.

'Do I understand that it is customary to embark additional men at Shetland whether or not men are pressed out of your ships?'

Harvey nodded cautiously. 'If we are bound for the Greenland fishery. If we are bound for the Davis Strait we recruit in Orkney. We also fill up our water casks.'

'And to which fishery are you bound, gentlemen?' He looked round expecting a further outbreak of argument but apparently this matter, at least, had been brought to a conclusion.

'We have resolved that, due to the advance of the season, sir, we shall repair to the Greenland fishery. Shoulds't the fish not prove to be swimming there we may then catch some favourable effects from rounding Cape Farewell and entering the Davis Strait. But this matter we hold in abeyance, to be decided upon later by a majority and for those that wish to try the enterprise.'

'Thank you, Captain Sawyers. Then I must advise you that I cannot winter in the ice . . .'

'We do not need you, Captain,' said the black bearded Ellerby aggressively, 'and we shall in any case fish where the whim takes us, so do not expect us to hang upon your skirts like frightened children.'

'I have no intention of so doing. I shall require that you attend me upon the passage as I have word that there are French cruisers already at sea. I shall cruise in company with those captains who wish for my protection on grounds of their own choosing. I further purpose we sail the instant we are ready. Shall we say the first of the ebb at daylight tomorrow morning?'

A murmur of surprise greeted this news and the Greenlanders debated briefly among themselves. After a while Sawyers rose.

'Thou hast our agreement.'

'Very well. You should each send a boat to the *Melusine* at six of the clock this evening for your written instructions. I shall include a table of signals to be used by us all for our mutual support and the direction of the convoy. The rendezvous will be Bressay Sound until the end of the first week in June. That is all, but for reminding you that I was informed in London that French private ships of war have sailed for the Polar regions, gentlemen. You may yet have need of *Melusine*.'

Drinkwater watched for reaction to this slight exaggeration. It would do no harm to induce a little co-operation from these independent ship-masters. He was quite pleased with the result. Even the black bearded ruffian Ellerby exchanged glances of surprise with a captain near him.

Drinkwater rose and picked up his hat. The meeting broke up into groups. The Hudson Bay Company officers made for the door. The one who had spoken introduced himself as Commander Learmouth and congratulated Drinkwater on taming 'the polar bears'. He repeated his invitation to dinner which Drinkwater declined on the grounds of insufficient time. Learmouth and Malim departed and Drinkwater paused only to thank the curious Quaker Sawyers for his help.

'Thou hast an evil calling, friend, but thou dost not discredit it.' Sawyers smiled. 'And now I shall attend the Custom House and tomorrow pilot thy ship to sea.'

Drinkwater moved towards the door and found himself behind the big, bearded Greenlander. Suddenly the man turned, barring the way so that Drinkwater almost bumped into him and was forced to take a step backwards.

Drinkwater looked up at the face. Beneath the mass of dark hair and the beard he noticed a sharpness of feature and the eyes were a peculiar pale blue which caused the pupils to seem unnaturally piercing.

'Have you ever been to the polar regions, Captain?'

'No, I have not.' The big man turned to his companion, the same whaler captain who had sat next to him.

'They send a novice to protect us, God damn and blast them.' The Greenlander turned on his heel. Behind him Drinkwater was aware of other men gathered in a group. His reserve snapped.

'Captain!' There was no response and Drinkwater stepped quickly into the corridor where his voice echoed: 'Captain!'

With ponderous contempt the big man turned slowly.

'What is your name?'

The big man retraced his steps, intimidating Drinkwater with his height. 'Ellerby, Jemmett Ellerby of the *Nimrod*.' Drinkwater put out his hand to prevent a further dismissal.

'I understood, Captain Ellerby,' he said quickly but in a voice that carried to the curious group behind him, 'I understood you had a *reputation* for good manners. It seemed I was mistaken. Good day to you, gentlemen.'

'No, sir, you may not go ashore. I require the services of three midshipmen as clerks this afternoon to make copies of my orders to the convoy. You must make the final rounds of the ship to ensure that she is ready to weigh tomorrow morning. We will refill our water casks in Shetland so you may stum a few casks in readiness. Tell me, did Captain Palgrave lay in a store of practice powder?'

'Yes, sir,' replied Lieutenant Germaney unhappily.

'Good. Will you direct the purser to attend me and extend to the gunroom my invitation to dinner. Mr Quilhampton and Mr Gorton are also invited. I shall rate Mr Gorton as master's mate. As for the rest of the young gentlemen I may make their acquaintance in due course.' He turned and peered through the stern windows at the high, white mare's tails in the west.

'We shall have a westerly breeze in the morning,' he rose, 'that is all.'

'Aye, aye, sir. There is a gentleman come aboard, sir, with a trunk and God knows what besides. He has a letter of introduction and says he is to sail with us.'

Drinkwater frowned. 'Sail with us? What imposition is this?'

Germaney shrugged. 'He is in the gunroom.'

'Send him in.'

'Yes, sir . . . sir, may I not take an hour . . .?'

'God's bones, Mr Germaney, can you not take no for an answer! We are about to sail for the Arctic, you have a hundred and one things to attend to. I have no objection to your sending a midshipman ashore on an errand. Send Dutfield or Wickham, neither can write a decent hand, judging from their journals. Now where the devil is that pen . . .?'

Drinkwater cursed himself for a fool. In the luxury of Palgrave's cabin he had forgotten he was without half of his own necessaries. Tregembo had not yet arrived and here he was giving orders to sail!

He swore again, furious with Palgrave, Ellerby and that cabal of whale-ship masters that had distracted him. Sudden misgivings about Germaney's competence and the fitness of his ship for Polar service seized him. He had made no preparations himself, relying on those made by Palgrave. But now Palgrave's whole reputation threw doubts upon the matter. He remembered Ellerby's taunt about being a novice in Arctic navigation. His eyes fell on the decanter and he half-rose from the table when a knock came at the door.

'Yes?'

The man who entered was dressed from head to foot in black. He was about thirty years of age with hair short cropped and thinning. His features were strong and his shaved beard gave his lantern jaw a blue appearance. His brown eyes were full of confidence and his self-assurance had led him into the centre of the cabin where the skylight allowed him to draw himself up to his full height.

38

'I give you good day, sir. My credentials.' He handed Drinkwater a packet sealed with the fouled anchor wafer of the Admiralty. It contained a second letter and simply instructed Captain Drinkwater to afford every facility to the bearer consistent with the service he was presently engaged upon, as was set out in the bearer's letter of introduction.

Drinkwater opened the enclosed letter. It was dated from London three days earlier.

Honourable Sir,

Having been lately acquainted with Their Lordships' Intention of despatching a ship into Arctic Regions, the Governors of this body conceived it their Christian Duty to carry the word of Christ to the peoples Domiciled upon the Coasts of Greenland. It is with this purpose in mind that you are asked to convey thither the bearer of this letter, the Reverend Obadiah Singleton, D.D.,M.D.

Your landing him at a Settlement of the Esquimaux, or causing him to be landed at some such Settlement, will assure you the Warmest Approbation from this Society for your furtherance in the Spread of the Christian Gospel.

The signature was illegible but was accredited to the Secretary of the Church Missionary Society.

Drinkwater put down the letter and looked up. He was beginning to feel the burden of command too great for him and the decanter beckoned seductively.

'Mr Singleton, pray take a seat. Will you take a glass of wine?' He rose.

'I do not drink intoxicating liquors, sir.' Drinkwater sat again, aware that the splendid isolation, the power and the purpose of command was, in reality, a myth. Only men like Palgrave sustained the illusion.

'Mr Singleton, are you aware of the extreme climate of the Arctic regions? Do you mean to winter there among the Eskimos?'

'I do, sir.'

'Entirely alone?'

'With God, sir,' Singleton answered with devastating simplicity. Drinkwater rose, a sense of helpless exasperation filling him. Almost defiantly he helped himself from the decanter, ignoring the disapproval in Singleton's eyes. Well damn Singleton! There would be much that Singleton did not approve of aboard a King's ship.

'But like me, Mr Singleton,' he said sipping the wine, 'you are flesh and blood.'

'Imbued with the Holy Spirit, sir, and the faith that can move mountains.'

'Let us hope,' remarked Drinkwater, 'that your faith sustains you.'

'Amen to that, sir.'

Drinkwater looked at the missionary, searching for some gleam of humour evident in the man. There was none. He was an alien amongst them, uncomprehending of their jack-ass humour, unable to understand the bawdy small talk, the rigid divisions that made a man-of-war. Singleton was an academic, a product of universities where the distilled wisdom of a thousand generations might be assimilated within the confines of a library. Drinkwater sighed and drained his glass. Singleton's insufferable self-righteousness would doubtless combine with an assumed right to criticise. That augured ill for the future and Drinkwater could see squalls ahead.

'Where have you been berthed, Mr Singleton? There is little room in the gunroom.'

'I do not think a *gun*room a fit place for a missionary, sir. No, Lieutenant Germaney has permitted me to use the cockpit.'

Drinkwater could well imagine it! The harassed lieutenant would not want the intrusion of a priggish irrelevance challenging his position in the gunroom.

'I doubt you will find it to your liking, but this is a small ship and there is no alternative.'

'It is true the air is mephitic, sir, but it will be a fit preparation for my ministry. The darkness alone will condition me to the Arctic winter.'

'It was not the darkness I had in mind, Mr Singleton, but no matter. You will see soon enough.' He ignored Singleton's puzzlement and went on: 'There is one thing you should know and that is that while you remain aboard this ship you are answerable for your conduct under the Articles of War as surely as if you were truly a midshipman. You will doubtless observe things that you do not approve of. Have you ever seen a flogging, sir? No? Well, it does not matter but you must accept that the usages of the naval service will come as a surprise to you and you would do well to remember that the wooden bulwarks behind which your church so comfortably nestles, are purchased at the price of blood, sweat and indignity.'

Singleton ignored this homily. 'When do you propose to land me, sir?'

'Land you? Good heavens, do not trouble me with such matters now. First I have to get these confounded ships out of this God-damned river!'

Drinkwater saw the look of shock on Singleton's face and found that it gave him a pleasurable sensation. 'Saving your cloth, Mr Singleton,' he said ironically and added, 'I should like you to join the officers and dine with me this evening. And I should like you to make no hasty judgements about the sea service; parsons have a bad reputation at sea, far worse than that of seamen ashore.'

He rose and smiled, dismissing Singleton abruptly as another knock came at the cabin door. The purser entered.

'You sent for me, sir?'

'I did, Mr Pater . . . I shall see you at dinner, Mr Singleton.'

'Your man has arrived, sir,' put in the purser, 'they are swinging your baggage aboard now.'

'Excellent. Will you take a glass, Mr Pater?'

'With pleasure, sir.'

'Thou should'st address the ship's head a half-point more to starboard.'

Drinkwater nodded at Hill as the master sought his approval. *Melusine* leaned slightly as the wind shifted forward a trifle as they altered course. The distant banks of the broad river were low and barely perceptible as the steeples and roofs of Hull dropped astern. Drinkwater raised his glass and studied the two vessels hoisting their topsails off Killingholme. The Hudson Bay Company's ships were superbly fitted, of a similar size to *Melusine* and with the appearance of sixth-rates of the smallest class. They were certainly a contrast to the squat whalers following *Melusine* down the river.

'Thou hast competition in the matter of elegance, Captain.'

'You object to elegance, Captain Sawyers?'

'It is irrelevant to the true meaning of life, Captain.'

'How will the *Faithful* fare with you piloting *Melusine* from the Humber?' asked Drinkwater, changing the subject and feeling preached at for the second time in as many days.

'My son is chief mate, Captain Drinkwater, a man as skilled as myself.'

'Come, sir,' put in Drinkwater grinning, 'that is immodest!'

'Not at all. Ability is a gift from God as manifest as physical strength or the fact that I have brown hair. I do not glory in it, merely state it.'

41

Drinkwater felt out-manoeuvred on his own quarterdeck and turned to look astern. Alone among the whale-ships foaming in their wake, *Faithful* was without a garland slung between fore and mainmasts. The ancient symbol of a Greenlander's love-tokens was absent from her topgallant rigging, neither were there so many flags as were flying from the other ships. Drinkwater wondered how many of Sawyers's crew shared his gentle and sober creed. Perhaps his rumoured success at the fishery reconciled them to a lack of ostentation as was customary on sailing day.

The other ships were under no such constraint. The otherwise dull appearance of the whale-ships was enlivened by streamers, ensigns and pendants bearing their names, lovingly fashioned by their wives and sweethearts whose fluttering handkerchiefs had long since vanished. The embroidered pendant that flew from *Nimrod*'s mainmasthead was fifty feet long, an oriflamme of scarlet, and Drinkwater could see the dominating figure of Jemmett Ellerby at the break of her poop.

Nimrod was crowding on sail and bid fair to pass *Melusine* as she slipped easily along at six knots, going large before the wind under her topsails and foretopmast staysail, leading the slower whalers towards the open waters of the North Sea.

'He hath the pride of Goliath before the Philistine Host,' Sawyers nodded in Ellerby's direction. 'He shall meet David at God's will.'

Drinkwater looked at the Quaker. He was not surprised that there were divisions of opinion and rifts between a group of individuals as unique as the whale-captains. Once on the fishing grounds there would be a rivalry between them that Drinkwater foresaw would make his task almost impossible. But the remark had either a touch of the venom of jealousy or of a confidence. Given what he had seen of Sawyers he doubted the man was a hypocrite and marked the remark as a proof of the Quaker's friendship. He responded.

'I am most grateful, Captain Sawyers, for your kind offer to pilot us clear of the Humber. It is an intricate navigation, given to much change, but I had not supposed that a gentleman of your persuasion would countenance boarding a King's ship.' He gestured towards the lines of cannon housed against the rail.

'Ah, but, thou hast also doubtless heard how those of my persuasion, as thou has it, are not averse to profit, eh?' Sawyers smiled.

'Indeed I have,' replied Drinkwater smiling back.

'Well I shall confess to thee a love of the fishery, both for its profits and its nearness to God. It seems that thy presence is indispensable

42

this season and so,' he shrugged, 'in order to practise my calling, sir, I have needs to assist thee to sea. Now, thou must bring her to larboard two points and square the yards before that scoundrel Ellerby forces you ashore on the Burcom.'

Nimrod was foaming up on their quarter, a huge bow wave hissing at her forefoot.

'May I give her the forecourse, sir?' asked Germaney eagerly.

'Aye, sir, he knows well enough to keep astern according to the order of sailing,' added Hill indignantly.

Drinkwater shook his head. 'This is not a race. Mr Q!'

'Sir?'

'Make to *Nimrod* "Keep proper station".'

'Aye, aye, sir.'

Drinkwater turned his full attention to the *Nimrod*. She was almost level with the *Melusine*'s mizen now, no more than a hundred feet off as she too swung to larboard.

In the waist of the sloop men milled about watching the whaler and looking aft to see the reaction of their new commander. Officers too, advised of the trial of strength taking place above, had come up from their watch below. Drinkwater saw Singleton's sober black figure watching from the rail while Mr Gorton explained what was happening.

Drinkwater felt an icy determination fill him. After the days of being put upon, of being the victim of circumstance and not its master, he secretly thanked Ellerby for this public opportunity. By God, he was damned if he would crowd an inch of canvas on his ship.

Quilhampton and little Frey were sending up the signal. It was a simple numeral, one of two score of signals he had circulated to his charges the evening before. Mr Frey had even tinted the little squared flags drawn in the margins with the colours from his water-colour box. Drinkwater smiled at the boy's keenness.

Amidships the newly joined Tregembo nudged the man next to him.

'See that, mate. When he grins like that the sparks fly.' There was renewed interest in the conduct of their captain, particularly as the *Nimrod* continued to surge past.

Drinkwater turned to his first lieutenant. 'Give him the larboard bow chaser unshotted, if you please.'

'Larbowlines! Spitfire battery stand by!'

It was all very modish, thought Drinkwater ruefully, the divisions told off by name as if *Melusine* had been a crack seventy-four. Still, the

43

men jumped eagerly enough to their pieces. He could see the disappointment as Germaney arrived forward and stood all the gun-crews down except that at the long twelve pounder in the eyes.

Germaney looked aft and Drinkwater nodded.

The gun roared and Drinkwater saw the wadding drop right ahead of *Nimrod*'s bowsprit. But still she came on.

'Mr Germaney! Come aft!'

Germaney walked aft. 'Sir?'

'Have your topmen aloft ready to let fall the forecourse, but not before I say. Mr Rispin!' The junior lieutenant touched his hat. 'Load that brass popgun with ball. Maximum elevation.'

'Aye, aye, sir.'

'Do you purpose to fire on him, friend?' There was anxiety in Sawyers's voice.

'Merely putting a stone in David's sling,' said Drinkwater raising his glass.

'But I do not approve . . .'

Drinkwater ignored him. He was staring at Ellerby. The Greenlander was pointing to the men ascending *Melusine*'s foremast and spreading out along the foreyard, casting off alternate gaskets.

'Pass me the trumpet, Mr Hill.' He took the megaphone and clambered up into the mizen rigging.

'Take station, Ellerby! do you hear me! Or take the consequences!'

He watched the big man leap into *Nimrod*'s mizen chains and they confronted one another across eighty feet of water that sloshed and hissed between them, confused by the wash of the two ships.

'Consequences? What consequences, eh, Captain?' There was a quite audible roar of laughter from *Nimrod*'s deck. Without climbing down Drinkwater turned his head.

'When his mainmast bears, Mr Rispin, you may open fire.'

Drinkwater felt the wave of concussion from the brass carronade at the larboard hance. The hole that appeared in Nimrod's main topsail must have opened a seam, for the sail split from head to foot. A cheer filled *Melusine*'s waist and Drinkwater leapt inboard. 'Silence there!' he bawled. 'Give her the forecourse, Mr Germaney.'

The big sail fell in huge flogs of billowing canvas. In an instant the waisters had tailed on the sheets and hauled its clews hard down. *Melusine* seemed to lift in the water and start forward. *Nimrod* fell astern.

'Tell me, Captain Sawyers,' Drinkwater asked conversationally, 'do you throw a harpoon in person?'

'Aye, Captain, I do.'

'And cause more harm than that ball, I dare say.' Drinkwater was smiling but the Quaker's eyes were filled with a strange look.

'That was a massive pride that thou wounded, Captain Drinkwater, greater than the greatest fish in the sea.'

But Drinkwater did not hear. He was sweeping the horizon ahead, beyond the low headland of Spurn and its slim lighthouse. There were no topsails to betray the presence of a frigate cruising for men.

'Mr Hill, please to back the main topsail and heave the *Faithful*'s boat alongside. Captain Sawyers, I am obliged to you, sir, for your assistance, but I think you may return to your ship.' He held out his hand and the Quaker shook it firmly.

'Recollect what happened to David, sir. I give you God's love.'

Chapter Four

The Captain's Cloak

Captain Drinkwater nodded to his first lieutenant. 'Very well, Mr Germaney, you may secure the guns and pipe the hammocks down.' He turned to the lieutenant of the watch. 'Mr Rispin, shorten sail now and put the ship under easy canvas.'

'Aye, aye, sir.'

Drinkwater paced aft, ignoring the stream of superfluous orders with which Mr Rispin conducted the affairs of the deck. He was tempted to conclude the young officer hid his lack of confidence beneath this apparent efficiency. It deceived no-one but himself. But in spite of misgivings about his lieutenants Drinkwater was well satisfied with the ship. *Melusine* handled like a yacht. He stared aft watching a fulmar quartering the wake, its sabre wings rigid as it moved with astonishing agility. He eased his shoulders beneath his coat aware that he could do with some exercise. There were other compensations besides the qualities of his former French corvette. Mr Hill, the master, had proved an able officer, explaining the measures taken in the matter of stores for the forthcoming voyage. Furthermore his two mates, Quilhampton and Gorton, seemed to be coming along well. Drinkwater was pleased with Hill's efficiency. He seemed to have assumed the duties of both sailing master and executive officer, and not for the first time Drinkwater regretted the system of patronage that promoted a man like Germaney and denied a commission to Stephen Hill.

Drinkwater turned forward and began pacing the windward side of the quarterdeck. Since they had returned Sawyers to his ship off the Spurn lighthouse the wind had held at west-north-west and they had made good progress to the north. Four more whalers had joined them from Whitby and this evening they were well to the eastward of the Firth of Forth, the convoy close hauled on the larboard tack and heading due north.

Drinkwater stopped to regard the whalers as the sun westered behind him. He could see a solitary figure on the rail of *Narwhal*. Taking off his hat he waved it above his head. Jaybez Harvey returned the salute and a few seconds later Drinkwater saw the feather of foam in the whaler's wake jerk closer to her stern as Harvey's men pulled in the cask at which *Melusine*'s gunners had been firing.

It had been a good idea to practise shooting in this manner. He had been able to manoeuvre up to, cross astern of and range alongside the cask, making and taking in sail for a full six hours while Harvey maintained his course. Finally to test both their accuracy and their mettle after so protracted an exercise, he had hauled off and let the hands fire three rounds from every gun, before each battery loosed off a final, concussive broadside.

The Melusines were clearly pleased with themselves and their afternoon's work. There was nothing like firing guns to satisfy a British seaman, Drinkwater reflected, watching the usual polyglot crowd coiling the train tackles and passing the breechings. He took a final look at the convoy. One or two of the whalers had loosed off their own cannon by way of competition and Drinkwater sensed a change of mood among the whale-ship masters. It was clear that preparations were under way for the arrival at the fishing grounds and he fervently hoped the differences between them were finally sunk under a sense of unanimous purpose.

He had stationed the Hudson Bay Ships at the van and rear of the convoy where, with their unusual ensigns, they gave the impression of being additional escorts, while *Melusine* occupied a windward station, ready to cover any part of the convoy and from where all her signals could be seen by each ship. He turned forward and looked aloft. The topmen were securing the topgallants and he could see the midshipmen in the fore and main tops watching over the furling of the courses. He considered himself a fortunate man in having such a proficient crew. Convoy escort could frustrate a sloop captain beyond endurance but the whalers, used to sailing in company and manoeuvring with only a handful of men upon the deck while the remainder were out in the boats after whales, behaved with commendable discipline. They were clearly all determined to reach the fishing grounds without delay. Even Ellerby seemed to have accepted his humiliation off the Spurn in a good grace, although it was at *Nimrod* that Drinkwater first looked whenever he came on deck.

'Beg pardon, sir.'

'Mr Mount, what is it?'

'I should like to try my men at a mark, sir, when it is convenient.'

'By all means. May I suggest you retain the gunroom's empty bottles and we'll haul 'em out to the lee foreyard arm tomorrow forenoon, eh?'

'Very good, sir.'

'Have the live marines fire at the dead 'uns,* eh?' Mr Mount's laughter was unfeigned and, like Hill, he too inspired confidence.

'Are there any fencers in the gunroom? Mr Quilhampton and I have foils and masks and I am not averse to going a bout with a worthy challenger.'

The light of interest kindled in Mount's eye. 'Indeed, yes, sir. I should be pleased to go to the best of . . .'

A scream interrupted Mount and both men looked aloft as the flailing body of a seaman fell. He smacked into the water alongside. Drinkwater's reaction was instantaneous.

'Helm a-lee! Main braces there! Starboard quarter-boat away! Move God damn you! Man overboard, Mr Rispin!' Mount and Drinkwater ran aft, straining to see where the hapless topman surfaced.

'Where's your damned sentry, Mount?'

'Here, sir.' The man appeared carrying a chicken coop. He hove it astern to the fluttering, squawking protest of its occupants.

'Good man.' The three men peered astern.

'I see him, sir.' The marine pointed.

'Don't take your eyes off him and point him out to the boat.'

Melusine was swinging up into the wind like a reined horse. Men were leaping into the quarter-boat and the knock of oars told where they prepared to pull like devils the instant the boat hit the water. Mr Quilhampton, holding his wooden hand out of the way as he vaulted nimbly over the rail, grabbed the tiller.

'Lower away there, lower away lively!'

The davits jerked the mizen rigging and the boat hit the water with a flat splash.

'Come up!' The falls ran slack, the boat unhooked and swung away from the ship, turning under her stern.

'Hoist *Princess Charlotte*'s number and "Man overboard".' Drinkwater heard little Frey acknowledge the order and hoped that Captain Learmouth would see it in time to wear his ship round into *Melusine*'s wake. The marine was up on the taffrail, one hand gripping a spanker vang, the other pointing in the direction of the drowning

---

A dead marine – naval slang for an empty bottle.

man. He must remember to ask Mount the marine's name, his initiative had been commendable.

'Ship's hove to, sir,' Rispin reported unnecessarily.

'Very well. Send a midshipman to warn the surgeon that his services will be required to revive a drowning man.'

'You think there's a chance, sir . . . Aye, aye, sir.' Rispin blushed crimson at the look in Drinkwater's eye.

Everyone on the upper deck was watching the boat. Men were aloft, anxiety plain upon their faces. They could see the boat circling, disappearing in the wave-troughs.

'Can you still see him, soldier?'

'No sir, but the boat is near where I last saw 'im, sir.'

'God's bones.' Drinkwater swore softly to himself.

'Have faith, sir.' The even features of Obadiah Singleton glowed in the sunset as he stopped alongside the captain. The pious sentiment annoyed Drinkwater but he ignored it.

'Do you see the coop, soldier?'

'Aye, sir, 'tis about a pistol shot short of the boat . . . there, sir!'

Drinkwater caught sight of a hard edged object on a wave crest before it disappeared again.

'What's your name?'

'Polesworth, sir.'

'Oh! May God be praised!' Singleton clasped his hands on his breast as a cheer went up from the Melusines. A man, presumably the bowman, had dived from the boat and could be seen dragging the body of his shipmate back to the boat. The boat rocked dangerously as willing hands dragged rescued and rescuer inboard over the transom. Then there was a mad scramble for oars and the boat darted forward. Drinkwater could see Quilhampton urging the oarsmen and beating the time on the gunwhale with his wooden hand.

The boat surged under the falls and hooked on. Drinkwater looked at the inert body in the bottom of the boat.

'Now is the time for piety, Mr Singleton,' he snapped at the missionary as the latter stared downwards.

'Heave up!' The two lines of men ranged along the deck ran away with the falls and held the boat at the davit heads while the body was lifted inboard. The blue pallor of death was visible to all.

'Where's Macpherson?'

'Below, sir,' squeaked Mr Frey.

'God damn the man. Get him to the surgeon and lively there!' Men hurried to carry the dripping body below. Drinkwater felt the sudden anger of exasperation fill him yet again. He was damned if he wanted to lose a man like this!

'Mr Rispin! Don't stand there with your mouth open. Clap stoppers on those falls and secure that boat, then put the ship on the wind.' The boat's bowman slopped past, his ducks flapping wetly about his legs, his knuckle respectfully at his forehead as he crossed the hallowed planking of the quarterdeck.

'What's your name?'

'Mullack, sir.'

'That was well done, Mullack, I'll not forget it. Who was the victim?'

'Jim Leek, sir, foretopman.'

'A messmate of yours?' Mullack nodded. 'Did you see what happened?' The seaman met Drinkwater's eyes then studied the deck again. 'No, sir.' He was lying, Drinkwater knew, but that was nothing to hold against him in the circumstances.

'Very well, Mullack, cut along now.' Drinkwater watched for a second as *Melusine* paid off to steady on her course again.

'Begging your pardon, sir,' offered Lord Walmsley, stepping forward, 'but the man was only skylarking, sir. Leek was dancing on the yardarm when he missed his footing.'

'Thank you, Mr Walmsley. He is in your division ain't he?'

'Yes, sir.'

'Kindly inform the midshipmen that they will be put over a gun-breech every time they permit a man in their division to fool about aloft . . . and Mr Rispin! Set the main t'gallant again, we are three miles astern of our station.'

The smell of tobacco smoke filled the dimly lit cockpit which housed the midshipmen. For a second Drinkwater was a 'young gentleman' again, transported back to an afternoon in Gibraltar Bay when he had caught a messmate in the throes of sodomy. As he paused to allow his eyes to adjust he took in the scene before him.

Leek's body was thrown over a chest, his buttocks bared while a loblolly boy held his abdomen face downwards. Behind him Surgeon Macpherson stood with a bellows inserted into Leek's anus. The clack-hole was connected to a small box in which tobacco was burning and, in addition to the aroma of the plug and the stink of bilge, the smell of rum was heavy in the foetid air.

'He's ejecting water,' said the loblolly boy. Drinkwater felt himself pushed aside in the darkness and looked round sharply as Singleton elbowed his way into the cockpit.

'What diabolical nonsense is this?' he snapped with uncommon force, opening a black bag. Macpherson looked up and his eyes narrowed, gleaming wetly in the flickering light of the two lanterns.

'The Cullenian cure,' he sneered, 'by the acrimony of the tobacco the intestines will be stimulated and the action of the moving fibres thus restored . . .'

'Get that thing out of his arse!' Macpherson and the loblolly boys stared at Singleton in astonishment as the missionary completed his preparations and pushed the drunken surgeon to one side.

Drinkwater had recovered from his shock. He was remembering something in Singleton's letter of introduction; the two letters 'M.D.'.

'Do as he says, Macpherson!' The voice of the captain cut through the gloom and Macpherson stepped back, his rum-sodden brain uncomprehending.

'By my oath . . . here, on his back and quickly now or we'll have lost him . . .'

Singleton waved two onlookers, Midshipmen Glencross and Gorton, to assist. Leek was laid face up on the deck and Singleton knelt at his head and shoved a short brass tube into his mouth. Pinching Leek's nose Singleton began to blow into the tube. After a while he looked at Gorton.

'Sit astride him and push down hard on his chest when I take my mouth away.'

They continued thus for some ten minutes, alternately blowing and punching down while the watchers waited in silence. About them *Melusine* creaked and groaned, her bilge slopping beneath them, but in the cockpit a diminishing hiatus of hope suspended them. Even Macpherson watched, befuddled and bewildered by what he was seeing.

Suddenly there was a contraction in Leek's throat. Singleton leapt up and pushed Gorton to one side, rolling Leek roughly over and slapping him hard between the shoulder blades. There was a massive eructation and Leek's chest heaved and continued to heave of its own accord. A quantity of viscid fluid ran from his mouth.

Singleton stood up and fixed Macpherson with a glare. 'I suggest you forget about Cullen, sir. The Royal Humane Society has advocated resuscitation since seventy-four.' He bumped into Drinkwater. 'Oh, I beg your pardon, sir.'

'That is quite all right, Mr Singleton. Thank you. Have that man conveyed to his hammock and excused watches until noon tomorrow, Mr Gorton.'

'Aye, aye, sir.'

Lieutenant Germaney leant on the rail and endeavoured to distract his preoccupied mind by concentrating upon the wine bottle at the yard arm. The pain was constant now and he thought his bowels were on fire and melting away.

The snap of a musket called his attention momentarily. The bottle swung intact, a green pinpoint at the extremity of the yard, catching the morning sun and twinkling defiantly.

A second musket spat and the bottle shattered. The marines were forbidden to cheer but there were congratulatory grins and one or two sullen faces. Mount was not under the same constraint.

'Ho! Good shooting, Polesworth. Next man, fire!' Mount's voice was bright with exhilaration and Germaney cursed him for his cheerfulness, seeing in the merriment of others a barometer of his own despair. Since the ship was witness to the remarkable medical talents of the Reverend Obadiah Singleton, Germaney had seen an opportunity to end his suffering. But fate had dealt him a mean trick, providing him with the means of a cure but entailing him in the awkward business of a confession before a gentleman of the cloth. Germaney writhed with indecision, an indecision made worse by the sudden popularity of Mr Singleton and the fact that he was seldom alone, was universally courted by all sections of the ship's company and encouraged in it by the captain, having seen the disgusting state of *Melusine*'s own surgeon.

The revival of Leek had also stimulated a sudden religious fervour, for the topman claimed he had died and seen God. While Singleton's attitude to his own medical abilities was purely professional, the theologian in him was intrigued. This circumstance seemed to make Germaney's distress the more acute.

A second bottle shattered and, a few minutes later, Mount dismissed his men. The Marine officer crossed the deck and removed his sword belt, sash, gorget and scarlet coat, laying them over the breech of the quarterdeck carronade next to Germaney. He doffed his hat and held it out.

'Be a good fellow, Germaney . . .' Germaney took the hat.

'What the deuce are you up to?'

Mount smiled and bent down to rummage in a canvas bag. He pulled a padded plastron over his shirt, produced a gauntlet, foil and mask and made mock obeisance.

'I go, fair one, to joust with the captain. Wilt thou not grant me a favour?'

'Good God.' Germaney was in no mood for Mount's humour but Mount was not to be so easily suppressed.

'See where he comes,' he whispered.

Commander Drinkwater had emerged on deck in his shirt sleeves and plastron. Germaney could see the extent of the rumoured wound. The right shoulder sagged appreciably and the reason for the cock of his head, that Germaney had dismissed as a peculiarity of the man, now became clear.

Drinkwater ignored the frank curiosity of the idlers amidships, whipped his foil experimentally, donned his mask and strode across the deck. He flicked a salute at his opponent.

'Best of seven, sir?' asked Mount, hooking the mask over his head.

'Very well, Mr Mount, best of seven.' Drinkwater lowered his mask and saluted.

Mount dropped his mask and came on guard. Both men called 'Ready' to Quilhampton, who was presiding, and the bout commenced.

The two men advanced and retreated cautiously, feeling their opponent by an occasional change of line, the click of the blades inaudible above the hiss of the sea and the thrum of the wind in the rigging.

There was a sudden movement. Mount's lunge was parried but the marine was too quick for Drinkwater, springing backwards then extending as the captain came forward to riposte.

Drinkwater conceded the hit. They came on guard again. Mount came forward, beat Drinkwater's blade and was about to extend and hit Drinkwater's plastron when the captain whirled his blade in a circular parry, stepped forward and his blade bowed against Mount's breast.

They came on guard again and circled each other. Mount dropped his left hand and threw himself to the deck, intending to extend under Drinkwater's guard but the captain pulled back his pelvis, then leaned forward, over Mount's sword and dropped his point onto the Marine officer's back.

'Oh, very good, sir!' There was a brief round of applause from the knot of officers assembled about the contest.

Mount scored two more points in quick succession before a hiatus in which each contender circled warily, seeking an opening without exposing himself. The click of the blades could be heard now as they slammed together with greater fury. Mount's next attack scored and he became more confident, getting a fifth hit off the captain.

Mount came in to feint and lunge for the sixth point. Drinkwater realised the younger man was quicker than Quilhampton and he was himself running short of breath. But he was ready for it. He advanced boldly, bringing his forte down hard against Mount's blade and executing a croisé, twisting his wrist and pulling his elbow back so that his sword point scratched against Mount's belly. He leaned forward and the blade curved. Mount straightened and stepped back to concede the point. The second he came on guard again Drinkwater lunged. It would have gratified M. Bescond. Mount had not moved and Drinkwater had another point to his credit.

The muscles in Drinkwater's shoulder were hurting now, but the two quick hits had sharpened him. He caught Mount's next extension in a bind and landed an equalising hit. The atmosphere on the quarterdeck was now electric and the quartermaster called the helmsmen to their duty.

Drinkwater whirled a *molinello* but Mount parried quinte. There was a gasp as the onlookers watched Mount drop his blade to attack Drinkwater's unguarded gut, stepping forward as he did so. But Drinkwater executed a brilliant low parry. The two blades met an instant before they collided *corps-à-corps*. They separated and came on guard again.

'A guinea on Mount,' muttered Rispin.

'Done!' said Hill, remembering the slithering deck of the *Draaken* one dull October afternoon off Camperdown.

Drinkwater scored again as Mount slipped on the deck then lost a point to the marine with an ineffectual parry. They came on guard for the last time. There was a *conversazione* of blades then Mount's suddenly licked out as he lunged low. Drinkwater stepped back to cutover but Mount seemed to coil up his rear leg and thrust himself bodily forward. His blade curved triumphantly against the captain's breast.

The fencers removed their masks, smiling and panting. They shook their left hands.

'By God you pressed me damned hard, sir.'

'You were too fast for me, Mr Mount.' Drinkwater wiped the sweat from his brow.

'You owe me a guinea, Mr Hill.'

'I shall win it back again, Mr Rispin, without a doubt.'

. . .

Drinkwater returned below, nodding acknowledgement to the marine sentry's salute as he entered the cabin. Tregembo had the tub of salt water ready in the centre of the cabin and Drinkwater immersed himself in it.

'I've settled all your things now, zur, but we have too many chairs.'

'Strike Palgrave's down into the hold. Get the sailmaker to wrap some old canvas round them.'

'I hope the pictures are to your liking, zur.'

He looked at the portraits by Bruilhac and nodded. Sluicing the icy water over his head he rose and took the towel from Tregembo.

'Don't cluck like an old hen, Tregembo. Don't forget I'm short of good topmen.'

'Aye, zur, I doubt you'll take to Cap'n Palgrave's lackey,' replied Tregembo familiarly, brushing Drinkwater's undress coat, 'but I'll exchange willingly, zur, I'm not too old yet.'

'D'you think I could stand Susan's reproaches if I sent you aloft again?' Drinkwater stepped out of the bath-tub. 'Where's Germaney put Palgrave's man?'

'He is mincing about the gunroom, sir,' replied Tregembo with a touch of ire and added under his breath, 'and 'tis the best bloody place for 'im.'

The Cornishman picked up the tub and sluiced its contents down the quarter gallery privy.

Dressing, Drinkwater sent for Mr Midshipman the Lord Walmsley. Donning his coat he sat behind his desk and awaited the appearance of his lordship. A glance out of the stern window showed the tail of the convoy. The sea was a dazzling blue and the wind still steady from the north of west, blowing fluffy cumulus clouds to leeward. It was more reminiscent of the Mediterranean than the North Sea: too good to last.

'Come in!' Lord Walmsley entered the cabin, his uniform immaculate, his hose silk. Drinkwater could imagine that he and his servant were popular in the confines of the cockpit.

'You sent for me, sir.'

'I did. The man Leek fell from the fore t'gallant yard yesterday, a consequence of skylarking didn't you say.'

Walmsley nodded. 'That is so, sir.'

'Skylarking upon the yards is irresponsible when it leads to losing men . . .'

'But sir, it was only high spirits, why Sir James . . .'

'Damn Sir James, Mr Walmsley,' Drinkwater said quietly. 'I

command here and I intend to flog Leek this morning.' He paused. 'I see that disturbs you. Do you have a weak stomach, or a feeling of solicitude for Leek? Eh?' Drinkwater suppressed the smile that threatened to crack his face as he watched perplexity cross his lordship's face. '*Do* you have any feeling for Leek?'

'Why . . . I, er . . . yes, er . . .'

'Is he a good seaman?'

'Yes, sir.'

'Then I rely upon you to intercede for him. Do you understand? When I call for someone to speak for him. Now, kindly tell the first lieutenant to pipe all hands aft to witness punishment and to rig the gratings.'

Drinkwater gave way to suppressed mirth as Walmsley retreated, his face a picture of confusion. The lesson would be better learned this way.

Half a minute elapsed before the marine drummer began to beat the tattoo. Drinkwater heard the pipes at the hatchways and the thump of marines' boots and the muffled slap of bare feet. He rose, hitched his sword and tucked his hat under his arm. He picked up the slim brown book that gave him the right to do what he was about to.

Germaney's head came round the door. 'Ship's company mustered to witness punishment, sir. Lord Walmsley tells me it's Leek.'

'That's correct, Mr Germaney.'

'Begging your pardon, sir, but I conceive it my duty to inform you that Sir James encouraged . . .'

'. . . Such rash bravado. I know. Walmsley has already informed me. But, Mr Germaney, I would have you know that I command here now and I would advise you to recollect that Sir James's example is not to be followed too closely.' He was unaware that his remark pierced Germaney to his vitals.

Drinkwater stepped on deck into the sunshine. Half a mile to leeward the convoy foamed along. Mount's marines glittered across the after end of the quarterdeck and the officers were gathered in uniform with their swords. Forward a sea of faces was mustered. 'Off hats!'

Drinkwater cleared his throat and read the Thirty-Sixth Article of War.

'All other crimes not Capital, committed by any Person or Persons in the Fleet, which are not mentioned in this Act, or for which no Punishment is hereby directed to be inflicted, shall be punished according to Laws and Customs in such cases used at Sea.'

It was colloquially known as the Captain's Cloak, a grim pun which covered every eventuality likely to be encountered in a man-of-war not dealt with by the other thirty-five Articles.

'Able-Seaman Leek step forward.' The murmur from amidships as Leek stepped out in utter surprise was hostile. 'Silence there! You stand condemned by the provisions of this Article, in that you did skylark in the rigging, causing risk to yourself and to others in your rescue, and that you did delay the passage of His Majesty's sloop *Melusine* engaged in the urgent convoy of other ships. What have you to say?'

Leek hung his head and muttered inaudibly. He was bewildered at this unexpected ordeal. He had never been flogged, he was a volunteer, he began to tremble.

Drinkwater's eye was caught by a movement on his right. Singleton was pushing through the midshipmen. Drinkwater turned his head and fixed Singleton with a glare. 'Stand fast there!' Singleton paused.

'I sentence you to one dozen lashes. Does anyone speak for this man?' He sought out Lord Walmsley. The young man came forward.

'Well, sir?'

'I, er . . . I wish to speak for the man, sir. He is a topman of the first rate and I have previously entertained no apprehensions as to his good behaviour, sir. I should be prepared to stand guarantor against his good conduct.'

Drinkwater bit his lip. Walmsley's speech was nobly touching and he had played his part to perfection.

'Very well. I shall overlook the matter on this occasion. But mark me, my lads, we are bound upon a service that will not tolerate the casual loss of good seamen. But for Mr Singleton, Seaman Mullack and Marine Polesworth, Leek, we would be gathered here this morning to send you over the standing part of the foresheet.* Do you reflect on that.' He turned to Germaney. 'Dismiss the men and pipe up spirits, Mr Germaney.'

Drinkwater chuckled to himself. Talk at dinner over the mess kids would be about this morning's theatricals. He hoped they would conclude that he would stand no nonsense, that although he might only be a 'job captain', temporarily commanding a post-captain's ship, he was not prepared to tolerate anything but the strictest adherence to duty.

---

* Naval slang for death or burial. Bodies were usually slid overside where the foresheet was belayed.

Bressay Sound

The wind held fair and they raised Sumburgh Head at daylight after a passage of three days from the Spurn Head. By previous agreement the Hudson Bay ships, usually escorted to longitude twenty west, left them off the Fair Isle. Due to the mild weather the convoy had kept together and by the afternoon all the ships had worked into the anchorage in Bressay Sound and lay within sight of the grey town of Lerwick.

That evening Drinkwater received a deputation of whale-ship masters in his cabin. It consisted of Jaybez Harvey, Abel Sawyers and another captain whose name he did not know. Sawyers introduced him.

'Captain Waller, Captain Drinkwater. Captain Waller is master of the *Conqueror*.'

'Your servant.' Drinkwater remembered him as having sat next to Ellerby at the meeting in Hull. He was surprised that Ellerby was not among the announced deputation. Drinkwater hoped Ellerby realised he was no longer dealing with a man of Palgrave's stamp and had come to his senses. In any event Waller seemed a mild enough character, leaving most of the talking to Sawyers.

'Well, gentlemen,' Drinkwater said when he had settled them with a glass and placed Palgrave's decanter on the table before them, 'to what do I owe this honour?'

'As thou knowest, Captain Drinkwater, since we cast anchor we have been taking water and augmenting our crews. The islanders are as eager as ourselves to avoid delay, the season already being far advanced. It is therefore hoped that within these twenty-four hours thou also wilt be ready to weigh.'

'I see no reason for thinking otherwise.'

'Very well. We have therefore to decide upon the procedures to be adopted when we reach the fishing grounds. Know therefore that we have agreed to consider ourselves free to pursue whales once we cross the seventy-second parallel. Opinion is divided, as to the most advantageous grounds, the mysticetus . . .'

'Mysticetus?' broke in Drinkwater frowning.

'*Baleana Mysticetus*, the Greenland Right Whale . . .' Drinkwater nodded as Sawyers continued, 'has become wary of the approach of man in recent years. There are those who advocate his pursuit upon the coast of Spitzbergen, those who are more disposed to favour a more westerly longitude, along the extremity of the ice.'

'I gather you favour this latter option?' Sawyers nodded while a silent shake of the head indicated that Waller did not. 'I see, please go on.'

'I do not think this late arrival on the grounds will inconvenience us greatly. It was our practice to spend the first month in the Greenland Sea in sealing, waiting for the ice to open up and spending the first days of continuous daylight in the hunting of seal, walrus and bear. However, those of us that have, of late, pursued mysticetus into the drift ice, have been rewarded by a haul as high as ten or even a dozen fish in a season, which amply satisfies us.'

It was clear that Harvey and Sawyers were of one mind in the matter. But if the whale-fleet dispersed his own task became impossible.

'Would you be kind enough to indicate the degree to which these options are supported by the other masters?' The three men consulted together while Drinkwater rose and pulled out a chart of the Greenland Sea. Seven hundred miles to the north-north-west of Bressay Sound lay the island of Jan Mayen. His present company, he knew, still referred to it as Trinity Island, after their own corporation.

'I think, sir,' said Harvey in his broad accent, 'that a few favour the Spitzbergen grounds while the majority will try the ice-edge.'

'Very well.' Drinkwater paused to think. He could not cover both areas so which was the better post to take up with the *Melusine*? During the last war Danish privateers had operated out of the fiords of Norway. Would these hardy men attempt to entrap British whale-ships on the coast of Spitzbergen? The battle of Copenhagen and Britain's new alliance with Russia must surely persuade Denmark that she had nothing to gain by provoking Britain from her Norwegian territories. Drinkwater cleared his mind of these diplomatic pre-occupations. His own responsibilities were to the whalers and he conceived the greater threat, as indicated at the Admiralty, to come from French privateers. Long experience of French corsairs had led Drinkwater to admire their energy. He did not share the contempt of

59

many of his contemporaries for French abilities. The Republican Navy had given the Royal Navy a bloody nose from time to time, he recalled, thinking that even the great Sir Edward Berry, one of Nelson's Band of Brothers, had nearly caught a tartar in the *Guillaume Tell* off Malta in 1800. And the corsairs were of greater resource than the Republican Navy. What of those Breton ships that had sailed north? Where were they now?

He looked at the chart. The huge area of the Greenland Sea was imperfectly surveyed. Hill had added every scrap of detail he could glean but it was little enough. Drinkwater concentrated on the problem from the French point of view. If the intention of the privateers was to harass British whalers then they would probably hide in the fiords of Iceland or around Cape Farewell. The former, ice free on its southern and eastern coasts would threaten the Greenland fishery whilst the less hospitable coast of Greenland would permit a descent upon the trade in the Davis Strait. Either station would give the ships a favourable cast well to the windward of British cruisers in the Western Approaches and a clear passage back to the French coast where they had only to run the British blockade to reach safety. And given the fact that they were unlikely to be making for the great French naval arsenals this would be relatively simple. It was clear that if the Hull ships were determined to fish in the Greenland Sea he must conceive the greater threat, if it existed at all, would come from Iceland and that he should support the whalers on the ice-edge.

'I shall make known to you that I shall cruise upon the ice-edge in company with the majority of ships. I would ask you therefore that you appoint one of your number to consult and advise me as to your intentions, that we may not be at cross-purposes.'

'That matter has already been settled, Captain. Abel Sawyers, here, has been elected to be our commodore.' Harvey's ugly face smiled.

'Then that is most satisfactory . . .'

'There is one thing, Captain.' Waller's apparent insignificance was enhanced by a thin voice with an insinuating quality.

'What is that, Captain Waller?'

'I do not think you understand the diversity of individual method employed by masters in the whale-fishery. We do not expect to be constrained by you in *any* way. We wish to be free to chase fish wherever we think it to our advantage.'

Drinkwater shrugged, irritated by the man's pedantic manner.

Alone among the whale-ship masters Waller seemed the least appropriate to his calling.

'Captain Waller, I have my orders and they are to *extend to you* the protection of a ship of war. I cannot prevent you from hunting the whale wherever you desire, but I can and have arranged a rendezvous and a distress signal to use if you are attacked.'

'And what do you propose?'

'My gunner is preparing Blue Lights for you. A Blue Light shot into the sky and accompanied by two guns may transmit your distress over a large distance and if this signal is used whenever strange sails are sighted I am sanguine that *Melusine* may be deployed to cover you.'

'And if we are attacked from two directions simultaneously?' asked Waller.

'I shall deal with hypothetical situations when they become real, sir, you ain't the only people used to active operations with boats, Captain.'

'And you are not the only people fitted with cannon. There have been instances where whale-ships have driven off an enemy . . .'

'Chiefly, I believe,' snapped Drinkwater, 'when the enemy was one of their own kind disputing the possession of a fish. Frankly, Captain Waller, since you have made it clear that you intend to fish off Spitzbergen I cannot see why you wish to enquire into the methods I intend to employ to protect the trade.'

Waller did not retort but lolled back into his chair. 'Aye, Captain, you will perfectly satisfy me if you do not interfere.'

Angrily Drinkwater looked at Harvey and Sawyers. They were clearly out of sympathy with Waller but said nothing as he equally obviously represented a body of opinion among this curious Arctic democracy. Drinkwater swallowed pride and anger. 'Another glass, gentlemen,' he conciliated. 'I suggest that we remain in company until the seventy-second parallel in eight degrees easterly longitude.' He laid a finger on the chart and the three men bent over the table. 'From here the Spitzbergen ships can detach.'

'I think that would be most agreeable,' said Sawyers.

'Agreed,' added Harvey.

Waller on the left, smoothed the chart out and nodded. 'Aye, 'twill do,' he said thoughtfully. Drinkwater saw his three visitors to their boats. The sun had disappeared behind a bank of cloud as they came on deck.

'I shall hoist the signal to weigh at noon tomorrow then, gentlemen.'

They all agreed. Drinkwater looked across the Sound at the whalers.

Odd shapes had appeared at their mastheads.

'Crow's nests,' explained Sawyers in answer to Drinkwater's question. 'It is necessary to provide an elevated lookout post both for sighting the fish and for navigating through the ice. I myself have spent many hours aloft there and have a nest of my own devising.'

'I see . . . Good night, Captain Waller.'

'They are also indispensable for shooting unicorns, Captain,' added Harvey.

'Unicorns? Come sir you haze me . . .'

'A name given to the Narwhal or Tusked Dolphin, Captain Drinkwater, after which my own ship is named. He may be hit from the masthead where a shot from the deck will be deceived by the refraction of the sea.'

'Ahhh . . . Your boat, Captain Harvey.'

Harvey's ugly face cracked into a grin and he held out his hand. 'If a King's Officer won't take offence from an old man, may I suggest that excessive concern will have a bad effect on you. Whatever heated air may have been blown about back in Hull, no-one expects the impossible. While we don't want to be attacked by plaguey Frenchmen we are more anxious to hunt fish.'

'I fear I cut a poor figure.'

'Not at all, man, not at all. You are unfamiliar with our ways and your zeal does you credit.'

'Thank you.'

'And I'll go further and say, speaking plainly as a Yorkshireman, you'm a damned sight better than that bloody Palgrave.' Harvey went over the side still smiling. Drinkwater turned to say farewell to Sawyers. The Quaker was staring aloft.

'Thou woulds't oblige thyself, Captain, by constructing a similar contrivance aloft.'

'A crow's nest? But it would incommode the striking of my t'gallant masts in a gale, Captain Sawyers.'

Sawyers nodded. 'Thou hast a dilemma, Friend; to keep thy lofty spars in order to have the advantage in a chase, or to snug thy rig down and render it practical.'

Drinkwater looked aloft and Sawyers added, 'Come, Friend, visit the *Faithful* tomorrow forenoon and familiarise yourself with the workings of a whale-ship.'

'I am obliged to you, Captain.' They shook hands and Sawyers clambered down into his boat. Drinkwater watched him pulled away, across the steel-grey waters of the Sound.

Immediately after Lieutenant Germaney had seen the captain over the side the following morning he returned to the gunroom and kicked out those of its occupants who lingered over their breakfasts. He took four glasses of blackstrap in quick succession and sent for the Reverend Obadiah Singleton.

'Take a seat, Mr Singleton. A glass of blackstrap?'

'I do not touch liquor, Mr Germaney. What is it you wish to see me about?'

'You are a physician are you not?'

Singleton nodded. 'Can you cure clap?'

Singleton's astonishment was exceeded by Germaney's sense of relief. The wine now induced a sense of euphoria but he deemed it prudent to restrain Singleton from any moralising. 'I don't want your offices as a damned parson, d'you hear? Well, what d'you say, God damn it?'

'Kindly refrain from blasphemy, Mr Germaney. I had thought of you as a gentleman.'

Germaney looked sharply at Singleton. 'A gentleman may be unfortunate in the matter of his bedfellows, Singleton.'

'I was referring to the intemperance of your language, but no matter. You contracted this in Hull, eh?'

Germaney nodded. 'A God da . . . a bawdy house.'

'Were you alone?'

'No. I was in company.'

'With whom, Mr Germaney? Please do not trifle with me, I beg you.'

'Captain Sir James Palgrave, the Lord Walmsley and the Honourable Alexander Glencross.'

'All gentlemen,' observed Singleton drily. 'May I ask you whether you have advertised your affliction to these other young men?'

'Good God no!'

'And why have you not consulted Mr Macpherson?'

'Because the man is a drunken gossip in whom I have not the slightest faith.'

'He will have greater experience of this sort of disease than myself, Mr Germaney, that I can assure you.'

Germaney shook his head, the euphoria wearing off and being again replaced by the dread that had been his constant companion since his first intimation of the disease. 'Can you cure me Singleton? I'll endow your mission . . .'

'Let us leave it to God and your constitution, Germaney. Now what are your symptoms?'

'I have a gleet that stings like the very devil . . .'

Germaney described his agony and Singleton nodded. 'You appear to be a good diagnostician, Mr Germaney. You are not a married man?'

'Affianced, Singleton, affianced, God damn and blast it!'

The deck of the *Faithful* presented a curious appearance to the un-initiated. Accompanied by Quilhampton, Gorton and Frey, Drink-water was welcomed by Sawyers who introduced his son and chief mate. He directed his son to show the younger men the ship and tactfully took Drinkwater on a private tour.

The *Faithful* gave an immediate impression of strength and utility, carrying five boats in high davits with three more stowed in her hold. Her decks were a mass of lines and breakers as her crew attended the final preparations for fishing and the filling of her water casks. The men worked steadily, with little noise and no attention paid to their commander and his guest as they picked their way round the cluttered deck.

Sawyers pointed aloft. 'First, Captain, the rig; it must be weatherly but easily handled. Barque rig with courses, top and t'gallant sails. Thou doubtless noticed the curious narrow-footed cut to our courses, well this clears the davits and allows me to rig the foot to a 'thwart-ships boom. The boom is secured amidships to those eyebolts on the deck and thus tacks and sheets are done away with. As thou see'st with course and topsail braces led thus, through that system of euphroes I can handle this ship, of three hundred and fifty tons burthen, with five men.'

'Ingenious.'

'Aye, 'tis indeed, and indispensable when working after my boats in pursuit of fish running into the ice. Now come . . .' Sawyers clam-bered up onto the rail and leaned his elbows on the gunwhale of one of the carvel-built whale-boats. Drinkwater admired the lovely sheer and sharp ends of the boat and at his remark a man straightened up from the work of coiling a thin, white hemp line into a series of tubs beneath the thwarts.

'Whale line,' explained Sawyers, 'six tubs per boat, totalling seven hundred and twenty fathoms. The inner end accessible to the boat steerer, so that the lines of another boat may be secured and thus extend the line. This is done in the event of a fish sounding deep or running under ice. The outer end at the bow is secured to the foreganger, a short line attaching it to the harpoon which is kept to hand here, on this rest.' The instrument itself was not in place and Sawyers added, 'This is Elijah Pucill, Captain, speksioneer and chief harpooner; a mighty hunter of mysticetus.' The man grinned and Sawyers pointed to various items in the boat.

'Five oars and a sixth for steering. We prefer the oar for steering as it doth not retard the speed of a boat like a rudder. By it the boat may be turned even when stopped. By sculling, a stealthy approach may be made to a fish caught sleeping or resting upon the surface of the ocean. Of course a whale-boat may, by the same method, be propelled through a narrow ice-lead where, by the lateral extension of her oars, she would otherwise be unable to go.'

Drinkwater nodded. 'The oars,' Sawyer tapped an ash loom, 'are secured by rope grommets to a single thole pin and may thus be trailed without loss, clearing the boat of obstruction and allowing a man two hands to attend to any other task.'

'Who commands the boat?'

'In our fishery the harpooner, although in America they are sufficiently democratic to prohibit the officer from pulling an oar and he combines the duties of mate and steersman. My boats are commanded by the chief and second mates and the speksioneer, here. They pick their boat-steerers and line managers and all are men with whom they have sailed for many seasons.

'Remember, Captain, the harpooner is the man who places the harpoon, who must cut the fish adrift if danger threatens and who, having exhausted the fish, finally comes up with him and attacks with the lance.' Sawyers pointed to half a dozen slim bladed, long shafted weapons like boarding pikes. 'The lance is plied until the vitals of the fish are found and he is deprived of life.'

'It is not against your sensibilities to deprive the fish of life, Captain?'

Sawyers looked surprised. 'Genesis, Captain, Chapter One, verses twenty-six to twenty-eight, "God gave man dominion over the fish of the sea, and over the fowl of the air, and every living thing that moveth upon the earth." And in the Eighth Psalm "the Almighty madest him to have dominion over the works of Thy hands; thou hast put all things under his feet . . . the fowl of the air, and the fish of the sea, and whatsoever passeth through the paths of the seas. O, Lord, our Lord, how excellent is thy name in all the earth . . .".'

'Amen.' The speksioneer added fervently and then Sawyers resumed his discourse as though nothing had interrupted it.

65

'It is ordained thus.' He looked at Drinkwater, 'But I do not hold with the practice used by Jaybez Harvey and others, including thy friend Ellerby, of discharging the harpoon from a gun. It is a method lately introduced and not much in favour among the more *feeling* masters. Now there,' he said indicating a massive vertical post set near the bow of the whale-boat, 'is the bollard, round which a turn of whale-line may be taken to retard his progress and the more quickly tire him. This is very necessary in the case of a young whale or one which swims under the ice. It is, as you see, deeply scored by the friction of the line and may require water, supplied by this piggin, to prevent it setting fire to the timber.'

'Good heavens, and the line is able to take this strain?'

'Aye. The line is of the very best hemp and the finest manufacture. I have seen a boat pulled under when a fish dives and towed along underwater until the fish surfaced exhausted.'

'And you recovered the boat?'

'Yes. It does not always occur and here is an axe with which the harpooner can, at any time, cut free. But once a boat is fast, the harpooner is reluctant to let it go and he may, as we say, give the fish the boat, to induce fatigue or drown it.'

'Drown it? I do not understand.'

'The fish breathes air, respiring on the surface. He is able, however, to sustain energetic swimming for many minutes before nature compels him to return to the surface for more air. Should he dive too deep, as is often the case with young fish, he may gasp many fathoms down and thus drown.'

'I see,' said Drinkwater wondering. 'It must be of the first importance to ensure that the line is properly coiled and does not foul.' The man in the boat grinned and nodded.

'Aye, Cap'n, for if it fouls and the line-tender or harpooner don't cut it through quick enough, it may capsize the boat and take a man down in its 'tanglement.'

'Thou hast seen that, Elijah, hast thou not?'

'Aye, Cap'n. Once in the Davis Strait and once off Hackluyt's Head.'

Drinkwater shook his head in admiration. 'I do not see a harpoon, Captain Sawyers, and am curious to do so.'

'Ah.' Sawyers regained the deck and led Drinkwater forward. Three men sat upon a hatch, each carefully filing the head of a harpoon. A forge was set up on deck, with bellows and anvil at which a fourth man was fashioning another.

66

'The harpoon is made of malleable iron allowing it to twist but not to break. Here, Matthew, pray show Captain Drinkwater what I mean.'

A huge man rose from the hatch and grasped the harpoon he was sharpening, holding it at each end of the shank. Drinkwater noted the narrow shank which terminated at one end in the barbed head and at the other in a hollow socket intended to take the wooden stock used by the harpooner to throw the deadly weapon.

The man Matthew walked to the rail and hooked the shank round a belaying pin. With a grunt he bent and then twisted it several times.

'The devil!'

'Old horseshoe nails, Captain, that is what the finest harpoons are made from.'

'And the barbs on the harpoon's head are sufficient to secure it in the flesh of the fish enough to tow a boat?' Drinkwater asked uncertainly.

'Aye, Friend. The mouth, or head as thou calls't it, has withered barbs as you see. The barbs become entangled in the immensely strong ligamentous fibres of the blubber and the very action of the fish in swimming away increases this. The reverse barb, or stop-wither, collects a number of the reticulated sinews which are very numerous near the skin and once well fast, it is unusual to draw it.'

They passed on along the deck. Sawyers pointed out the various instruments used to flens a whale. They were razor sharp and gleaming with oil as each was inspected.

'They are cleaner than my surgeon's catling.'

The two men peered into the hold where, Sawyers explained, the 'whale-bone' and casks of blubber would be stowed, 'If God willed it that they had a good season.'

Drinkwater followed Sawyers into his quarters. It was a plain cabin, well lit by stern lights through which Drinkwater could see *Melusine*.

'I see you have struck your main topgallant mast, Friend.'

'I took your advice.' Drinkwater took the offered glass of fine port, 'To the mortification of several officers, I am amputating the upper twelve feet.'

'You will not regret it.'

'Thank you for your hospitality, Captain Sawyers. I have to admit to being impressed.'

Sawyers smiled with evident pleasure. 'The ship is but a piece of *man's* ingenuity, Captain Drinkwater. You have yet to see the wonders of the Almighty in the Arctic Seas.'

PART TWO

The Greenland Sea

'Oh Greenland is a cold country,
And seldom is seen the sun;
The keen frost and snow continually blow,
And the daylight never is done,
      Brave boys!
And the daylight never is done.'

Sea-song, *The Man O' War's Man*

The Matter of a Surgeon

'You are entirely to blame, Mr Singleton,' shouted Drinkwater above the howl of the wind in the rigging. He stood at the windward rail, holding a backstay and staring down at the missionary who leaned into the gale on the canting deck.

'For what, sir?' Singleton clasped the borrowed tarpaulins tightly, aware that they were billowing dangerously. In an instant they were as wet with rain and spray as the captain's.

'For the gale!'

'The gale? *I* am to blame?' Singleton made a grab for a rope as *Melusine* gave a lee lurch. 'But that is preposterous . . .'

Drinkwater smiled, Singleton's colour was a singular, pallid green. 'Breathe deeply through the nose, you'll find it revivifying.'

Singleton did as he was bid and a little shudder passed through him. 'That is a ridiculous superstition, Captain Drinkwater. Surely you do not encourage superstition?'

'It don't matter what *I* think, Mr Singleton. The people believe a parson brings bad weather and you cannot deny it's blowing.'

'It is blowing exceedingly hard, sir.' Singleton looked to windward as a wave top reared above the horizon. *Melusine* dropped into the trough and it seemed to Singleton that the wave crest, rolling over in an avalanche of foam, would descend onto *Melusine*'s exposed side. Singleton's mouth opened as *Melusine* felt the sudden lift of the advancing sea imparted to her quarter. The horizon disappeared and Singleton's stomach seemed far beneath the soles of his feet. He gasped with surprise as the breaking crest crashed with a judder against *Melusine*'s spirketting and shot a column of spray into the air. As *Melusine* felt the full force of the wind on the wave-crest she leaned to leeward and dropped into the next trough. Singleton's stomach seemed to pass his eyes as the wind whipped the spray horizontally over the rail with a spiteful patter. Beside him an apparently heartless Captain Drinkwater raised his speaking trumpet.

'Mr Rispin, you must clear that raffle away properly before starting the fid or you will lose gear.' He turned to the missionary, 'It is an article of faith to a seaman, Mr Singleton,' he grinned, 'but it is, I agree, both superstitious and preposterous. As for the wind I must disagree, if only to prepare you for what may yet come. It blows hard, but not *exceedingly* hard. This is what we term a whole gale. It is quite distinct from a storm. The wind-note in the rigging will rise another octave in a storm.'

'Mr Bourne sent below to the cockpit to turn the young gentlemen out to strike the topgallant masts,' Singleton said, the colour creeping back into his cheeks and checking the corpse-like blue of his jaw. 'I had supposed the term to apply to some form of capitulation to the elements.'

Drinkwater smiled and shook his head. 'Not at all. The ship will ride easier from a reduction in her top hamper. It will lower her centre of gravity and reduce windage, thus rendering her both more comfortable and more manageable.' He pointed to leeward. 'Besides we do not want to outrun our charges.' Singleton stared into the murk to starboard and caught the pale glimpse of sails above the harder solidity of wallowing hulls that first showed a dull gleam of copper and then seemed to disappear altogether.

'And this,' Singleton said, feeling better and aware that any distraction, even that of watching the sailors, was better than the eternal preoccupation with his guts, 'is what Rispin is presently engaged upon?'

'Aye, Mr Singleton, that was my intention,' the speaking trumpet came up again. 'Have a care there, sir! Watch the roll of the ship, God damn it!' The trumpet was lowered. 'Saving your cloth, Mr Singleton.'

'I begin to see a certain necessity for strong expressions, sir.'

Drinkwater grinned again. 'A harsh environment engenders a vocabulary to match, Mr Singleton. This ain't a drawing-room at Tunbridge nor, for that matter, rooms at . . . at, er at whatever college you were at.'

'Jesus.'

'I beg your pardon?'

'Jesus College, Oxford University.' There was a second's pause and both men laughed.

'Ah. I'm afraid I graduated from the cockpit of a man o' war.'

'Not an *alma mater* to be recommended, sir, if my own experiences . . .'

'A cesspit, sir,' said Drinkwater with sudden asperity, 'but I do

72

assure you that England has been saved by its products more than by all the professors in history . . .'

'I did not mean to . . .'

'No matter, no matter.' Drinkwater instantly regretted his intemperance. But the moment had passed and it was not what he had summoned Singleton for. Such levity ill became the captain of a man o' war. 'We were talking of the wind, Mr Singleton, and the noise made by a storm, beside which this present gale is nothing. I believe, Mr Singleton, that the wind in Greenland is commonly at storm force, that the particles of ice carried in it can wound the flesh like buckshot and that a man cannot exist for more than a few minutes in such conditions.'

'Sir, the eskimos manage . . .'

'Mr Singleton,' Drinkwater hurried on, 'what I am trying to say is that I need your services here. On this ship, God damn it. If the eskimos manage so well without you, Mr Singleton, cannot you leave them in their primitive state of savagery? What benefits can you confer . . .?'

'Captain Drinkwater! You amaze me! What are you saying? Surely you do not deny the unfortunate natives the benefits of Christianity?'

'There are those who consider your religion to be as superstitious in its tenets as the people's belief that you can raise a gale, Mr Singleton.'

'Only a Jacobin Frenchman, sir! Not a British naval captain!' Singleton's outrage was so fervent that Drinkwater could not resist laughing at him any more than he could resist baiting him.

'Sir, I, I protest . . .' Drinkwater mastered his amusement.

'Mr Singleton, you may rest easy. The solitude of command compels me to take the occasional advantage . . . But I am in desperate need of a surgeon. Macpherson has, as you know, been in a strait-jacket for three days . . .'

'The balance of his mind is quite upset, sir, and the delirium tremens will take some time to subside. Peripheral neuritis, the symptom of chronic alcoholic poisoning . . .'

'I am aware that he is a rum-sodden wreck, devil-take it! That is why I need your knowledge as a physician.'

Melusine's motion eased as Rispin came across the deck and knuckled his hatbrim to report the topgallant masts struck. 'Very well, Mr Rispin. You may pipe the watch below.'

'Aye, aye, sir.'

'And send Mr Quilhampton to me.' He dismissed Rispin and

turned to Singleton. 'Very well, Mr Singleton. I admire your sense of vocation. It would be an unwarranted abuse of my powers to compel you to do anything.' He paused and fixed Singleton with his grey eyes. 'But I shall expect you to volunteer to stand in for Macpherson until such time as we land you upon the coast of Greenland. Ah, Mr Q, will you attend the quarterdeck with your quadrant and bring up my sextant. Have Frey bring up the chronometer . . .'

Singleton turned to windward as the captain left him. The wind and sea struck him full in the face and he gasped with the shock.

Mr Midshipman the Lord Walmsley nodded at the messman. The grubby cloth was drawn from the makeshift table and the messman placed the rosewood box in front of his lordship. Drawing a key from his pocket Lord Walmsley unlocked and lifted the lid. He took out the two glasses from their baize-lined sockets and placed one in front of himself and one in front of Mr Midshipman the Honourable Alexander Glencross whose hands shot out to preserve both glasses from rolling off the table.

'Cognac, Glencross?'

'If you please, my Lord.'

Walmsley filled both glasses to capacity, replaced the decanter and locking the box placed it for safety between his feet. He then took hold of his glass and raised it.

'The fork, Mr Dutfield.'

'Aye, aye, my Lord.' Dutfield picked up the remaining fork that lay on the table for the purpose and stuck it vigorously into the deck beam. The dim lighting of the cockpit struck dully off it and Walmsley and Glencross swigged their brandy.

'Damn fine brandy, Walmsley.'

'Ah,' said his lordship from the ascendancy of his position and his seventeen years, 'the advantages of peace, don't you know.' He frowned and stared at the two midshipmen at the forward end of the table then, catching Dutfield's eye raised his own to the fork above their heads. 'The fork, Mr Dutfield.'

Mr Frey looked hurriedly up from his book and then snapped it shut, hurrying away while Dutfield's face wrinkled with an expression of resentment and pleading. 'But mayn't I . . .?'

'You know damn well you mayn't. You are a youngster and when the fork is in the deck beam your business is to make yourself scarce. Now turn in!'

Mumbling, Dutfield turned away.

74

'What did you say?'

'Nothing.'

Walmsley grinned imperiously. 'Dutfield you have forgot your manners. I could have sworn he said "good night", couldn't you, Glencross?'

'Oh, indeed, yes.'

Dutfield began to unlash his hammock. 'Well, Dutfield, where *are* your manners? You know, just because The Great Democrat has forbidden any thrashing in the cockpit does not prevent me from having your hammock cut down in the middle watch. Now where are your manners?'

'Good night,' muttered Dutfield.

'Speak up damn you!'

'Good night! There, does that satisfy you?'

Walmsley shook his head. 'No, Dutfield,' said his lordship refilling his glass, 'it does not. Now what have I told you, Dutfield, about manners, eh? The hallmark of a gentleman, eh?'

'Good night, *my Lord*.'

'Ah . . .' His lordship leaned back with an air of satisfaction. 'You see, Glencross, he isn't such a guttersnipe as his pimples proclaim . . .'

'Are you bullying again?' Quilhampton entered the cockpit. 'Since when did you take over the mess, Walmsley?'

'Ah, the *harm*less Mr Q, together with his usual ineffable ch*arm* . . .' Walmsley rocked with his own wit and Glencross sniggered with him.

'Go to the devil, Walmsley. If you take my advice you'd stop drinking that stuff at sea. Have you seen the state of the surgeon?'

'Macpherson couldn't hold his liquor like a gentleman . . .'

'God, Walmsley, what rubbish you do talk. Macpherson drinks from idleness or disappointment and has addled his brain. Rum has rotted him as surely as the lues, and the same will happen to you, you've the stamp of idleness about you.'

'How dare you . . .!'

'Pipe down, Walmsley. You would best address the evening to consulting Hamilton Moore. I am instructed by the captain that he wishes to see your journals together with an essay upon the "Solution of the longitude problem by the Chronometer".'

'Bloody hell!'

'Where's Mr Frey?'

'Crept away to his hammock like a good little child.'

'Good. Be so kind as to tell him to present his journal to the captain tomorrow. Good night.' Quilhampton swung round to return to the deck, bumping into Singleton who entered the cockpit with evident reluctance.

'Cheer up, sir!' he said looking back into the gloom, 'I believe the interior of an igloo to be similar but without some of the *inconveniences* . . .' Chuckling to himself Quilhampton ran up the ladder.

'Good evening, gentlemen.' Singleton's remark was made with great forbearance and he moved stealthily as *Melusine* continued to buck and swoop through the gale.

He managed to seat himself and open the book of sermons, ignoring the curious and hostile silence of Walmsley and Glencross who were already into their third glass of brandy. They began to tell each other exaggerated stories of sexual adventure which, Singleton knew, were intended to discomfit him.

'. . . and then, my dear Glencross, I took her like an animal. My, there was a bucking and a fucking the like of which would have made you envious. And to think that little witch had looked at me as coy as a virgin not an hour since. What a ride!'

'Ah, I had Susie like that. I told you of Susie, my mother's maid. She taught me all I know, including the French way . . .' Glencross rolled his eyes in recollection and was only prevented from resuming his reminiscence by Midshipman Wickham calling the first watch. The two half-drunk midshipmen staggered into their tarpaulins.

Singleton sighed with relief. He had long ago learned that to remonstrate with either Walmsley or Glencross only increased their insolence. He put his head in his hands and closed his eyes. But the vision of Susie's French loving would not go.

Eight bells rang and Walmsley and Glencross staggered out of the cockpit. As he passed Dutfield's hammock, his lordship nudged it with his shoulder.

'Stop that at once, Dutfield,' deplored Walmsley in a matriarchal voice, 'or you will go blind!'

Captain Drinkwater looked from one journal to another. Mr Frey's was a delight. The boy's hand was bold and it was illustrated by tiny sketches of the coastline of east Scotland and the Shetlands. There were some neat drawings of the instruments and weapons used in the whale-fishery and a fine watercolour of *Melusine* leading the whalers out of the Humber past the Spurn Head lighthouse. The others lacked any kind of redeeming feature. Wickham's did show a little promise from the literary point of view but that of Lord Walmsley was clearly a hurried crib of the master's log. Walmsley disappointed him. After the business of Leek, Drinkwater had thought some appeal had been made to the young man's better feelings. He was clearly intelligent and led Glencross about like a puppy. And now this disturbing story about the pair of them being drunk during the first watch. Drinkwater swore. If only Rispin had done something himself, or called for Drinkwater to witness the matter, but Drinkwater had not gone on deck until midnight, having some paperwork to attend to. One thing was certain and that was that unpunished and drunken midshipmen could quickly destroy discipline. Men under threat of the lash for the least sign of insobriety would not thank their captain for letting two boys get drunk on the pretext of high spirits. And, thought Drinkwater with increasing anger, it would be concluded that Walmsley and Glencross were allowed the liberty because of their social stations.

He was on the point of sending for the pair when he decided that, last night's episode having gone unpunished though not unpublicised, he must make an example as public as the offence. And it was damned chilly aloft in these latitudes, he reflected grimly.

'Mistah Singleton, sah!' The marine sentry announced.

'Come in! Ah, Mr Singleton, please take a seat. What can I do for you?'

'First a message from Mr Bourne, sir, he says to tell you, with his compliments, that he has sighted the *Earl Percy* about three leagues to leeward but there is still no sign of the *Provident*.'

'Thank you. I had thought we might have lost contact with more ships during the gale but these whaling fellows are superb seamen. Now, sir. What can I do for you? It was in my mind that you might like to address the men with a short sermon on Sunday. Nothing too prolix, you understand, but something appropriate to our present situation. Well, what d'you say?'

'With pleasure, sir. Er, the other matter which I came about, sir, was the matter of the surgeon.'

'Ahhh . . .'

'Sir, Macpherson is reduced to a state of anorexy. I do not pretend that there is very much that can be done to save him. Already his groans are disturbing the men and he is given to almost constant ramblings and the occasional ravings of a lunatic.'

'You have been to see him?'

Singleton sighed. 'It seems you have carried the day, sir.'

Drinkwater smiled. 'Don't be down-hearted, Mr Singleton. I am sure that you would not wish to spend all your days aboard *Melusine* in

77

idleness. If my gratitude is any consolation you have it in full measure.'

'Thank you, sir. After you have landed me you will find that the whalers each have a surgeon, should you require one. I shall endeavour to instruct the aptest of my two mates.'

'That is excellent. I shall make the adjustments necessary in the ship's books and transfer the emoluments due to Macpherson . . .'

'No, sir. I believe he has a daughter living. I shall have no need of money in Greenland and the daughter may as well have the benefit . . .'

'That's very handsome of you.'

'There is one thing that I would ask, Captain Drinkwater.'

'What is that?'

'That we transfer Macpherson to the hold and that I be permitted to use his cabin.'

Drinkwater nodded. 'Of course, Mr Singleton, and I'm obliged to you.'

The gale increased again with nightfall and Drinkwater waited until two bells in the first watch. An advocate of Middleton's three watch system he liked to know who had the deck at any time during the twenty-four hours without the wearisome business of recollecting who had been the officer of the watch on his last visit to the quarterdeck. He wrapped his cloak about him and stepped out onto the berth deck. The marine sentry snapped to attention. Drinkwater ran up the ladder.

Melusine buried her lee rail and water rolled into the waist. The air was damp and cold, the clouds pressed down on the mastheads, obscuring the sky but not the persistent daylight of an Arctic summer. It was past nine in the evening, ship's time, and in these latitudes the sun would not set for some weeks.

Drinkwater made for the lee rail, took a look at the convoy, remarked the position of the *Nimrod* as sagging off to leeward.

'Mr Rispin, have the midshipmen of the watch make *Nimrod*'s number and order that he closes the commodore.'

'Aye, aye, sir.'

Drinkwater took himself across the deck to the weather rail where the vertical side of the ship deflected the approaching wind up and over his head, leaving its turbulence to irritate those less fortunate to leeward. He began to pace ruminatively up and down, feigning concentration upon some abstruse problem while he watched the two midshipmen carry out the simple order. After a little he called the lieutenant of the watch.

'Mr Rispin, I desired you that the midshipmen of the watch hoisted the signal. Send that yeoman forward. How else do you expect the young gentlemen to learn without the occasional advantage of practical experience?'

The wind was strong enough to require a practised hand at the flag-halliards.

Expecting a fouled line or even the loss of one end of the halliard Drinkwater was secretly delighted when he observed Number Five flag rise upside down from the deck.

'Mr Rispin!'

'Sir?'

'Have that yeoman called aft and instruct the young gentlemen in the correct manner to hoist numerals.' The exchange was publicly aired for the benefit of the watch on deck. There were a number of grins visible.

When the signal had been hoisted and *Nimrod's* attention been called to it by the firing of a gun, Drinkwater called the two midshipmen to him.

'Well, gentlemen. What is your explanation of this abysmal ignorance?'

'An error, sir,' said Walmsley. Drinkwater leaned forward.

'I detect, sir,' he said, 'that you have been drinking. What about you, Mr Glencross?'

'Beg pardon, sir.'

'We are not drunk, sir,' added Walmsley.

'Of course not, Mr Walmsley. A gentleman does not get *drunk*, does he now, eh?'

The midshipmen shook their contrite heads. Experience had taught them that submission would purchase them a quick release.

'The problem is that I am not greatly interested in your qualities as gentlemen. You will find gentlemen forward among the lord mayor's men, you will find gentlemen lolling at Bath or Tunbridge, you will find gentlemen aplenty in the messes of His Majesty's regiments of foot and horse. Those are places proper to gentlemen with no other abilities to support them beyond a capacity for brandy.

'You may, perhaps, also find gentlemen upon the quarterdeck of a British man-o'-war, but they have no *right* there unless they are first and foremost seamen and secondly officers, capable of setting a good example to their men.

'In a few years you will be bringing men to the gratings for a check-shirt for the offence your gentility has led you into. Now, Mr Glencross, the fore topmasthead for you; and Mr Walmsley the main. There you may reflect upon the wisdom of what I have just told you.'

He watched the two young men begin to ascend the rigging. 'Mr Rispin, bring them down at eight bells. And not a moment earlier.'

The First Whales

Drinkwater turned from the stern window and seated himself at the table: He drew the opened journal towards him. The brilliant sunlight that reflected from the sea onto the deckhead of the cabin was again reflected onto his desk and the page before him. He picked up his pen and began to write.

The ships favouring the Spitzbergen grounds left us in latitude 72° North and 8° East'ly longitude. Among those left under my convoy are Faithful, *Capt. Sawyers, and* Narwhal, *Capt. Harvey. Their appearance much changed as they disdain to shave north of the Arctic Circle. It fell calm the next morning and the air had a crystal purity. Towards evening I detected a curious luminosity to the northward, lying low across the horizon. This the whale-fishers denominate 'ice blink'. Towards midnight, if such it can be described with no need to light the binnacle lamps, a steady breeze got up, whereupon the ships crowded on sail and stood to the northwards. At morning the 'ice-blink' was more pronounced and accompanied by a strange viscid appearance of the sea. There was also an eerie and subtle change in the atmosphere that seemed most detectable by the olfactory senses and yet could not be called a smell. By noon the reason for these strange phenomenae was apparent. A line of ice visible to the north and west. I perceived immediately the advantages of a 'crow's nest'. All are well on board . . .*

He was interrupted by a loud and distant howl. It seemed to come from the hold and reminded Drinkwater of the unfortunate and now insane Macpherson.

. . . except for the surgeon, whose condition by its very nature, disturbs the peace of the ship.

But it was not Macpherson. The knock at the door was peremptory and Quilhampton's eager face filled with excitement. 'Whales, sir, they've lowered boats in chase!'

'Very well, Mr Q. I'll be up directly.'

At a more sedate pace Drinkwater followed him on deck. He saw the whales almost immediately, three dark humps, moving slowly through the water towards the *Melusine*. In the calm sea they left a gentle wake trailing astern of their bluff heads, only a few whirls visible from the effort of their mighty tails. One of them humped its back and seemed to accelerate. A fine jet of steamy spray spouted from its spiracle. They crossed *Melusine* 's stern not one hundred feet away, their backs marked by some form of wart-like growths. From the rail Drinkwater could clearly see the sphinctal contractions of the blow-hole as the mighty creature spouted.

The watch, scattered at the rails and in the lower rigging were silent. There was something profoundly awe-inspiring in the progress of the three great humps, as they moved with a ponderous innocence through the plankton-rich water. But then the boats passed in energetic pursuit and *Melusine*'s people began to cheer. Drinkwater marked Sawyers Junior, pulling the bow oar of *Faithful*'s number two boat. He wore a sleeveless jerkin and a small brimmed hat. In the stern stood the boat-steerer, leaning on the long steering oar, the coloured flag attached to a staff with which they signalled their ship fluttered like an ensign.

Drinkwater also noticed Elijah Pucill sweep past in *Faithful*'s number-one boat. There were more than a dozen boats engaged in the pursuit now, their crews pulling at their oar looms until they bent, springing from the water to whip back ready for the next stroke. Already the whalers were swinging their yards, to catch what breeze there was and work up in support of their boats.

'Don't impede the whalers, Mr Hill, let them pass before you trim the yards to follow.'

'Aye, aye, sir.'

He looked again at the whales and saw they had disappeared. The boats slowed and Drinkwater watched a few kittiwakes wheel to the south and wondered if they could see the whales. Within a few minutes the boats were under way again, following the kittiwakes. But two boats had veered away at a right angle and Drinkwater noticed with sudden interest that they were from *Faithful*. He hauled himself up on the rail and, leaning against the mizen backstays, pulled out his Dollond glass.

There was a flurry of activity among the boats to the south. One had struck and its flag was up as the whale began to tow it. The other boats set off in pursuit. Drinkwater swung his glass back towards Sawyers and Pucill. They were no more than eight cables away and Drinkwater could see both men standing up in the bows of their boats while the crews did no more than paddle them steadily forward.

Then there was a faint shout and Drinkwater saw the whale. He saw a harpoon fly and Sawyers's boat steerer throw up the flag. Pucill had dropped his harpoon and jumped back to his oar as Sawyers's boat began to slide forward. A faint cloud of smoke enveloped the harpoon and Drinkwater remembered the bollard and a snaking line. He could see the splash of water from the piggin and then the rushing advance of the whale stopped abruptly and it sounded. Pucill's boat came up alongside Sawyers's and lay on its oars. Through the glass Drinkwater could see Pucill stand up again, both he and Sawyers hefting their lances. They stayed in this position for several minutes, like two sculptures and Drinkwater began to tire of trying to hold the glass steady. He lowered it and rubbed his eye. He was aware now of a cloud of seabirds, gathered as if from nowhere over this spot in the ocean. He could hear their cries and suddenly the whale breached. For a split second he saw its huge, ugly head with its wide, shiny portcullis of a mouth and the splashes of whitened skin beneath the lower lip that curled like a grotesque of a negro's. The lances darted as the boats advanced and there was a splashing of foam and lashing of fins as the head submerged again and the back seemed to roll over. Then the tail emerged, huge, horizontally-fluked and menacing the boats as they back-watered. The crack as it slapped the water sounded like artillery, clearly audible to the watching Melusines. They saw the pale shape of a belly and the brief outline of a fin as the boats closed for the kill. The lances flashed in the sun and the beast seemed to ripple in its death flurry. Then Drinkwater was aware that the sea around the boats was turning red. Mysticetus had given up the ghost.

We passed into open pack ice, Drinkwater wrote, *shortly before noon on 13th June 1803, in Latitude 74° 25' North 2° 50' East. We have sighted whales daily and taken many. The masters speak of a good year which pleases me after our previous melancholy expectations. In light winds the watch are much employed in working the ship through the ice. The officers have greatly benefitted from this experience and I have fewer qualms about their abilities than formerly. Mr Q. continues to justify my confidence in him while I find Mr Hill's services as master indispensable. I believe Mr Germaney to be unwell, suffering from some torpor of the spirits. Singleton will say little beyond the fact that he suspects Germaney of suffering from the blue devils, which I conceive to be a piece of nautical conceit upon his part to deceive me as to the real nature of G's complaint.*

The people have been exercised at cutlass and small arms drill by Mr Mount and recently, when we had occasion, in the manner of the whale-ships, to moor to a large ice floe, they played a game of football.

There has been a plentiful supply of meat for the table, duck in particular being very fine. Seal and walrus have also been taken. While flensing, the carcases of the whales are frequently attacked by the Greenland Shark, a brown or grey fish some twenty odd feet in length. It is distinguished by a curious appendage from the iris of its eye. It makes good eating.

We have observed some fully developed icebergs. Their shapes are fantastical and almost magical and beggar description. In sunlight their colours range from brilliant white to a blue of . . .

Drinkwater paused. The strange and awesome sight of his first iceberg had both impressed and disquieted him for some reason that he could not fathom. Then it came to him. That pale ice-cold blue had been the colour of Ellerby's eyes. He shook his head, as though clearing his mind of an unpleasant dream. Ellerby was two hundred and fifty miles to the north-east and could be forgotten. He resumed his journal: . . . *impressive beauty. We have used them as a mark for exercising the guns which delights the people who love to see great lumps of ice flying from their frozen ramparts.*

Drinkwater laid down his pen and rubbed his shoulder. Frequent exercise with the foil had undoubtedly eased it, but the cold became penetrating in close proximity to the ice and his shoulder sometimes ached intolerably. Palgrave's decanter beckoned, but he resisted the temptation. Better to divert his mind by a brisk climb to his new-fangled crow's nest. He pulled the greygoe on and stepped out of the cabin. As he came on deck his nostrils quivered to the stimulating effect of the cold air. Swinging himself into the main shrouds he began to ascend the mainmast.

The crow's nest had been built by the carpenter and his mate. It was a deep box, bound with iron and having a trap in its base through which to enter. Inside was a hook for a speaking trumpet and a rest for a long-glass. Turning the seaman on duty out of it from the top gallant mast cross trees, Drinkwater ascended the final few feet and wriggled up inside.

'Nothink unusual, yer honour,' the lookout had reported as they passed in the rigging. Settling himself on the closed trap Drinkwater swept the horizon. He could see open water to the south and a whaler which he recognised as one of the Whitby ships. The drift ice closed to open pack within a mile of them and he counted the whalers still inside the ice within sight of the ship. Reckoning on visibility of some forty miles, he was pleased to identify all his charges and to note that most had boats out among the floes. One ship's boats were engaged in towing a whale, tail first, back to their ship while two vessels were engaged in flensing.

A number of tall, pinnacled bergs could be seen three or four miles away, while one huge castellated monster lay some ten miles off to the north-north-eastward.

Satisfied he lifted the trap with his toe by the rope grommet provided and eased himself down. Nodding to the waiting seaman at the cross trees. 'Very well, Appleyard, up you go again.'

'Aye, aye, sir.' The man scrambled up to the relative warmth of the nest and Drinkwater noted the scantiness of his clothing. He descended to the deck where Bourne, the officer of the watch, saluted him. Drinkwater was warmed by the climb and in a good humour. 'Mr Bourne, I'd be obliged if you and your midshipmen would join me for dinner.'

He went below and sent for the purser. When Mr Pater arrived Drinkwater ordered an issue of additional warm clothing at his own expense to be made to topmen. Then he sent for Mr Mount.

'Sir?' Mount stood rigidly to attention, promptly attentive to Drinkwater's summons.

'Ah, Mr Mount, I wish you to take advantage of every opportunity of taking seal and any bears to fabricate some additional warm clothing. Mr Pater informs me our stocks are barely adequate and I rely upon your talents with a musket to rectify the situation. See Mr Germaney and take a boat this afternoon. The signal for recall will be three guns.'

'Yes, sir, with pleasure.'

'I perceived a few seals basking about two miles to the east.'

'Thank you, sir. I'll take a party and see what we can accomplish.'

Drinkwater watched the hunting party leave. Fitting out the cutter for the expedition as if for a picnic Mount, Bourne, Quilhampton and Frey had been joined at the last minute by Lord Walmsley and Alexander Glencross. Mr Germaney had relieved Bourne of the deck and Mount had ensured the seamen at the oars each took a cutlass as a skillet for butchering the meat. Drinkwater toyed with the idea of watching their progress from the crow's nest but rejected it as a pointless waste of time and advised Germaney to keep a sharp watch for the onset of a fog and fire the recall the moment he thought it possible.

In the still air he heard an occasional pop through the open window of his stern lights as he recorded the air temperature and dipped a thermometer into the sea. Closing the sash frame he sat, blew on his hands and wrote:

Sawyers sends to me that he is confident this will be a good season. The sea is of a rich, greenish hue which he says indicates a plenitude of plankton and krill, tiny forms of life upon which Mysticetus feeds. He states that his men took a Razorback, an inferior species of fish which contains little oil and sinks on dying.

There is a strange remote beauty about these regions and they seem far from the realities of war. I begin to think my Lord St Vincent too sanguine in his expectations.

Drinkwater snapped the inkwell shut and leaned back in his chair. Five minutes later he was asleep. He was woken by a confused bedlam of shouts that pursuaded him they were attacked. He had slept for several hours and was stiff and uncomfortable. The sudden awakening alarmed him to the extent of reaching the door before he heard the halloos and the laughter. Muttering about the confounded hunting party he slumped back into his chair, rubbing his shoulder.

'Pass word for my coxswain!' he bawled at the sentry, listening to the order reverberate forward. Tregembo knocked and entered with the familiarity of a favoured servant. 'Coffee, zur?'

'Aye, and a bath.'

'A bath, zur?'

'Yes, God damn it! A bath, a cold bath of sea-water! You've seen three boats of whale-fishers upset in it and it'll not kill me.'

'Aye, aye, zur.' Tregembo's tone was disapproving.

'And find out what happened to Mr Mount's huntin' party.'

Despite his desire for invigoration the bath was unbelievably cold. But in the flush of blood as he towelled himself and put on the clean under-drawers laid out by Tregembo, he felt a renewal of spirits. What he had not written in his journal but which had taken root in his mind and filled it upon waking in such discomfort, was the growing conviction that *Melusine*'s services in the Arctic were going to be purely formal. The strange beauty of the ice and sea did not blind him to the dangers that a fog or storm could summon up, but the necessity of endangering his ship for such a needless cause, for working his crew hard to maintain their martial valour to no purpose, set a problematical task for their captain.

He drew the clean shirt over his head as his steward brought in the coffee.

'Thank you, Cawkwell, on the table if you please, and pass word to Mr Mount to come and see me.'

'Sir,' whispered Cawkwell, a shadow of a man who seemed in

86

constant awe of everybody. Drinkwater suspected Tregembo of specially selecting Cawkwell as his servant so that his own ascendant position was not undermined.

'I told Mr Mount to wait until you'd had your bath, zur,' he waited until Cawkwell had left the cabin, 'when you was less megrimish.'

Drinkwater looked up. 'Damn you for your insolence, Tregembo,' Tregembo grinned, 'you should try a bath, yourself.' Tregembo sniffed with disapproval and the knock of Mr Mount put an end to the familiarities.

'Enter!'

Mount, wrapped in his great-coat, stepped into the cabin. 'Ah, Mr Mount, what success did you have, eh?'

'A magnificent haul, sir, eleven seals and,' Mount's eyes were gleaming with triumph, 'a polar bear, sir!'

'A polar bear?'

'Yes, sir. Mr Frey discovered him asleep alongside a seal that he had partly eaten. He got the scent of us and made off into the water but, I suppose conceiving himself safe after putting a distance between us, clambered up onto another floe. Quilhampton and I both hit him and he made off, but we called up the boat and I got a second ball into his brain at about sixty paces.'

Drinkwater raised his eyebrows. 'A triumph indeed, Mr Mount, my congratulations.'

'Thank you, sir.'

'Now we will butcher the seals but have a party skin them and scrape the inside of the skins. I asked Mr Germaney to determine whether any of the people were conversant with tanning.'

'Yes, sir. Er, there's one other thing, sir.'

'Yes? What is it?'

'We brought back an eskimo, sir.'

'You did *what*?'

'Brought back an eskimo.'

'God bless my soul!'

After this revelation Drinkwater could no longer resist inspecting the trophies. The eskimo proved to be a young male, who appeared to have broken his arm. He was dressed in skins and had a wind-tanned face. His dark almond eyes were clouded with fear and pain and he held his left arm with his right hand. Mr Singleton was examining him with professional interest.

'A fine specimen of an innuit, Captain, about twenty years of age but with a compound fracture of the left tibia and considerable bruising. I understand he resisted the help of Mount and his party.'

'I see. What do you propose to do with him Mr Singleton? We can hardly turn him loose with his arm in such a state, yet to detain him seems equally unjust. Perhaps his family or huntin' party are not far away.' Drinkwater turned to Mount. 'Did you see any evidence of other eskimos?'

'No, sir. Mr Frey ascended an eminence and searched the horizon but nothing could be seen. He is very lucky, sir, we were some way from the ship and returning when we happened to see him. If he had not moved we would have passed him by.'

'And left him to the polar bears, eh?'

'Exactly so, sir.'

Singleton had reached under the man's jerkin and was palpating the stomach. Curiously the eskimo did not seem to mind but began to point to his mouth.

'He's had little to eat, sir, for some time,' Singleton stood back, 'and I doubt whether soap has ever touched him.' Several noses wrinkled in disgust.

'Very well. Take him below and get that arm dressed. Give the poor devil some laudanum, Mr Singleton. As for the rest of you, you may give me a full account of your adventure at dinner.' He turned aft and nearly bumped into little Frey. 'Ah, Mr Frey . . .'

'Sir?'

'Do you think you could execute a small sketch of our friend?'

'Of course sir.'

'Very good, I thank you.'

The meal itself proved a great success. The trestle table borrowed from the wardroom groaned under the weight of fresh meat, an unusual circumstance in a man-of-war. In an ill-disguised attempt to placate his commander Lord Walmsley had offered Drinkwater two bottles of brandy which the latter did not refuse. The conversation was naturally about the afternoon's adventure and Drinkwater learnt of little Frey's sudden, frightening discovery of the sleeping polar bear which the boy re-told, his eyes alight with wine and the excitement of recollected fear. He heard again how Quilhampton, his musket resting in his wooden hand, had struck the animal in the shoulder and how Mount had established his military superiority by lodging a ball in the bear's skull.

'By comparison Bourne's triumph's over the seals was of no account, sir, ain't that so, Bourne?' Mount said teasing his young colleague.

'That is an impertinence, Mount, if I had not had to secure the boat while you all raced in pursuit of quarry I should have downed the beast with a single shot.'

'Pah!' said Mount grinning, 'you should have left the boat to Walmsley or Glencross. I conceive it that you were hanging back from the ferocity of those somnolent seals.'

'Come, sir,' said Bourne with mock affront, 'd'you insinuate that I was frightened of an old bear who ran away at the approach of Mr Frey . . .'

Drinkwater looked at Frey. The boy coloured scarlet, uncertain how to take this banter from his seniors. Was Bourne implying the bear-was scared by his own size or his own courage? Or that polar bears really were timid and his moment of triumph was thereby diminished?

Drinkwater felt for the boy, particularly as Walmsley and Glencross joined the raillery. 'Oh, Mr Bourne, the bear was absolutely *terrified* of Frey, why I saw him positively roll his eyes in terror at the way Frey hefted his musket. Did you not see that, Glencross?' asked Lord Walmsley mischievously.

'Indeed I did, why I thought he was loading with his mouth and firing with his knees . . .' There was a roar of laughter from the members of the hunting party who had witnessed the excited midshipman ascend an ice hummock with a Tower musket bigger than himself. He had stumbled over the butt, tripped and fallen headlong over the hummock, discharging the gun almost in the ear of the recumbent bear.

Poor Frey was in no doubt now, as to the purpose of his senior's intentions. Drinkwater divined something of the boy's wretchedness.

'Come, gentlemen, there is no need to make Mr Frey the butt of your jest . . .'

There was further laughter, some strangled murmurs of 'Butt . . . butt . . . oh, very good, sir . . . very apt' and eventual restoration of some kind of order.

'Well, Mr Singleton,' said Drinkwater to change the subject and addressing the sober cleric, 'what d'you make of our eskimo friend?'

'He is named Meetuck, sir and is clearly frightened of white men, although he seems to have reconciled himself to us after he was offered meat . . .'

'Which he ate raw, sir,' put in Frey eagerly.

' 'Pon my soul, Mr Frey, raw, eh? Pray continue, Mr Singleton.'

'He claims to come from a place called Nagtoralik, meaning a place with eagles, though this may mean nothing as a location as we understand it, for these people are nomadic and follow their food sources. He says . . .'

'Pardon my interruption, Mr Singleton but do I understand that you converse with him?'

Singleton smiled his rare, dark smile. 'Well not converse, sir, but there are words that I comprehend which, mixed with gesture, mime and some of Mr Frey's quick drawings, enabled us to learn that he had found a *putulik*, a place with a hole in the ice through which he was presumably catching fish when he was attacked by a bear. He made his escape but in doing so fell and injured himself, breaking his arm. I think that *scuppers* the arguments of Mr Frey's persecutors, sir, that even an experienced hunter may fall in such terrain and also that the polar bear is capable of great ferocity.'

'Indeed, Mr Singleton, I believe it does,' replied Drinkwater drily. Cawkwell drew the cloth in his silent ghost-like way and the decanters began to circulate.

'Tell us, Mr Singleton how you came to learn eskimo,' asked Mount, suddenly serious in the silence following the loyal toast.

Singleton leaned forward with something of the proselytiser, and the midshipmen groaned inaudibly, but sat quiet, gulping their brandy avidly.

'The Scandinavians were the first Europeans to make contact with the coast of Greenland sometime in the tenth century. Their settlements lasted for many years before being destroyed by the eskimos in the middle of the fourteenth century. When the Englishman John Davis rediscovered the coast in 1585 he found only eskimos. Davis,' Singleton turned his gaze on the midshipmen with a pedagogic air, 'gave his name to the strait between Greenland and North America . . . The Danish Lutheran Hans Egedé was able to study the innuit tongue before embarking with his family and some forty other souls to establish a permanent colony on the West Coast of Greenland. When he returned to Copenhagen on the death of his wife he wrote a book about his work with the eskimos among whom he preached and taught for some fifteen years. His son Povel remained in Greenland and completed a translation of Our Lord's Testament, a catechism and a prayer book in eskimo. Povel Egedé died in Copenhagen in '89 and I studied there under one of his assistants.' Singleton paused again and this time it was Drinkwater upon whose face his gaze fixed.

'I refused to leave during the late hostilities and was in the city when Lord Nelson bombarded it.'

'That,' replied Drinkwater meeting Singleton's eyes, 'must have been an interesting experience.'

'Indeed, Captain Drinkwater, it persuaded me that no useful purpose can be served by armed force.'

A sense of affront stiffened the relaxing diners. To a man their eyes watched Drinkwater to see what reply their commander would make to this insult to their profession. From little Frey, ablaze with brandy and bravado; the arrogant insensitivity of Walmsley and Glencross and the puzzlement of Mr Quilhampton, to the testy irritation of a silent Mr Hill and the colouring anger of Mr Mount, the table seethed with a sudden unanimous indignation. Drinkwater smiled inwardly and looked at his first lieutenant. Mr Germaney had said not a word throughout the entire meal, declined the brandy and merely toyed with his food.

'That, Mr Singleton, is an interesting and contentious point. For my own part, and were the world as perfect as perhaps its maker intended, I should like nothing better than to agree with you. But since the French do not seem to be of your opinion the matter seems likely to remain one for academic debate, eh? Well, Mr Germaney, what do you think of Mr Singleton's proposition?'

The first lieutenant seemed at first not to have heard Drinkwater. Hill's nudge was far from surreptitious and Germaney surfaced unsure of what was required of him.

'I . . . er, I have no great opinion on the matter, sir,' he said hurriedly, hoping the reply sufficient. Remarking the enormity of Germaney's abstraction with some interest Drinkwater turned to the bristling marine officer.

'Mr Mount?'

'Singleton's proposition is preposterous, sir. The Bible is full of allusions to the use of violence, Christ's own eviction of the money-lenders from the Temple notwithstanding. Had he argued the wisdom of bombarding a civilian population I might have had some sympathy with his argument for it is precisely to preserve our homes that we serve here, but the application of force is far from useless . . .'

'But might it not become an end, rather than a means, Mr Mount?' asked Singleton, 'and therefore to be discouraged lest its use be undertaken for the wrong motives.'

'Well a man does not stop taking a little wine in case he becomes roaring drunk and commits some felonious act, does he?'

'Perhaps he should, Mr Mount,' said Singleton icily, raising a glass of water to his lips.

'I don't understand you, Mr Singleton,' said Hill at last. 'I can see you may argue that if Cain had never slain Abel the world might have been a better place but given that it is not paradise, do you advocate that we simply lie down and invite our enemies to trample over us?'

'To turn the other cheek and beat our swords into ploughshares?' added Mount incredulously.

'Why not?' asked Singleton with impressive simplicity. There was a stunned silence while they assimilated the preposterous nature of this suggestion. Then the table erupted as the officers leaned forward with their own reasons for the impossibility of such a course of action. The candle flames guttered under the discharge of air from several mouths. In the ensuing babel Drinkwater heard such expressions as 'march unchecked on London . . . dishonour our women . . . destroy our institutions . . . rape . . . loot . . . national honour . . .'

He allowed the reaction to continue for some seconds before banging sharply on the table.

'Gentlemen, please!' They subsided into silence. 'Gentlemen, you must have some regard for Mr Singleton's cloth. Preposterous as his idea sounds to you, your own conversations have disturbed him these past weeks. He doubtless finds equally odd your own assertions that you will "thrash Johnny Crapaud", "cut the throats of every damned frog" you encounter not to mention "flog any man that transgresses the Articles of War or the common usages of the service". Yet you appear devout enough when Divine Service is read, an act which Mr Singleton may regard as something close to hypocrisy . . . eh?' He looked round at them, his eyes twinkling as he encountered mystification or downright astonishment.

'Now, if you ignore abstract considerations and deal with the pragmatic you will see that we have all chosen professions which require zeal. In Mr Singleton's case religious zeal and in your case, gentlemen, the professional zeal of strict adherence to duty. Zeal is not something that admits of much prevarication or equivocation and since argument and debate might be said to be synonyms for quibbling, your two positions are quite irreconcilable. And if two opposing propositions are irreconcilable I would suggest the arguing of them a fatuous waste of time.'

Drinkwater finished his speech with his eyes on Singleton. The man appeared disappointed, as though expecting unreserved support from Drinkwater. He felt slightly guilty towards Singleton, as though owing him some explanation.

'I believe in providence, Mr Singleton, which you might interpret as God's will. To me it incorporates all the forces that you theologists claim as evoked by "God" whilst satisfactorily explaining those you do not. It is a creed much favoured by sea-officers.'

'Then you do not believe in God, Captain Drinkwater,' pronounced Singleton dolefully, 'and the power of your intellect prevents you from spiritual conversion.'

Drinkwater inclined his head. 'Perhaps.'

'Then I find that a matter of the profoundest sadness, sir,' Singleton replied quietly. The silence in the cabin was touching; even Walmsley and Glencross had ceased to wriggle, though their condition was more attributable to the brandy they had consumed than interest in polemics.

'So do I, Mr Singleton, so do I. But the moment when a man has to say whether God, as you theologists conceive him, exists or not is a profound one, not to be taken lightly. We cannot conceive of any form of existence that does not entail physical entity, witness your own archangels. Indeed even a devout man may imagine eternal life as some sort of transmigration of our corporeal selves during which all disabilities, uglinesses, warts and ill-disposed temperaments disappear. This is surely understandable, though not much above the primitive, something which our eskimo friend would comprehend.

'Now I ask you, as rational beings living in an age of scientific discovery and more particularly being seamen observing the varied phenomena of atmosphereology can you convince me of the whereabouts of these masses of corporeal souls? Of course not . . .'

'You deny the Resurrection, sir!'

Drinkwater shrugged. 'I have seen too much of death and too little of resurrection to place much faith in it applying it to common seamen like ourselves.'

'But you are without faith!' Singleton cried.

'Not at all, sir!' Drinkwater refilled his glass. 'Belief in atheism surrenders everything too much to hazard. I cannot believe that. I see only purpose in all things, a purpose that is made evident by science and manifests itself in the divine working of providence. As for the corporeal self why Quilhampton, Hill and I hold together like a trio of doubled frigates. If the enemy gets a further shot at our carcases there will likely be little left to refurbish for the life hereafter.'

The facetious jest raised a little laughter round the table and revealed that all three midshipmen were asleep.

'I agree with the Captain,' said Germaney suddenly. 'I recollect something Herrick wrote. Er,' he thought for a moment and then sat up and quoted: ' "Putrefaction is the end, of all that nature doth intend." There is great truth in that remark, great truth . . .'

Drinkwater looked sharply at his first lieutenant. Germaney's silence had seemed as uncharacteristic as his sobriety and now this sudden quotation seemed to be significant. It appeared that Singleton considered it so, for he seemed disinclined to pursue the discussion and Drinkwater himself fell silent. Mount rose and thanked him for his hospitality and the hint was taken up by the others. As the chairs scraped back the midshipmen awoke and guiltily made their apologies. Drinkwater waved them indulgently aside.

As he watched them leave the cabin he called Singleton back. 'A moment, Mr Singleton, if you please.'

Drinkwater blew out the candles that had illuminated the table. The cabin was thrown into penumbral gloom from the midnight daylight of the Arctic summer.

'You must not think that I wish to ridicule your calling. In my convalescence I met a priest of your persuasion possessed of the most enormous spiritual arrogance. I found it most distasteful. It is not that I disbelieve, it is simply that I *cannot* believe as you do. After the birth of my children I had the curious *natural* feeling that I had outlived my usefulness. My liberal ideals were in conflict with this, but I could not deny the emotion. It seemed that all thereafter was merely vanity.'

Singleton coughed awkwardly. 'Sir, I . . .'

'Do not trouble yourself on my account, Mr Singleton, I beg you. I hear that Leek is a faithful convert and protests not only the existence of God but can vouch for his very appearance.'

'Leek was very close to death by drowning, sir, perhaps a little of the great mystery was unfolded to him.' Singleton was deadly serious.

'But the intervention of science prevented it; *your* knowledge, Mr Singleton.'

'Now you do ridicule me.'

Drinkwater laughed. 'Not at all. Perhaps we are, as you said earlier, too well-informed for our own good, as it says in the Bible, "unless ye be as little children . . ." '

'That is perhaps the wisest thing you have said, sir,' Singleton at last smiled back.

'Touché. And good night to you.'

'Good night, sir.'

Drinkwater went on deck. Mr Rispin had the watch and pointed out the closer drift ice and identified the whalers in sight. There was scarcely a breath of wind and *Melusine* lay upon a sea that only moved slightly from the ground swell. Rispin's unconfident, fussy manner irritated Drinkwater until he reflected that he had been particularly lugubrious this evening and dominated the conversation. Well, damn it, it was a captain's privilege to talk nonsense.

Lieutenant Germaney sat in his hutch of a cabin contemplating the bundle of scented paper tied with a blue ribbon. After a while he opened the lantern and removed the candle tray. He began to burn the letters, a little pile of ash mounting up and spilling onto the deck.

When he had completed his task he turned to his cot and lifted the lid of the walnut case that lay upon it. Taking out one of the pair of pistols it contained, he checked its priming. Turning again to the candle he carefully replaced the tray inside the lantern and closed it, returning the thing to its hook in the deck-head.

Reseating himself he lifted the pistol, placed its muzzle in his mouth. For a moment he sat quite still then, with the cold steel barrel knocking his teeth he said, 'Putrefaction!'

And pulled the trigger.

Balaena Mysticetus

'Why in God's name was I not told of this?'

'The confidentiality which exists between a patient and his physician . . .'

'God's bones, Singleton, I will not bandy words with you. The man should have been on the sick book, along with the others that have lues and clap.' Drinkwater swore again in self reproach and added, 'I remarked some morbid humour in him.'

'I am not the ship's surgeon, Captain Drinkwater, a fact which you seem to have lost sight of . . .'

'Have a care, sir, have a care!' Both men glared angrily at each other across the cabin table. At last Singleton said, 'It seems we have adopted irreconcilable positions which, by your own account are a waste of time trying to harmonise.' The ghost of a smile crossed Singleton's dark features. Drinkwater sighed as the tension ebbed. He gestured to a chair and both men sat, thinking of the broken body of Lieutenant Francis Germaney lying in its cot. *Melusine* lay becalmed, rolling easily in a growing swell among the loose drift ice. On deck the watch fended off the larger floes while the sun shone brilliantly, dancing in coruscating glory from several fantastically shaped bergs to the north. Within the cabin the gloom of death hung like a stink.

'How long will he live?'

'Not very long. The condylar process of the left mandible is shattered, the squamous part of the temporal bone is severely damaged and there is extensive haemorrhaging from the ascending pharyngeal artery. How the internal carotid and the associated veins were not ruptured I do not know but a portion of the left lower lobe of the cortex is penetrated by pieces of bone.'

Drinkwater sighed. 'I marked some preoccupation in him from our first acquaintance, but I never guessed its origin,' he said at last. 'Might you have achieved a cure?'

Singleton shrugged. 'I believed that I might have achieved a clinical cure, he was receiving intra-urethral injections of caustic alkali and a solution of ammoniated mercury with opium. His progress was encouraging but I fear that his humour was morbid and the balance of his mind affected. He confided in me that he was affianced; I think it was this that drove him to such an extremity as to attempt his own life.'

Drinkwater shuddered, feeling a sudden guilt for his unsympathetic attitude to Germaney. 'Poor devil,' he said, adding 'you have him under sedation?'

Singleton nodded, 'Laudanum, sir.'

'Very well. And what of our other lost cause, Macpherson?'

'He will not last the week either.'

After Singleton had left the cabin Drinkwater sat for some minutes recollecting the numbers of men he had seen die. Of those to whom he had been close he remembered Madoc Griffiths, Master and Commander of the brig *Hellebore* who had died on the quarterdeck of a French frigate in the Red Sea; Blackmore, the elderly sailing master of the frigate *Cyclops* worn out by the cares and ill usage of the service. Major Brown of the Lifeguards had been executed as a spy and hung on a gibbet above the battery at Kijkduin as a warning to the British cutters blockading the Texel. More recently he thought of Mason, master's mate of the bomb vessel *Virago* who had died after the surgeon had failed to extract a splinter, of Easton, *Virago*'s sailing master, who had fallen at Copenhagen during a supposed 'truce'. And Matchett who had died in his arms. Now Germaney, a colleague who might, in time, have been a friend.

A sudden world-weariness overcame him and he was filled with a poignant longing to return home. To lie with Elizabeth would be bliss, to angle for minnows in the Tilbrook with his children charming beyond all reason.

But it was impossible. All about him *Melusine*, with her manifold responsibilities, creaked and groaned as the swell rolled her easily and the rudder bumped gently. He suddenly needed the refreshment of occupation and stood up. Flinging on his greygoe he went on deck.

A light breeze had sprung up from the westward and he received Bourne's report with sudden interest. Most of the whalers were flensing their catches, rolling the great carcases over as the masthead tackles lifted strips of pale blubber from the dead whales whose corpses were further despoiled by scores of Greenland sharks. Flocks of screaming and hungry gulls filled the air alongside each of the whalers and only one had her boats out in search of further prey.

'Very well, Mr Bourne, be so kind as to rig out the gig immediately. I shall require a day's provisions and, tell Mr Pater, two kegs of rum, a breaker of water well wrapped in canvas. One of the young gentlemen may accompany me and Mr Quilhampton is to command the boat. They may bring muskets. You will command in my absence.'

'Aye, aye, sir.' Drinkwater watched Bourne react to this news by swallowing hard.

He turned away to pace the quarterdeck while the boat was being prepared. A day out of the ship would do him good. He had a notion to cruise towards the *Faithful* or the *Narwhal* and renew his acquaintance with Sawyers or Harvey. The expedition promised well and already he felt less oppressed.

It was so very easy to forget Germaney dying in his cot. The wind steadied at a light and invigorating breeze which set the green sea dancing in the sunlight. The ice shone with quite remarkable colours which little Frey identified as varying tints of violet, cerulean blue and viridian. The larger bergs towered over the gig in wonderful minarets, towers and spires, appearing like the fantastic palaces of fairy folk and even the edges of the ice floes were eroded in their melting by the warmer sea into picturesque overhangs and strange shapes that changed in their suggestion of something else as the boat swept past.

Somehow Drinkwater had imagined the Arctic as a vast area of icy desert and the proliferation and variety of the fauna astonished him. Quilhampton suggested taking potshots at every seal they saw but Drinkwater forbade it, preferring to encourage Mr Frey's talents with his pencil. It seemed there was scarcely a floe that did not possess at least one seal. They saw several walruses while the air was filled with gulls, ivory gulls, burgomaster gulls, the sabre winged fulmar petrels and the pretty little kittiwakes with their chevron-winged young. The rapid wing beats of the auks as they lifted hurriedly from the boat's bow seemed ludicrous until they spotted a pair swimming beneath the water. The razorbills raced after their invisible prey with the agility of tiny dolphins.

Under her lugsail the gig raced across the water, Quilhampton's ingenious wooden hand on the tiller impervious to the cold.

'She goes well, Mr Q.'

'Aye, sir, but not as fast as the Edinburgh Mail.' Mr Q gazed dreamily to windward his thoughts far from the natural wonders surrounding him and filled only with the remembered image of Catriona MacEwan.

Shooting between two ice floes they came upon the *Faithful* in the very act of lowering after a whale. Captain Sawyers hailed them and Drinkwater stood up in the boat to show himself.

'I give you God's love, Captain, follow us by all means but I beseech thee to lower thy sail or the fish will see it and sound,' the Quaker called from his quarterdeck through a trumpet. 'Thou seest now the wonders of God, Captain . . .' Drinkwater recollected their valedictory remarks in Bressay Sound and waved acknowledgement.

'Douse the sail, Mr Q, let us warm the hands at the oars and, Tregembo, do you show these whale-men how they are not the only seamen who can pull a boat.'

'Aye, zur.'

Melusine's gig took station astern of *Faithful*'s Number One boat with the redoubtable Elijah Pucill at her bow oar. The gig's crew did their best, but their boat was heavier and it was not long before they were overtaken by young Sawyers and then left astern as a third boat from the whaler, her crew grinning at the out-paced naval officers as they sat glumly regarding the sterns of the racing whale-boats.

There were two spare oars in the boat and Drinkwater touched Quilhampton's arm and nodded at them. Quilhampton took the hint.

'Mr Frey, do you ship an oar and lay your back into it, eh? Better than looking so damned chilly,' he added with rasping kindness. The men lost stroke as Frey shipped an oar forward, but the boat was soon under way again and began to close upon the whalers.

'Come lads, pull there! We gain on them!' There were grins in the boat but Drinkwater, who had been studying events ahead cooled them.

'I fear, Mr Q, that you are not gaining. The others have stopped. I suspect the whale has sounded . . . there, see that flock of birds, the gulls that hover above the boats . . .'

'Oars!' ordered Quilhampton and the blades came up horizontally. The men panted over their looms, their breath cloudy and their faces flushed with effort. The boat lost way and they lay about half a cable from the whale-boats.

Carefully Drinkwater stood as Quilhampton ordered the oars across the boat.

'Issue a tot of grog, Mr Q,' said Drinkwater without taking his eyes from the patch of swirling water that lay between the whale-boats. In each of them the harpooners were up in their bows, weapons at the ready, while at the stern each boat-steerer seemed coiled over his steering oar. Drinkwater was aware of a fierce expectancy about the

99

scene and while in his own boat a mood of mild levity accompanied the circulation of the beaker, the whale-boat crews were tense with the expectation of a sudden order.

Just ahead of them the *Faithful*'s third boat lay, with Pucill's slightly broader on the starboard bow and Sawyer's to larboard.

Suddenly it seemed to Drinkwater that the circling gulls ceased their aimless fluttering. He noted some arm movements in the boat ahead, then it began to backwater fast. The gulls were suddenly overhead, screaming and mewing.

'Give way, helm hard a-starboard!'

Even as he shouted the instruction it seemed the sea not ten yards away disappeared and was replaced by the surfacing leviathan. The great jaw with its livid lower lip covered by strange growths seemed to tower over them. Then the blue-black expanse of the creature's back rolled into view as it spouted, covering them with a warm, foetid-smelling mist. The oar looms bent as the men pulled the boat clear and Quilhampton held the tiller over to bring the gig round onto a course parallel with that of the whale.

As the sea subsided round the breaching monster they caught a glimpse of its huge tail just breaking the surface. From somewhere Pucill's boat appeared and they saw the other two beyond the cetacean. The whale did not seem to have taken alarm and, pulling steadily, they managed to keep pace as Pucill raced past them. Drinkwater saw the specksioneer raise his harpoon as his boat drew level with the whale's hump and it spouted again.

The weapon struck the whale and for a second the monster seemed not to have felt it. Then it increased speed. Drinkwater could see the harpoon line snaking round the loggerhead and the faint wisp of smoke from the burning wood as Pucill paid it out. But the whale began to tow Pucill's boat. Already it was leaving *Melusine*'s gig behind and its flag was up to signal to the *Faithful* and the other boats on the far side of the whale that he was fast to a fish.

Then mysticetus lifted his mighty tail and sounded again. Pucill paid out line and Drinkwater judged the whale's dive to be almost vertical, as though the great animal sought safety in depth. Pucill's boat ceased its forward rush and the others, including the gig closed on him. Drinkwater saw frantic signals being made and Sawyers's boat ran alongside Pucill's to pass him more line. The speksioneer's boat began to move forward again, indicating the whale had levelled off and was swimming horizontally. Both the speksioneer's and the mate's boats were now in tandem, Sawyers's astern of Pucill's and

Drinkwater bade Quilhampton follow as the third of *Faithful*'s boats was also doing.

Although they had no real part in the chase it seemed to every man in the gig that it was now a matter not only of honour but of intense interest to keep up with the frightened and wounded whale. But it was back-breaking work and soon clearly a vain effort, for the towed boats swung north and headed inexorably for the ice edge where a large floe blocked their passage.

They could hear faint shouts. 'Cut! Cut!' and 'Give her the boat, Elijah! Give her the boat!' There was a scrambling of bodies from the speksioneer's boat into that of the young mate then the latter was cut free and swung aside. Pucill's boat was smashed against the edge of the floe under which the whale had passed yet the two remaining boats seemed to disregard this unhappy circumstance. Their courses diverging, they each headed for opposite extremities of the floe.

'I think, Mr Q, that it is time we set our sail again, I believe the wind to have strengthened.'

'Aye, aye, sir.'

Taking the nearer gap in the ice Quilhampton gave chase the instant the sail was sheeted home. Both the remaining whale-boats had hoisted flags and from occasional glimpses of these over the lower floes they were able to keep in touch. However it was soon apparent that the freshening of the wind was now to their advantage and they made gains on the nearer whale-boat as they wove between the ice. It was an exhilarating experience, for in the narrow leads the water was smooth yet the wind was strong as it blew over the flatter floes or funnelled violently between those with steeper sides. It seemed the whale was working to leeward. Unaware of the dangers of unseen underwater ledges of ice they were fortunate to escape with only a slight scraping of the boat as they rounded a small promontory of rotten ice from which half a dozen surprised seals plopped hurriedly into the sea, surfacing alongside to peer curiously at the passing gig.

Then, quite suddenly they came upon the death throes of the whale. Sawyers's boat was already alongside as the beast rolled and thrashed with its huge flukes. They let fly the sheets and watched as the unbarbed lances were driven into the fish again and again in an attempt to strike its heart. After a few minutes of agony it seemed to lie still and Quilhampton pointed to the approach of the second boat. Of the wrecked boat there was no sign, though the drag it had imposed upon the whale had clearly exhausted it. There was suddenly a boiling of the sea and a noise like gunfire. The whale's flukes struck the surface of the water with an explosive smack several times and then, as Sawyers continued to probe for its life, it twisted over and brought those huge flukes down upon the stern of its tormentor's boat. The Melusines watched in stupefied horror as the boat's bow flew into the air and her crew tumbled out and splashed into the sea.

But leviathan was dead. His heart had burst from the deadly incisions of Sawyers's lance and the muscle-rending effort of his dying act. The open water between the floes was red with its blood.

'Get that sail down, Tregembo! Give way and pick those men out of the water. Mr Frey, have the rum ready, the poor devils are going to need it.'

'Aye, aye, sir.'

'I thank thee for thy assistance, Friend.' Captain Sawyers raised his glass and Drinkwater savoured the richness of the Quaker's excellent port. A bogie stove in *Faithful*'s cabin burned cheerfully and Drinkwater felt warmed within and without. There remained only the ache in his neck and shoulder which he had come almost to disregard now. The sodden whale-boat's crew had been rolled in hot blankets and seemed little the worse for their experience, though Drinkwater had been chilled to the very marrow from a partial wetting in getting the hapless seamen out of the water. He remarked upon this to Sawyers.

'Aye, 'tis often to be wondered at. We have found men die of the cold long after being chafed with spirits and warmed with blankets. But the over-setting of a boat, whilst not common, is not unusual. Whalers are naturally hardy and wear many woollen undergarments, also the nature of their trade and the almost natural expectation of mishap, leads them to suffer less shock from the experience. These factors and a prompt rescue, Friend, I believe has preserved the life of many an immersed whale-man.'

'It was fortunate the fish turned down-wind or we could not have followed with such speed.'

'Aye, 'tis true that mysticetus will commonly run to windward but he sensed dense ice in that direction and from the exertions necessary to his escape had, perforce, to turn towards open water where he might breathe. Also, Friend, the wind freshened, which reminds me that if it backs another point or two thou shoulds't expect a gale of wind. For your assistance in rescuing my men I thank you as I do also for thy assistance in towing the fish alongside; there cannot be many who command King's ships who engage in such practices.' Sawyers smiled wryly.

Drinkwater tossed off his glass and picked up his hat. He grinned at the older man. 'The advantages of being a Tarpaulin officer, Captain, are better employed in the Arctic than in Whitehall.'

They shook hands and Drinkwater took his departure. Scrambling down the *Faithful*'s easy tumble-home he was aware that the cutting-in of the whale had already begun. Undeterred by his ducking, Elijah Pucill was already wielding his flensing iron as the try-tackles began to strip the blanket-piece from the carcase.

'By God, sir, remarked Quilhampton as he settled himself in the stern sheets of the gig, 'they don't work Tom Cox's traverse aboard there.'*

'Indeed not, Mr Q.'

'The ship bore east-nor'-east from the whaler's mizen top, sir, about two leagues distant.'

'Very well, Mr Q, carry on.'

'Wind's freshening all the time, Mr Hill.'

'And backing Mr Gorton, wouldn't you say?'

'Aye, and inclined to be a trifle warmer I think, not that there's much comfort to be derived from that.'

'Ah, but what should you deduce from that observation, Mr Gorton?'

Gorton frowned and shook his head.

'Fog, Mr Gorton, fog and a whole gale before the day is out or you may rate me a Dutchman. You had better inform Mr Bourne and then hoist yourself aloft and see if you can spot the captain's boat.'

'Aye, aye, sir.'

Bourne came on deck, anxiety plain on his face. 'Have you news of the Captain, Mr Hill?'

'No, Mr Bourne, but Gorton's going aloft with a glass.'

Bourne looked aloft. *Melusine* lay under her spanker and fore-topmast staysail, her reefed maintopsail aback. Hove-to she drifted slowly to leeward, ready to fill her topsail and work to windward. Bourne looked to starboard. The nearest ice lay a league under the sloop's lee.

'D'you know the bearing of the nearest whaler, Mr Hill?'

'*Faithful*'s west-sou'-west with the *Narwhal* and *Truelove* further to the west among heavier ice.'

'Very well. Fill the main tops'l, we'll work the ship towards the ice

* To work Tom Cox's traverse meant to idle.

103

to windward. That will be . . .' he looked at the compass.

'West-sou'-west,' offered Hill.

'Very well.' Bourne clasped his hands behind his back and walked to the windward rail. Standing at the larboard hance by Captain Palgrave's fussy brass carronade now covered in oiled canvas, Lieutenant Bourne felt terribly lonely. He began to worry over the rising wind while Hill had the watch brace the mainyards round. The last few days had demonstrated the dangers of the ice floes to a ship of *Melusine*'s light build. The speed with which the ice moved had amazed them and all their skill had been needed to manoeuvre the ship clear of the danger. Captain Drinkwater's written orders to his watch-keeping officers had been specific: *At all costs close proximity with the ice is to be avoided and offing is to be made even at the prospect of losing contact with the whalers*. To move *Melusine* to safety now meant that the captain might be unable to relocate them and with fog coming on there was no longer the refuge contained in Captain Drinkwater's order book: *If in any doubt whatsoever, do not hesitate to inform me*.

In a moment of angry uncertainty Bourne damned Germaney for his insanity. Then worry reasserted itself, worming in the pit of his stomach like some huge parasite. He looked again and looked in vain for the ice edge. Already a white fog was swirling towards them. He ran forward and lifted the speaking trumpet.

'Masthead there!'

'Sir?' Gorton leaned from the crow's nest.

'D'you see anything of the gig?'

'Nothing, sir.'

'God damn and blast it!' He thought for a moment longer and then made up his mind, hoping that Captain Drinkwater had remained safe aboard one of the whalers.

'Mr Hill! Put the ship about, course south, clear of this damned ice.'

Like the good sailing master he was, Hill obeyed the order of the young commissioned officer and brought *Melusine* onto the starboard tack. Then he crossed the deck and addressed Bourne.

'Mr Bourne, if the captain's adrift in this fog he'll lose the ship. My advice is to give him minute guns and heave to again after you've run a league to the southward.'

Bourne looked at the older man and Hill saw the relief plain in his eyes.

'Very well, Mr Hill, will you see to it.'

Already the white wraiths curled across the deck and the next instant every rope began to drip moisture and the damp chill of a dense fog isolated the ship.

The Mercy of God

It was intuition that told Drinkwater a change in the weather was imminent, intuition and a nervous awareness of altering circumstances. He was slowly awakened to a growing ache in his neck and a dimming of the brilliance of the ice which combined with a softening of its shadows. The day lost its colour and the atmosphere began to feel oddly hostile. The birds were landing on the sea and were airborne in fewer numbers.

He touched Quilhampton's arm as the boat ran between two ice floes some seven or eight feet tall. The lead through which they were running was some hundred yards across, with a patch of open sea visible ahead of them from which, when they reached it, they hoped to catch sight of *Melusine*. Quilhampton turned. 'Sir?'

'Fog, Mr Q, fog and wind,' he said in a low voice.

Their eyes met and Quilhampton replied, 'Pray God we make the ship, sir.'

'Amen to that, Mr Q.'

Quilhampton, who had been dreaming again of Catriona, pulled himself together and concentrated on working the gig even faster through the lead to reach the open water before the fog closed over them.

Drinkwater ordered Frey to pass another issue of rum to the men who sat shivering in the bottom of the boat. The warmth had gone out of the sun and the approaching fog made the air damp. He heard Quilhampton swear and looked up. The lead between the floes was narrowing as they spun slowly in the wind. He was conscious of a strong and unpleasant smell from the algae on the closing ice.

'Get the oars to work, Tregembo!' Drinkwater snapped and the men, looking round and grasping the situation at a glance, were quick to obey. Already the lead had diminished by half.

'Pull, damn you!'

The boat headed for the narrowing gap with perhaps a cable to run before reaching the open water. The men grunted with effort as they tugged the gig forwards while in the stern Drinkwater and Quilhampton watched anxiously. The gap ahead was down to twenty yards. The sail flapped uselessly as the wind died in the lee of the converging ice. Drinkwater looked anxiously on either side of them, seeking some ledge on the ice upon which they could scramble when the floes ground together and crushed the boat like an eggshell. But both floes were in an advanced state of melting, their waterlines eroded, their surfaces overhanging in an exagerrated fashion. In a minute or two the oars would be useless as there would be insufficient room to extend them either side of the boat. He wished he had a steering oar with which to give the boat a little more chance.

'Keep pulling, men, then trail oars as soon as you feel the blades touch the ice. Mr Frey, get that damned mast down.' He tried to keep his voice level but apprehension and a sudden bitter chill from the proximity of the ice made it shake. The floes had almost met overhead so that they pulled in a partial tunnel. Then there was a crash astern. Drinkwater looked round. The lead had closed behind them and a wave of water was rushing towards the gig's transom.

'Pull!' he shouted, turning forward to urge the men, but as he did so he saw them leaning backwards, the looms of their oars sweeping over their heads as they allowed them to trail. They tensed for the impact of the ice when the wave hit them. The boat was thrust abruptly forward as the ice met overhead. Lumps of it dropped into the boat and there were muttered curses as the midshipman, helped now by idle oarsmen got the mast into the boat not an instant too soon.

Suddenly they were in open water and, a moment later in a dense fog.

'Did anyone see the ship?' Drinkwater asked sharply.

There was a negative muttering.

'We have exchanged the frying pan for the fire, Mr Q.'

'Aye, sir.' Quilhampton sat glumly. The heart-thumping excitement of the race against the closure of the ice had had at least the advantage of swift resolution. Catriona might one day learn he had died crushed in Arctic ice and it seemed to him a preferable death to freezing and starving in an open boat. He was about to ask how long Captain Drinkwater thought they could survive when he saw the men exchange glances and Midshipman Frey looked aft, his face pale with anxiety. He pulled himself together. He was in command of the boat, damn it, despite the fact that *Melusine*'s captain sat beside him.

'Permission to re-ship the mast, sir.'

107

Drinkwater nodded. He looked astern. They were well clear of the ice and already feeling the effect of the wind. 'Aye, but do not hoist the sail.'

'Aye, aye, sir.' Quilhampton nodded at the junior midshipman. 'Step that mast forrard!'

There was a scrambling and a knocking as the stumpy spar with its iron traveller and single halliard was relocated in the hole in the thwart. The men assisted willingly, glad of something to do. When it was done they subsided onto the thwarts and again looked aft.

'Have all the oars secured inboard and two watches told off. You will take one and I the other. Tregembo pick the hands in Mr Quilhampton's watch and Mr Frey you will pick those in mine. I will take the tiller, Mr Q, whilst you make an issue of grog and biscuit. We will then set the watches and heave the gig to. At regular intervals the bowman will holloa and listen for the echo of his voice. If he hears it we may reasonably expect that ice is close but from what we saw there is little ice to leeward, though some may drift that way at a greater speed than ourselves. In this case we have only to put up the helm and run away from it while its protection to windward will reduce the violence of the sea. The watch below will huddle together to get what warmth it can. Captain Sawyers was only just relating many whale-boat crews have survived such circumstances so there is little to be alarmed about.'

The last sentence was a bare-faced lie, but it had its effect in cheering the men and they went about their tasks with a show of willingness.

With greater misgivings and the pain in his shoulder nagging at him appallingly, Drinkwater sat hunched in the stern-sheets.

Singleton looked at the blade of the catling as the loblolly boy held the lantern close. There was no trace of mist upon it. Francis Germaney had breathed his last.

'One for the sail-maker, eh sir?' The loblolly boy's grin was wolfish. It was always good to bury an officer, especially one who had the sense to blow his brains out. Or make a mess of it, the man thought, thereby casting doubts on whether he had them in the first place.

Singleton looked coldly at Skeete who stared back.

'I'll plug his arse and lay him out for the sail-maker, sir.'

'Be silent, Skeete, you blackguard!' snapped Singleton impatiently, rising and for the hundredth time cracking his head on the deckbeam above. He left the first lieutenant's cabin hurriedly to the accompaniment of Skeete's diabolical laughter. A loblolly 'boy' of some twenty years experience and some fifty years of age, Skeete was enjoying himself. To the added pleasure of witnessing the demise of an officer, a circumstance which in Skeete's opinion was all too rare an occurrence, he derived a degree of satisfaction from the office he was about to perform upon such an august corpse as that of Lieutenant Francis Germaney, Royal Navy. Further, since ridding themselves of the drunken oppression of Macpherson, Skeete and his mate had enjoyed an autonomy previously unknown to them. Mr Singleton's remarkable ability in reviving Leek had impressed the surgeon's assistants less than the rest of the crew. To Skeete and his mate, Singleton was not a proper ship's officer and, being a damned parson with pronounced views upon flogging and the Articles of War, could be insulted with a fair degree of impunity. Skeete could not remember enjoying himself so much since he last visited Diamond Lil's at Portsmouth Point.

In search of Drinkwater Singleton arrived on deck to be knocked to his knees by a seaman jumping clear as Number Nine gun fired and recoiled.

'Mind you f . . . Oh, beg pardon, sir,' the man grinned sheepishly and helped the surgeon to his feet. Somewhat shaken and uncertain as to the cause of the noise and apparent confusion as the gun crew reloaded and hauled up the piece, Singleton made his way aft.

'Is something the matter, Mr Hill?' he asked the master.

'Bosun's mate, take that man's name and tell him I'll give him a check shirt at the gangway the next time he forgets to swab his gun . . . matter, Mr Singleton? merely that there is a fog and the captain has yet to return.'

'Fog?' Singleton turned and noticed the shroud that covered the ship for the first time. He looked sharply at Hill. 'You mean that the captain's lost in this fog? In that little boat?'

'So it would seem, Mr Singleton. And the little boat is his gig . . . now if you will excuse me . . . Mackman, you Godforsaken whoreson, coil that fall the other way, God damn you bloody landsmen!'

Singleton pressed aft aware that not only was the *Melusine* shrouded in dense fog but that the wind was piping in the rigging and that the ship was beginning to lift to an increasingly rough sea as she came clear of the ice.

Mr Bourne, now in command, stood miserably at the windward rail with a worried looking Rispin, promoted abruptly and unwillingly to first lieutenant. It was clear, even to Singleton's untutored eye, that Stephen Hill was in real command. Although he realised with a pang that he felt very uneasy without Drinkwater's cock-headed presence on the quarterdeck, he felt a measure of reassurance in Hill's competence. Knowing something of the promotion-hungry desires of lieutenants and midshipmen Singleton wondered to what extent efforts were being made to recover the captain, then he recollected his duty and struggled across the deck towards Bourne.

A patter of spray flew aft and drove the breath from his body as he reached the anxious lieutenant. 'Mr Bourne!'

'Eh? Singleton, what is it?'

Bourne's cloak blew round him and his uncertainty seemed epitomised by the way he clutched the fore-cock of his hat to prevent it blowing away.

'Mr Germaney has expired.'

'Oh.' There seemed little else to say except, 'Thank you, Mr Singleton.'

Frozen to the marrow Singleton made his way to the companion-way. As he swung himself down a second dollop of spray caught him and Number Nine gun roared again. Reaching the sanctuary of his cabin he flung himself on his knees.

Afterwards Drinkwater was uncertain how long they nursed the gig through that desperate night, for night it must have been. Certainly the fog obscured much of the sunlight and prevented even a glimpse of the sun itself so that it became almost dark. After the twists and turns of their passage through the ice, and his preoccupation in avoiding damage to the boat, Drinkwater had to admit to being lost. The pain in his neck and the growing numbness of his extremities seemed to dull his brain so that his mental efforts were reduced to the sole consideration of keeping the boat reasonably dry and as close to the wind as they were able. He dare not run off before it for, although its effect would be less chilling, he feared far more the prospect of being utterly lost, while every effort he made to retain his position increased his chances of being not too far distant from the whalers or the *Melusine* when the fog lifted.

The boat's crew spent a miserable night and at one point he recovered sufficient awareness to realise he had his arm round the shoulders of little Frey who was shuddering uncontrollably and trying desperately to muffle the chattering of his teeth and the sobbing of his breath. Tregembo and Quilhampton huddled together, their familiarity readily breaking down the barriers of rank, while further forward the other men groaned, swore and crouched equally frozen.

Occasionally Drinkwater rallied, awakened to full consciousness by a sudden, agonising spasm in his shoulder, only to curse the self-indulgence that had led to this folly and probable death. He realised with a shock that he was not much moved by the contemplation of death, and with it came the realisation that his hands and feet felt warmer. For a second sleep threatened to overwhelm him and he knew it was the kiss of approaching death. A picture of Charlotte Amelia and Richard Madoc swam before his eyes, he tried to conjure up Elizabeth but found it impossible. Then he became acutely aware that the boy beside him was his son, not the baby he had left behind, but Richard at ten or eleven years. The boy's face was glowing, his full lips sweet and his eyes the deep brown of his mother's.

'Farewell, father,' the boy was saying, 'farewell, for we shall never meet again . . .'

'No, stay . . .!' Drinkwater was fully conscious, his mind filled with the departing vision of his son. A seaman whose name he could not remember looked aft from the bow. Drinkwater came suddenly to himself, aware that the extremities of his limbs were lifeless. He tried to move the midshipman. Mr Frey was asleep.

'Mr Frey! Mr Frey! Wake up! Wake up, all of you! Wake up, God damn it . . . and you, forrard, why ain't you holloaing like you were ordered . . . Come on holloa! All of you holloa and sing! Sing God damn and blast you, clap your hands! Stamp your feet! Mr Frey give 'em grog and make the bastards sing . . .'

'Sing, sir?' Frey awoke as though recalled from a distant place.

'Aye, Mr Frey, sing!'

Realisation awoke slowly in the boat and men groaned with the agony of moving. But Frey passed the keg of grog and they drained it greedily, the raw spirit quickening their hearts and circulation so that they at last broke into a cracked and imperfect chorus of 'Spanish Ladies'.

And just as suddenly as Drinkwater had roused them to sing, he commanded them to silence. They sat, even more dejected now that the howl of the wind reasserted itself and the boat bucked up and down and water slopped inboard over them.

The minute gun sounded again.

'A six-pounder, by God!'

'M'loosine, zur,' said Tregembo grinning.

'Listen for the next to determine whether the distance increases.' They sat silent for what seemed an age. The concussion came again.

111

' 'Tis nearer, zur.'

'Further away . . .'

They sat through a further period of tense silence. The gun sounded yet again.

Three voices answered at once. They were unanimous, 'Nearer!'

'Let us bear off a little, Mr Q. Remain silent there and listen for the guns, but each man is to chafe his legs . . . Mr Frey perhaps you would oblige me by checking the priming of those muskets. Then you had better rub Mr Q's calves. His hand may be impervious to the cold but his legs ain't.'

Half an hour later they were quite sure the *Melusine*'s guns were louder, but the sea was rising and water entering the boat in increasing amounts. The hands were employed baling and Drinkwater decided it was time they discharged the muskets. They waited for the sound of the guns. The boom seemed slightly fainter.

The muskets cracked and they waited for some response. Nothing came. The next time the minute gun fired it was quite definitely further away.

The fog lifted a little towards dawn. Those on *Melusine*'s quarterdeck could see a circle of tossing and streaked water some five cables in radius about them.

'With this increase in visibility, Mr Bourne, I think we can afford to take a chance. I suggest we put the ship about and stand back to the northward for a couple of hours.'

Bourne considered the proposition. 'Very well, Mr Hill, see to it.'

Melusine jibbed at coming into the wind under such reduced canvas as she was carrying and Hill wore her round. She steadied on the larboard tack, head once more to the north and Hill transferred the duty gun-crew to a larboard gun. It was pointless firing to windward. After a pause the cannon, Number Ten, roared out. *Melusine* groaned as she rose and fell, occasionally shuddering as a sea broke against her side and sent the spray across her rail.

'Sir! Sir!' Midshipman Gorton was coming aft from the foremast where he had been supervising the coiling of the braces.

'What is it?'

'I'm certain I heard something ahead, sir . . .'

'In this wind . . . ?'

'A moment, Mr Rispin, what did you hear?'

'Well sir, it sounded like muskets, sir . . .'

The quarterdeck officers strained their eyes forward.

'Fo'c's'le there!' roared Hill. 'Keep your eyes open, there!'

'There sir! There!' Midshipman Gorton was crouching, his arm and index finger extended over the starboard bow.

'Mark it, Mr Gorton, mark it. Leggo lee mizen braces, there! Mizen yards aback!'

'Thank God,' breathed Mr Rispin.

'Thank Hill and Gorton, Mr Rispin,' said Lieutenant Bourne.

Mr Frey saw the ship a full minute before Mr Gorton heard the muskets.

'Drop the sail, Mr Q! Man the oars my lads, your lives depend upon it!'

They were clumsy getting the oars out, their tired and aching muscles refusing to obey, but Tregembo cursed them from the after thwart and set the stroke.

Drinkwater took them across *Melusine*'s bow to pull up from leeward. He could see the sloop was hove-to and making little headway but he felt easier when he saw the mizen topsail backed.

As they approached it was clear that even on her leeward side it was going to be impossible to recover the boat. He watched as several ropes' ends were flung over the side and men climbed into the chains to assist. The painter was caught at the third and increasingly feeble throw and the gig was dashed against *Melusine*'s spirketting and then her chains. The tie-rods extending below the heavy timbers of the channels smashed the gunwhale of the boat, but as the gig dropped into the hollow of the sea Drinkwater saw one pair of legs left dangling over the ledge of the chains where willing hands reached down. It was not a time for prerogative and Drinkwater refused to leave the boat until all the others were safe. He had little fear for the seamen, for all were fit, agile and used to scrambling about. But Frey was very cold and his limbs were cramped. Drinkwater called for a line and a rope snaked down into the boat. He passed a bowline round Frey's waist as the men scrambled out of the boat. As the gig rose and the rope was hauled tight, Drinkwater tried to support the boy. Suddenly the boat fell, half rolling over as the inboard gunwhale caught again and threatened to overset it. Frey dangled ten feet overhead, the line rigged from the cro'jack yardarm had plucked him from the boat. One of his shoes fell past Drinkwater as he grabbed a handhold. He looked down to find the gig half full of water. The mizen whip was already being pulled inboard and Drinkwater shouted.

'Mr Q! Up you go!' Quilhampton waited his moment. As the boat rose he leapt, holding his wooden left hand clear and extending his right. He missed his footing but someone grabbed his extended arm and his abdomen caught on the edge of the channel. Hands grabbed the seat of his trousers and he was dragged inboard winded and gagging.

Only Drinkwater was left. He felt impossibly weak. Above him the whole ship's company watched. He was aware of Tregembo, wet to the skin and frozen after his ordeal, leaning outboard from the main chains. One hand was extended.

'Come *on*, zur!' he shouted, a trace of his truculent, Cornish independence clear in his eyes.

Drinkwater felt the boat rise sluggishly beneath him. She would not swim for many more minutes. He leaped upwards, aware that his outstretched arm was only inches from Tregembo's hand, but the boat fell away and he with it, suddenly up to his waist in water as the gig sank under him.

'Here, zur, here!'

He felt the rope across his shoulders and with a mighty effort passed a bight about his waist, holding the rope with his left hand and the loose end with his right. He felt himself jar against the barnacled spirketting and the weight on his left arm told where he hung suspended by its feeble grip, then that too began to slide while he tried to remember how to make a one-handed bowline with his right hand. Then *Melusine* gave a lee roll and a sea reached up under his shoulders. He was suddenly level with the rail, could see the faces lining the hammock nettings. In an instant the sea would drop away again as the sloop rolled to windward. He felt the support of the water begin to fall yet he was quite unable to remember how to make that first loop.

Then hands reached out for him. He was grabbed unceremoniously. The sea dropped away and he was pulled over the nettings and laid with gentle respect upon the deck. He looked up to see the face of Singleton.

'The mercy of God, Captain Drinkwater,' he said, 'has been extended to us all this day . . .'

And the fervent chorus of 'Amens' surprised even the semi-conscious Drinkwater.

The Seventy-second Parallel

'Sir! Sir!'

Drinkwater swam upwards from a great depth and was aware that Midshipman Wickham was shaking him. 'Eh? What is it?'

'Mr Rispin's compliments, sir, but would you come on deck.'

'What time is it?'

'Nearly eight bells in the morning watch, sir.'

'Very well.' He longed to fling himself back into his cot for he had been asleep no more than three or four hours and every muscle in his body ached. He idled for a moment and heard a sudden wail of pipes at the companionways and the cry for all hands as *Melusine*'s helm went down and she came up into the wind. Two minutes later, in a coat and greygoe that were still wet under his tarpaulin, he was on deck.

'The smell made me suspicious, sir,' cried Rispin, his voice high with anxiety, 'then the wind fell away and then we saw it . . .' He pointed.

Drinkwater's tired eyes focussed. Half a mile away, rearing into the sky and looming over their mastheads the iceberg seemed insubstantial in the grey light. But the smell, like the stink he had noticed in the ice lead, was strongly algaic and the loss of wind was evidence of its reality. *Melusine* seemed to wallow helplessly and, although Rispin had succeeded in driving her round onto the larboard tack, there seemed scarcely enough wind now to move her as the mass of ice loomed closer.

Drinkwater stood stupefied for a moment or two, trying to remember what he had learned from fragments of conversation with the whale-ship captains. It was little enough, and he felt the gaps in his knowledge like physical wounds at such a moment.

He had read of the submerged properties of icebergs, that far more of them existed below the level of the sea than above. Part of the monster that threatened them might already be beneath them.

'A cast of the lead, Mr Rispin, and look lively about it!'

Above his head *Melusine*'s canvas slatted idly. 'T'gallant halliards there, topman aloft and let fall the t'gallants! Fo'c's'le head there! Set both jibs!' The waist burst into life as every man sought occupation. Drinkwater was left to reflect on Newton's observations upon the attraction of masses. Ship and iceberg seemed to be drawn inexorably together.

'By the mark seven, sir!'

'That'll be ice, sir,' Hill remarked, echoing his own thoughts.

'Aye.'

'Let fall! Let fall!' Lieutenant Bourne had taken the deck from Rispin and the topgallants hung in folds from their lowered yards.

'Hoist away!' The yards rose slowly, their parrels creaking up the slushed t'gallant masts as the topmen slid down the backstays.

'Sheet home!'

'Belay!'

Amidships the braces were ready manned as the halliards stretched the sails. Watching anxiously Drinkwater thought he saw the upper canvas belly a little.

'By the mark five, sir!' The nearest visible part of the iceberg was half a musket shot away to starboard. Drinkwater sensed *Melusine*'s deck cant slightly beneath his feet. He was so tense that for a moment he thought they had touched a spur of ice but suddenly *Melusine* caught the wind eddying round the southern extremity of the berg. Her upper sails filled, then her topsails; she began to move with gathering swiftness through the water.

'By the deep nine, sir!'

Drinkwater began to breathe again. *Melusine* came clear of the iceberg and the wind laid her on her beam ends. Just as suddenly as it had come the fog lifted. The wind swung to the north-north-west and blew with greater violence, but the sudden shift reduced the lift of the sea, chopping up a confused tossing of wave crests in which *Melusine* pitched wildly while her shivering topmen lay aloft again to claw in the topgallants they had so recently set.

As the visibility cleared it became apparent that the gale had dispersed the ice floes and they were surrounded by pieces of ice of every conceivable shape and size. Realising that he could not keep the deck forever, Drinkwater despatched first Bourne and then Rispin aloft to the crow's nest from where they shouted down directions to the doubled watches under Drinkwater and Hill, and for three days, while the gale blew itself out from the north they laboured through this vast and treacherous waste.

The huge bergs were easy to avoid, now that clear weather held, but the smaller bergs and broken floes of hummocked ice frequently required booming off from either bow with the spare topgallant yards. Worst of all were the 'growlers', low, almost melted lumps of ice the greater part of whose bulk lay treacherously below water. Several of these were struck and *Melusine's* spirketting began to assume a hairy appearance, the timber being so persistently scuffed by ice.

Drinkwater perceived the wisdom of a rig that was easily handled by a handful of men as Sawyers had claimed at Shetland. He also wished he had had the old bomb vessel *Virago* beneath his feet, a thought which made him recollect his interview with Earl St Vincent. It seemed so very far distant now and he had given little thought to his responsibilities during the last few days, let alone the possibility of French privateers being in these frozen seas. He wished St Vincent had had a better knowledge of the problems of navigation in high latitudes and given him a more substantial vessel than the corvette. Lovely she might be and fast she might be, but the Greenland Sea was no place for such a thoroughbred.

They buried Germaney the day following Drinkwater's return to *Melusine*. It was a bleak little ceremony that had broken up in confusion at a cry for all hands to wear ship and avoid a growler of rotten ice. Singleton's other major patient, the now insane Macpherson, lay inert under massive doses of laudanum to prevent his ravings from disturbing the watch below.

On the fifth day of the gale they sighted *Truelove* and made signals to her across eight miles of tossing ice and grey sea. She was snugged down under her lower sails and appeared as steady as a rock amid the turmoil about her. A day later they closed *Diana*, then *Narwhal*, *Provident* and *Earl Percy* hove in sight, both making the signal that all was well. On the morning that the wind died away there seemed less ice about and once again *Faithful* was sighted, about ten miles to the north-west and making the signal that whales were in sight.

Greatly refreshed from an uninterrupted sleep of almost twelve hours, wrote Drinkwater in his journal, *I woke to the strong impression that my life had been spared by providence . . .* He paused. The vision of Midshipman Frey as his son had been a vivid one and he was certain that had he not awakened to full consciousness at that time he would not have survived the ordeal in the open boat. The consequences of his folly in leaving the ship struck him very forcibly and he resolved never to act so rashly again. In his absence Germaney had died and he still felt pangs of conscience over his former first lieutenant. He shook off the 'blue devils' and his eye fell upon the portraits upon the cabin bulkhead, and particularly that of his little son. He dipped his pen in the ink-well.

The conviction that I was awoken in the boat by the spirit of my son is almost impossible to shake off, so fast has it battened upon my imagination. I am persuaded that we were past saving at that moment and would have perished had I not been revived by the apparition. He paused again and scratched out the word *apparition*, substituting *visitation*. He continued writing and ended: *the sighting of* Faithful *reassured me that my charges had made lighter of the gale than ourselves, for though nothing carried away aloft* Melusine *is making more water than formerly.* Faithful *made the signal for whales almost immediately upon our coming up and the whale ships stood north where, inexplicably, there seems to be less ice. The cold seems more intense.*

He laid his pen down, closed his journal and slipped it into the table drawer.

'Pass word for Mr Hill!'

He heard the marine sentry's response passed along and rose, pulling out the decanter and two glasses from the locker where Cawkwell had secured them.

'Come in,' he called as Hill knocked and entered the cabin. 'Ah, take a seat, Mr Hill, I am sure you will not refuse a glass on such a raw morning.'

'Indeed not, sir . . . thank you.'

Drinkwater sipped the blackstrap and re-seated himself.

'Mr Hill, we have known each other a long time and now that Germaney is dead I have a vacancy for a lieutenant . . . no, hear me out. I can think of no more deserving officer on this ship. I will give you an acting commission and believe I possess sufficient influence to have it ratified on our return. Now, what d'you say, eh?'

'That's considerate of you, sir, but no, I . . .'

'Damn it, Bourne's told me that without you he'd have been hard pushed to work the ship through the fog, he's a good fellow and does you the credit you deserve. With a master's warrant you'll never get command and the advancement you should have. Recollect old James Bowen, Earl Howe's Master of the Fleet, when asked what he would most desire for his services at the First of June, asked for a commission.'

'Aye, sir, that's true, but Bowen was made prize agent for the fleet, he'd no need to worry about the loss of pay. I've no private income and have a family to support. Besides, Bowen still had the earl's patronage whilst I, with all due respect to yourself, sir, would likely remain a junior lieutenant for the rest of my service. At least now I receive ninety-one pounds per annum, which even less five guineas for the income tax, is more than a junior lieutenant's pay. In addition, sir, with my warrant I'm a standing officer and even if the ship is laid up I still receive pay. Thank you all the same, sir.'

Drinkwater refilled Hill's glass. It was no less than he expected Hill to say and he reflected upon the stupidity of a system which denied men of Hill's ability proper recognition.

'Very well then. Whom do you think I should promote? Gorton has his six years almost in and is the senior, Quilhampton is but a few months his junior but holds a certificate from the Trinity House as master's mate. I am faced with a dilemma in that my natural inclination is to favour Quilhampton because he is known to me. I would welcome your advice.'

Hill sighed and crossed his legs. 'I have seen neither of them in action, sir, but I would rate both equally.'

'The decision is invidious, but you incline to neither . . .?'

'Sir, if I may be frank . . .?'

'Of course.'

'Then I should favour Mr Gorton, sir. Mr Quilhampton is both junior and a mite younger, I believe. Your favouring him would seem like patronage and I think that his hand might prove a handicap.'

Drinkwater nodded. 'Very well, Mr Hill. I do not approve of your pun but your reasoning is sound enough. Be so kind as to have a quiet word with Mr Q, that his disappointment is tempered by the reflection that he has not lost my confidence.'

'Aye, aye, sir.' Hill rose.

'One other thing . . .'

'Sir?'

'Do not mention the matter of the hand as deciding one way or another. I do not really think it a great disadvantage. It is quite impervious to cold, d'you know.'

Singleton looked with distaste at what had once been the person of Mr Macpherson the surgeon. He lay stupefied under ten grains of laudanum, his face grey, the cheeks cadaverous and pallid with a sheen of sweat that gleamed like condensation on a lead pipe under the lantern light.

He could almost *feel* Skeete grinning in the shadows next to him.

Singleton thought a very un-Christian thought, and was mortified by the ferocity of it. Why, why did Macpherson not die? Rum had long since destroyed his brain and now deprivation of it had turned him into a thrashing maniac. Yet his punished organs refused to capitulate to the inevitable, and he came out of his stupor to roll and rave in his own stink until Skeete cleaned him up and Singleton sedated him once more.

Singleton forbore to hate what Drinkwater had trapped him into accepting. He saw it as a God-given challenge that he must overcome his revolted instincts. This was a testing for the future and the squalor of life among the eskimos. He tried to thank God for the opportunity to harden himself for his coming ordeal. Attending Macpherson was as logical a piece of divine intervention as was the discovery of Meetuck, and Singleton knew he had been right, that men's cleverness did indeed obscure the obvious. Was it not crystal clear that God himself had intervened in thus providing him with means of preparing himself for the future?

There was also the matter of Drinkwater's survival in the gig. It appalled Singleton that the matter was taken so lightly on board. It struck Singleton as a kind of blasphemy. He was not used to the thousand tricks that fate may play a seaman in the course of a few days. He could not lie down and forget how close he had been to death a few hours ago, and worse, he could not forget how the ship had missed the steadying presence of her commander. There had been no doubt as to Hill's competence, indeed it was enhanced by the lower deck opinions he had heard about the other officers, but Hill had been alone and his isolation emphasised the loss of Drinkwater.

From the rough, untutored tarpaulin of first impression, Singleton had come to like the sea-officer with the cock-headed figure and the lined face. The mane of brown hair pulled impatiently behind his head in a black-ribboned queue told of a still youthful man, a man in his prime, a man of implicit reliability. Singleton began to lose his unfortunate prejudice against the profession of arms, though his own principles remained admirably steadfast. They might appear impractical to the world of sophistry, the world in which Drinkwater was enmeshed, but Singleton was bound upon a mission inspired by the Son of God. Among the primitive peoples of the earth he would prove a theory practical, a theory more shattering in its simplicity than the prolix vapourings of the Revolutionary pedagogues that had apostrophised the French Revolution. He would prove practical the Gospel of Christ.

But although he was motivated by the spirit, Singleton was unable to ignore reality, and he had become aware that without Drinkwater he would be unlikely to find the kind of co-operation he required to land upon the coast of Greenland. He began to be obsessed with the preservation of Drinkwater's health, particularly since the ordeal in the open boat, after which the captain had become thin and drawn. Looking down on the inert body of the *ci-devant* surgeon he decided there were more pressing things for him to attend to.

'Try and get some portable soup into him,' he said dismissively to Skeete, and turned in search of the companionway and the freezing freshness of the upper deck.

And there Singleton found further evidence of the beneficence of the Almighty in the person of Meetuck engaged, with two seamen as his assistants to supplement his broken arm, in completing the preparations of the bear and seal skins. Meetuck's conversation had enabled Singleton to turn the theoretical knowledge he had acquired at Copenhagen into a practical instrument and already Meetuck had submitted himself to baptism.

But in his eagerness to converse colloquially, to perfect his knowledge of the eskimo tongue and to test his ability to spread the gospel of Christ, Singleton had paid little attention to those things he might have learned from the eskimo. Beyond the knowledge that Meetuck had lost touch with his companions in a fog, fallen and injured himself, losing his kayak in the process, Singleton learned only that he came from a place called Nagtoralik, and called his people the Iker-miut, the people of the Strait. Some prompting from a more curious, though preoccupied Drinkwater, elicited the information that this 'strait' was far to the westward, and thus, by deduction, on the coast of Greenland. In his heart Singleton believed that it was where he would establish his mission on behalf of the Church Missionary Society. Eager to convert Meetuck it never occurred to Singleton that a male of Meetuck's maturity ought to have survived better on the ice, and the eskimo's lack of intelligence never prompted him to volunteer information he was not specifically asked for. All Meetuck knew was that Singleton was a *gavdlunaq*, a white man, and that he seemed to be a good one. In his simple mind Meetuck strove to please the men that had rescued him and fed him so well.

Seeing Singleton, Meetuck looked up and smiled, his thin lips puckering the wind-burned cheeks and his mongol eyes became dark slits. He said something and indicated the skins, particularly that of the polar bear, which he gently smoothed.

'It was a great bear,' Singleton translated for the puzzled seamen, 'and he who killed it was a mighty hunter . . .' The two men seemed to think this a quaint turn of phrase and giggled, having been much amused by Meetuck's antics and incomprehension at their inability to speak as did Singleton. Singleton was affronted by their attitude, his almost humourless disposition unable to see the amusement caused by the eskimo. 'Like Nimrod . . .' His voice trailed away and he turned aft to see the captain coming on deck, his boat cloak over the greygoe in the intense cold. It struck him that Drinkwater would benefit himself from warmer clothing and he turned below again in search of Mount.

The marine lieutenant was dicing with Rispin when he entered the gunroom.

'Ho, there, Singleton, d'you come to taste the delights of damnation then?' Mount grinned at the sober missionary whose disapproval extended to almost all the leisure activities of both officers and midshipmen, especially, as was now the case, it was accompanied by the drinking of alcohol. Singleton swallowed his disapproval and gave one of his rare, dry smiles.

'Ah, Mount, I wish you to prove that you deceive my eyes and are not yet sunk to a depravity that is beyond redemption.'

Mount rolled his eyes at Rispin, 'Lo, Rispin, I do believe I am being granted a little Christian forbearance. What is it you want?'

'Your polar bear's hide.'

'Egad,' Mount smote his breast in mock horror, 'you press me sore, good sir. Why?'

'I wish to have it for a good cause.'

'Ah-ha! Now it becomes clear, Mr Singleton, you wish to deprive me of the spoils of my skill so that I shall freeze and you will be warm as an ember, eh?'

'You misunderstand . . .'

Mount held up his hand, 'Are you aware what trouble I went to to stop that whelp Quilhampton from claiming the damned animal was his. He had the nerve to claim that without his winging the brute I should not have struck him. There! What d'you think of that, eh?'

'I think it most likely, certainly he did very well to hit a target with his wooden hand.'

'Oh, I do not think you need worry about Mr Q's abilities. He does not seem in any way handicapped. No, Mr Singleton, you want the bear's pelt and so do I. Now what do you suggest we do with it, Rispin? How would you, old Solomon, decide between the two of us, eh?' Mount's eyes fell significantly upon the dice.

'But, Mount, it is not for myself that I wish to have the skin, I have already purchased several of the seal-skins.'

'What is it for then? Not that damned eskimo friend of yours?'

'No. For the Captain, I fear he may have taken a chill and you know that in this weather a chill may become bronchitic or worse, induce a pulmonary inflammation.'

'Why this *is* Christian charity . . . come, Singleton, let us ask Rispin to resolve the matter.'

'Very well,' said Singleton, refusing to rise to Mount's bait. 'Mr Rispin?'

'Let the dice decide,' Rispin said, incurring a furious glare from Singleton.

'That is dishonourable, Mr Rispin, you know I do not approve . . .'

'But it would be amusing, Singleton, come, let us see whether the Almighty will influence the dice . . .'

'That's blasphemy, Mr Mount! I do not mind you having your joke at my expense but I will not tolerate this.' Singleton turned on his heel indignantly and smashed his forehead against a deck-beam. 'God-damn!' he swore, leaving the gunroom to the peals of laughter from the two officers.

Drinkwater lowered his glass and addressed Bourne. 'Heave-to under his stern, Mr Bourne.'

'Aye, aye, sir.' Raising the telescope again Drinkwater stared at *Narwhal*. It was the third time that forenoon she had lowered her boats after whales and the third time she had recovered them as the beasts eluded the hunt and swam steadily north-west. For two days the *Narwhal*, *Faithful*, *Diana*, *Earl Percy* and *Provident* and *Truelove* had worked their way north-west with *Melusine* accompanying them. Only Captain Renaudson of the *Diana* had hit a whale using his brass harpoon gun, and that had turned out to be a razorback.

As *Melusine* came up under *Narwhal*'s lee, Drinkwater hoisted himself onto the rail, holding onto the mizen rigging.

'*Narwhal*, ahoy!' He saw Jaybez Harvey's pock-marked features similarly elevate themselves and he waved in a friendly fashion. 'No success, Captain?'

Harvey shook his head. 'No, there be sommat curious about the fish,' he shouted. ' 'Tis unusual for them to swim north-west in such schools. Happen they know sommat, right whales is slow, but these

123

devils aren't wanting to fill the lamps of London Town, Captain, that I do know.'

Drinkwater jumped down on deck as *Narwhal*'s hands squared her yards and she moved forward again, bumping aside an ice floe upon which a seal looked up at her in sudden surprise.

'If I hit him, may we lower, sir?' asked Walmsley, eagerly lifting a musket. Drinkwater looked at the seal as it rolled over.

'It's hardly sport, Mr Walmsley, ah . . . too late . . .' Drinkwater was saved the trouble of a decision as the seal, worried by the shadow of the *Narwhal* that passed over it, sought the familiarity of the sea.

Drinkwater saw the grin of pleasure that it had escaped cross Mr Frey's face as he sorted the signalling flags with the yeoman. 'Bad luck, Mr Walmsley, perhaps another time.'

'Aye, aye, sir.' Walmsley grimaced at Frey who grinned back triumphantly. 'God knows what you'll do when you meet a Frenchman, Frey, ask him to sit for his bloody portrait I shouldn't wonder . . .'

Drinkwater heard the jibe, but affected to ignore it. Walmsley's concern was unnecessary, the likelihood of their meeting a Frenchman so remote a possibility that Drinkwater considered Mr Frey's talents with pencil and watercolour box the only profitable part of the voyage.

They braced the yards round and *Melusine* reached east, across the sterns of the *Narwhal*, the *Diana* and the *Faithful*, tacking at noon in a sea that was scattered with loose floes. Only a dozen ice bergs were visible from the deck and the light north-easterly breeze had re-established clear weather. It was still bitterly cold, but the wind was strong enough to keep the surface of the sea moving, otherwise Drinkwater suspected it might freeze over. Although this would be unseasonable it was a constant worry for him as he inspected the readings of the thermometer in the log book.

Another problem he had faced was that of employment in the ship. During the days since the abatement of the gale there had been less danger from the ice, and they had worked slowly north in the wake of the whalers under easy sail. The diversions they had used on the passage north from the Humber had been re-started, although the weather was too cold for fencing, making the foil blades brittle. But the cutter had been lowered to pursue seals, for Drinkwater wanted all hands to be better clad than Palgrave's slops would allow, and hunting had ceased to be the prerogative of the officers. Marines and topmen trained in the use of small arms under Lieutenant Mount's direction, made up the shooting parties and it was certain that *Melusine* was the best fed warship in the Royal Navy. This fresh meat was most welcome and thought to be an excellent anti-scorbutic.

Drinkwater devised what amusements he could, even to the extent of purchasing some of the baleen from the whalers, in order that the seamen might attempt to decorate it in the same manner as the men in the whale-ships. As he looked along the waist where Meetuck supervised the cleaning of a fresh batch of seal skins and the gunner checked the flints in the gun-locks, he felt that the ship's services were somewhat wasted. They still went to quarters twice a day and exercised the guns with powder every third day; the unaccustomed presence of a marine sentry at his door and the pendant of a 'private' ship of war at the mainmasthead were constant reminders that *Melusine* was a King's ship, a man-of-war.

But Drinkwater was aware of a feeling seeping through the ship that she had undergone some curious enchantment, that, for all the hazards they had and would encounter, these were natural phenomena. He could not throw off the growing feeling that they were on some elaborate, dangerous but nevertheless curiously pleasurable yachting excursion. Preoccupied with this consideration he was surprised at the little party of officers that suddenly confronted him.

'Beg pardon, sir.'

'Yes, Mr Mount, what is the matter?' It seemed like some deputation and for a moment his heart missed a beat in alarm, for his thoughts had run from yachting to naval expeditions like Cook's and, inevitably, Bligh's. He looked at the officers. With Mount were Rispin and Hill, Gorton, Quilhampton.

Walmsley, Glencross, Dutfield and Wickham with an angry Obadiah Singleton apparently bringing up the rear with some reluctance. They seemed to be carrying a bundle.

'We thought, sir, that you might consider accepting a gift from us all . . .'

'A gift, Mr Mount . . .?'

'Something to keep you warm, sir, as Mr Hill informs me we crossed the seventy-second parallel at noon.'

They offered him the magnificent pelt of the polar bear.

Greatly daring Mount said, 'The Thirty-sixth Article of War is of little use in a boat sir.' It was an impropriety, but an impropriety made in the spirit of the moment, in tune with the bitingly cold, clean air and the sunshine breaking through the clouds. It was all thoroughly unreal for the quarterdeck of a sloop of war.

'Thank you, gentlemen,' he said, 'thank you very much. I am indebted to you all.'

Bourne crossed the deck to join them. 'Perhaps, sir, at a suitable occasion you will honour the gunroom for dinner.'

Drinkwater nodded. 'I shall be delighted,' he said, removing cloak and greygoe and flinging the great skin around him. 'What happened to the animal's head?'

'We had him *Mount*ed, sir,' said Walmsley mischievously and they drifted forward in high spirits, just as if they were on a yachting cruise.

The Great Hunt

Mr Quilhampton swung the glass from larboard beam to starboard bow. At first he saw nothing unusual for they had been aware that the loose floes would give way to close pack ice and probably to an ice shelf, from the ice blink that had been in sight for some twelve hours. He was taking some comfort from the isolation of the crow's nest to nurse his wounded pride. He was disappointed at Mr Gorton's advancement, and although he acknowledged the kindness of Mr Hill in mollifying him, it did not prevent him from suffering. He would have liked to return home a lieutenant, to indulge in a little swagger with a new hanger at his hip and a cuff of buttons instead of the white collar patches of the novice, when he entered the Edinburgh drawing-room of Catriona MacEwan. He had already furnished and popula-ted the room in his imagination, but he was still perfecting the manner of his entrance, torn between an amusing frightening of Catriona's perfectly awful aunt with his wooden hand, or the upstaging of a languid rival who would probably be wearing the theatrical uniform of a volunteer yeomanry regiment. Although amusing, he had already astonished the old lady with his hand, and, in any case, the jape smacked more of the cockpit he wished to leave, than the gunroom to which he aspired. No, the discomfiture of the rival it must be, then . . .

'Masthead there!' He looked down. The master was looking aloft. 'Sir?'

'*Narwhal*'s signalling, what d'you make of it?'

Recalled to his duty Quilhampton levelled the big watch glass. The six whalers were bowling along on the larboard tack. *Melusine* was slightly to leeward of them all, but astern of *Narwhal*. The whaler's signal flaps streamed out in a straight line towards the sloop and were impossible to read. He struggled with the glass but could not make head or tail of the flag hoist. He hailed the deck and told Hill. Looking round the horizon again he saw the reason almost at once. The fast moving school of whales that they had so patiently followed for three days now, beating to windward as the great fish swam with steady purpose to the north-west had slowed. They were circling and there were more of them. Quilhampton wondered if it was the entire school on the surface at the same time or whether they had made som· sort of rendezvous for breeding purposes. And then he saw something else, something quite extraordinary.

Opening up upon their larboard beam was a great channel in the ice shelf. Quilhampton realised the extent of his preoccupation in not noticing it before. Apart from loose floes he estimated the opening was several miles wide, partly hidden by a low raft of hummocked ice. In the channel the water appeared greener, forming a eutrophid strait between great continents of ice. Here was the reason for the whales' mysterious migration, a krill and plankton-rich sea which they had sensed from a distance.

Already *Narwhal* had two boats in the water. *Provident, Earl Percy* and *Faithful* were heaving to. *Diana* had still to come up and *Truelove*, fallen off to the eastward, had seen *Narwhal*'s signal and altered to the west.

Quilhampton swung himself through the trapdoor and hurried down the mainmast rigging.

Drinkwater realised the significance of the great ice-free lead as soon as he reached the crow's nest. He was perceptive enough to know that the strange channel that seemed to exist as far as the eye could see to the westward was unusual. Entering the channel the right whales had slowed. He could see twenty or thirty at any one time on the surface, their spouts so numerous as to form a cloud above them as they vented through their spiracles. From time to time a great, blunt head would appear, the baleen gleaming in a rigid grin while sea-water poured from the corners of the gaping mouth as the fibrous whale-bone strained the tiny organisms from the sea.

He sensed, too, a change of tempo from the pursuing whalers. As he swung his glass on the two nearer ships he counted the boats already in the water. *Narwhal* and the nearer ships had all their boats out, *Diana*, a little to the east was lowering, while *Truelove* had hoisted her topgallants in her haste to join the great hunt.

Surprisingly he saw a boat from *Narwhal* turn away from the whales towards the sloop and through the glass he could see Harvey himself standing in the bow. He swung his glass once more to the west. The open lead, with hardly a floe loose on its extraordinary surface, beckoned them to the westwards. It seemed to Drinkwater that the ice shelf had suddenly split, moved by some elemental force, and pulled apart. Momentarily he wondered whether that force might be reversed, that if they entered the channel they might be trapped and crushed. Shaking off his apprehension he made his way below, arriving on the quarterdeck as Harvey's boat came up under the quarter and Lieutenant Rispin, at a nod from Drinkwater, invited Harvey on board.

Harvey's eyes were shining with excitement, illuminating his snub-nosed face and eradicating the disfigurements of the small-pox. Drinkwater immediately warmed to him. 'Good morning, Captain Harvey, I am surprised you are not in hot pursuit of the fish.'

Harvey grinned and dispensed briefly with the formalities. 'There will be enough pickings here, Captain, if we can hold the whales, to fill all our empty casks and send us safe back to Hull, but we want your assistance.'

'How so?'

'Well, the whales will likely follow th'krill and all into yonder lead. Once we get amongst them they'll swim to west, like. If you'd put this ship ahead of the fish and drop cannon fire ahead of them it'll slow them like, stop them escaping . . . will you do it?'

A quick kill, a short voyage, the success of a task that had seemed once so very difficult and French privateers a figment of the First Lord's overworked imagination. He had only one reservation, and his inexperience in ice nagged him.

'How far into the lead will they go, Captain Harvey? That looks like dense shelf ice to me, if it closes you may survive but this ship will be crushed like an egg-shell.'

Harvey shook his head. 'I've heard of this happening once before, Captain Drinkwater, in my father's day, sixty-eight or nine, I think. Happen if the whales take themselves into the lead then it'll not close.'

Drinkwater could see Harvey's argument, but it was imperfect. The whales might turn and swim back faster than a ship could beat to windward, the wind might shift and blow the ice to the south-west of them to the north again. He said as much to Harvey and watched the disappointment in the Yorkshireman's eyes.

'The ice'll not close, not for a week at least, and we'll have our casks full by then . . .' The lust of the hunter was strong in him. Drinkwater could sense his sudden impatience to be gone, to be pointing the harpoon gun that gleamed dully in the bow of his whale-boat.

A short voyage. Home and an end to the ache in his shoulder. Elizabeth . . .

'Very well, three days, damn you.' He grinned and Harvey grinned and smacked him painfully upon his shoulder. The *lèse-majesté* caused the waiting officers to hide their grins and the instant Harvey had regained his boat Drinkwater called for all hands. He would make them pay for their impertinence, damn it!

'Set the t'gallants, Mr Rispin!'

'Set t'gallants, sir.' He watched Rispin pick up the speaking trumpet as the watch below tumbled up the hatchways. The lieutenant launched into his customary stream of largely superfluous orders.

'After guard to hoist the main t'garns'ls. Bosun's mate, send the after guard to man the main t'garns'l halliards, there! Corporal of marines, send the marines aft to man the mizen t'garns'ls halliards. Master at arms! Send below and turn up the idlers, stewards and servants, messmen, cooks-mates, sweepers and loblolly boys!'

This volley of orders was answered by the petty officers who thumped the fife-rails for good effect with their starters, cursing and shouting at the men.

'Topmen aloft, aloft ...' Rispin's strange, hysterical system seemed to galvanise the hands, as though they were all suddenly aware that the hunt for whales had taken on a new, more primitive flavour. And yet, watching from the larboard hance, one foot upon the slide of Palgrave's fancy brass carronade, Drinkwater once again received the strong impression that they were engaged upon a yachting excursion. Perhaps it was just the excitement, perhaps the extravagance of Rispin's fancy orders that had about it that ritual quality he had observed aboard such craft as the Trinity House Yacht back in eighty-eight, or perhaps it was the fantastic cake-icing seascape that surrounded him that induced the Arctic calenture.

'Let fall! Sheet home!' The yards rose as the canvas fell.

He shook off the ridiculous feeling. 'Mr Quilhampton!'

'Sir?'

'Aloft with you, we shall run into the ice lead and work ahead of the whales.'

'Aye, aye, sir.' Drinkwater looked at the compass.

'Steer west by north.'

'West by north, sir ... west by north it is, sir.'

'Sheet home there! Belay!' Rispin at last pronounced topgallants hoisted.

'Square the yards, Mr Rispin, course west by north.'

Rispin acknowledged the order and his voice rose again as he bawled through the trumpet.

'After guard and marines to the weather mainbrace! Forebrace there! Bosun's mate start those men aft here! Haul in the main brace, pull together damn you and mind the weather roll! That's very well with the main yard! Belay there! Belay! Belay the foreyard, don't come up any . . .!'

It went on for some minutes before Mr Rispin, fussing under his captain's eye, was satisfied with the trim of the yards and *Melusine* had already gathered way. From her leeward position she was up among the whalers and their boats now. Two boat-flags were already up, with *Narwhal*'s colours on them, Drinkwater noticed. He raised his hat to Harvey's mate who conned the whaler while his commander was out after the fish. He saluted Abel Sawyers as *Melusine* swept past the Quaker in his boat, his men pulling furiously to catch a great bull whale a musket shot on the sloop's starboard bow. Then they were in among the whales, the air misty with their breathing, a foetid taint to it. The humps of the shining backs, the flick of a great tail and once a reappearance of that great ugly-noble head as it sluiced the water through the baleen in an ecstasy of surfeit.

'Beat to quarters, Mr Rispin,' Drinkwater said it quietly, watching the young officer's reaction. He noted the surprise and the hesitation and then the acknowledgement.

Pipes squealed again and the marine drummer began to beat the *rafale*. Men ran to their stations and knelt by the guns, the officers and midshipmen drew their dirks and swords and the gun-captains raised their hands as their guns became ready.

'Sail trimmers, Mr Hill. We'll heave-to and fire a broadside ahead of the leading whales!' Hill was at his station and had relieved Rispin. There was now an economy of orders as Hill deployed the men chosen to trim the *Melusine*'s sails and spars in action. Bourne too was beside him, ready to pass orders to the batteries. 'Load ball, Mr Bourne, all guns at maximum depression, both broadsides to be ready.'

'Aye, aye, sir.'

Melusine had entered the lead now. On either side the backs of whales still emerged, their huge tails slowly thrusting the water as they drove majestically along. Beyond the whales, close to larboard and some miles distant to starboard, the ice edge glittered in the sunlight, full of diamond brilliants shading to blue shadows with green slime along the waterline.

He was aware of Mr Singleton on the quarterdeck. 'Should you not be at your station?' he asked mildly.

'I beg your pardon, sir, I took it to be another of these interminable manoeuvres that . . .'

'Never mind, never mind. You may watch now you are here.'

Singleton turned to see Meetuck pointing excitedly from the fo'c's'le as a female whale rolled luxuriously on her side, exposing her nipple for her calf. 'It seems scarcely right to kill these magnificent creatures,' he muttered to himself, remembering the *Benedicite*. The mother and calf fell astern.

'Down helm, Mr Hill, you may heave the ship to . . .' There were more orders and *Melusine* swung to starboard, easing her speed through the water to a standstill.

'Larboard battery! Make ready!' The arms went up and he nodded to Bourne.

'Fire!'

The broadside erupted in smoke and flame with a roar that made the ears tingle. The balls raised splashes, a cable to leeward where two big whales had been seen. Through the drifting smoke Drinkwater saw one huge fluke lift itself for a moment as the whale dived, but he had no idea whether he had reversed its course.

'Reload!' There was a furious and excited activity along the larboard waist. There was nothing to compare with firing their brute artillery that so delighted the men, officers and ratings alike.

'You may give them another broadside, Mr Bourne.'

Again the arms went up and again the shots dropped ahead of the whales. Drinkwater turned to starboard, to look back up the strait. The whalers were three miles away and between them and the *Melusine* was a most extraordinary sight. The sea seemed to boil with action. He could see more than a dozen boats. Three were under tow by harpooned whales, others were in the act of striking, their harpooners up in the bows as the tense steersmen brought their flimsy boats into the mass of whales that had now taken alarm and were swimming south-west, along the line of the lead. Beyond these two boat's crews were lancing their catches, probing for the lives of the great beasts as their victims rolled and thrashed the water with their great tails. Through his glass Drinkwater could see the foam of their death agonies tinged with blood. A few flags were up on dead carcases and these were either under tow to the whalers or awaiting the few boats that could be spared for this task.

Drinkwater saw at once that he could not fire his starboard guns without endangering the boats but their crews were excitedly awaiting the order that would send their shot in amongst the whales.

'By God,' he heard Walmsley mutter to Glencross, 'this is better than partridge.'

'Secure the starboard guns, Mr Bourne, and draw the charges!' He heard the mutter of disappointment from the starbowlines. 'Silence there!'

A new danger suddenly occurred to him. The sloop lay in the path of the advancing animals. The death of some of their number had communicated an alarm to the others and their motion was full of turbulent urgency. He did not wish to think what effect one of those bluff heads would have upon *Melusine*'s hull. 'Haul the mainyard, Mr Hill and put the ship before the wind . . .' Hill grasped the sudden danger and *Melusine* turned slowly to larboard as she again gathered headway. She had hardly swung, presenting her stern to the onrushing whales when their attention was attracted by shouts to the south, to larboard. One of the boats that had been fast to a fish had been dashed to fragments on the ice edge two miles away as the tortured beast had dived under the ice. The alarm had been raised by another boat, towing past *Melusine*'s stern, who hailed the sloop to request her rendering assistance and allowing them to hold onto their whale. It was while clearing away the quarterboat that a whale struck them. A large gravid female in the last stages of her pregnancy had been terrified by the slaughter astern of her. The ship shook and the stunned animal rolled out from under the quarter, almost directly beneath the boat. Her astonished crew, half-way down to the water's surface looked down into the tiny eye of the monster. The whale spouted, then dived, her flukes hitting the keel of the suspended boat but not upsetting it.

A few minutes later, under the command of Acting Lieutenant Gorton the boat was pulling across a roil of water, avoiding the retreating whales with difficulty, on her way to rescue the crew of the smashed whale-boat. It did not appear that *Melusine* had suffered any damage from the collision.

The whalers hunted their quarry for fifty hours while the sun culminated and then began its slow unfinished setting, its azimuth altering round the horizon to rise again to each of two successive noons. *Melusine* was quite unable to stem the escape of the whales and in the end Drinkwater agreed to the boats securing their captured whales to her sides.

'As fenders!' Harvey had hailed, his eyes dark and sunken in his head with the fatigue of the chase, 'in case the ice closes on you!' The

133

jest was made as he went in pursuit of his eighth whale, his cargo almost complete. Now the five ships lay secured along the ice edge on the northern side of the lead, tied up as though moored to a quay, their head and stern lines secured to ice anchors. Each had a pair of whales alongside, between hull and ice, while rafted outboard in tier after tier lay the remainder of the catch. While *Melusine*'s company stood watch, the exhausted whalers turned below to sleep before the flensing began. They had taken more than thirty whales between them and the labour of cutting up the blubber and packing it in casks took a further two days of strenuous effort.

Melusine's midshipmen went out on the ice with Mount and a party of marines and took some more seals, returning to the ship to pick off the brown sharks that clustered round the whale corpses as they sank after flensing. The fine weather held and the whale-captains expressed their good fortune, accepting an invitation to dine with Drinkwater the instant the flensing was completed. Even Sawyers seemed to be un-Quakerishly cheerful, and Drinkwater, anticipating an early departure from the Greenland Sea, ordered Tregembo to get Palgrave's carvers, silver and plate out of storage.

The high good humour that seemed to infect them all after the success of the last few days allayed his worries about the possible closure of the ice. Besides, he twice-daily ascended the mainmast to the crow's nest, spending as much as half an hour aloft with the big watch glass and making note of the bearings of familiar ice hummocks with a pocket compass. The variation in their positions was minimal, the movement of the ice, like the weather, seemed suspended in their favour. His own natural suspicions, those fine tunings of his seaman's senses, were blunted by the triumphant confidence of Harvey, Renaudson, Sawyers and Atkinson of the *Truelove*.

As they gathered in Drinkwater's cabin sipping from tankards of mimbo, a hot rum punch that Cawkwell concocted out of unlikely materials, their elation was clear. So great had been their success that the customary jealousy of one whaler who had done less well than his more fortunate colleague was absent. It was true that Harvey's harpoon gun had proved its value, netting him the largest number of whales, but he endured only mild rebukes from Sawyers who claimed the method un-Godly.

'Never a season like it, Captain,' Renaudson said, his face red from the heat in the cabin and the effects of the mimbo. 'Abel bleats about God like your black-coated parson,' he nodded in Singleton's direction, 'but 'tis luck, really. A man may fish the Greenland Seas for a lifetime, like, then, ee,' he shook his head slightly, a small grin of disbelief in his good fortune crossing his broad, sweating features, 'his luck changes like this.' He became suddenly serious. 'Mind you, Captain, it'll not happen again. No. Not in my lifetime, any road. I've seen the best and quickest catch I'm ever likely to make and I doubt my son'll see owt like it himself, not if he fishes for twenty year'n more. Abel's lucky there, both him and his son together in one great hunt.' He drained the tankard. 'I see tha's children of thee own, Captain.' He nodded at the portraits on the bulkhead, his accent thickening as he drank.

'Yes,' said Drinkwater, sipping the mimbo more cautiously. It was not a drink he greatly cared for, but his stocks of good wine were almost exhausted and Cawkwell had suggested that he served a rum punch to warm his guests. Harvey joined them.

'Ee, Captain, your guns weren't as much good as mine.' He grinned, clearly happy that his beloved harpoon gun had established its reputation for the swift murder of mysticetae. 'I shall patent the modifications I've made and make my fortune twice over from this voyage.' He nudged Renaudson. 'Get th'self a Harvey's patent harpoon gun for next season, Thomas, then th'can shoot whales instead of farting at them.' The dialect was thick between them and Drinkwater turned away, nodding to Atkinson, a small, active man with a lick of dark hair over his forehead, who was talking to Mr Gorton. Drinkwater had invited only Hill, Singleton and the lieutenants to the meal, there was insufficient room for midshipmen. Besides, he knew the whalemen would not want the intrusion of young gentlemen at their celebrations.

He found himself confronted by Singleton's blue jaw. His sobriety was disquieting amongst all the merriment. 'Good evening, Mr Singleton.'

'Good evening, sir. A word if you please?'

'Of course.'

'I deduce this gathering to mark the successful conclusion of the fishery.'

'So it would appear. Is that not so, Captain Sawyers?' He turned to the Quaker who had, as a mark of the relaxation of the occasion, removed his hat.

'Indeed it is, although a few of us have an empty cask or two left. The Lord has provided of his bounty . . .'

'Amen,' broke in Singleton, who seemed to have some purpose in his abruptness. 'Then may I ask, sir, when you intend landing me?'

'Landing thee . . .?' Sawyers seemed astonished and Drinkwater again explained for Sawyers's benefit.

'It seems the Almighty smiles upon all our endeavours then, Friend,' he said addressing Singleton, 'and perhaps thine own more than ours.' He smiled. 'This lead towards the south-west will bring you close to the coast of East Greenland, somewhere about latitude seventy. I have heard the coast is ice-free thereabouts, although I have never seen it close-to myself. You may see the mountain peaks in clear weather for a good distance. *Nunataks*, the eskimos call them . . .'

'Then we had better land you,' Drinkwater said to Singleton, 'but I am still uncertain of the wisdom of following this lead into the ice shelf. Do you not think it might prove a cul-de-sac?'

Sawyers shook his head. 'No, the fish would not have entered it if some instinct had not told them that the krill upon which they feed were rich here, and that open water did not exist ahead of them . . .'

'But surely,' Singleton put in, his scientific mind engaged now, 'the whales may dive beneath the ice. My observations while you have been hunting them show they can go prodigious deep.'

'No, Friend,' Sawyers smiled, 'their need of air and their instinct will not pursuade them to dive beneath such an ice shelf as we have about us now. Surely,' he said with a touch of irony, the dissenter gently teasing the man of established religion, 'surely thou sawest how, even in their terror, they made no attempt to swim under the ice?'

Singleton flushed at the mocking of his intelligence. Sawyers mollified him. 'But perhaps in the confusion of the gun smoke thine eyes were misled. No, mysticetus will dive only under floes in the open sea and beneath bay ice through which he breaks to inhale . . .'

'Bay ice?' queried Drinkwater.

'A first freezing of the sea, Captain, through which he may appear with a sudden and majestic entrance . . .'

They sat to dinner, cod, and whale meat steaks with dried peas and a little sour-krout for those who wanted it, all washed down with the last bottles of half-decent claret that Tregembo had warmed slightly in the galley. As was usual in the gloom of the cabin despite the low sunshine outside, Drinkwater had had the candles lit and the spectacle of such a meal etched itself indelibly upon his mind. Alternating round the table the whale-ship masters and the naval officers made an incongruous group. In eccentric varieties of their official uniform the lieutenant and the master agreed only in their coats. Beneath these they wore mufflers, guernseys and an assortment of odd shirts.

Gorton, presumably slightly over-awed to be included in the company, wore shirt and stock in the prescribed manner, but this was clearly over some woollen garment of indeterminate shape and he presented the appearance of a pouter pigeon. The whale-captains were more fantastic, their garb a mixture of formality, practicality and individual choice.

Sawyers, with the rigidity of his sect, appeared the most formal, clearly possessing a thick set of undergarments. His waistcoat and coat were of the heaviest broadcloth and he wore a woollen muffler. Renaudson, on the other hand, marked the perigee of Arctic elegance, in seal-skin breeches over yellow stockings, a stained mustard waistcoat and a greasy jacket, cut short at the waist and made of some nondescript fur that might once have been a seal or a walrus. Atkinson was similarly equipped, although his clothes seemed a little cleaner and he had put on fresh neck-linen for the occasion, while Harvey, his neckerchief filthy, sported a brass-buttoned pilot jacket. Drinkwater himself wore two shirts over woollen underwear, his undress uniform coat almost as salt-stained as Harvey's pilot jacket. But he was pleased with the evening. The conviviality was infectious, the wine warming and the steaks without equal to an appetite sharpened by cold.

The conversation was of whales, of whale-ships and captains, of harpooners and speksioneers and the profits of owners. There were brief, good-natured arguments as one challenged the claims of another. For the most part the whalers dominated the conversation, the young naval officers, under the eye of their commander and overwhelmed by the ebullience of their guests, playing a passive part. But Drinkwater did hear Singleton exchanging stories of the eskimos with Atkinson who seemed to have met them whilst sealing, and they were debating the reasons why they took their meat raw, when methods of cooking it had been shown to them on many occasions. Thus preoccupied he was suddenly recalled by Sawyers on his right. Above the din Sawyers had been shouting at him to catch his attention.

'I beg your pardon, Captain, I was distracted. What was it you were saying?'

'That thy guns were of little use, Friend.'

'In the matter of stopping the whales? Oh, no . . . very little, but it allowed my people to share the excitement a little, although,' he recollected with the boyish grin that countered the serious cast to his cock-headed features, 'I think that my order to secure the starboard guns without them being fired, near sparked a mutiny.'

'That was not quite what I meant, Friend. I had said that we had no *need* of thy guns, that thy presence here has proved unnecessary. Oh, I mean no offence, but whatever hobgoblins the enemy were supposed to have in the Arctic seas have proved imaginary.'

Drinkwater smiled over the rim of his glass as he drained it, leaning back so that Cawkwell could refill it. 'So it would seem . . .'

'Sir! Sir!' Midshipman Frey's face appeared at the opposite end of the table and the conversation died away.

'*Narwhal*, sir! *Narwhal*'s taken fire . . .!'

Fortune's Sharp Adversity

From *Melusine*'s deck they saw *Narwhal* already blazing like a torch. Great gouts of flame bellied from her hold and tongues of fire leapt into the rigging. She was moored beyond *Truelove*, ahead of the sloop, and her crew could be seen rushing down upon the ice. For a second the diners stood as though stunned, then they made for the gangplank onto the ice, led by Harvey.

Pausing only to call for all hands and the preparation of the ship's fire-engine, Drinkwater followed, impelled by some irrational force that caused him to do anything but stand in idleness. Men were pouring down *Truelove*'s gangplank unrolling a canvas hose that was obviously too short to reach much beyond the barque's bowsprit. As he came abreast of *Narwhal*'s stern and among the milling of her crew, Drinkwater realised they were mostly drunk. Harvey was roaring abuse at them, his face demonic in his rage, lit by a blaze that spewed huge gobbets of flame into the sky as casks of whale kreng exploded. Harvey struck two men in his agony before he turned to his ship. He staggered forward into the orange circle of heat where the ice gleamed as it melted, holding his arms up before his face. He was still shouting, something more persistent than abuse, and Drinkwater was about to start after him when Bourne and Quilhampton arrived with a party of marines and seamen lugging the fire-engine.

'Just coming, sir!'

'Suction into the sea, Mr Q! And get two jets playing on the gangplank . . .'

To save the ship was clearly impossible, but there seemed some doubt among the men assembled on the ice as to the whereabouts of two or three of *Narwhal*'s company.

Harvey had already reached the gangplank and edged cautiously forward. Above his head the mainyard was ablaze, the furled canvas of the sail burning furiously. Ahead of him the main hatchway vented flame like a perpetually firing mortar and the deck planks could be seen lifting and curling back. The bulwarks had yet to catch and Harvey reached their shelter, hanging outboard of them and peering over the rail. Drinkwater stepped forward and the heat hit him, searing his eyes so that he stopped in his tracks. It was intense and the roaring of the fire deafening.

A man was crouching beside Drinkwater and he turned to see the marine Polesworth pointing the nozzle of the hose and shouting behind him to the men at the handles. The gurgle of the pump was inaudible and the jet, when it came in spurts to start with, quite inadequate. He felt Quilhampton pulling his left arm.

'Come back, sir, come back!'

'But Harvey, James, what the hell does he think he's doing?'

'They say there's a boy still aboard . . .'

'My God! But no-one could live in that inferno!'

Quilhampton shook his head, his face scarlet in the reflection of the flames. Their feet were sinking into the melting ice as they stared at Harvey. He was attempting to make his way aft outside the hull, by way of the main chains, but the hand by which he clutched the rail was continually seared and he was making painfully slow progress. And then Drinkwater saw the object of Harvey's foolhardy rescue attempt. The figure was lit from within the cabin where the bulkheads were already burning, silhouetted against the leaded glass of the larboard quarter-gallery. By contrast to the conflagration above, *Narwhal*'s hull was dark as lamp-black but as their eyes adjusted, the pale face with its gaping mouth pressed against the glass in a silent scream, riveted their attention.

'Polesworth! Direct your hose upon the quarter-gallery!' The marine obeyed and Drinkwater hoped he might thereby delay the fire spreading to the place. Harvey had scrambled the length of the main chains and was feeling for a footing to cross twenty feet of hull to the mizen chains. He found some plank land, a perilous footing, but he kept moving steadily aft.

'Rope, we need rope. From *Truelove*, Mr Q!' He saw Renaudson among the appalled crowd. 'Rope, Captain, rope from your ship!'

There was a hurried exchange of orders and men began to run towards *Truelove*.

Harvey gained the mizen chains and had leant outboard from their after end to find a footing on the leaded top of the quarter-gallery. But he was too late.

With a roar an explosion shook *Narwhal*'s stern, the windows of the gallery shattered outwards and a small rag of humanity was ejected into the blackness. Harvey was blown off into the water.

As the explosion died away Drinkwater heard several voices shout that *Narwhal*'s small powder magazine was beneath the cabin aft, and then their attention was claimed by a great cracking and splitting of wood as the mainmast, closest to the origin of the fire, burnt through and toppled slowly over onto the ice, bringing the fore and mizen masts with it. The crowd of men moved backwards in fear and when the rope arrived, Renaudson, Quilhampton and Drinkwater made their way to the edge of the ice amid burning spars. Their footing was treacherous. The surface ice was reduced to slush, slush that had no longer the sharp edge of the ice shelf. It now formed a lethal declivity into the freezing black waters of the sea.

They looked down upon Harvey's pale face, curiously blotched and appearing like the head of John the Baptist upon Salome's salver. 'Quick! The rope!'

It snaked over Drinkwater and fell alongside Harvey, but his eyes closed and he did not seem to have seen it.

'God's bones!' Drinkwater began to struggle out of his coat but Quilhampton was quicker, splashing into the water as soon as he saw what the matter was. Drinkwater hesitated a second, concerned that Quilhampton's wooden hand might hamper him, remembering his own pathetic attempts to make a bowline.

But Quilhampton needed no help. He shouted to the men on the ice and Drinkwater stumbled back up the ice-slope to get men to tail onto the line and drag Harvey and Quilhampton to safety, while *Narwhal*'s hull finally erupted, splitting open along her topsides as the fire consumed her.

Despite the fierce heat both rescued and rescuer were shivering. Blankets miraculously appeared and Singleton arrived with an improvised stretcher and the surgeons of the *Truelove* and the *Narwhal* herself.

In seconds Harvey and Quilhampton were on their way back to *Melusine* and in their wake men followed, drifting away from the fire now that there was no longer anything that could be done.

'Captain Renaudson, ah, and you, Captain Sawyers. A word if you please . . .' The two men approached, sober faces reflecting the glare of the fire, even though it was the midnight of an arctic summer and quite light.

'What do we do with these men, gentlemen?' Drinkwater asked.

'Hang the lubbers, God blast their bloody stupidity.' Renaudson turned on the shifty eyed and shamefaced Narwhals as they stood on the ice disconsolately, 'You should starve here, if I had my way . . . drunken bastards!' he said with venom.

'Steady, Friend . . .' put in Sawyers, putting out a restraining arm.

'A pox on your damned cant, Abel. These harlots' spawn deserve nothing . . .'

'You do not know that they all . . .'

'I do not need to know more than that Jaybez Harvey will not live to see his wife again, nay, them art shit,' and he spat for emphasis and turned away.

Drinkwater looked at the crowd of men. 'Which of you is the chief officer?'

The mate stepped forward. 'I'm the mate, Captain, John Akeroyd.'

'How did the ship catch fire?'

'I'm not certain, sir, I was below, turned in.'

'Who had the watch?' Drinkwater addressed the question to the huddle of men. There seemed to be some shoving and then a man came forward.

'Me.'

'What is your name?'

'Peter Norris, third mate . . . men got among the spirits, sir, there was some sort o'fight over a game o'cards . . . tried to stop it but it was too late . . .'

Drinkwater saw the raw bruising round Norris's left eye which indicated he spoke the truth. 'Hhmmm . . .'

'There is a custom, Friend, in the fishery,' offered Sawyers helpfully, 'that when a disaster such as this occurs the crew of the vessel lost is split up among the other vessels. Perhaps, Mr Akeroyd, thou would'st care to divide the men.' Sawyers caught Drinkwater's arm and turned him away. 'Come, Friend, this is not a naval matter.'

'But there is some degree of culpability . . . if Harvey should die . . .'

'The fishery has its own ways, Captain Drinkwater.' Sawyers was tugging him as he tried to turn back, 'Come away, they have lost everything and will go home as beggars . . .'

'But, damn it, Sawyers, Harvey is like to die and that boy . . .'

'Aye, Friend, thou mayst be right, but thou cannot flog them and they will be penitent ere long. Come.' And Drinkwater returned reluctantly to *Melusine*.

Rispin met him formally at the side. 'I beg pardon sir, the sideboys are . . .'

'Oh, damn the sideboys, Mr Rispin, where is Mr Singleton?'

'He took the injured man below, sir, with the surgeons from two of the whaling vessels, sir.'

'Thank you.'

'And sir, the wind's freshening.'

'And damn the wind too!'

Drinkwater found Quilhampton in the cockpit, a mug of mimbo before him and blankets and midshipmen close about him. He was recovering in good company and although the midshipmen drew deferentially aside Drinkwater offered Quilhampton no more than a nod and the terse observation that he had 'Done very well'.

'Bit tight with the compliments, Q, old chap,' muttered Lord Walmsley as Drinkwater moved forward to where the midshipmen's chests had been dragged into a makeshift table.

'How is he?' The three surgeons turned, grunted and bent over Harvey. The pock-marked face was crusted with burnt flesh, the beard singed and smelling foully. Alongside lay the roll of Singleton's instruments, the demi-lunes, daviers and curettes gleaming in the light of the two battle lanterns suspended from the low beams. Drinkwater looked at the palms of the hands. They were black and swollen.

Singleton straightened. 'How is he?' Drinkwater repeated the question.

'We have administered laudanum as an anodyne, Captain Drinkwater, and *I* am of the opinion that the wounds *must* be debrided without delay.'

'If you cannot agree, gentlemen,' said Drinkwater with a sudden edge to his voice addressing the whale-ships' surgeons, 'then you may leave the patient to my doctor.' The surgeon of the *Narwhal* looked up angrily. He was a man of nearer seventy years than sixty, Drinkwater judged.

'I've been with Cap'n Harvey these last twenty-six years, Cap'n, an' I'll not leave him . . .'

'Then you will hold your tongue, sir, since you have nowhere else to go, you may remain. As for you,' he turned to the other man, 'I suggest you return and offer Captain Renaudson what assistance he requires in the matter of examining those of *Narwhal*'s crew that join *Truelove*.' He ignored the sullen glares in the two men's eyes. 'Now, Singleton, how is he?'

143

'We will debride the wounds, sir, while he is still in a state of shock, those about the face particularly, but . . .'

'Well . . .'

'Well what?'

'I have auscultated the pulmonary region and,' he paused, shaking his head, 'the trachea, the bronchia and larynx, indeed it appears the lungs themselves have been seared severely, by the intake of such hot air, sir.'

'Then there is little hope?'

'I fear not, sir.'

Drinkwater looked at the *Narwhal*'s surgeon. 'Who was the boy?'

'Cap'n Harvey's sister's son.'

Drinkwater sighed. His eye caught the edge of the circle of lamp-light. A face, disembodied in the darkness of the cockpit, seemed to leer at him and for a second Drinkwater imagined himself in the presence of the personification of death. But it was only the loblolly 'boy', Skeete.

He turned in search of the fresh air of the deck, pausing at the foot of the ladder. 'You had better lie him in my cot. And you would best do your curettage in the cabin. There is more light.'

Lieutenant Rispin met him at the companion. 'Ah, sir, I was about to send for you. The wind continues to freshen, sir, and we are ranging a little.'

Drinkwater looked at the ice edge above the rail.

'Only a little, Mr Rispin, pray keep an eye upon it.'

'Aye, aye, sir.' Rispin touched the fore-cock of his hat and Drinkwater fell into a furious pacing of the deck. Forward the bell struck two and the sentries called their ritual 'All's well' at hatch, companionway and entry, on fo'c's'le and stern. It was two bells in the middle watch, one o'clock in the morning, bright as day and beneath his feet another man was dying.

It was the waste that appalled him most, that and the consideration that the loss of *Narwhal*, though it in no way affected the *Melusine* directly, seemed of some significance. He had liked Harvey, a tarpaulin commander of the finest sort, able, kindly and, in the end, heroic. Drinkwater began to see *Narwhal*'s loss as an epitome, a providential instruction, an illumination of a greater truth as he paced his few yards of scrubbed planking.

The folly of many had destroyed in a twinkling their own endeavours, a few had been victims of the consequence of this folly (for they had later learned that, in addition to the boy, two men were also missing). And one, upon whom all the responsibility had lain, was to be sacrificed; to die to no ultimate purpose, since *Narwhal* had been lost. Drinkwater could only feel a mounting anger at the irresponsibility of the men who had got among the spirits aboard the whaler. Renaudson had been furious with them, damning them roundly with all the obscene phrases at his disposal and yet Drinkwater began to feel a degree of anger towards himself. Perhaps he should not have had the masters to dinner; had Harvey been aboard *Narwhal*, his men might not have run wild. In that case Harvey would have been alive.

He clutched at his hat. 'God damn it!' he muttered to himself, suddenly mindful of his duty. Rispin had been right, the wind had an edge to it that promised more. He looked aloft, the pendant was like a bar, stretching towards the south-west as the gale began to rise from the north-east.

Drinkwater strode forward to the main rigging. Swinging himself onto the rail he began the ascent of the mainmast.

He felt the full violence of the gale by the time he reached the main top. It threatened to pluck him from the futtocks as he hung, back downwards. At the topgallant crossing, it tore at his clothes. He cursed as he struggled into the crow's nest, realising that his preoccupation had lasted too long. Commanders of ships should not indulge in morbid reflections. Even before he had levelled the long glass he knew something was wrong.

To the north-east the lead was not only filling with loose ice floes, blown into it by the gale, but it was narrower; quite noticeably narrower. The great ice raft to which they were moored which had cracked away from the shelf to the north and west of them and which was, perhaps, some fifty or sixty miles square, must have been revolving. Drinkwater tried to imagine the physical reasons for this. Had it just been the onset of the gale? Could a few hours of rising wind turn such a vast island of ice so quickly? The logic of the phenomena defeated him. What was certain was that the lead had closed to windward; he did not need to take bearings to see that. He swung the glass the other way. If the ice island revolved, then surely the strait ought to open in that direction. It did not. Its unwillingness to obey the laws of nature as he conceived them disturbed Drinkwater. He was once again confronted by his ignorance. Kicking open the trapdoor, he dangled his legs for the topgallant ratlines.

Regaining the deck and without the ceremony required by the usages of the navy, he hastened precipitately down the makeshift gangplank onto the ice. Hurrying aboard *Faithful* he woke Sawyers with the news. The Quaker's eyes told him what he already felt in his bones.

'Thou dids't right, Friend. Happen the Lord was about to punish our pride. We must make sail without delay and take this fair wind to the south-west. We have no need to linger. I pray thee do not delay, thy ship is not fit to withstand a single fastening in the ice. Go, go!'

The watches were swiftly alerted on the other whalers and within a few minutes the hands were being tumbled up on all the ships. *Diana*, the leewardmost would have to leave first, for the wind pinned them slightly onto the ice, but her sturdy sides withstood a scrape or two before her rudder bit and her head came off. *Truelove*'s bow nudged the remnants of *Narwhal* that had rested, half sunk, upon a ledge of ice, and she to stood out into the lead, her hands dropping the forecourse as well as setting the topsails. *Melusine* followed, her spirketting grinding on *Narwhal* as her bow was thrust out into open water. As the hands dropped the forecourse in its buntlines it occurred to Drinkwater, as one of those savage ironies truth thrust before him, that had not *Narwhal*'s burnt timbers lain like a fender ahead of them, the onshore wind might have pinned *Melusine*'s hull against the ice forever.

He looked astern as *Diana*, *Earl Percy* and *Provident*, bumped off the wreck and out into the safety of open sea. Then the six ships stood south-west, aware that the lead, once so wide and inviting, so apparently permanent and alive with whales, was already narrowing on either beam.

There was no longer any sign of a single whale.

PART THREE

The Fiord

'(Men) live like wild beasts in a deep solitude of spirit and will, scarcely any two being able to agree since each follows his own pleasure or caprice.'

Giambattista Vico (1668–1744)

The Fate of the 'Faithful'

Drinkwater kept the deck for three days. By the end of this time he was reduced to a stupor of fatigue, suffering from a quinsy and incipient toothache. But *Melusine* and the whalers had broken out of the lead to the south-west and, but for the presence of a thousand ice floes, were in what passed for 'open' water. Their escape from being set fast and crushed had been remarkable, as much for the danger to the ship as to the frequency of its occurrence. Perhaps twenty or thirty times, Drinkwater had lost count, they tacked, wore, or threw all aback to make a stern-board clear of impending doom. Many more times than this the hands bore lighter floes off with the spare spars. There were several minor injuries, one rupture and a case of crushed ribs amongst the men. The days of hunting parties were long forgotten, the yachting atmosphere paid for ten times over. Despite their best endeavours *Melusine* was several times jarred by collision with floes and the increasing number of growlers that bore witness to the high summer of the region.

There was little conviviality in gunroom or cockpit. On the berth deck the men rolled in or out of their hammocks as the watches changed, dog-tired, cold and miserable. Amid this atmosphere Macpherson ceased his ravings and quietly gave up the ghost, while Harvey now awash with opiates, continued to breathe with increasing difficulty. The internal routines of the ship went on, hammocks were piped up, the decks scrubbed, spirits served and the hands piped to their dinners. The mess kids were scoured and the hammocks piped down. The cook and his mates swore and blasphemed at the coppers, the bosun's mates cursed at the hatchways, the loblolly boys in the cockpit as they cleared night soil from the sick.

On the quarterdeck Hill and Bourne bore the brunt of the activity, for Drinkwater had doubled the watches, and Rispin and Gorton were stationed in the waist, or forward, supervising the staving off of the ice.

And through it all Drinkwater kept the deck, his mind numbed with weariness, yet continually aware of every influence upon the movement of his ship. At moments of greatest peril he was the first to be aware of a sudden set towards a berg, the swirl of undertow suggesting the submerged presence of a growler or the catspaw of a squall from the turbulent lee of a large ice hummock. And it was Drinkwater who first suspected there might be something wrong with the rudder. It was nothing serious, a suspicious creaking when he listened from the privacy of the quarter-gallery latrine, a certain sluggishness as *Melusine* came to starboard. In fact it was at first only a suspicion, a figment, he thought, of an over-anxious mind. In the face of more pressing problems he tended to dismiss it. When he came below at the end of his three-day vigil as they drifted into the 'open' water and the wind, perversely, fell to a dead calm, he flung himself across his cot in grateful oblivion.

But when he woke, with *Melusine* rolling gently on a long, low swell, he heard again the creak from the rudder stock below.

Wearily he came on deck to find Hill on watch.

'What time is it, Mr Hill?'

'Six bells in the afternoon watch, sir.'

'I have slept the clock round . . . tell me, do the quartermasters complain of the steering?'

'No, sir.' Drinkwater looked at the two men at the wheel.

'How does she steer?'

'She seems to drag a little, sir, a-coming to 'midships.'

'When you've had helm which way?'

'Larboard, I think, sir.'

'Why didn't you report it?'

The man shrugged. 'Only noticed it today, sir, while we've bin tryin' to catch this fluky wind, sir.'

'Very well.' He turned to Hill. 'I'm mystified, Mr Hill, but we'll keep an eye on it. Damned if I don't think there's something amiss, but what, I'm at a loss to know.'

'Aye, aye, sir, I'll take a look in the steerage if you wish.' Drinkwater nodded and Hill slipped below to return a few minutes later shaking his head.

'Nothing wrong, sir. Not that I can see.'

'Very well.'

'That whale hit the rudder, sir, and we've had a fair number of these damned ice floes . . .'

'Deck there!' They both looked aloft. 'Deck there! Think I can see gun-fire three points to starboard!'

The two officers looked at each other, then Drinkwater shouted, 'Silence there!' They stood listening. A faint boom came rolling over the limpid water. 'That's gun-fire, by God!' Drinkwater ran forward and swung himself up into the main rigging. As he climbed he stared about him, trying to locate the whalers, aware that they had become widely dispersed in their struggle through the ice. He could see *Diana,* about five miles away to the eastward and ahead of them eight, perhaps ten miles distant was *Truelove.* Yes, her barque rig could be plainly seen beneath the curved foot of the main topgallant. *Earl Percy* and *Provident* were also to the east. He struggled up into the crow's nest as Leek slid agilely down.

'Where away?' gasped Drinkwater with the effort of his climb.

'Four points now, sir. I think it's where I last saw *Faithful,* sir, lost her behind a berg.'

'Very well.' He picked up the glass and stared to the south-west. He could see nothing. 'Leek!'

'Sir?'

'Away to Mr Hill, ask him to rig out the booms and set stun's'ls aloft and alow.'

'Stun's'ls aloft 'n' alow, aye, sir.' He watched Leek reach out like a monkey, over one hundred feet above the deck, and casually grab a backstay. The man diminished in size as he descended and Drinkwater levelled his glass once more. He felt the mast tremble as the topmen mounted the shrouds, he heard the mates and midshipmen as they supervised the rigging of the booms and the leading of outhauls and downhauls, heel-ropes and sheets. And then, as his patience was running out, he felt *Melusine* heel as she increased her speed. Five minutes later he located the *Faithful.*

She was fifteen or twenty miles away, perhaps more, for it was hard to judge. Her shape was vertically attenuated by refraction. She seemed to float slightly above the surface of the sea amid a city of the most fantastic minarets, a fairy-tale picture reminiscent of the Arabian Nights displaced to a polar latitude. But Drinkwater's interest was diverted from the extraordinary appearance of refracted icebergs by the unusual shape alongside the *Faithful.* At first he took it for a mirror image of the whaler. But then he saw the little points of yellow light between the ships. Sawyers was a Quaker and carried no guns. The second image was a hostile ship; an enemy engaging *Faithful.* Drinkwater swore; he was seven leagues away in light airs at the very moment Earl St Vincent had foreseen his presence would be required to protect the whalers.

.   .   .

'An enemy sir?'

'Yes, Mr Bourne, at a guess twenty miles distant and already with a prize crew on board the *Faithful,* damn it . . . Mr Hill, bear up, bear up! D'you not see the growler on the starboard bow . . .' Drinkwater broke off to cough painfully. His throat was rasped raw by the persistent demands made on him to shout orders, but he felt an overwhelming desire to press after the ship that had taken one of his charges from under his very nose.

'I have a midshipman at the masthead and want a pair of young eyes kept on the enemy and prize until they're both under our lee. The midshipman that loses sight of them will marry the gunner's daughter!' He coughed again. 'Now double the watches, Mr Bourne, this may prove a long chase.'

'Aye, aye, sir.' Bourne hesitated, unwilling to provoke a captain whom he knew to be short-tempered if his orders were not attended to without delay. 'Beg pardon, sir, but what about the other ships?'

'I have made them a signal to the effect that I am chasing an enemy to the south-west. My orders to them oblige them to close together. Let us hope they do what they are told, Mr Bourne.'

Bourne took the hint, touched the fore-cock of his hat and hurried off. Drinkwater swallowed with difficulty, swore, and set himself to pace the quarterdeck, leaving the business of working the ship through the ice to Hill until he was relieved by Bourne himself at eight bells. He was beyond shouting orders, feeling a mild fever coming on and worrying over the loss of the *Faithful* and the ominous creaking that came from the rudder. But *Melusine* handled well enough and after another hour Tregembo appeared to announce Drinkwater's dinner, served late, as had become his custom in high latitudes to try and differentiate between day and night in the perpetual light.

It was while he was eating that Mr Frey came below to report they had lost the wind and the enemy.

'What . . .?' His voice whispered and he tried to clear his throat, 'Upon what point of sailing was the enemy and prize when last seen, Mr Frey?'

'Both ships were close hauled on the starboard tack, sir. They had a fair breeze before the fog closed in.'

'And their heading?'

'South-west, sir.'

'Very well. Tell Mr Bourne to strike the stun's'ls, and reduce to all plain sail. Double the forward lookouts and make good a course towards the south-west. A man to go to the mainmast head every hour to see if the enemy masts are above the fog. Kindly call me in two hours time.'

'Aye, aye, sir.' Frey hesitated in the doorway.

'Well, what is it?'

'If you please, sir, Mr Bourne said I was to ask you if you wanted Mr Singleton to attend you?'

'Damn Mr Bourne's impertinence, Mr Frey, you've your orders to attend to . . .' The boy fled and, rolling himself in his cloak, Drinkwater flung himself across his cot shivering.

Two hours later Mr Frey called him. Staggering to his feet, his head spinning, Drinkwater ascended to the quarterdeck. Although the thermometer registered some 36° Fahrenheit it seemed colder. Every rope and spar dripped with moisture and the decks were dark with it. Mr Bourne touched his hat and vacated his side of the quarterdeck. It could not by any stretch of the imagination be described as the 'windward side' for *Melusine* lay wallowing in a calm. Almost alongside her a ridge of ice, hummocked and cracked with apparent age gleamed wetly in the greyness. It was not daylight, neither was it night. The ship might have been the only living thing in an eternity of primordial mist, an atmosphere at once eerie and oppressive through which each creak of the ship's fabric, each slat of idle canvas or groan of parrel as she rolled in the low swell, seemed invested with a more than ordinary significance. The grinding creak from the rudder stock seemed deafening now. Drinkwater was too sick to attribute this heightened perception to his fever, and too unsteady on his legs to begin to pace the deck. Instead he jammed himself against the rail close to the mizen rigging and beckoned Bourne over.

'Sir?'

'Mr Bourne, my apologies. I was short with Frey when he offered the services of the doctor.'

' 'Tis no matter, sir, but I thought you looked unwell . . .'

'Yes, yes, Mr Bourne, thank you for your kindness. I will see Singleton in due course. But I am more concerned with the rudder. Had you noticed the noise?'

'Mr Hill drew it to my attention. The ship has long lost steerage way, sir. But I had no reason to doubt much was wrong, sir. She answered the helm well enough when last the wind blew.'

Drinkwater nodded, then spoke with great difficulty. 'Yes, yes, but I fear the matter is a progressive disintegration of some sort. No matter, there is nothing to be done at the moment. You have had no sign of those ships?'

'None, sir.'

'Very well. That is all, Mr Bourne.'

Bourne turned away and Drinkwater hunched his shoulders into his cloak. His right shoulder ached with the onset of the damp weather, his throat was sore and his toothache seemed to batter his whole skull.

The fog lasted for four days and was followed by a south-westerly gale during which the visibility never lifted above half a mile. The air was filled with particles of frozen rain so that Drinkwater was obliged to secure the *Melusine* to a large ice floe. At the height of the gale he submitted to the ministrations of Mr Singleton and suffered a brief agony which ended his toothache by the extraction of a rotten molar. But the removal of the tooth also signalled the end of his quinsy. On the advice of Singleton he kept his cabin and his cot while the *Melusine* was alongside the ice. There was, in any case, little he could do on deck and, as Singleton pointed out, his recovery would be the quicker and he would be fitter to attend his duties, the instant the gale abated and the visibility lifted.

He did not protest. His general debility was, he realised himself, his own fault. In circumstances of such peril as *Melusine* had so often been, it was physically impossible to keep the deck permanently. His confidence in his lieutenants had not initially been high and he had found it very difficult to go below in circumstances of broad daylight. However, the days of working the ship through the ice had improved the proficiency of Bourne and Gorton. Even Rispin showed more firmness and self-confidence, while Hill and the other warrant officers appeared to carry out their duties efficiently. In addition to the worry and sense of failure at the capture of *Faithful*, his shoulder plagued him, reducing his morale and subjecting him to fits of the 'blue devils' while the fever lasted. All the while the rudder ground remorselessly below him, like a long-fused petard waiting to explode. Despite its comparative idleness while they were secured to the floe, it continued to grind and groan as *Melusine* ranged and bumped the ice, rolling and sawing at her moorings as the gale moaned in the rigging. Meanwhile the watch stumbled about the deck, wound in furs, greygoes, even blankets, to combat the stinging particles in the air.

Ten days after the onset of the fog there came a change in the weather that was as abrupt as it was unexpected and delightful. A sense of renewed hope coincided with this change, sending Drinkwater on deck a fit man, all traces of quinsy and fever gone. He was burning to resume the pursuit of the unknown enemy ship that had taken the *Faithful* from under his nose. The situation of the *Melusine* had been transformed. The sun shone through a fine veil of cloud producing a prismatic halo upon the horizontal diameter of which appeared two parhelia, faint false suns, the results of atmospheric refraction. This phenomena was exciting some comment from the watch on deck and had so far absorbed Mr Rispin's interest that he had neglected to inform Drinkwater of the dramatic change in the weather. It was bitterly cold. On every rope and along the furled sails the moisture had frozen into tiny crystals which were glinting in the sunshine. Drinkwater sniffed the air and felt its chill tingle the membranes of his nasal passages. The resultant sneeze recalled Rispin belatedly to his duty.

'Oh, good morning, sir. As you see, sir, the wind has dropped and the visibility is lifting . . .'

'Yes, yes, Mr Rispin, I can see that for myself . . .' Drinkwater replied testily. The appearance of the twin sun dogs alarmed him, not on any superstitious account, but because he recollected something Harvey had said about their appearance indicating a change of weather. That much was obvious, but there had been something said about wind. He looked at the weft on the windward dog-vane. It hung down motionless. Casting his eyes aloft he saw that the masthead pendant was already lifting to a light air from the north. He also saw the crow's nest was empty.

'Mr Rispin!'

'Sir?'

'Direct a midshipman aloft upon the instant to look out for any sails, then have the topsails hard reefed and loosed in their buntlines, the foretopmast stays'l and spanker ready for setting and the longboat hoisted out and manned ready to pull the ship's head off.'

Rispin's mouth opened, then closed as his eyes filled with comprehension. He might be slow on the uptake, thought Drinkwater as he forced himself to a patience he was far from feeling, but Mr Rispin certainly made up for what he lacked in intelligence by a veritable out-pouring:

'Mr Glencross, aloft at once with a glass and cast about for sails. Bosun's mate! Pipe the watch aloft to loose topsails, topmen to remain at the yard arms and the bunts and await the order "let fall" Corporal of marines! Turn up the marines and send 'em aft to man the yard tackles. Master at Arms! Turn up the idlers below to man the stay tackles. Look lively there!' Rispin turned frantically, waving the speaking trumpet. 'Mr Walmsley! Have the afterguard cast loose the stops on the spanker. Fo'c's'le there! Cast loose the fore topmast stays'l!' Rispin's brow wrinkled in thought as he mentally ticked off the tasks Drinkwater had set him.

Already the dogvanes pointed north and the wefts were lifting. Drinkwater watched a catspaw of wind ripple the surface of the clear water to starboard. A low raft of ice a cable to windward seemed to be perceptibly nearer.

'You may cut the moorings, Mr Rispin!'

'Cut the moorings, aye, aye, sir.' Rispin's relief was noticeable. He had clearly forgotten the necessity of putting a party onto the ice and the difficult business of recovering them by boat once the ship had got clear.

Hill and Bourne had come on deck, alarmed by the bellowing at the hatchways. Drinkwater nodded to them. 'We are about to get a blow from the north, gentlemen, I want the ship off this ice floe before we are trapped. The boat is about to be launched to pull her head off.'

Both Hill and Bourne acknowledged the immediacy of Drinkwater's alarm. There was already a perceptible breeze from the north, icy and dry after the south-westerly gale. 'Turn up the watch below, Mr Bourne!'

The longboat was already swaying up from the waist, the marines stamping aft as they leant their weight to the yard tackles that hoisted the boat out over the side. Mr Quilhampton was standing on the rail in charge of the launching party.

'Walk back all!' The boat descended below the rail as the last of her crew tumbled in. A second or two later she hit the water. 'Come up all!' Marines and idlers relaxed as the tackles went slack and on the fo'c's'le Walmsley's party, having prepared the staysail, made a line ready for the boat. A carpenter's party was hacking through the moorings and in the tops Frey, Wickham and Dutfield held up their hands to indicate the topsails were ready.

A glance at the dog-vanes showed the wefts horizontal. It was not a moment too soon. There were pronounced white caps on the water to windward and *Melusine* was rubbing against the ice with some violence.

Drinkwater could feel the sensation of physical discomfort churning the pit of his stomach as his body adjusted to the state of acute worry. Ten minutes neglect by Rispin and they might remain pinned on the floe. He thought of setting sail in an attempt to spin the floe, but he had only the vaguest idea of its size. He was grasping at straws. Officers were reporting his preparations complete and he ordered the yards braced sharp up on the larboard catharpings. The boat was attempting to pull *Melusine*'s head round towards the wind and, although the bow came some six feet off the ice they seemed to be unable to increase that distance. Forward a resourceful Mr Gorton was getting out a spare topgallant yard and lashing it to prevent losing what the longboat had gained. Meanwhile Mr Quilhampton was urging his boat's crew to further efforts, but *Melusine* seemed unwilling to move. On the last occasion this had occurred they had bounced off the remains of *Narwhal*. This time they did not have such help.

'Mr Bourne!' The lieutenant's face turned anxiously towards him. 'Sir?'

'Man the larboard guns, two divisions to fire unshotted cartridges alternately. The breechings to be set up tight. We'll use the recoil to throw the ship off.'

'Aye, aye, sir! Larbowlines! Larboard battery make ready . . .!'

It took several minutes, much longer than if the men had been at their stations for action. But there was no-one on deck, except perhaps Meetuck, who was not seaman enough to appreciate the nature of their situation. Hill was dragging a pudding fender aft to heave over the larboard quarter.

'Well done, Mr Hill . . .'

Drinkwater watched the dog-vanes, his stomach churning. He felt his isolation from the comforting expertise of the whale-ship masters acutely. It prompted him to hail the mainmasthead.

'Masthead there!'

Glencross's head appeared. 'D'you have anything in sight?'

'No, sir! There seems to be clear water to leeward of this floe, but no sails, sir.'

'Very well.' Drinkwater directed his thoughts to the fate of the *Faithful*. In which direction should he chase once he got clear of their present situation? He tried not to think of the possibility of their failing to clear the floe. *Melusine* was not fit for such work in these latitudes. He began to see the weaknesses of St Vincent's reforms undertaken in a mere temporary truce, while the protagonists of this great war caught their breath. But he had no time for further considerations. Bourne reported the guns ready.

'Very well. Forward battery to fire first and to reload as fast as possible. Fastest guns' crew will receive a double tot of rum. But no rolling fire, Mr Bourne, half broadsides only, to make best use of the recoil.'

'Aye, aye sir. I took the liberty of double-loading . . .'

'Have a care then, one round only doubled, Mr Bourne. See to it yourself and open fire without delay.'

Drinkwater clasped his hands behind his back with anxiety as Bourne ran along the deck. It would certainly make the ship recoil, double charging the guns like that. But it might also blow the chambers of the guns . . .

'Fire!' The forward division of guns jerked back against their lashed breechings and their crews leapt round them, swabs and rammers plied as *Melusine* trembled. Drinkwater leaned over the side to see the rope to the longboat curve slightly.

'Pull, Mr Q! Pull!'

He saw Quilhampton wave as a sea swept over the bow of the boat. The after division of the larboard battery roared, the guns leaping against the capsquares on the restrained carriages.

Drinkwater strode to the larboard side and looked overboard. There was a slight gap between the *Melusine*'s tumblehome and the ice edge. He raised his glance forward to see Gorton rigging out another foot of spare spar. They would not lose what they had gained. He must remember to congratulate Gorton on his initiative.

'Fire!' The forward division of six pounders roared again and this time Drinkwater saw the sloop move, her head falling off as Gorton rigged out his spar a little more. Aft, Hill let the fender down so that the larboard quarter could set in on the ice, increasing the angle with the floe. If they could achieve an angle of two points, twenty-two and a half degrees, they might theoretically sail off, but in practise a greater angle would be required, for they would fall back towards the ice as they got the ship underway. The after division fired a second time.

There was no doubt that they were gaining on the wind! But that too was increasing. The forward division fired a third time.

Gorton's spar jerked out again, but Drinkwater could see the strain it was bearing.

'Mr Bourne! Hold the after battery and reload the forrard. All guns to fire simultaneously!'

'Tops there! Let fall the instant the guns discharge!' The three midshipmen acknowledged. 'And, Mr Hill, direct the sheets to be hove to the yardarms the instant the buntlines are slackened!'

'Very well, sir!'

Drinkwater was sweating with excitement despite the numbness of his hands. Quilhampton's boat was a liability now, but he dare not cast it off just yet.

'Ready sir.'

'Very well, Mr Bourne. Fire!'

Melusine shuddered throughout her entire length. Somewhere amidships an ominous crack sounded. But it was not the spar. Gorton's party grunted and swore with effort as their yard, hove out with an extempore tackle at its heel, took up two feet of increased gap. Astern *Melusine*'s larboard quarter ground against the pudding-fender.

Above his head the sails creaked and cracked with ice as the men at the sheets hove down on the frozen canvas.

'Hoist away fore and aft!' The staysail rose from the fo'c's'le head and behind him the spanker was hauled out upon its gaff and boom.

'I can't hold her, sir!' Gorton cried from forward. Drinkwater's heart thumped with anxiety as *Melusine* gathered way.

'No matter, Mr Gorton . . .' The last words were drowned in the splitting crack that came from Gorton's breaking topgallant yard. *Melusine*'s head fell back towards the floe, but she was already gaining speed.

'Mr Gorton, cut the longboat free and hoist the jib!'

Drinkwater stared forward. 'Steady, keep her full and bye, quarter-master. Not an inch to loo'ard.'

'Nothing to loo'ard, sir, aye, aye.'

But she was falling back. The gap between the ice and *Melusine*'s hull was narrowing.

It was too late to order another broadside prepared. He gritted his teeth and watched the inevitable occur. The shock of collision was jarring, knocking some unsuspecting men to the deck, but *Melusine* bounced clear and began to stand off the ice. Half an hour later she hove-to in comparatively clear water and waited for the longboat to come up.

Drinkwater looked up from the chart and tapped it with the dividers. Bourne and Hill bent over the table at the broken and imperfect line that delineated the east coast of Greenland. There were a few identifiable names far to the south, Cape Farewell and Cape Discord, then innumerable gaps until Hudson's anchorage of Hold with Hope.

'I believe our present situation to be here, some sixty leagues west-nor'-west of Trinity Island.

'I believe that the enemy approached from, and retired to, the south-west. We should have seen him earlier had he attacked from any other quarter and it argues favourably to my theory that it was *Faithful* he took, the ship most advanced into that quarter. In addition the last sighting of him and his prize was to the south-west and sailing on the same point. I therefore propose that we chase in that direction. It is inconceivable that he did not experience the fog and south-westerly gale that we have just had and it may be that he is not far away.'

'What about the other whale ships, sir?' asked the cautious Bourne.

Drinkwater looked at the young man. 'There are times when it is necessary to take risks, Mr Bourne. They are armed and alerted to the presence of enemy cruisers while *Faithful was* unarmed and *is* a prize. It argues for our honour as well as our duty that we pursue *Faithful* with a view to retaking her.'

'D'you think there are more French cruisers in the area, sir?'

'It's a possibility that there are. I have reason to believe there may be.'

'You were aware of the possibility?' asked Hill.

'Yes,' Drinkwater nodded. 'That is why *Melusine* was appointed escort to the whale-fleet.'

Drinkwater understood what Hill was implying. It made the capture of *Faithful* highly discreditable to *Melusine* and her commander, despite the practical impossibilities of policing the whole Greenland Sea.

'What about the Spitzbergen ships, sir?'

Drinkwater shrugged. 'One can only be in one place at one time, Mr Hill. Besides I believe that the capture of *Faithful* at least argues to our being in the right area, if not in the right position to prevent the capture. At all events, now it is our duty to reverse that. Do you have any more questions?'

First lieutenant and master shook their heads.

'Very well, gentlemen. In the meantime there is no need to impress upon you the necessity of keeping a sharp lookout.'

The Corsair

Drinkwater awoke from a dream that had not disturbed him for many months since the nightmares of his delirium following the wounding he had received off Boulogne. But it terrified him as much as upon the first occasion he had experienced it, as a callow and frightened midshipman on the frigate *Cyclops*. Again the terrifying inability to move laid him supine beneath the advance of the ghastly white lady who over-rode his body to the accompanying clanking of chains. Over the years the white lady had assumed different guises. She had appeared to him with the face of Hortense Santhonax, sister to one of the French Republic's most daring frigate captains and secret agents, or as the sodomite tyrant of *Cyclop*'s cockpit, the unspeakably evil Augustus Morris. Now she had a visage as cold as the icebergs that had given him so many nightmares of a more tangible nature in recent weeks. Her eyes had been of that piercing and translucent blue he had noticed forming in the shadows of ice pinnacles and spires. Although she changed her appearance Drinkwater knew the white lady had not lost the power to awake in him a strong feeling of presentiment.

He lay perspiring, despite the fact that his exposed feet were registering air at a temperature well below the freezing of water. He began to relax as he heard the rudder grind. It had been grinding so long now with so little apparent ill-effect that he had almost ceased to worry about it. Was he being cautioned by fate to pay it more attention? He tossed aside the blankets and with them such a childish notion. He was about to call the sentry to pass word for Tregembo when he considered it was probably still night, despite the light that came through the cabin windows.

He had almost forgotten the dream as he ascended to the deck. But its superstitious hold was once more thrown over him as he stepped clear of the ladder.

Meetuck turned from the rail where he seemed to have been looking at something, and his almond eyes fell upon Drinkwater with an almost hostile glare. The eskimo, whom Drinkwater had not seen for several days, took a step towards him. Meetuck was muttering something: then he halted, looked at his arm, which was still splinted, shrugged and turned forward.

Mystified by this pantomime Drinkwater nodded to Mr Bourne, who had the deck, and swung himself into the main rigging, reaching the crow's nest and ousting Glencross who appeared to have made himself comfortable with a small flask of rum and a bag of biscuit.

'You may leave that there, Mr Glencross. I doubt you'll be requiring them on deck.' The midshipman cast a rueful glance at the rum and mumbled, 'Aye, aye, sir.'

'I shall return the flask, Mr Glencross, in due course.'

Drinkwater settled himself down with the telescope. In five minutes all thoughts of dreams or eskimos had been driven from his mind. The wind had held steady from the north and they sailed through an almost clear sea, the bergs within five miles being largely decayed and eroded into soft outlines. More distant bergs presented a fantastic picture which increased in its improbability as he watched. Munching his way through Glencross's biscuit and warmed by the rum, he had been aloft for over an hour, enjoying the spectacle of increasing refraction as the sun climbed. The distant icebergs, floes and hummocks seemed cast into every possible shape the imagination could devise. He sighted a number of polar bears and numerous seals lay basking upon low ice. Once the ship passed through a school of narwhals, the males with their curious twisted swords. He saw, too, a number of grampuses, their black and livid white skin a brilliant contrast to the sea as they gambolled like huge dolphins in *Melusine*'s wake as she pressed south-west. Drinkwater was reminded of Sawyers and the whale-captain's regard for the works of God in Arctic waters. He was also reminded of Sawyers's present plight.

It was four bells into the morning watch before Drinkwater saw what he had been looking for, amid the ice pinnacles on their starboard bow, almost indistinguishable from them except to one who had a hunter's keenness of purpose. The edges of sails, betrayed by the inverted image of two ships, their waterlines uppermost, jutted dark into the glare of the sky. They were perhaps thirty miles away and the easing of the wind and the comparative simplicity of navigation through such loose ice suited the slight and slender *Melusine*.

Descending to the deck, Drinkwater passed orders for the course to be amended three points closer to the wind and the corvette to hoist a press of sail. He doubted if *Melusine* presented such a conspicuous picture to the enemy, given her relative position to the sun, but if they were spotted he felt sure the ship's speed would close the gap between them and the distant *Faithful*, whose sea-keeping qualities were far superior to her speed.

At noon the distance between them had closed appreciably and at the end of the first dog-watch the enemy could be clearly seen from the head of the lower masts.

Drinkwater dined with Singleton and Bourne, remarking on the way the eskimo had startled him that morning.

'You mean you thought he had some hostile intent, sir?' asked Singleton.

'Oh, I conceived that impression for a second or two. His appearance was aggressive, but he seemed suddenly to recall some obligation relative to his arm.'

'So he damned well should,' said Bourne.

'Can you recall what he said to you, Captain?' asked Singleton, ignoring Bourne.

Drinkwater swallowed his wine and frowned. 'Not perfectly, but I recall something like "gavloonack" . . .'

'*Gavdlunaq?*'

'Yes, I think that was it. Why? Does it signify to you?'

'It means "white man". Was there anything else?'

Drinkwater thought again. 'Yes, nothing I could repeat though. Oh, he mentioned that place he said he came from . . .'

'*Nagtoralik?*'

'Aye, that was it, *Nagtoralik*.' Drinkwater experimented with the strange word. 'A place with eagles, didn't you say?'

'Yes, that's right, but I don't recall eagles being mentioned by Egedé . . .'

Drinkwater threw back his head and laughed. 'Oh, come, Mr Singleton, you academics! If a thing ain't in print in some dusty library it don't signify that it don't exist.' Bourne joined in the laughter and Singleton flushed.

'There is a Greenland Falcon, the *Falco Rusticolus Candicans* of Gmelin which the innuits, in their unfamiliarity with the order Aves, may mistake for eagles. It is possible that an error in nomenclature took place in translation . . .' Bourne chuckled at Singleton's seriousness as Drinkwater said, somewhat archly, 'Indeed that may be the case, Mr Singleton.'

A silence filled the cabin. Singleton frowned 'To return to Meetuck, sir. You can recall nothing further, nothing specific, I mean?'

163

Drinkwater shook his head. 'No. He was looking over the side, saw me, turned and advanced, uttered this imprecation, looked at his arm and went off forward. I can scarcely expect anything better from a savage.' Then Drinkwater became aware of something preoccupied about Singleton. 'What is it, Mr Singleton? Why are you so interested in an incident of no importance?'

Singleton leaned back in his chair. 'Because I believe it may indeed be of some significance, sir. I understand you are chasing to the south-west, chasing an enemy ship, a French ship perhaps?'

Drinkwater looked at Bourne enquiringly. The first lieutenant shrugged. 'Yes,' said Drinkwater, 'that is correct.'

'Why do you think this ship is running south-west, sir?'

'Well, Mr Singleton, the wind is favourable, she is luring us away from our other charges and the sea is less encumbered by ice in this direction.'

'It is also in the direction of the coast, sir.'

'And . . .?'

'And I believe Meetuck, though he is not very intelligent, even for an eskimo, has seen white men before, white men who have been hostile to him. I believe that before setting out on the ice he may have come from the Greenland coast where white men were . . .'

'Frenchmen?' broke in Bourne.

'It is possible,' said Singleton, turning to the lieutenant.

'It is indeed,' said Drinkwater thoughtfully, remembering the cautionary words of Lord Dungarth in his room at the Admiralty.

'You have some information upon that point, Captain?' asked Singleton shrewdly, but before Drinkwater could reply the cabin door burst open. Midshipman Lord Walmsley stood in the doorway. His usual look of studied contempt was replaced by alarm.

'An enemy, sir, to windward a bare league . . .'

Drinkwater rose. 'Beat to quarters, damn it!'

Mr Rispin had been caught out again. The enemy ship had clearly sighted the pursuing sloop and whether she knew *Melusine* for a naval ship or took her for a whaler, she had left *Faithful* to head west-south-west alone and doubled back unobserved, to lurk behind a berg until *Melusine* came up. Drinkwater reached the quarterdeck as the marine drummer beat the *rafale*.

'Who was your masthead lookout, Mr Rispin?' he asked venomously, casting round for the enemy. He saw the Frenchman immediately, frigate-built and with the tricolour flying from her peak.

'As bold as bloody brass,' said Hill, taking up his station on the quarterdeck alongside the captain.

'Well sir?' Drinkwater stared unblinkingly at Rispin.

'Lord Walmsley, sir.'

'God damn and blast his lordship!'

'D'you wish me to take in sail, sir?'

'Aye, Mr Hill, turn down-wind and get the stuns'ls in. Mr Bourne, don't show our teeth yet, all guns load canister and ball but hold 'em inboard with closed ports.'

Hill altered course and Drinkwater watched the yards squared and the topmen work aloft, stiff monkeys in the frozen air as the studding sails fluttered on deck. He looked astern. A dozen burgomaster gulls flew in their wake and a few fulmars swept the sea to starboard but he no longer had time for such natural wonders. He was studying the strange ship coming up on their starboard quarter.

She was bigger than themselves, a frigate of twenty-eight guns, he reckoned, more than a match for the *Melusine* and wearing French colours.

A shot plunged into the water just astern of them. A second following a minute later struck the hull beneath his feet. Drinkwater hoped Cawkwell had lowered the window sashes. A third ball plunged under their stern. Her guns were well served and there was no doubt that, whether a national frigate or a well-appointed corsair, she was determined upon making a prize of the *Melusine*.

Drinkwater set his mouth in a grim line. He had fought the *Romaine* off the Cape of Good Hope from a position of disadvantage, but now there were no British cruisers in the offing to rescue him.

'Ship's cleared for action, sir.' Bourne touched his hat. Drinkwater turned forward and looked along the deck. The gun crews were kneeling at their posts, the midshipmen with their parties in the fore and main tops, two men at each topgallant crossing and marines aloft in the mizen top. The sail trimmers were at the rails and pins; on the fo'c's'le the bosun stood, his silver whistle about his neck. The helm was in the hands of the two quartermasters with Mr Quilhampton standing casually alongside, his wooden hand holding the log slate. Gorton and Rispin commanded the two batteries, seconded by Glencross and Walmsley, while Mr Frey attended the quarterdeck, with Drinkwater, Hill, Bourne and Lieutenant Mount, whose marines lined the hammock nettings.

'Very well, Mr Bourne.' He raised his voice. 'Starboard battery make ready. I intend to haul our wind and rake from forward.' He paused as another enemy ball found their stern. 'You may fire as you bear, Mr Rispin, but take your time, my lads, and reload as if the devil was on your tail.' He nodded to Hill, 'Very well, Mr Hill, starboard tack, if you please.'

Melusine began to turn, heeling over as she brought the wind round on her beam. Gun captains pulled up their ports and drove home more quoins to counter-act the heel. Rispin, leaped from gun to gun, his hanger drawn.

'God damn! Mr Frey, pass word to Tregembo to get my sword . . . Where the devil have you been, Tregembo?'

'Sharpening your skewer, zur, 'twas as rusty as a church door knocker . . .' Tregembo buckled on the sword and handed Drinkwater a pair of pistols. 'An' I took down the portraits, zur.' He reproached Drinkwater, his old face wrinkling with a kind of rough affection.

Drinkwater managed a half smile and then turned his attention to the ship. Above their heads the braces were swinging the yards. From forward he heard the report of the first gun and watched the enemy for the fall of shot. He saw splinters fly from the vessel's knightheads. Each gun fired in turn as *Melusine* crossed the stranger's bow, and although one or two holes appeared in the Frenchman's fore course and several spouts of water showed on either bow, most seemed to strike home. But as *Melusine* stretched out on the starboard tack she too exposed her stern to the enemy. They fired a broadside and several balls furrowed the deck, one wounded the mizen topmast and holes opened in the spanker. Somewhere below there rose the most horrible howl of agony and Drinkwater was aware of little Frey shaking beside him.

'Mr Frey,' said Drinkwater kindly, 'I don't believe anyone has loaded Captain Palgrave's fancy carronades. Would you and your two yeomen attend to it, canister might be useful later in the action, wouldn't you say?'

Frey focussed his eyes on the two brass carronades that Captain Palgrave's vanity had had installed at the hances. They still slumbered beneath oiled canvas covers. Frey nodded uncertainly and then with more vigour. 'Aye, aye, sir.' It would be good for the child to have something to do.

Astern of them the enemy hauled into their wake. The *Melusine*'s French build began to take effect. She started to open the distance between them.

'Mr Bourne, pass word for the gunner to report to me.'

166

The gunner was called for at the hatchways and made his appearance a moment or two later, his felt slippers sliding incongruously upon the planking.

'Ah, Mr Meggs, I want a caulked keg of powder with a three-minute fuse sealed up in canvas soon as you are able to arrange it.'

The gunner frowned, raised an eyebrow and compressed his toothless mouth. Then, without a word, knuckled his forehead and waddled below. Drinkwater turned to Bourne.

'Well, Mr Bourne, whatever our friend is, he'll not get a gun to bear at the moment.'

Hill came up. 'D'you intend to mine him, sir?'

Drinkwater grinned. 'We'll try. It's a long shot, but I'm not certain that he's a national frigate. I have an idea that he may be a letter-of-marque, in which case he'll be stuffed full of men and we cannot risk him boarding.'

'I am of the same opinion, sir. There's something about him that marks him as a corsair.'

'Yes. Now, we don't want him to see the keg dragging down on him so we will put it over forrard and lead the line out of a forrard port. That way he will not observe any activity around the stern here . . .'

'Use the log-line, sir? It's handy and long enough,' asked Hill.

'Very well. Do that if you please.' Drinkwater looked forward. 'But first, I think you had better luff, Mr Hill.'

'Jesus!' Hill's jaw dropped in alarm as the berg reared over them. Drinkwater held his breath lest *Melusine* struck some underwater projection from the icy mass that towered over the mastheads. 'Down helm!'

Melusine swooped into the wind, her sails shivering, then paid off again as the berg drew astern. Their pursuer, his attention focussed ahead, had laid a course to pass almost as clear as his quarry. That the *Melusine* could shave the berg indicated that it was safe for him to do so, and Drinkwater remarked to Hill on the skill of their enemy.

'Aye, sir, and that argues strongly that he's a letter-of-marque.'

Drinkwater nodded. 'And he'll be able to read our name across our stern and know all about our being a French prize.'

Hill nodded and Bourne rejoined them. 'Meggs says he'll be a further ten minutes, sir, before the keg is ready.'

'Very good, Mr Bourne. Will you direct Rispin to take watch on the fo'c'sle and warn us of any ice ahead. Take over the starboard battery yourself.'

167

Bourne looked crestfallen but acknowledged the order and moved forward to the waist.

Meggs brought the wrapped keg to the quarterdeck in person.

'Three-minute fuse, sir,' he said, handing over the keg to Hill who had mustered three sail-trimmers to carry the thing forward, together with the log-line tub. Five minutes later Drinkwater saw him straighten up and look expectantly aft. Drinkwater nodded and leaned over the side. The keg drifted astern as *Melusine* rushed past, the log-line paying out. Snatching up his glass Drinkwater knelt and focussed his telescope, levelling it on the taffrail and shouting for Quilhampton.

'Mr Q! The instant I say, you are to tell Hill to hold on.'

'Hold on, aye, aye, sir.'

Drinkwater could see the canvas sack lying in the water. It jerked a few times, sending up little spurts of water as the ship dragged it along when the line became tight, but in the main it drifted astern without appreciably disturbing the wake. He wondered if his opponent would have a vigilant lookout at the knightheads. He did not seem a man to underestimate.

Suddenly in the image glass he saw not only the keg, but the stem of the advancing ship. The bow wave washed the keg to one side.

'Hold on!'

'Hold on!' repeated Quilhampton and Drinkwater saw the line jerk tight and then the persistent feather of water as *Melusine* dragged the keg astern, right under the larboard bow of the pursuing Frenchman.

He wondered how long it had taken to veer the thing astern. Perhaps no more than a minute or a minute and a half. He wondered, too, how good a fuse Meggs had set. It was quite likely that the damned thing would be extinguished by now. It was, as he had admitted to Hill, a long shot.

'Stand by to tack ship, Mr Q!'

Quilhampton passed the order and Drinkwater stood up. He could do no more, and his shoulder hurt from the awkward position it was necessary to assume to stare with such concentration at the enemy's bow. The keg blew apart as he bent to rub his knees.

'Larboard tack!'

He felt the deck cant as the helm went down and Hill ran aft telling his men to haul in the log-line. Struggling down on his knees again he levelled his glass. At first he thought they had achieved nothing and then he saw the Frenchman's bowsprit slowly rise. The bobstay at least had suffered and, deprived of its downward pull the jibs and staysails set on the forestays above combined with the leeward pull of the foremast to crack the big spar. He saw it splinter and the sails pull it in two. There was a mass of men upon the enemy fo'c's'le.

He spun to his feet. 'We have him now, by God!' But *Melusine* had ceased to turn to starboard. She was paying off before the wind.

'She won't answer, sir! She won't answer!'

It was then that Drinkwater remembered the rudder.

The Action with the 'Requin'

Drinkwater did not know how much damage he had inflicted upon the enemy, only that his own ship was now effectively at the mercy of the other. It was true the loss of a bowsprit severely hampered the manoeuvrability of a ship, but by shortening down and balancing his loss of forward sail with a reduction aft, the enemy still had his vessel under command. And there was a good enough breeze to assist any manoeuvre carried out in such a condition.

As for themselves, he had no time to think of the loss of the rudder, beyond the fact that they were a sitting duck. But the enemy could not guess what damage had been inflicted by fortune upon the *Melusine*.

'Heave the ship to under topsails, Mr Hill!' Drinkwater hoped he might convey to his opponent the impression of being a cautious man. A man who would not throw away his honour entirely, but one who considered that, having inflicted a measure of damage upon his enemy, would then heave to and await the acceptance of his challenge without seeking out further punishment.

Despatching Hill to examine and report upon the damage to the rudder Drinkwater called Bourne aft.

'Now, Mr Bourne, if I read yon fellow aright, he ain't a man to refuse our provocation. It's my guess that he will work up to windward of us then close and board. I want every man issued with small arms, cutlasses, pikes and tomahawks. The larboard guns you are to abandon, the gun crews doubling to starboard so that the fastest possible fire may be directed at his hull. Canister and ball into his waist. Mr Mount! Your men to pick off the officers, you may station them where you like, but I want six marines and twenty seamen below as reinforcements. You will command 'em, Mr Bourne, and I want 'em out of the stern windows and up over the taffrail. So muster them in my cabin and open the skylight. Either myself, Hill or Quilhampton will pass word to you. But you are not to appear unless I order it. Do you understand?'

'Aye, aye, sir.'

'Oh, and Mr Bourne, blacken your faces at the galley range on your way below.'

'Very good, sir.'

'And you had better warn Singleton what is about to take place. Tell him he'll have some work to do. By the way who was hit by that first ball?'

'Cawkwell, sir. He's lost a leg, I believe.'

'Poor devil.'

'He was closing the cabin sashes, sir.'

'Oh.'

Drinkwater turned away and watched the enemy. As he had guessed, the Frenchman was moving up to windward. They had perhaps a quarter of an hour to wait.

'Mr Frey!'

'Are your two carronades loaded?'

'Aye, sir.'

'I think you may have employment for them soon. Now you are to man the windward one first and you are not to fire until I pass you the express order to do so. When I order you to open fire you are to direct the discharge into the thickest mass of men which crowd the enemy waist. Do you understand?'

The boy nodded. 'I need a cool head for the job, Mr Frey.' He lowered his voice confidentially. 'It's a post of honour, Mr Frey, I beg you not to let me down.' The boy's eyes opened wide. He was likely to be dead or covered in glory in the next half-hour, Drinkwater thought.

'I will not disappoint you, sir.'

'Very good. Now, listen even more carefully. When you have discharged the windward carronade you are to cross to the other and train it inboard. If you see a number of black-faced savages come over the taffrail you are to sweep the waist ahead of them with shot, even, Mr Frey, even if you appear to be firing into our own men.'

The boy's eyes opened wider. 'Now that is a very difficult order to obey, Mr Frey. But that is your duty. D'you understand me now?'

The boy swallowed. 'Yes, sir.'

'Very good.' Drinkwater smiled again, as though he had just asked Frey to fetch him an apple, or some other similarly inconsequential task. He went to the forward end of the quarterdeck and called for silence in the waist, where the men were sorting out the small arms, joking at the prospect of a fight.

'Silence there, my lads.' He waited until he had their attention.

'When I order you to fire I want you to pour in as much shot across his hammock nettings then hold him from boarding. If he presses us hard you will hear the bosun's whistle. That is the signal to fall back. Seamen forward under Lieutenants Rispin and Gorton. Marines aft under Mr Mount. When Mr Bourne's reserve party appears from aft you will resume the attack and reman your guns as we drive these impertinent Frenchmen into the sea. I shall then call for the fore course to be let fall in order that we may draw off.'

A cheer greeted the end of this highly optimistic speech. He did not say he had no intention of following the enemy and taking their ship. He did not know how many men knew the rudder was damaged, but some things had to be left to chance.

'Very well. Now you may lie down while he approaches.'

Like an irreverent church congregation they shuffled down and stretched out along the deck, excepting himself and Mount who kept watch from the quarterdeck nettings.

The enemy ship was almost directly to windward of them now and also heaving to. As Drinkwater watched, the side erupted in flame, and shot filled the air, whistling low overhead, like the ripping of a hundred silk shirts.

The second broadside was lower. There were screams from amidships and the ominous clang as one of the guns was hit on the muzzle and a section of bulwark was driven in. A marine grunted and fell dead. Drinkwater nudged Mount. It was Polesworth. Drinkwater felt his coat-tails being tugged. Mr Comley, the bosun, was reporting.

'I brought my pipe aft, sir.'

'Very good, Mr Comley. You had better remain with me and Mr Mount.'

'Aye, sir.'

'Have you served in many actions, Mr Comley?' asked Drinkwater conversationally.

'With Black Dick in the *Queen Charlotte* at the Glorious First, sir, with Cap'n Rose in the *Jamaicky* at Copenhagen, when you was in the *Virago*, sir, an' a score o' boat actions and cuttin' outs and what not . . .'

A third broadside thudded home. Aloft rigging parted and the main top gallant mast dangled downwards.

'You were with the gun brigs then, on the 2nd April?'

'Aye, sir. An' a precious waste of time they were, an' all. I says to Cap'n Rose that by the time we'd towed 'em damned things across to

172

Denmark and then half the little barky's got washed ashore here an' there . . .'

But Drinkwater never knew what advice Mr Comley had given Captain Rose in the battle with the Danish fleet. He knew that the *Melusine* could stand little more of the pounding she was taking without fighting back.

'Open fire!' He yelled and immediately the starboard guns roared out. For perhaps ten whole minutes as the larger ship drove down upon the smaller, the world became a shambles of sights and sounds through which the senses peered dimly, assaulted from every direction by destructive forces. The shot that whistled and ricochetted; the canister that swept a storm of iron balls across the *Melusine*'s deck; the musket balls that pinged off iron-work and whined away into the air; the screams; the smoke; the splinters that crackled about, made it seem impossible that a man could live upon the upperdeck and breathe with anything like normality. Even more astonishing was the sudden silence that befell the two ships' companies as they prepared, the one to attack, the other to defend. It lasted perhaps no more than ten seconds, yet the peace seemed somehow endless. Until that is, it too dissolved into a bedlam of shouting and cursing, of whooping and grunting, of killing and dying. Blades and arms jarred together and the deck became slippery with blood. Drinkwater had lost his hat and his single epaulette had been shot from his left shoulder. It was he who had ended the silence, ordering Frey's brass carronade to sweep the enemy waist from its commanding position at the hance. He had pushed the boy roughly aside as he placed his foot on the slide to repel the first Frenchman, a young officer whose zeal placed himself neatly upon the point of Drinkwater's sword.

Simultaneously Drinkwater discharged his pistol into the face of another Frenchman then, disengaging his hanger, cut right, at the cheek of a man lowering a pike at Mount.

'Obliged, sir,' yelled Mount as he half-turned and shrugged a man off his shoulder who had tried leaping down from the enemy's mizen rigging. The smoke began to clear and Drinkwater was suddenly face to face with a man he knew instinctively was the enemy commander. Drinkwater fell back a step as the small dark bearded figure leapt through the smoke to *Melusine*'s deck. It was a stupid, quixotic thing to do. The man did not square up with a sword. He levelled a pistol and Drinkwater half-shielded his face as Tregembo hacked sideways with a tomahawk. The Frenchman was too quick. The pistol jerked round and was fired at Tregembo. Drinkwater saw blood on the old

Cornishman's face and lunged savagely. The French captain jumped back, turned and leapt on the rail. Drinkwater's hanger caught him in the thigh. A marine's bayonet appeared and the French Commander leapt back to his own deck. Drinkwater lost sight of him. He found himself suddenly assailed from the left and looked down into the waist. The defenders were bowed back as a press of Frenchmen poured across.

'Mr Comley, your whistle!' Drinkwater roared.

He had no idea where Comley was but the whistle's piercing blast cut through the air above the yelling mob and Drinkwater was pleased to see the Melusines give way; he skipped to the skylight.

'Now, Bourne, now, by God!'

A retreating marine knocked into him. The man's eyes were dulled with madness. Drinkwater looked at Frey. The boy had the larboard carronade lanyard in his hand.

'Fire, Mr Frey!' The boy obeyed.

Drinkwater saw at least one Melusine taken in the back, but there seemed a hiatus in the waist. Most of his men had disengaged and skipped back two or three paces. The marines were drawn up in a rough line through which Bourne's black-faced party suddenly appeared, passing through the intervals, each armed with pike or tomahawk. Bourne at their head held a boarding axe and a pistol. The hiatus was over. The bewildered Frenchmen were suddenly hard-pressed. Drinkwater turned to Comley.

'Let fall the fore course, Mr Comley!'

The bosun staggered forward. 'Mr Frey!'

'Sir?'

'Reload that thing and get a shot into the enemy waist from there.'

'Aye, aye, sir.'

Slowly the Melusines were recovering their guns. There were dead and wounded men everywhere and the decks were red with their blood. Drinkwater followed Bourne down into the waist, joining Mount's marines as they bayoneted retreating Frenchmen. The quarterdeck was naked. If the French took advantage of that they might yet lose the ship. Drinkwater turned back. Two or three of the enemy were preparing to leap across. He shot one with his second pistol and the other two were suddenly confronting him. They looked like officers and both had drawn swords. They attacked at once.

Drinkwater parried crudely and felt a prick in his right leg. He felt that his hour had come but smote hard upon the blade that threatened his life. Both his and his assailant's blades snapped in the cold air and they stood, suddenly foolish. Drinkwater's second attacker had been beaten back by a whooping Quilhampton who had shipped his hook, caught the man's sword with it and twisted it from his grip. With his right he was hacking down at the man's raised arm as he endeavoured to protect his head. The tomahawk bit repeatedly into the officer's elbow.

'Quarter, give quarter, Mr Q!'

Drinkwater's own opponent was proffering his broken sword, hilt first as Tregembo, his cheek, hanging down like a bloody spaniel's ear, the teeth in his lower jaw bared to the molars, pinned him against the rail.

Drinkwater was aware of the hull of the enemy drawing slowly astern as the foresail pulled *Melusine* clear. The French began to retreat to orders screamed from her deck and the two ships drifted apart. As they did so the enemy swung her stern towards the retiring *Melusine*. Drinkwater could see his opponent's name: *Requin*, he read.

Drinkwater bent over the table and pointed at the sketch he had drawn. The cabin was crowded. With the exception of Mr Rispin, who had been wounded, and Mr Gorton, who had the deck, every officer, commissioned and warrant, was in the room, listening to Drinkwater's intentions, offering advice on technical points and assisting in the planning of the rigging of a jury rudder.

For eight hours *Melusine* had run dead before the wind under a squared fore course which was occasionally clewed up to avoid too heavy a crash as she drove helplessly through the ice. There was no way they could avoid this treatment to the ship. His own cuts and scratches he had dressed himself, the wound in his thigh no more than an ugly gash. Since the action Drinkwater had had Singleton question Meetuck. It had been a long process which Singleton, exhausted after four hours of surgery, appalled by the carnage after the fighting and strongly disapproving of the whole profession of arms, had accomplished only with difficulty. But he had turned at last to Drinkwater with the information he wanted.

'Yes, he says there are places from which the ice has departed at this season and which our big *kayak* can come close to.'

But Drinkwater could not hope to close a strange coast without a rudder. In order to refit his ship with a rudder capable of standing the strain of a passage back to Britain he had to have one capable of allowing him to close the coast of Greenland. It was this paradox that he was engaged in resolving.

He straightened up from the table. 'Very well, gentlemen. If there are no further questions we will begin. Mr Hill, would you have the fore course taken in and we will unrig the mizen topmast without delay.'

There was a buzz of conversation as the officers filed out of the cabin. Drinkwater watched them go then leaned again over the plan. How long would it take them? Six hours? Ten? Twelve? And still the masthead lookout reported the *Requin* in sight to the east-north-east. He wondered what damage they had really inflicted on her. How seriously had her commander been wounded? Would his wound deter him, or goad him to resume the pursuit? The action had ceased by a kind of mutual consent. Each party had inflicted upon the other a measure of damage. He was certain the *Requin* was a letter-of-marque. It would be an enormous feather in the cap of a corsair captain to bring in a sloop of the Royal Navy, particularly one that was a former French corvette. First Consul Bonaparte might be expected to find high praise and honours for so successful a practitioner of *la guerre de course*. But his owners might not be pleased if it was at the expense of extensive damage to their ship, or too heavy a loss amongst their men. Privateering was essentially a profit-making enterprise. The *Requin* had clearly been built on frigate lines intended to deceive unwary merchantmen entering the Soundings. Certainly, ruminated Drink-water, it argued that her owners had not spared expense in her fitting-out.

He sighed, hearing overhead the first thumps and shouts where the men began the task of rigging the jury rudder.

Sending down the mizen topmast was a matter of comparative sim-plicity. A standard task which the men might be relied upon to carry out in a routine manner. *Melusine* lay stationary, rolling easily upon a sea dotted with floes, but comparatively open. After an hour's labour the topmast lay fore and aft on the quarterdeck and was being stripped of its unwanted fittings. The topgallant mast was removed from it, but the cross-trees were left and the upper end of the topmast itself was rested on the taffrail. It was lashed there until the carpen-ter's mate had adzed a notch in the handsome carving. Meanwhile the carpenter had begun to build up a rudder blade by raising a vertical plane on the after side of the mast, coach-bolting each baulk of timber to its neighbour. In the waist the forge was hoisted up and a number of boarding pikes heated up to be beaten into bars with which to bind the rudder blade.

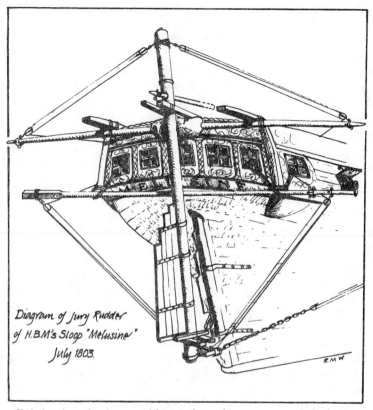

Diagram of Jury Rudder
of H.B.M's Sloop "Melusine"
July 1803.

R.M.W.

Fabricating the jury rudder and stock was comparatively easy. What exercised Drinkwater's ingenuity was the manner of shipping it so that it could be used to steer the ship. After some consultation with the warrant officers, particularly regarding the materials available, it was decided that an iron ring to encircle the masthead could be fabricated from the head-iron at the top of the mizen lower mast. This was of a sufficient diameter to encompass the heel of the mizen topmast so, by fitting it to the lesser diameter of the topmast's other end, there was sufficient play to allow the mast to rotate. The head-iron also had the advantage of having a second ring, a squared section band, which capped the mizen lower masthead. To this could be secured two chains, made from the yard slings from the main yard and elongated by those from the foreyard. These could then be led as far forward as was practical and bowsed taught at the fore-chains. This head-iron would thus become the new heel-iron for the rudder stock, a kind of stirrup.

The first part of the work went well. Some considerable delay was experienced in driving the head-iron off the mizen lower mast, but while Bourne and the bosun were aloft struggling with wedges, two stout timbers were prepared to be lashed either side of the vertical mizen topmast when it was lowered upside down, over the stern. A large pudding-fender was also slung over the side and lashed against the taffrail. The jury rudder stock would then turn against this well-slushed fender, restrained from moving to left or right by the side timbers.

There remained two problems. The first was to keep tension on the heel arrangement which it would be impossible to attend to once the thing was hoisted over the side. And the other would be to fabricate a method of actually turning the rudder.

Drinkwater estimated that *Melusine*'s forward speed would contribute greatly to the first as long as her alterations of direction were small, such as would occur while steering a course. Terrific strain would be imposed if large rudder angles were necessary, as would be the case with tacking or wearing or, God help them, if they had to fight another action with the *Requin*. To this end Drinkwater had the mizen topgallant yard slung over the stern and lashed below the level of his quarter galleries. From here tackles were led to the mizen topmast-head which would, of course, be the heel of the rudder stock when rigged. The cross-jack yard was similarly readied across the upper taffrail from quarter to quarter and lashed to the stern davits. From here two tackles could be rigged to the upper end of the topmast which would extend some feet above the rail and give good leverage to steady the spar.

The problem of rigging some steering arrangement proved the most difficult. The idea of lashing a tiller was rejected owing to the great strain upon it which would almost certainly result in the lashing turning about the round mast. In the end it was found necessary to bore the mast, a long task with a hand auger that occupied some four hours work. Into the mortice thus made, the yard arm of the mizen topgallant yard was prepared to go to become a clumsy tiller.

While these works were in progress Drinkwater frequently called for reports from the masthead about the movement of the *Requin*. But she, too, seemed to be refitting, although her inactivity did not remit the anxiety Drinkwater felt on her account, and he fumed at every trivial delay.

His impatience was unjust for, as he admitted to himself, he could not have been better served, particularly by Hill, Bourne, Gorton and

Quilhampton. Comley, the bosun and Mr Marsden, the carpenter were indefatigable, while the men, called upon to exert themselves periodically in heaving the heavy timbers into position, in fetching and carrying, in the rigging of tackles and the frequent adjustment of leads until all was to the demanding exactness Drinkwater knew was the secret of such an operation, carried out their multifarious orders willingly.

There were considerable delays and a few setbacks, but after eight hours labour the timbers assembled on the quarterdeck looked less like a lowered mast and more like a rudder and stock. In one of these delays Drinkwater took himself below to attend the wounded.

Melusine had suffered greatly in the action, not only in her fabric, but in her company. As Drinkwater made his way below to the cockpit he refused to allow his mind to dwell on the moral issues that crammed the mind in the aftermath and anti-climax of action. No doubt Singleton would hector him upon the point in due course and Drinkwater felt a stab of conscience at the way he had been instrumental in turning little Frey from a frightened boy to a murderous young man who had killed in the service of his King and Country. Still, Drinkwater reflected, that was better than fulfilling that mendacious platitude: *Dulce et decorum est, pro patria mori.*

But it was not Singleton's face that reproached him in the gloom of the cockpit. Skeete leered at him abruptly, holding up the horn lantern to see who it was.

'Are 'ee wounded, Cap'n, sir?' The foul breath of Skeete's carious teeth was only marginally worse than the foetid stink of the space, crammed as it was with wounded men. They lay everywhere, some twisted in agony, some slumped under the effects of laudanum or rum, some sobbed and cried for their wives or mothers. Singleton looked up as Drinkwater leaned over the body of Mr Rispin. Their eyes met and Singleton gave the merest perceptible shake to his head. Drinkwater knelt down beside the lieutenant.

'Well now, Mr Rispin. How goes it, eh?' he asked quietly.

Rispin looked at him as though he had no idea who it was. There was very little left of Rispin's chest and his eyes bore testimony to the shock his body had received. His pupils were huge: he was already a dead man, astonished to be still alive, if only for a little longer.

Drinkwater turned aside. He almost fell over one of the ship's nippers, a boy of some nine years of age named Maxted, Billy Cue Maxted, Drinkwater remembered from the ship's books, named for the battleship *Belliqueux*, from whence his father had come to ruin the reputation of poor Mollie Maxted. Now little Billy was a cripple. He had been carrying powder to his gun when a ball knocked off both his legs. They were no more than dry sticks and he was conscious of their loss. Drinkwater knelt down beside him.

The child's eyes alighted on the captain and widened with comprehension. He struggled to rise up, but Drinkwater pushed him back gently, feeling the thin shoulder beneath the flannel shirt.

'Oh, Cap'n Drinkwater, sir, I've lost both my legs, sir! Both on 'em, and this is my first action, sir. Oh, sir, what'm I going to do, sir? With no legs, who'll carry powder to my gun, sir, when next we fights the Frogs, sir?'

. 'There, Billy, you lie back and rest. It's for me to worry about the guns and for you to be a good boy and get well . . .'

'Will I get well, sir?' The boy was smiling through his tears.

'Of course you will, Billy . . .'

'And what'll happen to me, sir?' Drinkwater swallowed. How could you tell a nine-year-old he was a free-born Briton who would never be a slave? He was free to rot on whichever street corner took his fancy. He might get a pension. Perhaps ten pounds a year for the loss of two legs, if someone took up his case. Drinkwater sighed.

'I'll look after you, Billy. You come and see me when you're better, eh? We'll ship you a pair of stumps made of whale ivory . . .'

'Aye, sir, an a pair o' crutches out o' the Frog's topgallant yards, eh, Cap'n?'

An older seaman lying next to Billy hoisted himself on one elbow and grinned in the darkness. Drinkwater nodded, rose and stepped over the inert bodies. Rispin had died. Somewhere in the stinking filth of the orlop his soul sought the exit to paradise, for there were no windows here to throw wide to the heavens, only a narrow hatchway to the decks above. At the ladder Drinkwater paused to look back.

'Three cheers for Cap'n Drinkwater!' It was little Billy's piping voice, and it was answered by a bass chorus. Drinkwater shuddered and reached for the ladder man-ropes.

Dulce et decorum est . . .

He had not seen Tregembo in the cockpit, he realised as he passed the marine sentry stationed outside his cabin. He opened the door only to find a party of men under Mr Quilhampton completing the lashings of the mizen topgallant mast across the stern.

'We had to break two of the glazings, sir,' said Quilhampton apologetically, pointing at the knocked-out corners of the stern windows.

'No matter, Mr Q. How does it go?'

'Just passing the final frappings now.'

'Very well.' Drinkwater paused and looked hard at one of the men. The fellow had his back to Drinkwater and was leaning outboard. 'Is that Tregembo?'

'Yes, sir. He refused to stay in the cockpit,' Quilhampton grinned, 'complained that he wasn't having a lot of clumsy jacks in *his* cabin.'

Drinkwater smiled. 'Tregembo!'

The Cornishman turned. 'Aye, zur?' His head was bandaged and he spoke with difficulty.

'How is your face?'

'Aw, 'tis well enough, zur. Mr Singleton put a dozen homeward bounders in it an' it'll serve. I reckon I'll be able to chaw on it.'

Drinkwater wondered what sort of an appearance Tregembo would make, his cheek crossed by the scars of Singleton's sutures. If they ever reached Petersfield again he could expect some hard words from Susan. He nodded his thanks to the man for saving his life. The Cornishman's eyes lit. There was no need for words.

'Very well.'

'You've broke your sword, zur.' Tregembo was reproachful. The French sword had hung on his hip since he had taken it from the dead lieutenant of *La Creole* twenty-odd years ago off the coast of Carolina. He had forgotten the matter.

'You'd better have Mr Germaney's, zur. For the time bein'.'

Drinkwater nodded again, then turned to Quilhampton.

'Carry on, Mr Q.'

'Aye, aye, sir.'

They were ready to heave the jury rudder over the taffrail when he returned to the deck. All the purchases were manned, each party under the direction of an officer or midshipman. The former mizen topmast, the ball from the *Requin* prised out of it and the improvised rudder blade bound to it, jutted out over the stern. The heel-iron at its extremity was fitted with the requisite chains and hackles and the head of the mast was, where it passed through the heel-iron, well slushed with tallow to allow free rotation.

'All ready, sir.' Bourne touched his hat.

'Very good, Mr Bourne. Let's have it over . . .'

181

'Aye, aye, sir. Set tight all. Ready, Mr Gorton?' Gorton was up on the taffrail, hanging overboard with two topmen.

'Ready, sir.'

Bourne lifted the speaking trumpet and turned forward. 'Mr Wickham! Mr Dutfield! Your parties to take up slack only!'

'Ay, aye, sir!' The tackles from the heel iron came inboard at the chess-trees and here the two midshipmen had half a dozen men each to set the heel of the rudder tight.

'Very well, Mr Comley, haul her aft.'

'Haul aft, aye, aye . . . '

The mast was pushed aft, the tackles overhauling or tightening as necessary. At the point of equilibrium the weight was slowly taken on the side tackles that led downwards from the mizen topgallant mast, Mr Gorton shouting directions to Quilhampton in the cabin below, where the hauling parts came inboard.

'Some weight on the retaining tackle, Mr Comley . . . '

'Holding now, sir.' They had rigged a purchase from the base of the mizen mast to the upper end of the rudder stock. This now took much of the weight until the stock approached a more vertical angle and the full weight was taken by Quilhampton's quarter tackles. The rudder blade dipped down and entered the sea. There was an ominous jerk as Comley eased his purchase and the weight came upon the quarter tackles. But they were heavy blocks, with sufficient mechanical advantage to handle the weight. The rudder stock approached the vertical, coming to rest on the pudding fender and, further down, the cross member formed by the mizen topgallant mast.

'I think some parcelling there, Mr Gorton, together with a loose frapping will make matters more secure,' said Drinkwater, leaning over the stern by the starboard stern davit.

'Aye, aye, sir.' He called down to Quilhampton and explained what Drinkwater wanted. Looking down, Drinkwater could see Quilhampton's quarter tackles disappear into the water. They were bar-tight. Above his head Comley was removing the purchase to the mizen mast and setting up two side purchases, stretched out to the arms of the cross-jack yard which was lashed up under the boat davits. This was to ease some of the effects of torsion the improvised rudder could be expected to undergo.

Forward Wickham and Dutfield were hauling their tackles tight under Bourne's direction. As Comley clambered down Drinkwater directed him to set up some additional bracing lines to support the extremities of the mizen topgallant mast and the cross-jack yard. He felt his anxiety subside and rubbed his hands with satisfaction.

'Well done, Mr Bourne, a splendid achievement.'

'Thank you, sir.'

Drinkwater hailed the masthead. Mr Frey looked over the rim of the crow's nest.

'Any sign of the *Requin*, Mr Frey?'

'No change, sir! East-nor'-east, distant three or four leagues, sir!'

'Very well!' Drinkwater turned to Bourne. 'Heave the ship to, Mr Bourne, then set an anchor watch. Pipe "Up spirits", all hands to have a double tot and then send 'em below. We'll lie-to, then get under way in four hours. The masthead is to be continually manned. Carry on.'

Drinkwater was cheered for the second time that day, only on this occasion he felt less guilty.

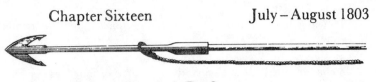

A Providential Refuge

'We therefore commit their bodies to the deep, to be turned into corruption, looking for the resurrection of the body (when the sea shall give up her dead) . . . '

Obadiah Singleton, the stole of ordained minister of the Church of England about his muffled neck, read the solemn words as *Melusine*'s entire company stood silently in the waist. Drinkwater nodded and the planks lifted. From beneath the bright bunting of the ensigns the hammocks slid over the standing part of the fore-sheet, to plunge into the grey-green sea.

There were fifteen to bury, with the likelihood of a further seven or eight joining them within a day or two. They did not go unmourned. Among *Melusine*'s company, friends grieved the loss of shipmates. For Drinkwater there was always the sense of failure he felt after sustaining heavy losses and among those rigid bundles lay Cawkwell, his servant. He wondered whether he had been wise to have held *Melusine*'s fire for so long, and yet he knew he had inflicted heavy casualties upon the *Requin*, that her reluctance to renew the action could only in part have been due to the physical damage they had done to her fabric. From what he had seen of her commander the purely commercial nature of privateering would not prevent him from seeking a chance of glory. Drinkwater knew that the ablest of French seamen were not in the Republic's battle-fleet, rotting in her harbours, penned in by the Royal Navy's weary but endless blockade. France's finest seamen were corsairs, aboard letters-of-marque like the *Requin*, as intrepid and daring as any young frigate captain in the Royal Navy. They were pursuing that mode of warfare at which they excelled: the war against trade, wounding the British merchants in their purses and thus bringing opposition to the war openly into Parliamentary debate. It was not without reason that First Consul Napoleon Bonaparte described the British as 'a nation of shopkeepers'. Singleton closed the prayerbook as the Melusines mumbled their final 'Amens'.

'On hats!'

Drinkwater turned away for the companionway and his cabin. Already Bourne was piping the hands to stations for getting under way.

Drinkwater looked up at the stump of the mizen mast. They would set no more than the spanker on that, but the wind, although it had swung round to the south, remained light. It had brought with it a slight lessening of the visibility and they had not seen the *Requin* for three hours.

However, although Drinkwater's anxiety was eased he was still worried about the rudder and had ordered Bourne to hoist only spanker, main topsail and foretopmast staysail to begin with. It was one thing to devise extempore measures and quite another to get them working. But while Bourne brought the ship onto a course for the Greenland coast there was something else Drinkwater had to attend to, an inevitable consequence of death.

'Pass word for Mr Quilhampton,' he said to the marine sentry who came to attention as Drinkwater opened the cabin door. Drinkwater took off his full-dress coat and changed it for the stained undress he wore over the blue guernsey that had become an inseparable, if irregular, part of his uniform clothing. The air had warmed slightly with the onset of the southerly breeze, but it had also become damp again and Drinkwater felt the damp more acutely in his bones and shoulder than the very cold, drier polar airstream of the northerly.

Drinkwater heard the knock at the door. 'Enter!'

'You sent for me, sir?'

'Ah, yes, sit down a moment. Pray do you pour out two glasses there.' He nodded at the decanter nestling between the fiddles on the locker top. Quilhampton did as he was bid while Drinkwater opened a drawer in his desk and removed a paper.

'Far be it from me to rejoice in the death of a colleague, James, but what may be poison to one man, oft proves meat to another.' He handed the sheet to Quilhampton who took it frowning. The young man's brow cleared with understanding.

'Oh . . . er, thank you, sir.'

'It is only an acting commission, Mr Q, and may not be ratified by their Lordships, and although you have passed your Master's Mate's examination you have not yet sat before a Captains' board to pass for lieutenant . . . you understand?'

Quilhampton nodded. 'Yes sir, I understand.'

'Very well. You will take Mr Rispin's watch . . . and good luck to you.' Drinkwater raised his glass and they sipped for a moment in companionable silence. Quilhampton gazed abstractedly through the stern windows, the view was obscured by the spars and lashings of the jury rudder but he was unaware of them. He was thinking of how he could now swagger into Mrs McEwan's withdrawing-room, to make a leg before the lovely Catriona, and send that damned lubber of a Scottish yeoman to the devil!

'I see,' said Drinkwater turning, 'that you are watching the effects of the ship getting under way upon the rudder.'

'Eh? Oh, oh, yes sir . . . ' Quilhampton focussed his eyes as Drinkwater drained his glass, rose and picked up his hat.

'Well, Mr Q, let us go and see how it answers our purpose . . .'

It answered their purpose surprisingly well. Kept under easy sail after a little experimenting with balancing the rig, and running tiller lines to the mizen royal yard in a manner which best suited steering the ship, *Melusine* made west-north-west. There was a thinning of the floes and although the wind remained from the south, it began to get colder. Fog patches closed in and from these circumstances Drinkwater deduced that the coast of Greenland could not be very far distant. There were other indications that this was so; an increase in the number of birds, particularly eider ducks, and a curious attentive attitude on the part of Meetuck who, having hidden during the action with the *Requin* to the amusement of the Melusines, now hung about the knightheads sniffing the air like a dog.

Then, shortly before eight bells in the morning watch the next day he was observed pointing ahead with excitement. He repeated the same word over and over again.

'*Nunataks! Nunataks!*'

The hands, with their customary good-natured but contemptuous ignorance, laughed at him, tapping their foreheads and deriving a good deal of fun at the eskimo's expense. Quilhampton had the watch and was unable to see anything unusual. Nevertheless he went forward and had Singleton turned out of his cot to translate.

'What the devil does he mean, Obadiah? Noon attacks, eh?'

Singleton stared ahead, nodding as Meetuck pulled at his arm, his eyes shining with excitement.

'You need to elevate your glass, Mr Quilhampton. Meetuck refers to the light on the peaks of Greenland.' There was an uncharacteristic note of awe in Singleton's voice, but it went unnoticed by the practical Quilhampton.

'Well, I'm damned,' he said shortly, looking briefly at a faint jagged and gleaming outline in the lower clouds to the west. It was the sun shining on the permanent ice-cap of the mountains of Greenland.

'Mr Frey! Be so good as to call the captain ... '

Drinkwater raised his glass for the hundredth time and regarded the distant mountains. They were distinguishable from icebergs by the precipitous slopes of dark rock on which the snow failed to lie. He judged their distance to be about twenty miles, yet he could close the coast no further because of the permanent coastal accretion of old ice, its hummocks smoothed, its ancient raftings eroded by the repeated wind-driven bombardment of millions upon millions of ice spicules. So far there was no break in that barrier of ice and mountains that indicated the existence of an anchorage. Drinkwater swore to himself. He was a fool to think a primitive savage of an eskimo could have any idea of the haven that he sought. And, he reflected bitterly, he was a bigger fool for actually looking. But he peered through his glass yet again in the fast-shrivelling hope that Meetuck might be right.

'It's a remarkable sight, isn't it?' Beside him Obadiah Singleton levelled the battered watch-glass he had borrowed from Hill.

Drinkwater could see little remarkable in the distant coast. It was as cold and forbidding as that of Arabia had been hot and hostile and his irritation was increased by the knowledge that Singleton had ceased to think like the *ad hoc* surgeon of *Melusine* and had reverted to being an Anglican divine sent on a mission to convert the heathen by a London Missionary society. When he had persuaded Singleton to assume the duties of surgeon Drinkwater had imagined it would prove regrettably impossible to find the time or opportunity to close the coast and land the missionary. Now it would be impossible to refuse, even if it meant landing Singleton on the ice.

'Don't you think it remarkable, sir?' asked Singleton again.

'I would think it so if I found an ice-free anchorage with a fine sandy bottom in five fathoms at low water, Mr Singleton. I should consider that highly remarkable.'

'But the colour, the colour, to what do you suppose it is due?'

'Eh?' Drinkwater took his glass from his eye and looked where Singleton was pointing. He had been scanning the coast ahead and failed to notice the strange coloration of the snow on the slopes of a mountain which plunged into the ice on the south side of what they took to be an ice-covered bay. This slope, just opening on their larboard beam was a dark, yet brilliant red.

'An outcrop of red-hued rock, perhaps . . . ' he said with only a mild curiosity. 'The rocks and cliffs of Milford Haven are a not dissimilar colour . . . '

'No, that is too smooth and even for rock. It's snow . . . red snow. Egedé did not mention red snow . . . '*

'To the devil with red snow, Mr Singleton. Get that damned eskimo aft here and quiz him again. Is he sure, absolutely sure of this anchorage for big kayaks? Have you explained that we must anchor our ship, Singleton, not run it up the beach like a bloody dugout?'

Singleton sighed. 'I have asked him that several times, sir . . . '

'Well get him aft and ask him again.' Drinkwater raised his glass and trained it forward to where a cape jutted out. There was the faint shadow of further land. Could that be the expected opening in the coast that Meetuck assured them existed? And if it was, how the hell were they to break through this fast-ice with a leaky old hull and a jury rudder, a stump mizen and a truncated mainmast?

They had drawn maps for Meetuck, but he did not seem to comprehend the concept of a bird's eye view and Drinkwater was increasingly sceptical of Singleton's assurances of his use of other faculties.

The olfactory organs did not rate very highly as navigational aids, in Drinkwater's opinion, especially as they seemed to be permanently clouded by the eskimos's own inimitable musk. Drinkwater had scoffed at Singleton's adamant assertions, privately considering that whatever inner faith makes a man a priest, also betrays he lacks common sense.

Drinkwater smelled Meetuck's presence and lowered the telescope. Since their dawn encounter Meetuck had appeared uneasy in Drinkwater's presence. He stuck close to Singleton and nodded as he fired the same questions yet again.

Meetuck answered, his flat speech with its monotonous modulation and clicking, minimal mouth movements seemed truly incomprehensible, but after some minutes Drinkwater thought he detected an unusual enthusiasm in Meetuck's answers.

Singleton turned to Drinkwater. 'He says, yes, he's sure that Nagtoralik is to the north, only a little way now.' Singleton gestured on the beam. 'This is *aqitseq*, a nameless place. It is also *anoritok*, very windy, and there are no fish, especially capelin. Soon, he says, we will

* Caused by a single-celled plant: *Chlamydomonas nivalis.*

188

see *uivak*, which is a cape to be skirted and beyond it we will see *ikerasak*, the strait upon the northern shores of which his people live.' At each innuit word Singleton turned to Meetuck, as if for confirmation, and on each occasion the eskimo repeated the word and grunted agreement.

'He says it is *upernavsuak*, a good location to dwell in the spring, by which I assume he means that by this time of the year it is ice free, but again he repeats that there are bad white men near Nagtoralik, white men like you, sir. He seems to have conceived some idea that you are connected with them after the action with the *Requin*. I cannot make it out, sir . . .'

'Perhaps your preaching has turned him into a proper Christian, Mr Singleton. Meetuck seems terrified by the use of force,' said Drinkwater drily. 'He certainly absented himself from the deck during the action. Ask him if that,' Drinkwater pointed to the distant cape, 'is the promontory to be skirted, eh?'

Meetuck screwed his eyes up and stared on the larboard bow. Then something odd happened. His weathered skin smoothed out as he realised this was indeed the cape they sought. He turned to speak to Singleton as if to confirm this and his face was so expressive that Drinkwater knew that, whatever the cape hid, and however it answered their purpose, Meetuck had brought them to the place he intended. But his eyes rested on Drinkwater and his expression changed, he muttered something which ended in a gesture towards the nearest gun and the noise 'bang!' was uttered before he ran off, disappearing below.

'Upon my soul, Mr Singleton, now what the devil's the meanin' of that?'

Singleton frowned. 'I don't know, sir, but he has an aversion to you and cannon-fire. And if I'm not mistaken it has something to do with the bad white men of Nagtoralik.'

'No bottom . . .' The leadsman's chant with its attenuated syllables had become a mere routine formality, a precaution for it was obvious that the water in the strait was extraordinarily deep.

'D'you have a name for the cape, sir?' asked Quilhampton who, with Hill and Gorton was busy striking hurried cross bearings off on a large sheet of cartridge paper pinned to a board.

'I think it should be named for the First Lord, Mr Q, except that he took his title off a Portuguese cape . . .' Drinkwater was abstracted, watching the dancing catspaws of increasing wind sweep down from

189

the mountainous coast two miles to the southwards.

'How about Cape Jervis, sir,' suggested Quilhampton who, if the captain did not decide quickly would name the promontory Cape Catriona.

'A capital idea, Mr Q,' then to the quartermaster, 'Meet her, there, meet her.'

The katabatic squall hit the *Melusine* with sudden, screaming violence and the tiller party shuffled and tugged at the clumsy arrangement. It had succeeded in steering through an ice strewn lead that was now opening into what Meetuck called *Sermiligaq*: the fiord with many glaciers. *Melusine*, under greatly reduced canvas, leaned only slightly to the increased pressure of the wind and began to race westward with the cold wind coming down from the massive heights to larboard.

'No-o botto-o-m . . .'

Curiosity had filled the quarterdeck. Those officers not engaged in the sailing of the ship or the rough surveying of the coast, formed in a knot around Singleton. The missionary's eyes were alight with a proprietary fire as he pointed to the dark rock that rose in strata after horizontal strata, delineated by a rind of snow as erosion reduced successive layers, giving the appearance of a gigantic series of steps.

'. . . It is more impressive, gentlemen,' Singleton was saying, 'than either Crantz or Egedé had led me to believe, more remarkable, perhaps, than those bizarre stratifications found in the Hebrides because of the enormous extent of this coastline . . . Is it not possible to imagine such a land as inflaming the imagination of the old Norse harpers when they composed their sagas? A land wherein giants dwelt, eh?'

Drinkwater strode up and down, catching snatches of Singleton's lyrical enthusiasm, watching the progress of the ship and casting an eye over the hurried mapping of the coastline. Hill had just completed a neat piece of triangulation from which he had established the elevation of the mountains closest to the extremity of Cape Jervis as 2,800 feet. From this he deduced a summit ten miles inland to the westward to be about 3,000 feet from its greater height. His proposal to name it after *Melusine*'s commander was gently rebuffed.

'I think not, Mr Hill, flattering though it might be. Shall we call it after the ship, eh?'

So Mount Melusine it became, a name of which nature seemed to approve because even as they made the decision there came a crack like gunfire. For an instant all the faces on the deck looked round apprehensively, until Singleton laughingly drew their attention to the calving glacier, one of many frozen rivers that ran down to the sea in the valleys between those mighty summits.

They watched with awe the massive lump of ice as it broke clear of the glacier and rolled with an apparent gentle slowness into the sea, finding its own floating equilibrium to become just one more iceberg in the Arctic Ocean.

'Nature salutes our eponymous ship, sir,' said Singleton turning to Drinkwater.

'Let us hope it is a salutation and not an omen, Mr Singleton. By the by, where is Meetuck?'

Singleton pointed forward. 'Upon what I believe you term "the knightheads", keeping a lookout for his kin, the *Ikermiut*.'

'Their village lies hereabouts, on this inhospitable shore?' Drinkwater indicated the mountains to the southward.

'No sir, to the north, where the land is lower. That is what I believe Meetuck means when he says we will find an anchorage at Nagtoralik.

A lower coastline presented itself to them the following afternoon, but the lead failed to find the bottom and Meetuck was insistent that this was not the place. Nevertheless they stood close inshore and half a dozen glasses were trained upon the patches of surprising green undergrowth that sprouted between the dark outcrops of rock. There were flocks of eider ducks and geese paddling upon the black sandy beaches and Mr Frey spotted a whirring brace of willow grouse that rose into the air.

Melusine tacked offshore and Drinkwater luxuriated in the amazing warmth of the sun. It struck his shoulders, seeping into aching muscles and easing some of the tension he felt in his anxiety both for the ultimate safety of *Melusine* and also that of Sawyers and the *Faithful*. Forward, Meetuck still kept his self-appointed vigil, staring ahead and Drinkwater felt an odd reassurance in the sight, a growing confidence that the eskimo was right.

The sun was delicious and it was clear that its heat melted the snows, and the moraine deposits brought from higher ground by the action of the ice had deposited enough of a soil to root the chickweed and ground willow that covered the low shore. It argued an area that might support life, if only there was an anchorage . . .

They went about again and rounded a headland of frowning black rocks. It was a salient of the mountains that rose peak above peak to the distant, glistening *nunataks*. Standing close in, the dark, deeply fissured rocks showed a variety of colours in the sunshine where lodes of quartz and growths of multi-hued lichens relieved the drabness. They were also made uncomfortably aware of the existence of mosquitos, a surprising discovery and one that made even the philosophical Singleton short tempered.

Squatting on a carronade slide little Frey recorded the drab appearance of the rocks as a shrewdly observed mixture of greys, deep red and dark green. His brush and pencil had been busy since they had first sighted land and the active encouragement of the captain had silenced the jeers of Walmsley and Glencross, at least in public.

Above them the cliff reared, precipitous to man, but composed of a million ledges where the stains of bird-lime indicated the nesting sites of kittiwakes and auks. A number still perched on these remote spots, together with the sea-parrots whose brilliant coloured beaks glowed like tiny jewels in the blazing sunshine.

Alongside, an old bull seal rose, his nostrils pinching and opening, while two pale cubs, the year's progeny, dived as the shadow of the ship fell upon them. As they cleared the cape open water appeared to the westward, bounded to the northern shore by another distant headland. From forward came a howl of delight from Meetuck. He pointed west, down the channel where distant mountains rose blue against the sky.

Singleton crossed the deck, his ear cocked to catch Meetuck's words.

'It seems, sir, that the anchorage of Nagtoralik lies at the head of this fiord.'

Drinkwater nodded. 'Let us hope that it is the providential refuge that we so desperately need, Mr Singleton.'

'And where you can land me,' answered Singleton in a low voice, staring ahead.

Daylight diminished to a luminous twilight for the six hours that the sun now dipped beneath the horizon. The brief arctic summer was fast fading and with its warmth gone the wind dropped and a dripping fog settled over the ship. Lines hung slack and the sails slatted impotently. After the warmth of the day the chill, grey midnight struck cold throughout the ship, though in fact the mercury in the thermometer had fallen far lower among the ice-bergs of the Greenland Sea.

Shivering in his cabin Drinkwater wrote up his journal, expressing his anxiety over the state of *Melusine*'s steering gear and his inability to find and rescue Sawyers.

Assuming that we are able to effect repairs to the rudder by hauling down I am not optimistic of locating the Faithful. *The lack of belligerence in Captain Sawyers made of him and his ship a gift to the marauding French and it is unlikely that we shall be of further use to him.*

He paused, unwilling to admit to himself the extent of his sense of failure in carrying out Earl St Vincent's orders. At the moment the very real anxieties of a safe haven, the possibility of carrying out effective repairs and of returning to join the whalers for the homeward convoy were more immediately demanding. With a sigh he turned to a more domestic matter.

My desire to anchor will, of necessity, rob me of the services of Mr Singleton who is determined to pursue his mission among the eskimo tribes. I am torn between admiration and . . . He paused. He had been about to write 'contempt', but that would not be accurate, despite the fact that he considered Singleton a fool to think he could either convert the eskimos or survive himself. He did not doubt that men imbued with Singleton's religious zeal could endure incredible hardships, but his own years of seafaring had taught him never to gamble with fate, always to weigh the chances carefully before deciding upon a course of action. He had never seen himself as a dashing sea-officer of the damn-the-consequences type. Drinkwater sighed again. He admired Singleton for his fortitude and he was in awe of his faith. He scratched out his last sentence and wrote:

I admire Singleton's courage at undertaking his mission, but I do not understand the power of his faith. His presence on board as a surgeon will be sorely missed, but I fear my remonstrances fall upon deaf ears and he is determined to remain upon this coast.

Soon afterwards Drinkwater's head fell forward upon his chest and he dozed.

'Captain, sir! Captain, sir!'

'Eh? What is it?' Drinkwater woke with a start, cold and held in a rigor of stiff muscles.

'Mr Quilhampton's compliments, sir, and there's a light easterly breeze, sir.'

'Thank you, Mr Frey, I'll be up.'

The boy disappeared and Drinkwater dragged himself painfully to his feet. On deck he found the fog as dense as ever, but above his head the squared yards spread canvas before the light wind. Quilhampton touched his hat.

'Mornin' sir.'

'Mornin' Mr Q.'

'Wind's increasing sir. Course west by north. Beggin' your pardon sir, but d'you wish us to heave to, sir, or, if we stand on to sound minute guns?'

'D'you sound minute guns, Mr Q, and post a midshipman forrard to sing out the instant he hears an echo. We will put the ship on the wind and the moment that occurs on a course of east-nor'-east.'

'Aye, aye, sir.'

Drinkwater fell to pacing the quarterdeck. Before the fog closed down they had seen the fiord open to the westward. They could stand down it with a reasonable degree of safety, provided of course that they heard no echoes close ahead from the towering cliffs in answer to their minute guns. Eight bells rang, the end of the middle watch, four o'clock in the morning and already the sun had risen. He longed for its warmth to penetrate the nacreous vapour, consume the fog and ease the pain in his shoulder.

It was six hours later before the fog began to disperse. The wind had fallen light again and their progress had been slow, measured only by the anxious barking of the minute gun and the hushed silence that followed it. They saw distant mountain peaks at first and it became clear that they were reaching the head of the fiord for they lay ahead, on either bow and either beam. Snow gleamed as the sun seemed suddenly fierce and the fog changed from a pervasive cloud to dense wraiths and then drew back to reveal a little, misty circle of sea about them while the cliffs seemed to reach downwards from the sky.

It was a fantastic effect, but their vision was still obscured at sea level, and for a further hour they moved slowly westward, Drinkwater still anxiously pacing the quarterdeck while on the knightheads Meetuck waited with the expectancy of a dog.

And then, about five bells in the morning watch, the visibility suddenly cleared. *Melusine* was almost at the head of the fiord. To the south stretched the cliffs and mountains that culminated in the cape beneath whose fissured rocks they had tacked the previous afternoon. This wall of rock curved round to the west and north, bordering the fiord. The northern shore was comprised of mountains but these were less precipitous, the littoral formed of bays and inlets some of which were wooded with low conifers. At the head of the fiord, where once a mighty glacier had calved bergs into the sea, was a bay, backed by rising ground, an alpine meadow-land that turned to scree, then buttresses of dark rock rising to mountain peaks.

On the fo'c's'le Meetuck pointed triumphantly, capering about and clapping his hands, his lined face creased with happiness.

'My God!' exclaimed Drinkwater fishing for his glass. It was an anchorage without a doubt. Not a mile from them five ships lay tranquilly at anchor. One of them was the *Requin*, flying the tricolour of France.

An instant later she opened fire.

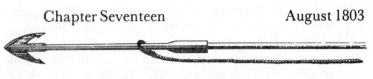

Nagtoralik Bay

'Beat to quarters, Mr Bourne!'

Drinkwater ignored the bedlam surrounding him while *Melusine* was put into a state to fight. He swept the anchorage, pausing only briefly on each ship to determine its force. But it occurred to him as he did so that there was something remarkable about three of the ships in the bay. Identification of the *Requin* was simple. She must have arrived off Cape Jervis well ahead of the *Melusine* and now she was swung, a spring on her cable, every gun pointing at the British ship which, by its minute guns, had warned her of its approach.

Drinkwater swore, for he realised that anchored to the south of the *Requin* was a large lugger, a *chassé marée*, and to the east of her, the unpierced topsides of the *Faithful*. To find Sawyers's ship in such circumstances was hardly reassuring, given that *Melusine* still laboured under her jury rudder.

To the west of *Requin* two more vessels lay at anchor and Drinkwater knew them instantly for whale ships. They were not immediately familiar and as Bourne reported the sloop cleared for action, Drinkwater ordered the course altered to starboard, risking raking fire, but anxious to close the distance a little before responding to *Requin*'s guns. Drinkwater began to calculate the odds. The big, French privateer made no obvious move to get under way. She would sit at anchor, in the centre of her captures, relying upon her superior weight of metal to keep *Melusine* at a distance. When she had driven off *Melusine* she would come in pursuit, to administer the *coup de grace*.

Drinkwater swore again. Their jury rudder and obvious reduction of rig bespoke their weakness. He looked again at the *Requin* for signs of damage to her bow. She had a bowsprit, perhaps a trifle shorter than when they had first met, and therefore a jury rig, but it looked perfectly serviceable.

'That's the bloody *Nimrod*!' Hill called in astonishment, 'and the *Conqueror*!'

Drinkwater swung his glass left. The extent of his own ineptness struck him like a blow even as Bourne replied to the sailing master.

'They must have been taken off Spitzbergen, by God!'

Was Bourne right? Had the *Requin* taken *Nimrod* and *Conqueror* off Spitzbergen and cruised with complete impunity throughout the Greenland Sea? If so, *Melusine*'s presence had been a farce, a complete charade. Every exertion of her company a futile waste of time. He could see again the contempt for his own inexperience in Captain Ellerby's pale blue eyes. How mortifyingly justified that contempt was now proved. He had bungled his commission from Lord St Vincent and failure stared at him from every one of *Requin*'s gun muzzles.

Drinkwater swallowed hard. He felt as though he had received a physical blow.

'Make ready the larboard battery, Mr Bourne. Put the ship on the wind, Mr Hill, starboard tack. We will open fire on the *Requin*, Mr Bourne, all guns to try for the base of her mainmast.' His voice sounded steady and assured despite his inner turmoil.

He nodded as the two officers acknowledged their orders, then he raised his glass again, anxious to hide his face.

Melusine headed inshore, her bowsprit pointing at the stern of the *Faithful* as *Requin* fired her second broadside. It was better pointed than the first as the British sloop stood well into range. Drinkwater felt shots go home, holes appeared in several sails and he felt acutely vulnerable with his clumsy jury steering gear. But a plan was formulating in his mind. If he could lay *Melusine* alongside the *Faithful* he might be able to launch a boat attack on the *Requin* while partially protecting *Melusine*'s weak stern from the *Requin*'s heavier guns.

'Larboard battery ready, sir,' Bourne reported, and Drinkwater took his glass from his eye only long enough to acknowledge the readiness of the gunners.

'Fire when you bear, Mr Bourne.'

They were closing *Faithful* rapidly and more shots from *Requin* arrived, striking splinters from forward and sending Meetuck scampering aft and down the companionway like a scuttering rabbit. A roar of laughter ran along the deck and then *Melusine*'s guns replied, the captains jerking their lanyards in a rolling broadside.

'Mr Mount! Your men are to storm the whaler *Faithful* when I bring the ship under her lee. I doubt she has more than a prize crew aboard and . . . '

'Bloody hell!' A heavy shot thumped into the quarter rail and smashed the timbers inboard. It was perilously close to Mr Hill as he stood by the big tiller and he swore in surprise. Drinkwater looked up to determine the source of the ball and another hit *Melusine*, dismounting an after larboard gun. It was carronade fire.

'It's the fucking *Nimrod*, by God!' howled Hill, his face purple with rage as he capered to avoid the splinters. Whatever it was it was dangerous and Drinkwater decided to retire.

'Larboard tack, Mr Hill, upon the instant!'

Hill jumped to the order with alacrity and Drinkwater swung his glass onto the whaler *Nimrod*. Smoke drifted away from her side and he saw another stab of yellow fire and a second later was drenched in the spray from the water thrown up no more than five yards astern.

'By Christ . . . ' Drinkwater saw a black-bearded figure standing on the rail. There was no doubt about it being Jemmett Ellerby and he was waving his hat as yet another shot was fired from his carronades.

Drinkwater's blood froze. He wanted to make sure of what he saw and studied the big figure intently. Yes, there could be no doubt about it. *Nimrod* flew no colours while above his own head the British ensign snapped out as *Melusine* lay over to the larboard tack, exposing her stern, but rapidly increasing her distance from the enemy.

'Ship full and bye on the larboard tack, sir,' Hill reported. Drinkwater nodded, his brain still whirling with the evidence his senses presented him with. It seemed impossible, but then, as the ship stood out of danger to the eastward and he could order the gun crews stood easy, he gave himself time to think.

'Beat to windward, Mr Hill. You may reduce sail and have the men served dinner at their guns . . . '

'Look at that, sir! Do you see it?' Lieutenant Bourne cried incredulously. He pointed astern to where, beyond the anchored ships what looked like stone huts, low and almost part of the beach, showed beyond the anchored ships. There was a flagpole and from it flew the unmistakable colours of Republican France.

Drinkwater attempted to make sense of the events of the forenoon. At first he was bewildered but after a while he set himself the task of assembling the evidence as he saw it. He retired to his cabin as *Melusine* stood eastward under easy sail, making short tacks. On a piece of paper he began to list the facts and as he wrote he felt a quickening of his pulse. Under the stimulus of a glass or two his memory threw up odd, remembered facts that began to slot neatly together. He was seized by the conviction that his reasoning was running true and he sent for Singleton, explaining that he would land

198

the missionary as soon as it was safe to do so but what appeared to be Frenchmen held the post at Nagtoralik.

'I want you to question Meetuck exhaustively, Mr Singleton. His attitude to the guns has been odd, so has his attitude to myself. You recollect he talked of "bad" white men.' Drinkwater explained and Singleton nodded.

'I do not expect he is able to tell the difference between British, French, Dutch or Russians, all of whom have frequented these seas from time to time. He could not be expected to comprehend a state of war exists between us and the men occupying his village.'

'You saw a village then?'

Singleton nodded. 'I saw twenty or so *topeks* and a number of kayaks drawn up on the beach.'

Drinkwater sighed, biting off a sarcasm that Singleton would have been better employed in the cockpit. The divine was no longer bound to serve there, he was free to go ashore when circumstances permitted and, thank God, *Melusine* had suffered no casualties thanks to Drinkwater's timely withdrawal.

'Very well. Be a good fellow and see what information you can extort from our eskimo friend. I am almost certain that Ellerby, the master of the *Nimrod*, is in league with whoever is ashore there. He opened fire on us.'

Singleton nodded. 'I wish to land in a place untainted by such doings, Captain Drinkwater. I shall see what I can do.'

After he had gone Drinkwater again gathered his thoughts. Of course St Vincent had not guessed that the French would attempt to make settlements in Greenland. Drinkwater could only imagine what privations the inhabitants endured during the Arctic winter. But since the loss of Canada forty years earlier France had held St Pierre and Miquelon and it was not inconceivable that now she dominated Denmark, the country that claimed sovereignty over these remote coasts, France might not attempt such a thing. St Vincent had mentioned Canada and had seemed certain that some moves were being made by Bonaparte's government or its agents, official or entrepreneurial, in these northern seas. 'This is no sinecure,' the Earl had said, 'and I charge you to remember that, in addition to protecting the northern whale-fleet you should destroy any attempt the French make to establish their own fishery . . .'

Was that what they were doing? It seemed possible. The Portuguese hunted the whale from island bases and, although the winter ice would close the bay, the collusion of a traitor like Ellerby to supply whales, blubber, oil and baleen to them began to make a kind of sense. He began to consider Ellerby and as he did so the figure of Waller insinuated itself into his mind. *Conqueror* was the other ship in the anchorage. Was Waller tied up with Ellerby? Had *Conqueror* also fired into *Melusine* unobserved?

Drinkwater thought back to Hull. Waller had seemed like Ellerby's familiar then. They had clearly acted together, Drinkwater concluded, as he recollected other things about the two men. Ellerby's hostility to Palgrave had resulted in a duel. It occurred to Drinkwater that whatever his prejudices against a man of Palgrave's stamp the quarrel might have been deliberately provoked. And there was Ellerby's affirmation at the Trinity House that he intended to fish for whales where the whim took him. 'Do not expect us to hang upon your skirts like frightened children,' he had said insolently. The recollection stimulated others. When Drinkwater had mentioned the menace of French privateers and the sailing of enemy ships for the Arctic seas he had intended a deliberate exaggeration, a hyperbole to claim attention. He remembered the look of surprise that the black-bearded Ellerby had exchanged with the master sitting next to him. That man had been Waller.

Later, in Bressay Sound, Waller had shown considerable interest in Drinkwater's intentions. It was with some bitterness that Drinkwater realised he had taken little note of these events at the time and had been hoist by his own petard to some extent. And there was something else, something much more significant and, to a seaman much less circumstantial. Waller's attitude to Drinkwater's offer of protection had been dismissive. How dismissive and how ineffectual that offer had been, now burned him with shame; but that was not the point. Waller had stated that the masters of whalers resented interference and when Drinkwater had nominated the rendezvous position Waller had smoothed the chart out. He had been on the left of Drinkwater, looking at the west Greenland coast, yet he and Ellerby intended to hunt whales off Spitzbergen!

The deception was simple. Ellerby, who had already attempted and failed to intimidate Drinkwater, took a back seat and sent Waller to the conference at Bressay Sound. Waller checked Drinkwater's methods and intentions, sounded him and gauged his zeal and ability before reporting back to Ellerby. Drinkwater cursed under his breath. It explained why, after his public humiliation leaving the Humber, Ellerby's *Nimrod* had behaved with exemplary regard for the convoy regulations. Yet Sawyers himself had remarked upon Ellerby's 'massive pride', spoken figuratively of David and Goliath and warned

Drinkwater about Ellerby. For a fleeting second Drinkwater thought Sawyers too might be a part of the conspiracy, given his religious contempt for war and the rights and wrongs of the protagonists. Allied with the well-known Quaker liking for profit it made him an obvious suspect. But *Faithful* had been captured under Drinkwater's very nose and Sawyers's behaviour did not really give any grounds for such a suspicion.

Drinkwater sat back in his chair, certain that he had solved the riddle. For some reason the French had established a settlement on the Greenland coast in a position that was demonstrably ice-free, to use for shipping whale products back to France. The risks were high, given the closeness of the British blockade. How much easier to establish contact with British ship-masters who could facilitate the return of the cargoes to France via the good offices of a smuggler or two. From Hull the coast of the Batavian Republic was easily access-ible and Drinkwater, like every other officer in the Navy, had heard that French soldiers preferred to march in Northampton boots, rather than the glued manufactures of their own country.

The provision of a powerful French privateer, more frigate than corsair, argued in favour of his theory. Encountered at sea she gave nothing away about official French involvement with the settlement, thus avoiding problems with the Danes, and her loss, if it occurred, would cause no embarrassment to First Consul Bonaparte.

Drinkwater nodded with satisfaction, convinced of Ellerby's treachery, almost certain of Waller's and then, with a start, recollec-ted that Earl St Vincent would not so easily be satisfied.

A knock came at his door. Frey's head was poked round the door when Drinkwater called him in.

'Beg pardon, sir, but Mr Hill says to tell you that there's three ships crowding on sail astern.'

'Very well, Mr Frey. My compliments to the first lieutenant and he's to issue spirits to all hands and then we'll give these fellows a drubbin', eh?'

'Aye, aye, sir.'

Drinkwater sat a moment longer and considered the news. One of the ships would be *Requin* and the second almost certainly *Nimrod*. Was the third *Conqueror* or that damnable lugger? He sighed. He would have to go on deck to see. Whatever the third ship was, Drinkwater was uncomfortably aware that he was outnumbered, outgunned and might, in an hour, have followed Germaney and Rispin into the obscurity of death.

·   ·   ·

The third ship turned out to be the lugger, her big sails proving more efficient to windward than the other two. He had been right about them. They were indeed *Requin* and *Nimrod*. He studied them through his glass. *Nimrod* was astern of *Requin*, hiding behind the more numerous guns of the big privateer, but ready to bring the smashing power of those heavy carronades to bear upon a *Melusine* that, in her captain's mind's eye, was already a defenceless hulk under the *Requin*'s guns.

Drinkwater summoned Singleton and requested his help after the action which, he confided, he expected to be bloody. He also asked about Meetuck's interrogation.

.'It is a complicated matter, but there is much about a big, bearded man with eyes the colour of, er, "shadowed ice", if that makes sense to you.'

'I am indebted to you.' Drinkwater smiled and Singleton felt an immense compassion for the cock-headed captain and his terrible profession. 'And now, Mr Singleton, I'd be further obliged to you if you would read us the Naval Prayer.' Drinkwater called the ship's company into the waist. Seamen and officers bared their heads and Obadiah Singleton read the words laid down to be used before an action.

'Oh most powerful and Glorious Lord God, the Lord of Hosts, that rulest and commandest all things . . .'

When it was over Singleton exceeded his brief and led the ship's company into the Lord's Prayer with its slurred syllables and loud, demotic haste. He finished with the Naval Prayer and Bourne, casting an agonised look at the closing enemy, hastily ordered the men back to their stations.

Scarcely less impatient, Drinkwater ordered more sail and turned to Hill, explaining his intentions and those he thought that would be the enemy's.

'*Requin* will seek to disable us, Mr Hill, aiming high from a range that will favour her long guns. The instant we are immobilised he will board while the *Nimrod* ranges alongside and pummels us with those damned carronades. He hasn't many of them, but I'll wager they'll be nasty.'

'Beg pardon, sir, but is *Nimrod* manned by a prize crew?'

'I don't believe she is, Mr Hill. I'm not certain, but I am sure that she's commanded by her British master, one Jemmett Ellerby who deserves to swing for his treachery.'

'Jesus . . .'

'Very well. Now we will bear up and put the ship before the wind. Mr Bourne! A moment of your time. We will run down on the lugger. She is in advance of the other vessels and is doubtless ready to run alongside and pour in men when *Requin* boards. If we can hit her hard with round shot and canister I'll be happy. Then I intend to man-oeuvre and avoid *Requin*, using *our* long guns to come up with *Nimrod* and disable her . . .' He outlined Ellerby's treachery for Bourne's benefit and saw the astonishment in his expression harden to resolu-tion. Drinkwater did not say that he intended to destroy *Nimrod* in the belief that they stood little chance of ultimate survival after an action with *Requin*.

He knew now that word of Ellerby's treachery would spread like wildfire and his men fight better for the knowledge. He smiled at his first lieutenant and sailing master. 'Very well, gentlemen. Good luck. Now you may take post.'

They bore down on the lugger which attempted to sheer away. Drinkwater had decided that the jury rudder would take such strains that their manoeuvring might throw upon it. If the enemy did not shoot it away *Melusine* might be relied upon to handle reasonably well, despite the leaky condition a few months in the ice had caused. Her superior height and the fury of her fire cleared the lugger's deck and wounded her mainmast, but her doggedness worried Drinkwater. He was almost certain the officer commanding her had been trying to work round his stern, within range of his light carriage guns to attempt to hit the rudder. This intention to disable the British sloop argued that they knew all about her weak spot. Whatever their intent, the enemy's first move had been thwarted, now he had to deal with the real threat. The *Requin* was on their starboard bow, close hauled on the larboard tack. In a few minutes she would cross their bow, rake them and then bear up astern, holding the weather gauge and assail-ing their vulnerable rudder.

Drinkwater ordered the course altered to starboard, to bring *Melusine*'s guns to bear as the two ships passed.

'For what we are about to receive, may the Lord make us truly grateful.'

A murmur of blasphemous 'Amens' responded to Hill's facetious remark.

Ellerby

'Fire!'

The gun captains jumped back, jerking their lanyards and snapping the hammers on the gunlocks. *Melusine*'s larboard six-pounders recoiled inboard against their breechings and as their crews moved forward to sponge and reload them the storm of shot from *Requin*'s broadside hit them. Uncaring for himself Drinkwater watched its effect with anxiety, knowing his enemy possessed the greater weight of metal and the risk he had taken in turning back instead of running from his pursuers. But he knew any chase would ultimately lead to either damage to *Melusine*'s exposed jury rudder or capture due to her being overtaken under her cut-down rig. Besides, he had already determined that Ellerby should reap the just reward of his treachery and that duty compelled him to exercise justice.

He therefore watched the smoke clear from the waist and saw, with a pang of conscience, that Bourne was down and perhaps eight or nine other men were either killed or badly wounded.

'Mr Gorton! Take command of the batteries!' Gorton crossed the deck and saw Bourne carried below as Drinkwater swung round to study *Requin*, already half a cable astern on the larboard quarter. The big privateer had been closed hauled on the wind and her gunnery had suffered from the angle to *Melusine* and the heel of her deck. Nevertheless it was a heavy price to pay for a single broadside. Drinkwater hoped the effects of his own shot, fired from the more level deck of a ship before the wind, had had greater effect. He could see *Requin*'s sails begin to shiver as her captain brought her through the wind to bear down on *Melusine*'s undefended stern. If her gunners were anything like competent they could catch the British sloop with a raking broadside.

Drinkwater turned resolutely forward and raised his glass. They were already very close to *Nimrod*. Ellerby's big figure jumped into the image lens with a startling clarity. Drinkwater closed the glass with a vicious snap.

'Starboard battery, make ready!' Quilhampton looked along the line of guns, his sword drawn. He nodded at Gorton.

'All ready, canister and ball.'

Drinkwater raised his speaking trumpet. 'Sail trimmers to their posts,' he turned to Hill. 'Bear up under his stern, Mr Hill, I want that broadside into his starboard quarter.'

'Aye, aye, sir.'

They raced down upon the approaching whaler. Her bulk and ponderous motion gave her an appearance of greater force than she possessed. Her gunwhales were only pierced for three carronades on each side, but they were of a heavy calibre.

Drinkwater ran forward to the starboard cathead and raised the speaking trumpet again. The two ships were already level, bowsprit to bowsprit.

'Captain Ellerby! Captain Ellerby! Surrender in the King's name before you consign your men to the gallows!'

Ellerby's violent gesture was all that Drinkwater knew of a reply, although he saw Ellerby was yelling something. Whatever it was it was drowned in the roar of his guns, their wide muzzles venting red and orange flame at point-blank range.

Drinkwater nodded at Quilhampton and as Hill put the helm down and *Melusine* began to lean over as she turned, the starboard guns poured ball and canister into the whaler's quarter. Drinkwater fought his way aft, through the sweating gun crews and the badly maimed who had been hit by the langridge from Ellerby's cannon. A man bumped into him. He was holding his head and moaning surprisingly softly seeing that several assorted pieces of iron rubbish protruded from his skull. Drinkwater regained the quarterdeck and looked astern. *Nimrod* continued apparently unscathed on an easterly course.

'Put her on the wind, Mr Hill, and then lay her on the starboard tack!'

Hill began to give orders as the waist was cleared of the dead and wounded, the guns reloaded and run out again. The days of practice began to pay off. Each man attending to his allotted task, each midshipman and mate supervising his half-division or special party, each acting-lieutenant, marking his subordinates, attending to the readiness of his battery while Hill, quietly professional on the quarterdeck, directed the trimming of the yards and sheets to get the best out of the ship.

Melusine turned into the wind, then swung her bowsprit back towards the *Nimrod*, gathering speed as she paid off on the starboard tack. Beyond the whaler, Drinkwater could see the *Requin* and was seized by a sudden feeling of intense excitement. He might, just *might*, be able to pull off a neat manoeuvre as *Requin* and *Nimrod* passed each other on opposite courses. He pointed the opening out to Hill.

'She'll do it, sir,' Hill said, after a moment's assessment.

'Let's hope so, Mr Hill.'

'Never a doubt, sir.'

Drinkwater grinned, aware that *Melusine* with her jury rudder and ice-scuffed hull was no longer the yacht-like 'corvette' that had danced down the Humber in the early summer.

They crossed *Nimrod*'s stern at a distance of four cables. Not close enough for the six-pounder balls to have much effect on the whaler's massive scantlings. But there was no response from the *Nimrod*'s carronades and Drinkwater transferred his attention to the *Requin*, whose bearing was opening up on the sloop's starboard bow.

'He's not going to let us do it, Mr Hill . . .' They had hoped to cross the *Requin*'s stern too, and pour the starboard broadside into her but the privateer captain was no fool and was already turning his ship, to pass the British sloop on a reciprocal course. They would exchange broadsides as before . . .

'Up helm! Up helm!' Drinkwater shouted. 'Starbowlines, hold your fire!'

'Stand by the lee braces, there!' Hill bawled at his sail-trimmers, suddenly grasping Drinkwater's intention.

'Pick off the officers!' Drinkwater yelled at the midshipmen and marines in the tops. *Melusine* was already turning, an ominous creaking coming from the rudimentary steering gear as a terrific load came on it. *Requin*'s guns roared as the *Melusine*'s stern swung away from the arc of her fire, and although a shower of splinters flew from the taffrail the rudder stock and supporting timbers and spars were untouched.

'Steady her and then bring her round onto the larboard tack. So far so good.'

Drinkwater felt the exhilaration of having called the tune during the last half hour, despite the losses *Melusine* incurred. He was aware of a mood of high elation along the deck where the men joked and relived the last few moments with an outbreak of skylarking equally uncaring in the heady excitement for those below undergoing the agonies of Singleton's knife.

Melusine clawed back to windward while her two enemies came round in pursuit again. Already they were a mile away to the north-west and Drinkwater thought he could keep them tacking in his wake for an hour or two yet while he sought a new opening.

'That lugger's out of the running, sir,' offered Hill, pointing to the *chassé marée* half a mile away. Her crew had sweeps out and were pulling her desperately out of the path of the approaching British sloop which seemed to be bearing down upon them with the intention of administering the *coup de grace.* In fact Drinkwater had long since forgotten about the lugger, although it had been no more than forty or fifty minutes since they had fired into her.

He nodded at Gorton with the good-natured condescension of a school-master allowing his pupils an indulgent catapult shot at sparrows. The larboard guns fired as they passed and several balls struck home, causing evident panic among the lugger's crew.

Drinkwater was seized by a sudden feeling that things had been too easy and recalled the dead and wounded. He turned and called sharply to the midshipman who was in attendance to the quarterdeck and whose obvious pleasure at still being alive had induced a certain foolish garrulousness with the adjacent gun crews.

'Mr Frey!'

'S . . . Sir?'

'Pray direct your attention to the surgeon, present him with my compliments and ascertain the extent of our losses. I am particularly concerned about Mr Bourne.'

'Aye, aye, sir.'

After Frey had departed Drinkwater called for reports of damage and the carpenter informed him that they had a shot between wind and water, but that otherwise most of the enemy's fire had been levelled at personnel on the upper deck.

Pacing up and down Drinkwater tried to assess the state of his enemies. He had not succeeded in forcing *Nimrod* to surrender and his chances of annihilating the *Requin* were slight. But the whaler had failed to take advantage of a clear shot at *Melusine*'s stern. Did that argue her untrained crew had simply missed an opportunity or that, having fired into a King's ship they might have taken heed of Drinkwater's earlier hail?

Discipline was not so tight on a merchantman and a crew might be seduced from its nominal allegiance to their master by the threat of the gallows. Drinkwater considered the point. Did it also signify that *Requin*'s fire had been at *Melusine*'s deck, not at her rigging? In the place of the privateer Captain Drinkwater thought he might have wanted the naval vessel disabled from a distance, without material damage to the *Requin* herself.

Unless, argued Drinkwater, *Requin's* superiority was over-estimated. Perhaps her crew were less numerous than he supposed and therefore to decimate the British had become a priority with *Requin's* commander.

'Wind's veering, sir.' Hill interrupted his train of thought.

'Eh?'

'Hauling southerly, sir.'

It was true. The wind had dropped abruptly and was chopping three, no, four points and freshening from the south-east. Drinkwater stared to the south, there was a further shift coming. In ten minutes or so the wind would be blowing directly off the mountain peaks to the southward. All the ships in the fiord would be able to reach with equal facility. It altered everything.

'That puts a different complexion on things, Mr Hill.'

Hill turned from directing a trimming of the yards and nodded his agreement. For a few moments Drinkwater continued pacing up and down. Then he came to a decision.

'Put the ship on an easterly course, Mr Hill. I want her laid alongside the *Nimrod* without further delay.'

It was a decision that spoke more of honour than commonsense, yet Drinkwater was put in an invidious position by his orders. It was doubtful if St Vincent could have foreseen the extent of the French presence in the Arctic, or of the treachery of Ellerby and, presumably, Waller. Yet Drinkwater's orders were explicit in terms of preventing any French ascendancy in the area. The red rag of honour was raised in encouragement; not to use his utmost endeavour was to court a firing squad as Byng had done fifty years before.

Requin's shot stove in the gunwhale amidships, dismounted a gun and wiped out two gun crews. The maintopmast was shot through and went by the board and the big privateer bore up under *Melusine's* stern. The single report of a specially laid gun appeared to annihilate the four men steering by the clumsy tiller.

Then Drinkwater realised that the rudder stock had been shot to pieces and the tiller merely fallen to the deck, taking the men with it. They picked themselves up unhurt, but Drinkwater's eyes met those of Hill and both men knew *Melusine* was immobilised. Two minutes later she bore off before the wind and with a jarring crash that made her entire fabric judder she struck *Nimrod* amidships.

'Boarders awa-a-ay!' Mad with frustration and anger Drinkwater lugged out his borrowed sword and grabbed a pistol from his waistband and ran forward. Men left the guns and grabbed pikes from the racks by the masts and cutlasses gleamed in the sunshine that beat hot upon their backs as they crowded over the fo'c's'le and scrambled down onto the whaler's deck.

Quilhampton was ahead of Drinkwater and had reached the *Nimrod*'s poop where Ellerby stood aiming his great brass harpoon gun into the *Nimrod*'s waist as Drinkwater led his boarders aft. A cluster of men had gathered round him but the majority of his crew, over twenty men, were dodging backwards into whatever shelter the deck of the whaler offered, making gestures of surrender and calling for quarter.

'Mr Q! Stand aside, damn it!' Drinkwater called, his voice icy with suppressed fury. He saw Ellerby raise the huge gun, saw its barrel foreshorten as the piece was aimed at his own breast and heard the big Yorkshireman yell:

'Stand fast, Cap'n Drinkwater! D'you hear me! Stand fast!'

But Drinkwater was moving aft and saw the smoke from the gun. He felt the rush of air past his cheek as the harpoon narrowly missed him and a second later he was shoving Quilhampton aside.

Somebody had passed Ellerby a whale-lance and its long shaft kept Drinkwater at a distance. 'You traitorous bastard, Ellerby. Put that thing down, or by God, I'll see you swing . . .'

Drinkwater was forced backwards, stumbled and fell over as Ellerby, his face a mask of hatred, stabbed forward with the razor-sharp lance. Suddenly Ellerby had descended the short ladder from *Nimrod*'s poop and stood over Drinkwater.

Aware of the quivering lance and the fanatical light in Ellerby's pale blue eyes Drinkwater could think only of the pistol he had half fallen on. Even as Ellerby stabbed downwards Drinkwater rolled over, his thumb pulling the hammer back to full cock and his finger squeezing the trigger.

He felt the lance head cut him, felt the cleanness of the keen edge with a kind of detachment that told him that it was not fatal, that the lance had merely skidded round his abdomen, through the thin layer of muscles over his right ribs. He stood up, bleeding through the rent in his coat.

Ellerby was leaning drunkenly on the lance that, having wounded Drinkwater, had stuck in the deck. The beginnings of a roar of pain were welling up from him and streaming through his beard in a shower of spittle. Drinkwater could not see where the ball had entered Ellerby's body, but as he crashed forward onto the deck its point of egress was bloodily conspicuous. His spine was shattered in the small of his back and the roar of impotence and pain faded to a wheezing respiration.

Drinkwater pressed his hand to his own flank and looked down into his fallen foe. Ellerby's wound was mortal and, as the realisation spread men began to move again. The whale-ship crew threw down their weapons and James Quilhampton, casting a single look at Drinkwater, gave orders to take possession of the *Nimrod*.

Drinkwater turned, aware of blood warm on his hand. Before him little Mr Frey was trying to attract attention.

'Yes, Mr Frey? What is it?'

Frey pointed back across *Melusine*'s deck to where the *Requin* could be seen looming out of the smoke.

'B . . . beg pardon, sir, but Mr Hill's compliments and the *Requin* is bearing up to windward.'

As if to lend emphasis to the urgency of Frey's message the multiple concussion of *Requin*'s broadside filled the air, while at Drinkwater's feet Ellerby gave up the ghost.

The Plagues of Egypt

Drinkwater felt the relief of the broad bandage securing the thick pledget to his side. He stared through the smoke trying to ignore Skeete who was tugging his shirt down after completing the dressing.

'That'll do, damn it!' he shouted above the noise of the guns.

'Aye, aye, sir.' Skeete grinned maliciously through his rotten teeth and Drinkwater tucked his shirt tails impatiently into his waistband still trying to divine the intentions of *Requin*'s commander.

Leaving Lord Walmsley in command of *Nimrod* Drinkwater and the boarding party had returned to *Melusine* although the whaler and sloop still lay locked together. *Requin* lay just to windward, firing into the British ship with her heavier guns. At every discharge of her cannon they were swept by an iron storm. There were dead and dying men lying on the gratings where their mates had dragged them to be clear of the guns and from where the surgeon's party selected those worthy to be carried below to undergo the horrors of amputation, curettage or probing. The superficially wounded dressed themselves from the bandage boxes slotted into the bar-holes in the ship's capstans, and held against such an eventuality. Drinkwater saw that stained bandages had sprouted everywhere, that the larboard six-pounders were being served by men from both batteries and that Gorton was wounded.

The noise was deafening as the Melusines fired their cannon as fast as each gun could be sponged, charged and laid. Ropes and splinters rained down from aloft and below the mainmast three bodies lay where they had fallen from the top. Only the foremast stood intact, the foretopsail still filled with wind.

The stink of powder smoke, the noise and the confusion and above all the unbelievably hot sun combined with the sharp pain in his flank to exhaust Drinkwater. It crossed his mind to strike, if only to end the killing of his men and the intolerable noise.

Something of this must have been evident in his face, for Hill was looking at him.

'Are you all right, sir?' Hill shouted.

Drinkwater nodded grimly.

'Here sir . . .' Hill held out a flask and Drinkwater lifted it to his lips. The fiery rum stirred him as it hit the pit of his stomach.

'Obliged to you, Mr Hill . . .' He looked up at the spanker. It was too full of holes to be very effective, but an idea occurred to him.

'Chapel that spanker, Mr Hill, haul it up against the wind. Let us swing the stern round and try and put *Nimrod* between us and that bloody bastard to windward!'

A shower of splinters were struck from the adjacent rail and Drinkwater and Hill staggered from the wind of the passing ball, gasping for breath. But Hill recovered and bawled at the afterguard. Drinkwater turned. He must buy time to think. He saw Mount's scarlet coat approaching after posting his sentries over the prisoners aboard *Nimrod*.

'Mr Mount!'

'Sir?'

'Mr Mount, muster your men aft here . . .'

The katabatic squall hit them with sudden violence, screaming down from the heights to the south of them, streaking the water with spray and curling the seas into sharp, vicious waves in the time it takes to draw breath. The air at sea level in the fiord had been warmed for hours by the unclouded sun. Rising in an increasing mass, this air was replaced by cold air sliding down from its contact with the ice and snow of the mountain tops to spread out over the water as a squall, catching the ships unprepared.

Melusine's fore topgallant mast, already weighed down by the wreckage of the main topmast and its spars, carried away and crashed to leeward. But the chapelled spanker, hauled to windward by Hill's men, spun the sloop and her prize, while *Nimrod*'s sails filled and tended to drive both ships forward so that their range increased from their tormentor.

But it was a momentary advantage for, hove to, the *Requin* increased her leeway until the strain on her own tophamper proved too much. Already damaged by *Melusine*'s gunfire, her wounded foremast went by the board. Dragged head to wind and with her backed main yards now assisting her leeward drift, *Requin* presented her stern to Drinkwater and he was not slow to appreciate his change of fortune. A quick glance at *Nimrod*'s sails and he saw immediately that he might swiftly reverse their turning moment and bring *Melusine*'s battered larboard broadside to bear on that exposed stern.

'Belay that Hill!' He indicated the spanker. 'Brail up the spanker! Forrard there! Mr Comely! Foretopmast staysail sheets to windward . . .' His voice cracked with shouting but he hailed *Nimrod*.

'*Nimrod! Nimrod* 'hoy! Back your main and mizen tops'ls, Mr Walmsley, those whalemen that help you to be pardoned . . .' It was a crazy, desperate idea and relied for its success on a swifter reaction than the *Requin*'s captain could command. Drinkwater waited in anxious impatience, his temper becoming worse by the second. He raised his glass several times and studied the *Requin*, each time expecting to see something different but all he could distinguish with certainty was that the big privateer was drifting down on them. And then *Melusine* and her prize began to turn again, swinging slowly round, rolling and grinding together as the continuing wind built up the sea.

The katabatic squall had steadied to a near gale and swept the smoke away. The sun still shone from a cloudless sky although its setting could not be far distant. The altered attitude of the ships had silenced their gunfire and the air was filled now with the scream of wind in rigging and the groaning of the locked ships.

Drinkwater shook his head to clear it of the persistent ringing that the recent concussion of the guns had induced and raised his speaking trumpet again.

'Larboard guns! Gun captains to lay their pieces at the centre window of the enemy's stern. Load canister on ball. Fire on the command and then independently!'

He saw Quilhampton in the waist acknowledge and wondered what had become of Gorton. He raised his glass, aware that Mount was still beside him awaiting the instructions he was in the process of giving when the squall hit them.

'Any orders, sir?' Mount prompted.

Drinkwater did not hear him. He was watching *Melusine*'s swing and waiting for the raised arms that told him his cannon were ready. The last gun captain raised his hand. He waited a little longer. A quick glance along the gun breeches showed them at level elevation. They traversed with infinite slowness as *Nimrod* and *Melusine* cartwheeled . . . Now, by God!

'Fire!'

Noise, smoke and fire spewed from the ten six-pounders as sixty pounds of iron and ten pounds of small ball hit *Requin*'s stern. Drink-water was engulfed in the huge cloud of smoke which was as quickly rent aside by the wind. Then the six-pounders began independent fire, each captain laying his gun with care. *Requin*'s stern began to cave in, beaten into a gaping wound, her carved gingerbread-work exploding in splinters.

'Sir! Sir!' Mr Frey was dancing up and down beside him.

'What the devil is it, Mr Frey?' Drinkwater suddenly felt anxious for the boy whose presence on the quarterdeck he had quite forgotten.

'She strikes, sir! She strikes!'

Drinkwater elevated his glance. The tricolour was descending from the gaff in hasty jerks.

'Upon my soul, Mr Frey, you're right!'

'Any orders, sir,' repeated the hopeful Mount.

'Indeed, Mr Mount. You and Frey take possession!'

Drinkwater jerked himself awake with a start. The short Arctic night was already over. His wound, pronounced superficial by an ex-hausted Singleton, throbbed painfully and his whole body ached in the chill of dawn. He rose and stared through the stern windows. *Melusine* and her assorted prizes lay at anchor in Nagtoralik Bay. The battered British sloop to seaward, a spring on her cable, covering any signs of trouble in the other ships. He had prize crews aboard the lugger *Aurore*, the *Requin* and the *Nimrod*, although the *Nimrod* had assumed the character of consort, having towed the helpless *Melusine* into the anchorage.

They had been met by boats from the whalers *Conqueror* and *Faithful* as the last of the daylight faded from the sky and the wounded ships had come to their anchors. It was clear from the expression of Captain Waller of the *Conqueror* that he had put an entirely different interpreta-tion on the sight of *Melusine* towing in astern of *Nimrod* than was the case. His false effusions of congratulation had been cut short by Drinkwater arresting him and having him placed in the bilboes.

'Thou hast done right, Friend,' said Sawyers, holding out his hand. But Drinkwater gently dismissed the Quaker, pleading tiredness and military expediency for his bad manners. There would be time enough for explanations later, for the while it was enough that *Faithful* was recaptured and *Requin* a prize.

Drinkwater turned from the stern windows and slumped back in his chair. The low candle-flame in the lantern fell upon the muster book. In the two actions with the *Requin* he had lost a third of his ship's

214

company. They were terrible losses and he mourned Lieutenant Bourne who had died of head wounds shortly after the *Requin* surrendered.

Hardly a man had not collected a scratch or a splinter wound. Little Frey had received a sword cut on his forearm which he had bravely bandaged until Singleton spotted the filthy linen and ordered the boy below. Tregembo had been knocked senseless and of the quarterdeck officers only Mount and Hill were unscathed.

He blew the sand off the muster book and closed it. Amid all the tasks that awaited him this morning he must bury the dead. His eyelids dropped. On deck Mr Quilhampton paced up and down, the watch ready at the guns. Mount was aboard *Requin* with a strong detachment of marines; Lord Walmsley commanded *Nimrod* and the Honourable Alexander Glencross the *Conqueror*.

He could allow himself an hour's sleep. He was aware that providence had chastened him but that luck had saved him. His head fell forward onto his breast and his ears ceased to ring from the concussion of guns.

'Will you receive the deputation now, sir?' Drinkwater nodded at Mr Frey's figure standing in the cabin doorway. It was frightening how fast the maturing process could work. Frey stood aside and half a dozen whale-men came awkwardly into the cabin under the escort of Mount's sergeant and two private marines.

'Well,' said Drinkwater coldly, 'who is to speak for you?'

A man was pushed forward and turned a greasy sealskin hat nervously in his hands. Addressing the deck he began to speak, prompted by shame faced shipmates.

'B . . . beg pardon, yer honour . . .'

'What is your name?'

The man looked about him, as if afraid to confess to an identity that separated him from the anonymous group of whale-men.

'Give an answer to the captain!' Frey snapped with a sudden, surprising venom.

'J . . . Jack Love, sir, beggin' yer pardon. Carpenter of the *Nimrod*, sir . . .'

'Go on, Love. Tell me what you have to say.'

'Well sir, we went along of Cap'n Ellerby, sir . . .'

'An' of Cap'n Waller, sir . . .' another piped up to a shuffling chorus of agreement.

'Pray go on.'

215

'Well sir, there was a fair profit to be made, sir, during the peace like . . .' He trailed off, implying that trade with the French under those circumstances was not illegal.

'In what did you trade, Love? Be so good as to tell me.'

'We brought out necessaries, sir . . . comestibles and took home furs . . .'

'Furs?'

'Aye, sir,' an impatient voice said and a small man shoved forward. 'Furs, sir, furs for the Frog army what Ellerby could sell at a profit . . .'

Drinkwater digested the news and a thought occurred to him.

'Do you know anything about two Hull whale ships that went missing last winter?' He looked round the half-circle of faces. Love's hand rubbed anxiously across his mouth and he shook his head, avoiding Drinkwater's eyes.

'We don't want no traitorous doin's, sir. We was coerced, like . . .' He fell silent. The word had been rehearsed, fed him by some sea-lawyer and he was lying, although Drinkwater knew there was not a shred of evidence to prove it. They would have profited under Ellerby, war or peace, so long as no supercilious naval officer stuck his interfering nose into their business.

Love seemed to have mustered his defences, prodded on by some murmuring behind him.

'When we realised what Ellerby was doing, sir, we wasn't 'aving none of it. We didn't obey 'im sir . . .' Drinkwater remembered *Nimrod*'s failure to take full advantage of her position during the action.

'And *Conqueror*'s people. How are they circumstanced?'

'We were coerced too, sir. Cap'n Waller threatened to withhold our proper pay unless we co-operated . . .'

Drinkwater stared at them. He felt a mixture of contempt and pity. He could imagine them under the malign influence of Ellerby and he remembered the ice-cold fanaticism in his eyes. The men began to shuffle awkwardly under his silent scrutiny. They were victims of their own weakness and yet they had caused the death of his men by their treachery.

'Would you wish to prove your loyalty to King and Country, then?' he asked, rising to his feet, the picture of a patriotic naval officer. Their eagerness to please, to fall in with his suggestion, verged on the disgusting.

'Very well. You will find work enough refitting the ships under the direction of my officers. You may go now. Return to your ships; but I warn you, the first man that fails to show absolute loyalty will swing.'

Their delight was manifest. It was the kind of thing they had hardly dared hope for. They nodded their thanks and shambled out.

'You may discharge the guard, sergeant.' Drinkwater addressed Mr Frey. 'Do you go to the two whale ships, Mr Frey, and ransack the cabins of Captain Ellerby and Captain Waller. I want the press-exemptions of every man-jack of those whale-men.'

Drinkwater regarded Waller with distaste. Without Ellerby he was pathetic and Drinkwater was conscious that, as a King's officer, he represented the noose to Waller. Somehow hanging was too just an end for the man. He had tried a brief, unconvincing and abject attempt at blustered justification which Drinkwater had speedily ended.

'It is useless to prevaricate, Captain Waller. Ellerby fired into a British man-o'-war wearing British colours and I am well aware, from information laid before me by men from *Nimrod* and *Conqueror*, that you and he were in traitorous intercourse with the enemy for the purposes of profit. That fact alone put you in breach of your oath not to engage in any other practice other than the pursuance of whale-fishing. What I wish to know, is to what precise purpose did you trade here and with whom?'

Waller's face had drained. Drinkwater slammed his fist on the cabin table. 'And I want to know *now!*'

Waller's jaw hung slackly. He seemed incapable of speech. Drinkwater sighed and rose. 'You may,' he said casually, 'consider the wisdom of turning King's Evidence. I *do* have enough testimony against you to see you swing, Waller . . .'

Drinkwater's certainty was overwhelmingly persuasive. Waller swallowed.

'If I turn King's Evidence . . .'

'Tell me the bloody truth, Waller, or by God I'll see you at the main yardarm before another hour is out!'

'It was Ellerby . . . he said it couldn't fail. We did well out of it during the peace. There seemed no reason not to go on. When the war started again, I tried to stop it. Aye, I said it weren't worth the risk like. But Ellerby said it were worth it. Happen I should have know'd better. Anyroad I went along wi' it . . .'

The dialect was thick now. Waller in the confessional was a man turned in upon himself, contemplating his weaknesses. Again Drinkwater felt that surge of pity for a fool caught up in the ambitions of a strong personality.

'Went along with what?' he asked quietly.

'Furs. French have this settlement. Just before Peace of Amiens Ellerby had run into a French privateersman, Jean Vrolicq. This Vrolicq offered us a handsome profit if we carried furs to England, like, and smuggled them across t'Channel. Easier, nay, safer than Vrolicq trying to run blockade. Furs for the French army taken to France in English smuggling boats . . .'

'Furs?' It was the second time Drinkwater queried the word, only this time he was more curious about the precise nature of the traffic and less preoccupied by the fate of the man before him.

'Aye, Cap'n. Furs for French army. They have bearskins on every cavalry horse, fur on them hussars . . .'

Drinkwater recollected the cartoons of the French army, the barefoot scarecrows motivated by Republican zeal . . . and yet he did not doubt Waller now.

'We ran cargoes of fox, ermine, bear and hares . . . four hundred pounds clear profit on top o' what the fish brought in . . .'

'Very well, Captain Waller. You may put this in writing. I shall supply you with the necessaries.'

Drinkwater called the sentry and Waller was taken out.

It was a strange tale, yet, thinking back to his interviews with Earl St Vincent and Lord Dungarth he perceived the first strands of the mystery had been evident even then. That he had stumbled on the core of it was a mixture of good and bad luck that was compounded, for those who liked to think of such matters in a philosophical light, as the fortune of war.

He poured a glass of wine and listened to the noise around him. *Melusine*'s jury rudder was being lifted and the blacksmith from *Faithful* was fashioning a yoke iron so that tiller lines might be fitted to its damaged head and so rigged for the passage home. Spars were being plundered from the *Requin* to refit the sloop and the *Aurore* was being put in condition to sail to Britain.

Mindful of the political strictures St Vincent had mentioned in respect of the whale fishery, Drinkwater was anxious that both *Nimrod* and *Conqueror* returned to the Humber. But his own desperate shortage of men prevented him from taking *Requin* home as a prize. He intended burning her before they left Nagtoralik Bay.

A knock at the cabin door preceded the entry of Obadiah Singleton. His blue jaw seemed more prominent as his face was haggard with exhaustion.

'Ah, Mr Singleton. What may I do to serve you?'

218

'I consider that I have completed my obligations to the sick, Captain Drinkwater. I shall leave them in the hands of Skeete . . .'

'God help them . . .'

'Amen to that. But there is work enough for me ashore . . .'

'You cannot be landed here, Mr Singleton, there is a French settlement . . .'

'Your orders were to land me, Captain Drinkwater. There are eskimos here. As for the French, I cannot think that you would invite them on board your ship . . .'

'My orders, Mr Singleton,' Drinkwater replied sharply, 'are to extirpate any French presence I find in Arctic waters. To that end I must root out and take prisoner any military presence ashore.'

'I think your concern for your own ship will not permit that,' Singleton said with a final certainty.

'What the devil d'you mean by that?'

'I mean that Mr Frey, whom you sent ashore for water, has returned with information that leads me to suppose the poor devils ashore here are afflicted with all the plagues of Egypt, Captain Drinkwater.'

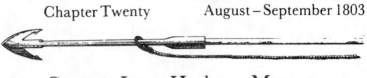

Greater Love Hath no Man

They had assembled all the French prisoners ashore prior to burning the *Requin*. Flanked by Mount and Singleton and escorted by a file of marines, Drinkwater inspected the hovels that made up the French settlement. Drawn apart from the privateersmen and regarded with a curious hostility by a crowd of eskimos, an untidy, starveling huddle of men watched their approach cautiously. They wore the remnants of military greatcoats, their feet bound in rags and their shoulders covered in skins. Most hid their faces. They were Bonaparte's Arctic 'colonists'.

Explanation came slowly, as though the revelation of horror should not be sudden. They were military ghosts, two companies of *Invalides*, a euphemism for the broken remnants of Bonaparte's vaunted Egyptian and Syrian campaigns. A handful of men who had regained France after the desertion of Bonaparte and the assassination of his successor Kleber; men who had returned home from annexed Egypt where their accounts of what had happened and the decay of their bodies were a double embarrassment to the authorities.

Drinkwater remembered the purulent eyes of the men he had fought hand to hand off Kosseir on the Egyptian coast of the Red Sea. Perhaps some of these poor devils had been in the garrison that had so gallantly resisted the British squadron under Captain Lidgbird Ball. He surveyed the diseased remnants of French ambition who had been trepanned to Greenland in an attempt to form a trading post to acquire furs for the French army. Here they could supply the voracious wants of the First Consul's armies at the expense of degrading the eskimos, exchanging liquor for furs, liquor that came through the agency of British whalers.

Under Drinkwater's scrutiny several of the Frenchmen drew themselves up, still soldiers, such was the power of military influence. The rags fell away from their faces. The ravages of bilharzia, trachoma-induced blindness, skin diseases, frostbite and God alone knew what other contagions burned in them.

Drinkwater turned aside, sickened. He met the eyes of Singleton. '*Dulce et decorum est pro patria mori*,' said the missionary softly.

'Where is this man Vrolicq?' Drinkwater muttered through clenched teeth.

Mount had the privateer's commander and officers quartered in a wretched stone and willow-roofed hovel. They stood blinking in the pale sunshine that filtered through a thin overcast and stared at the British officers.

Jean Vrolicq, corsair, republican opportunist and war-profiteer regarded Drinkwater through dark, suspicious eyes. He was a small man whose hardiness and energy seemed somehow refined, as though reduced to its essence in these latitudes, and disdaining a larger body. His face was bearded, seamed and tanned, his eyes chips of coal. Drinkwater recognised the man who had wounded him during their first action with the *Requin*.

'So, Captain, today you remember you have prisoners, eh?' Vrolicq's English was good, his accent suggesting a familiarity with Cornwall that was doubtless allied to the practice of 'free trade'.

'Tell me, M'sieur, was this trade you had with Captain Ellerby profitable to yourself?'

Perhaps Vrolicq thought Drinkwater was corruptible instead of merely curious, angling for a speculative cargo aside from his duty.

'But yes, Captain, and also for the carrier.' The man grinned rapaciously. 'You British are expert at making laws from which profits can be made with ease. You are equally good at breaking your own laws, which is perhaps why you make them, yes? Ellerby, he traded furs for cognac, his friends traded gold for cognac. We French now have gold in France and cognac in Greenland. Ellerby has furs which he also trades. To us French. So we have gold, cognac and furs. Ellerby has a little profit. It is clever, yes? And because your King George has a wise Parliament who all like a little French cognac.' The disdain was clear in Vrolicq's voice. But it was equally clear why Ellerby had not wanted Drinkwater's presence in the Greenland Sea, yet needed his protection in soundings off the British coast where an unscrupulous naval officer might board him in search of men and discover he had tiers of furs over his barrels of whale blubber. If Ellerby's plan had not been disrupted he and Waller would have been at the rendezvous off Shetland at the end of September and allowed Drinkwater to escort them safely into the Humber. And how assiduously Drinkwater had striven to afford Ellerby the very protection he needed for his nefarious trade!

'It is quite possible,' said Vrolicq, breaking into Drinkwater's thoughts, 'that you might yourself profit a little . . .'

'Go to the devil!' snapped Drinkwater, turning away and striding down the beach towards the waiting boat.

Drinkwater stood on the quarterdeck wrapped in the bear-skin given him by the officers. It was piercingly cold, the damp tendrils of a fog reaching down into the bay from the heights surrounding them. The daylight was dreary with mist; the Arctic summer was coming to its end.

'Boat approaching, sir.' Drinkwater acknowledged Frey's report and watched one of the *Nimrod*'s boats, commandeered to replace *Melusine*'s losses, as it was pulled out from the curve of dark sand and shingle that marked the beach at Nagtoralik. He waited patiently while Obadiah Singleton clambered over the rail, nodded him a greeting, then ushered him below to the sanctuary of the cabin.

'Well Obadiah, you received my note. I am about to sail. All the ships are ready and the wind, what there is of it, will take us clear of the bay as soon as this fog lifts. This is the last chance to change your mind.'

'That is out of the question, Nathaniel.' Singleton smiled his rare smile. All pretence at rank had long since vanished between the two men. Singleton's determination to stay and minister to the human flotsam on the shores of the bay ran contrary to all of Drinkwater's instincts. He could not quite believe that Singleton would remain. 'Oh, I know what you intend to say. "Remember whom you are to cope withal; a sort of vagabonds, rascals and runaways, a scum of Bretagnes, and base lackey peasants whom their o'er cloyéd country vomits forth to desperate ventures, and assured destruction . . ." King Richard the Third, Nathaniel. That last clause is most appropriate. Scarcely any will survive the coming winter. There is evidence of typhus . . .'

'Typhus!'

'Yes, what you call the ship or gaol fever . . .'

'I know damned well what typhus is . . .'

'Well then you know that as a divine I should urge you to take mercy upon them, to have compassion even at the risk of infecting your ship's company. As a physician I warn you against further contact with them. There is not only typhus, there is . . .'

'I know, I know. I do not wish to reflect upon the whole catalogue of ills that infests this morbid place. So you advise me to take no action. To leave them here to rot.'

'This is the first time, Nathaniel, that I have seen you indecisive.' Singleton smiled again.

'There is no need to enjoy the experience, damn it!'

'Forgive me. Perhaps one thing I have learned during our acquaintance is that true decisions are seldom made upon philosophical lines. Sometimes the burdens of your position are too great for one man to bear. It is God's will that I surrogate for your conscience.'

'And what will happen to you, Obadiah? Eh?'

'I do not know. Let us leave that to God. You were bidden to land me upon the coast of Greenland. You have done your duty.'

'And Vrolicq?'

'Vrolicq is an agent of the devil. Leave him to me and to God.'

'I have already offered you whatever you wish for out of the ships. Surely you will take my pistols . . .'

'Thank you, no. I have taken such necessaries as I thought desirable out of the *Requin* before you fired her yesterday. I have everything I need.' He paused. 'I am at peace, Nathaniel. Do not worry on my account. It is you who work for implacable masters. It was Christ's essential gospel that we should love our enemies.'

'I do not understand you, damned if I do.'

'John, fifteen, verse thirteen,' he held out his hand. 'Farewell, Nathaniel.'

'Have you any questions, gentlemen?'

The assembled officers shook their heads. Sawyers of *Faithful* had loaned his speksioneer, Elijah Pucill, to assist Mr Quilhampton in bringing home *Nimrod*. Gorton was sufficiently recovered to command *Conqueror*, seconded by Lord Walmsley. Sawyers's son was assisting Glencross in the *Aurore*. The crews of the two whalers had been tempered by prize crews from *Melusine* while those elements whose loyalty might still be in doubt were quartered aboard the sloop herself. Drinkwater dismissed them, each with a copy of his orders. They filed out of the cabin. Captain Sawyers hung back.

'You wished to speak to me, Captain Sawyers?'

'Aye, Friend. We have both been busy men during the past five days. I wished for a proper opportunity to express to thee my gratitude. I have thanked God, for the force of thine arm was like unto David's when he slew Goliath, yet I know that to be an instrument of

God's will can torture a man severely.'

Drinkwater managed a wry smile at Sawyer's odd reasoning. 'I am considering it less hazardous to be surrounded by ice than by theologians. But thank you.'

'I have left thy servant, the Cornishman, a quantity of furs. Perhaps thou might find some use for them better than draped over the horses of the un-Godly.'

Drinkwater grinned. Some explanation of Sawyers's activities in the last few days suggested itself to Drinkwater. It occurred to him that Sawyers knew all along of Ellerby's treachery but his religious abhorrence of war enabled him to overlook it. Besides, now the shrewd Quaker had most of *Nimrod*'s cargo of furs safely stowed aboard the *Faithful*.

'What have you entered in your log book concerning your capture?'

'That I was taken by a French privateer, conducted to an anchorage and liberated by thyself. I have no part in thy war beyond suffering its aggravations.'

'Good. It was not my intention to advertise this treachery. Much distress will be caused thereby to the families of weak and defenceless men.'

Sawyers raised an eyebrow. 'Canst thou afford such magnanimity? Seamen gossip, Friend.'

'Captain Sawyers, if you were to come upon two unmanned whalers anchored inside the Spurn Head, would you ensure they came safely home to their owners?'

A gleam of comprehension kindled in Sawyers's eyes. 'You mean to press the crews when you have anchored the ships?'

'There are a few of your men already on board to claim salvage. I am not asking you to falsify your log, merely amend it.'

Sawyers chuckled. 'A man who cannot write a log book to his own advantage is not fit to command a ship, Captain Drinkwater.' He paused. 'But what advantage is there to thee?'

Drinkwater shrugged. 'I have a crew again.'

'Patriotism is an unprofitable business and thy acumen recommends thee for other ventures. But have you considered the matter of their press exemptions?'

'I had them collected from the two ships. They burned with *Requin*.'

'And Waller?' asked Sawyers, raising an eyebrow in admiration.

Drinkwater smiled grimly. 'Ellerby may take the burden of treachery dead. Waller can expiate his greed if not his treason by serving the King along with the rest of the whale-men. It is better for them to dance at the end of the bosun's starter rather than a noose. Besides, as Lord St Vincent was at pains to point out to me, loss of whale-men means loss of prime seamen. It seems a pity to deprive His Majesty of seamen to provide employment for the hangman.'

Sawyers laughed. 'I do not think that it is expiation, Friend. It seems to be *immolation*.'

Drinkwater lingered a while after the Quaker had departed, giving him time to return to *Faithful*, then he reached for his hat and went on deck to give the order to weigh anchor.

Drinkwater stared astern. Gulls dipped in *Melusine*'s wake and beside him the jury rudder creaked. As if veiling itself the coast of Greenland was disappearing in a low fog. Already Cape Jervis had vanished.

Far to the west, above the fog bank, disembodied by distance and elevation, the *nunataks* of the permanent ice-cap gleamed faintly, remote and undefiled by man.

Drinkwater turned from his contemplation and began to pace the deck. He thought of Meetuck who had disappeared for several days, terrified of the guns that rumbled and thundered over his head. He had reappeared at last, driven into the open by hunger and finally landed a hero among his own people. He remembered the thirty odd Melusines that would not return, Bourne among them. And the survivors; Mr Midshipman Frey, Gorton, Hill, Mount and James Quilhampton. And little Billie Cue about whose future he must write to Elizabeth.

He looked astern once more and thought of Singleton, ministering to the sick veterans of an atheist government who were corrupting the eskimos. Singleton would die attempting to alleviate their agonies and save their souls whilst proclaiming the existence of a God of universal love.

There was no sense in it. And yet what was it Singleton had said? 'Mr Frey!'

'Sir?'

'Be so kind as to fetch me a Bible.'

'A Bible, sir?'

'Yes, Mr Frey. A Bible.'

Frey returned and handed Drinkwater a small, leatherbound Bible. Drinkwater opened it at St John's Gospel, Chapter Fifteen, verse thirteen. He read:

Greater love hath no man than this, that a man lay down his life for his friends.

Then he remembered Singleton's muttered quotation as they had stared at the French veterans: '*Dulce et decorum est pro patria mori.*'

'It's all a question of philosophy, Mr Frey,' he said suddenly, looking up from the Bible and handing it back to the midshipman.

'Is it, sir?' said the astonished Frey.

'And the way you look at life.'

The Nore

'Square the yards, Mr Hill, and set t'gallants.'

Drinkwater watched the departing whalers beat up into the Humber, carried west by the inrush of the flood tide. He had at least the satisfaction of having obeyed his orders, collecting the other ships, the *Earl Percy, Provident, Truelove* and the rest, at the Shetland rendezvous. He had now completed their escort to the estuary of the River Humber and most of them were taking advantage of the favourable tide to carry them up the river against the prevailing wind. Only *Nimrod, Conqueror* and *Faithful* remained at anchor in Hawke Road while Sawyers shipped his prize crews on board to sail the remaining few miles to the mouth of the River Hull.

Amidships Drinkwater watched Mr Comely's rattan flick the backsides of reluctant whalemen into *Melusine*'s rigging. Their rueful glances astern at their former ships tugged at Drinkwater's conscience. It had been a savage and cruel decision to press the crews of the *Nimrod* and *Conqueror*, but at least his action would appear to have the sanction of common practice and no-one would now hang for the treachery of Jemmett Ellerby. The irony of his situation did not escape him. A few months earlier he had given his word that no-one would be pressed from his convoy by a marauding cruiser captain intent on recruiting for the Royal Navy here off the Spurn. Now he had done the very thing he deplored. He did not think that waterfront gossip in Hull would examine his motives deeply enough to appreciate the rough justification of his action. But it was not local opinion that he was worried about.

He had collected all his scattered parties now, after the weary voyage home from Greenland. Aboard *Melusine* the watches had been reduced to the drudgery of regular pumping and Drinkwater himself had slept little, his senses tuned to the creaks and groans of the jury steering gear, every moment expecting it to fly to pieces under the strain. But it had held as far as Shetland where they had again overhauled it as the rest of the whalers prepared to sail south, and it would hold, God-willing, until they reached the Nore.

They passed *Faithful* as they stood out of the anchorage. She was already getting under way and Drinkwater raised his hat in farewell to Sawyers on his poop. The Quaker stood to make a small fortune from the voyage now that the 'salvage' of *Nimrod* and *Conqueror* could be added to his tally of profits on baleen, whale oil and furs. Drinkwater wished him well. He had given an undertaking to drop a few judicious words to any of the Hull ship-owners who sought to press the Government for reparation for the excessive zeal of a certain Captain Drinkwater in pressing their crews. Drinkwater was aware of the benefit of a precedent in the matter.

But there were other matters to worry Drinkwater. Sawyer's reassurances now seemed less certain as *Melusine* stood out to sea again. It was true Drinkwater had spent nearly two days in composing his confidential despatch to the Secretary of the Admiralty. In addition he had sent Mr Quilhampton to Hull on board the *Earl Percy* to catch the first London mail, a Mr Quilhampton who had been carefully briefed in case he was required to answer any question by any of their Lordships. Drinkwater doubted there would be trouble about the pressing of the whalemen. The Admiralty were not fussy about where they acquired their seamen. But what of Waller? Supposing Drinkwater's decision was misinterpreted? What of his leaving to their fate those pitiful French '*invalides*'? The Admiralty had not seen their condition. To the authorities they might appear more dangerous than Drinkwater knew them to be. As for Singleton, what had appeared on his part of an act of tragic courage, might now seem oddly fatuous. Drinkwater had carried a letter from Singleton to the secretary of his missionary society and had himself also written, but God alone knew what would become of the man.

'She's clear of the Spit, sir.'

'Very well, Mr Hill, a course for The Would, if you please.'

Drinkwater turned from contemplating the play of light upon the shipping anchored at the Nore. He had been thinking of the strange events of the voyage and the clanking of *Melusine*'s pumps had reminded him of his old dream and the strange experience when he had been lost in the fog. He came out of his reverie when Mr Frey reported the approach of a boat from Sheerness. Instinctively Drinkwater knew it carried Quilhampton, returning from conveying Drinkwater's report to Whitehall. He sat down and settled a stern self-control over the fluttering apprehension in his belly.

The expected knock came at the door. 'Enter!'

Mr Quilhampton came in, producing a sealed packet from beneath his boat cloak.

'Orders, sir,' he said with indecent cheerfulness. Drinkwater took the packet. To his horror his hand shook.

'What sort of reception did you receive, Mr Q?' he asked, affecting indifference as he struggled with the wax seals.

'They kept me kicking my heels all morning, sir. Then the First Lord sent for me, sir. Rum old devil, begging your pardon. He sat me down, as polite as ninepence, and asked a lot of questions about the action in Nagtoralik Bay, the force of the *Requin*, sir . . . I formed the impression he was judging the force opposed to us . . . then he got up, paced up and down and looked at the trees in the park and turned and dismissed me. Told me to wait in the hall. Kept me there two hours then a fellow called Templeton, one of the clerks, took me into the copy-room and handed me these,' he nodded at the papers which had suddenly fallen onto the table as Drinkwater succeeded in detaching the last seal.

'It was rather odd, sir . . .'

'What was?' Drinkwater looked up sharply.

'This cove Templeton, sir. He said, well to the best of my recollection he said: "You've smoked the viper out, we knew about him in May when we intercepted papers en route to France, but you caught him red-handed".' Quilhampton shrugged and went on. 'Then he asked after Lieutenant Germaney and seemed rather upset that he'd gone over the standing part of the foresheet . . .'

But Drinkwater was no longer listening. He began to read, his eyes glancing superficially at first, seeking out the salient phrases that would spell ruin and disgrace.

The words danced before his eyes and he shuffled the papers, looking from one to another. Quilhampton watched, uncertain if he was dismissed or whether further intelligence would be required from him.

With the silent familiarity of the trusted servant Tregembo entered the cabin from the pantry. He held a filled decanter.

'Cap'n's got some decent wine, at last, zur,' he said to Quilhampton conversationally. 'Happen you've a thirst since coming from Lunnon, zur . . .'

Quilhampton looked from the Cornishman's badly scarred face to the preoccupied Drinkwater and made a negative gesture.

'Give him a glass, Tregembo, and pour me one too . . .'

It was not unqualified approval. St Vincent considered Waller should have been handed over:

Bearing in mind the political repercussions upon the sea-faring community of Kingston-upon-Hull I reluctantly endorse your actions, acknowledging the extreme measures you were forced to adopt and certain that service in any of His Majesty's ships under your command will bring the man Waller to an acknowledgment of his true allegiance . . .

Drinkwater was aware of a veiled compliment. Perhaps Dungarth's hand was visible in that. But he was not sure, for the remainder of the letter was pure St Vincent:

It is not, and never has been, nor shall be, the business of the Royal Navy to make war upon sick men, and your anxieties upon that score should be allayed. The monstrous isolation which the Corsican tyrant has condemned loyal men to endure, only emphasises the nature of the wickedness against which we are opposed . . .

Drinkwater relaxed. He had been believed. He picked up the other papers somewhat absently, sipping the full glass Tregembo had set before him.

. . . I am commanded by Their Lordships to acquaint you of the fact that the condition of the sloop under your command being, for the present unfit for further service, you are directed to turn her over to the hands of the Dockyard Commissioner at Chatham and to transfer your ship's company entire into the frigate Antigone *now fitting at that place . . .*

'Good Heavens, James. I am directed to turn the ship's company over to the *Antigone*! Our old prize from the Red Sea!'

' 'Tis a small world, sir. Does that mean *Melusine* is for a refit?'

Quilhampton's anxiety for his own future was implicit in the question. Drinkwater nodded. 'I fear so, James.'

'And yourself, sir . . .?'

'Mmm?' Drinkwater picked up the final sheet and the colour left his face. 'God bless my soul!'

'What is it, sir?'

'I am posted to command her. Directly into a thirty-six gun frigate, James!'

'Posted, sir? Why my heartiest congratulations!'

Drinkwater looked at his commission as a Post-Captain. It was signed by St Vincent himself, a singular mark of the old man's favour.

'About bloody time too, zur,' muttered Tregembo, refilling the glasses.

Author's Note

It is a fact that damage was inflicted upon the northern whale-fishery by French cruisers during the Napoleonic War. For details of the fishery itself, Scoresby Jnr has been my chief authority. There are significant differences between the hunting of the Greenland Right whale and the better known Sperm Whale fishery of the South Pacific. Chief among these was the practice of not reducing the blubber to oil as the comparative brevity of the voyage did not warrant it. Similarly I have used the noun 'harpooner' in preference to the Americanism 'harpooneer'. Although it was well-known that the whale breathed air, it was still extensively referred to as a 'fish'. At this period the Right Whale was thought to have poor hearing but acute eye-sight. Although known to overset boats, Mysticetus was a comparatively docile animal, far less aggressive than the Sperm Whale.

The delay in the sailing of the Hull ships is my own fiction but it is based on the fact that in 1802, during the Peace of Amiens, the government removed some of the press-exemptions extended to the officers of whalers in anticipation of further hostilities. It is therefore not difficult to excuse the whale-ship masters their suspicions. There were indeed plans of Hull and the Humber discovered en route to France in early 1803 and this forms the basis for Ellerby's treachery. In addition he was not only acting traitorously but illegally, since he had breached an oath required of whaler captains that they would not profit from any activity in the Arctic Seas than that of whaling.

The extraordinary opening in the ice corresponds roughly to that found by Scoresby in 1806. It was however 1822 before the eponymous Scoresby discovered the great fiord, an inlet of which forms Nagtoralik Bay. Of Scoresby Sound the Admiralty Sailing Directions say 'This ice-free land consists mainly of rugged mountains but . . . near the open sea the vegetation is luxuriant and game is plentiful.' It is also 'considered to be the most easily accessible part of the coast of East Greenland.'

Drinkwater's reasons for suppressing his discovery are clear. When

Beaufort was appointed Hydrographer to the Navy his habit of personally scrutinising all surveys combined with the remoteness of the locality to delay the publication of a spurious and anonymous survey of 'Nagtoralik Bay and its surroundings'. By this time, of course, Scoresby's name had become firmly connected with the area.